Mummy's Little Girl

JANE ELLIOTT

Mummy's Little Girl

A desperate race
to save a lost child

HARPER

HARPER

an imprint of
HarperCollins*Publishers*
77–85 Fulham Palace Road,
Hammersmith, London W6 8JB

www.harpercollins.co.uk

First published by HarperCollins*Publishers* 2008

1

A catalogue record of this book
is available from the British Library

ISBN 978-0-00-726397-4

Printed and bound in Great Britain by
Clays Ltd, St Ives plc

Fact

In the UK alone, a child goes missing every five minutes.
Some of these children are found; others become
the focus of high-profile media campaigns.

A few are never seen again.

Mummy's Little Girl

Prologue

December 1996. London. Evening

The pains had started just after lunch – not that meal-times meant much in her house.

Had little Hayley Clark known what the sudden rush of water was, the one that had dampened her sheets in the small hours of the morning, she might have known to expect the contractions sometime soon. But she didn't. No one had explained it to her. There had been no visits to the doctor; no scans; no midwives to reassure her or tell her what was likely to happen, or when. It would have been unthinkable to wake her mum and admit that her bed was wet and she didn't know why, just as it would have been unthinkable in the first place to tell her that she thought she was going to have a baby.

It had been five months ago that Hayley had realised she was pregnant, a few weeks after she had met the boys who lived at the other end of the estate. She had left the flat out of necessity that summer's evening – Mum and Dad were shouting at each other, and she didn't know how it would end. The arguments didn't always spill over into her tiny bedroom, but they had happened enough times for her to feel scared to the pit of her stomach whenever she heard raised voices. Strangely it was her mum she feared more than her dad in those situations. Dad would just shout at her, telling her she was lazy and ugly and why the hell didn't she get out there and find some fucking friends, before stumbling into bed to sleep off the cheap booze. Mum, on the other hand, was more physical: she would pull her long, jet-black hair and hit her. One time she had given her a black eye, and Hayley had to pretend to the teachers at school that she'd been in a fight on the way home. Mum would hurl abuse at her too, but unkind words she could deal with. It was the punches that hurt.

That night back in the summer, she had sensed it would be in her interests to leave the house. They were drunker than usual, for one thing – it was the time of the month when they had more money, so there was no danger of running out of drink. And she had heard them talking about her. Yelling about her, actually. Hayley was only young, but she knew what that meant, and was smart enough to get out of there before things turned nasty for her.

She hadn't needed a coat – it was a warm evening – and so she slipped out of the flat wearing only the same jeans and T-shirt that she always wore, knowing that Mum and Dad would probably not even hear the door. She walked down the concrete stairwell, avoiding the nasty smell that always made her feel a little bit sick, and emerged at the front of the tower block. It was late, but still just light, and little crowds of people were standing around in cliques. Some of them were smoking, some of them were drinking. A lot of them had music blaring from their car stereos.

Hayley didn't like coming out here by herself, especially at this time of night. During the day there was a police presence, but come nightfall even they knew to steer clear of the estate. When they did show up, they tended to ignore most of what was going on. Cleaning this place up was like pushing sand uphill, Hayley had heard a grown-up say once.

It was scary. None of the groups of people seemed to talk to each other; none of them looked as if they *dared* talk to each other. Hayley walked quickly, with her head down, hoping that she wouldn't be noticed.

Hayley was the sort of girl people didn't normally notice. But that was about to change.

A wolf-whistle filled the air. Hayley felt her stomach lurch and she kept her eyes on the pavement as she continued walking, desperately hoping that the whistle hadn't been directed at her. Almost immediately, though, it was followed up by the sound of footsteps, and before Hayley knew what was happening, two boys were standing in front of her.

They were older than her – seventeen, maybe, or eighteen – and Hayley thought she knew their faces. They were definitely the sort of boys she would go out of her way to avoid, but that wasn't saying much: Hayley went out of her way to avoid most people. They both wore baggy jeans and hooded tops; the only thing that really made them look different from each other was that one of them had a tooth missing.

'Where you going?' the toothless one demanded. He chewed noisily on some gum.

Hayley almost automatically looked down at the ground. She said nothing.

She could sense the two boys grinning at each other. 'Going to come and hang with us?' the other boy said. It didn't sound much like a question.

'No thanks,' she mumbled.

But as she spoke, one of them grabbed her arm. She looked around her in alarm, but none of the other groups noticed what was going on; or if they did, they stayed well clear. It was the boy with the full set of teeth who had grabbed her, and his grip was strong. He pulled her over towards where they had been standing, by a car whose four doors were wide open. There were others here, mostly boys, but a couple of girls too, who looked at Hayley with nasty stares. They didn't say anything, however.

'Have a drink,' the toothless boy said to her. He put a bottle of something into her hand.

'I don't want to—' she started to say, her voice trembling slightly.

'*I don't want to!*' a female voice mimicked from somewhere. Hayley felt her skin flush.

'Drink it,' the boy insisted.

Hayley had never drunk alcohol before. She'd heard the other children at school talking about it, of course, talking about how they would get drunk on Friday nights, but she wasn't popular enough to be invited to their parties; and anyway, she was hardly likely to touch the stuff, knowing what sort of effect it had on her mum and dad. But as she stood there that night, with these intimidating people standing round and staring at her, she knew that she couldn't say no; so she put the bottle timidly to her lips.

The mouth of the bottle was already wet from somebody else's saliva, and it made Hayley shiver with revulsion. She closed her eyes, though, and tipped the bottle up further. The alcohol was incredibly sweet – a bit like the fizzy drinks she occasionally tasted – and to her surprise she found that she quite liked it. Seconds later, however, the kick of the alcohol hit the back of her throat and she started to cough.

The others laughed, and Hayley felt her skin suddenly burning with embarrassment. But what happened next surprised even her. Ashamed of her inability to handle the drink, she took another pull at the bottle, two hefty gulps. This time she didn't cough, and she handed the bottle back to the toothless boy with a tiny look of defiance. The boy looked at his friend with a smile – a smile Hayley could tell meant something, but she didn't know what. He took a swig at the bottle, and then handed it round.

'What's your name, then, gorgeous?' he said, his accent thick with south London, just like Hayley's.

'Hayley.'

That look again.

'Not seen you around much, Hayley.' A giggle from one of the group.

The alcohol had created a warm feeling in her chest. 'Yeah,' she said. 'So?' The boldness of her response astonished her.

'So … you gonna come with us?'

Hayley's eyes flickered up towards the top of the tower block and she felt a sudden thrill of rebellion. Mum and Dad probably still didn't know she'd left; even if they did, they wouldn't care.

'All right,' she said.

The boy grinned. He took her by the arm again, but not so roughly this time, and led her away from the group. His friend followed.

'Where you fucking going?' a voice screeched. It was one of the girls in the little crowd around the car. They stopped and turned round, and Hayley watched as the girl approached the two boys. She was mixed race, and wore tight clothes against her curves which made Hayley feel like the little girl she was, and her lips and nose were pierced.

'Fuck you,' the toothless boy muttered. He pushed her to one side, took Hayley by the arm again and led her off.

'I'll be looking out for you, you little bitch!' the girl called after her, her voice loaded with hate. 'I'll be looking out for you!'

Any other time, Hayley would have been petrified; but on that summer's evening six months previously, with the alcohol doing its work, she felt something different. Carelessness. Recklessness. Whenever she thought back on it, she cringed at her own stupidity.

The boys didn't tell her their names, and she didn't ask. They led her to a different tower block on the south side of the estate, and into a flat several storeys up. It was a dingy place, but Hayley was used to that – her own home was hardly luxurious. Thick, dirty blankets were pinned up against the windows, and the only light came from a lava lamp on the floor in the corner. There was no furniture – just a few stained mattresses lying here and there, and a selection of blue and green milk crates scattered around instead of chairs. The kitchen area was covered with fast-food packaging, and there was a strange mixture of smells. Rotting food, of course, but also something else. A thick, musty smell.

As soon as they were in the flat, the boy without the missing tooth shut the door; then he collapsed on to one of the mattresses and pulled out a pouch of tobacco and some cigarette papers. Hayley watched as he licked the gummed edges of two papers and stuck them together, before sprinkling some tobacco into the middle. He then removed a small lump of something brown and held it in the flame of a lighter before breaking bits off and crumbling them onto the tobacco. He rolled the cigarette up and lit it; instantly Hayley could tell where that sweet smell came from.

He took a deep drag on the joint, and then passed it to Hayley. Suddenly timid again, she shook her head. A look of annoyance passed the boy's face as he handed the joint to his friend. 'You want another drink?' he asked Hayley.

Not knowing what else to do, Hayley nodded her head.

She didn't see him pour the drink; nor did she question why he was giving it to her in a dirty glass rather than straight out of the bottle as before. She drank it quickly, hoping it would give her more of the warm feeling that it had done when they were outside.

'Why you looking at me like that?' she asked the two boys when she had finished it. They were standing, watching her, as if they were waiting for something. She took another sip of her drink, trying her best to look grown-up.

It was from that moment that she started to lose her memory. She couldn't remember what was said between them, or what she did; all she knew was that after a little while a terrible sickness hit her, a nausea that seemed to run through her whole body. She felt dizzy, the blood in her veins ran hot and she lost control of her limbs as she fell to the ground.

And falling to the ground was the last thing that she remembered.

When she woke up, her head was pounding, as though someone was beating the inside of her skull. But the pain in her head was nothing compared to the shocking, sinister stabbing she felt in her stomach, as though hot knives were slashing into her. She looked down and saw, to her horror and shame, that the bottom half of her body was naked. She was lying on one of the mattresses; the two boys were on the other side of the room, fast asleep.

She started to tremble with a mixture of sickness, fear and self-loathing. Slowly she sat up, and as she did so she became aware of streaks of blood down her legs.

Her jeans and underwear were lying on the floor near the boys. Wincing with pain, she got to her feet and crept towards them, quiet and terrified, to pick them up. As she started to get dressed, tears came to her eyes; her jeans became tangled as she pulled them on, and the more she struggled, the slower she became. She tried desperately to keep quiet, but she couldn't help a sudden, loud sob escaping her lips.

The toothless boy stirred and drowsily opened his eyes. Hayley froze, her jeans still only halfway up her legs.

The boy leered at her, and then pushed himself up to a sitting position. 'Get over here,' he said.

Hayley felt her body start to shake. She pulled her jeans up over her hips and walked towards him. He grabbed her hand and pulled her down to the floor; she did her best to master another wave of nausea as he took her face roughly in one of his hands. It hurt, and she whimpered. They were face to face now, and she could smell the tobacco on his breath. 'You can come back here any time, bitch,' he whispered. 'But tell anyone and I'll kill you. Understand?'

Terrified, Hayley nodded her head.

'Then get the fuck out of here.'

Hayley fled.

The sickness lasted for several hours, the discomfort in her belly for a few days; the shame endured for much longer than that. Hayley barely left her bedroom for the whole of the school holidays – she was too scared of seeing either the boys or the girl who had threatened her, and not even the prospect of a beating from her mum was enough to get her to leave the flat.

Hayley was not a worldly girl, but she wasn't stupid. She knew she had been raped that night, probably by both boys. She knew she should tell someone, but there was no one to tell, and anyway, she was scared. Scared of the boys who had done it to her, and scared of what people would think. Much better to forget about it. Pretend it had never happened. Put it from her mind.

But that was not possible.

When her period was late, she ignored the little voice that nagged inside her head. Hayley was only young, and far from regular; it was nothing to worry about. But a week passed, and then two. She started to feel sick. Of course, she kept it from her mum and dad. Mum especially always reacted badly when she said she felt unwell. She didn't go to the doctor, and even if she had had the courage to walk into a pharmacy and ask for a pregnancy test, she had no money to buy one.

And so the pregnancy progressed. Hayley knew she couldn't keep it a secret for ever, but nine months was a long time. Maybe by the time the baby was born, something would have changed in her life.

But it hadn't been nine months. Only five, when once again she slipped out of the flat without her mum and dad knowing. The pains were happening every fifteen minutes, and when they came she felt like doubling over in agony. There was no way she would be able to hide this from her mum, so she had to get out of there.

It was raining outside, a heavy, cold, persistent rain that saturated her clothes almost immediately. The sun had set, and there was no one outside in this weather – no one to see when Hayley bent over, clutching her belly and crying out. She staggered out of the estate and on to the main road that ran alongside it. There were few pedestrians here, but plenty of cars and buses, their headlamps on as they splashed their way through the rain.

If any of them saw the fifteen-year-old girl, stumbling along the puddle-ridden pavement with a look of unabated agony on her face, they didn't stop to help.

Charity Thomson took the lift down from the maternity ward and walked through the clattering corridors of the hospital to the café by the entrance on the ground floor. She could get coffee on the ward, of course, but sometimes you just had to get out of there, away from the stress and the urgency and the shouting. Fifteen minutes of time to herself and she would, she knew, be re-energised and ready to bring a few more souls into the world.

Charity had been a midwife all her working life – thirty years, near enough. In all that time she had never met a colleague who didn't have some complaint to make about the job – the conditions, the pay, the hours – but Charity had always loved it. There were difficult days, of course; there were deliveries that went wrong, that ended in heartbreak; and she would never be a rich woman. But on the whole Charity felt blessed to be doing what she was doing.

She bought her drink and took a seat on one of the plastic chairs. It was seven in the evening, but the hospital was still busy, and she watched as people rushed in and out of the large main doors – visitors, doctors, patients – all of them creating a throng of activity. Charity sat quietly for five minutes, absorbing it all in a kind of daydream.

It was the sight of the girl that brought her back to her senses. She was standing in the doorway, her clothes sopping wet and her matted black hair stuck to the side of her face. She was pale – deathly pale – and she looked around her as though she was completely lost and confused. Then she doubled over, her hands clutching the side of her belly. She stayed like that for perhaps twenty seconds. When she straightened up, she looked so scared that it caught Charity's breath.

Charity had been a midwife for long enough to know what those twenty seconds of agony were. She got to her feet and hurried over to where the girl was standing.

'Come on, love,' she said, her voice automatically slipping into the kindly bedside manner she used with all pregnant women. 'Let's get you upstairs. Can you walk? Best if you do, eh?'

The girl stared at her as though she hadn't understood a word.

Charity put her arm around the girl's shoulders and started ushering her in. 'Look at you,' she said, carrying on talking brightly. 'You're wet through. Sooner we get you out of these clothes and into something dry, the better, eh? Got someone here with you, have you, love? Baby's father?'

The girl shook her head violently.

'Mum?'

Again she shook her head. Poor dear, Charity thought. It happened like that sometimes. They walked slowly towards the lift.

On the way up to the maternity ward, Charity took a better look at this strange girl with the matted hair and the soaking wet clothes. She seemed young, and her belly was barely swollen. It wasn't so uncommon for that to happen – you might not even have known she was pregnant if you hadn't seen the signs – but Charity couldn't help wondering how far gone she was. 'How many months, love?' she asked as the doors hissed open on to the maternity ward.

'Five,' the girl replied hesitantly.

It was all Charity could do not to let the worry show in her face. She held her security card up to the panel by the entrance door and, when it clicked open, hurried the girl through.

'What's your name, love?' she asked.

No reply.

'How old are you?'

'S–seventeen,' the girl stuttered a bit too quickly. It was obviously a lie, but Charity couldn't worry too much about that just at the moment. Her job was to look after the girl and deliver a desperately premature baby against the odds. Everything else could wait until later.

A nurse was standing at reception. 'We're going to need a doctor,' Charity told her quietly. 'And make sure there's room in Special Care.'

The nurse looked at her quizzically.

Five months. Charity mouthed the words silently to the nurse, whose expression immediately changed to one of concern. The midwife nodded meaningfully, and then continued to walk with the girl towards the delivery suite.

Her patient was shaking violently, and Charity knew she wasn't far off now.

Hayley did not get the chance to hold her baby girl before she was taken away. But she saw her in the hands of the midwife, and she heard the tiny squawk of her little voice. She was so small. So desperately, impossible small – barely larger than the midwife's hands – and, despite her absolute exhaustion, Hayley felt an overwhelming need to reach out and touch the child. She pushed herself up on to her elbows, but her strength had left her and she could do nothing but look as the baby was placed in a clear Perspex cot and wheeled out of the birthing room.

Then the nice midwife was there, standing by her bed and tightly holding her shaking hand. 'You can see her in a bit, love. She's very frail, and we need to take her into Special Care and put her on a respirator. You're going to have to be very brave, but the doctors will do everything they can to give her the best chance.'

Hayley looked up at her with wide eyes, feeling them brim with tears. She was so kind. Nobody was ever that kind to her, and she was glad that her baby was being looked after by people like that.

'Thank you,' she said.

'Now listen, love,' the midwife continued. 'I *know* you're not really seventeen. No one here is going to judge you or think the worse of you. All we want to do is look after you and make sure that you and your baby are all right. But we need to know your name, and we need to get in touch with your mum and dad to let them know what's happened. You do have a mum and dad, don't you, love?'

Hayley nodded.

'Good girl.' The midwife squeezed her hand. 'Now we don't have to hurry. I'm going to leave you to rest for half an hour. You need anything at all, you press this button here. When I come back, we'll go down to Special Care to see your baby, and then we'll fill in all the pieces of paper that we need to. Then we'll call your mum and dad. Do you want to do it, or shall I?'

Hayley didn't answer.

The midwife squeezed her hand. 'You think about it, love,' she said with a reassuring smile. 'I'll be back in a bit.' She squeezed her hand a second time, and then left.

Hayley lay there, alone and confused. In the last hour, her world had changed. For months she had been terrified – terrified of what her parents would say and do if they found out the dirty truth about their daughter; terrified of encountering the boys again. Now it was all different. She was still scared, but scared for a different reason. Scared for her baby. Scared of what would happen when she took her home. Scared of the life she would have.

As these thoughts ran through her head, Hayley wondered whether this was what it was like to be a grown-up.

About five minutes after the midwife had left she summoned up the energy to get out of bed. Her legs felt weak as she steadied herself by the side of her bed, and she was sore from the birth; but she took a couple of tentative steps towards the chair over which her wet clothes had been laid. She took off her stained hospital robes, and with difficulty pulled on the still damp jeans and T-shirt, which were clammy and cold on her skin. Gingerly, she stepped towards the door and out into the corridor.

It was almost midnight, but the maternity ward was still buzzing with activity. Mums in labour walked up and down the corridor, some of them pushing drip stands along with them. Harassed hospital workers rushed in and out of rooms. Nobody paid any attention to a young girl walking unobtrusively past the reception desk and out of the main body of the hospital.

It was a relief for Hayley when she saw that the rain had stopped. If she'd had the money, she would have taken a bus home, but she didn't, so there was nothing for it but to walk. It took an hour and a half to get back to the estate, and by the time she got home, her mum and dad were fast asleep. She crept silently into the bathroom, where she removed her clothes before moistening some tissue and using it to wipe away the stubborn streaks of blood from her inner thigh. Then she rolled her clothes up into a little ball, returned to her room, climbed into bed and pulled the blankets tightly around her.

As she lay there, waiting for sleep to come, Hayley felt as though a part of her had been torn away. She felt a desperate, gaping emptiness. She felt as though she was no longer whole. Her body ached for the little girl she had only glimpsed for a matter of seconds.

Yet what else could she have done? Bring her back here, to this place? At least now her child had a chance – a chance of life in the hands of the kind doctors, and a chance of happiness in the hands of whoever she ended up with.

A chance of happiness. If she could give her little girl that, then perhaps she wasn't so worthless. It wasn't much to cling on to, but it was something.

A chance of happiness.

The words echoed around Hayley's head as she lay there in her little bed until eventually, overcome with exhaustion and emotion, she slipped into a troubled, dream-filled sleep.

It was a bit more than half an hour after she'd left Hayley that Charity returned to the girl's room. She didn't know why, but somehow she wasn't surprised to see that she was no longer there.

She felt a pang. On some level, she had hoped that maybe she had been getting through to the girl, but now she realised how thoughtless she had been to leave her alone. If anyone needed help, company and security, it was the frightened little thing who had given birth in that room less than an hour ago. She sighed.

There were procedures in place for this kind of event. Charity immediately informed hospital security what had happened; then the police were called. There would be statements and interviews in due course, but Charity knew it would all be in vain – the girl had not given any information about herself, not even her name. The midwife found herself wondering whether she had come into the hospital intending to abandon her child, but she soon brushed away that thought. Chances were that the girl didn't even know herself. Chances were that she was too scared even to get her childish thoughts together.

Charity did everything that was required of her in a kind of daze. Her shift was supposed to end at midnight, but it was past two o'clock by the time it was all done. Even then, tired though she was, she didn't leave for home. There was something she wanted to do first. She slipped down to the shop on the ground floor. It was empty, apart from the bored, pimply young man behind the counter. Charity couldn't afford much, so she chose the smallest toy she could – a little pink and blue teddy bear, not much bigger than her hand. She paid for it, and then headed back to the maternity suite.

It was never easy going into the Special Care Baby Unit, but tonight's trip was more difficult than most. She walked into the observation room and saw them lined up, those fragile little bundles of life. There were seven of them tonight, all lying in their sterile incubators, their stillness giving no clue to the desperate struggle each of them was making for their very existence.

The little girl the midwife had delivered lay at the end of the row. She was the smallest of them all, and she lay so still that had it not been for the regular pinging of the heart monitor by her side, you might never have known she was alive. A feeding tube had been inserted into her impossibly tiny nose, and a little oxygen mask covered her face. The baby was bathed in the glow of ultra-violet light to prevent jaundice.

How long Charity stood and stared at the child she could not have said. Eventually, though, she was awakened from her dream-like state by a voice.

'You should go home.'

She turned around. One of the doctors was standing just by her, a quietly spoken Asian man by the name of Sunil, whom she had always found to be very friendly.

'I just wanted to see how she was getting on,' she said quietly.

Sunil nodded and gave a sad little smile. 'Too early to say.' Charity was pleased that he didn't offer any platitudes – they both knew that the baby's life hung in the balance, and it would have been disrespectful of him to pretend that wasn't the case.

'Is this the one?' he asked. 'The one whose mother left?'

The midwife nodded.

'Did you deliver her?'

'Yes,' she whispered.

'Well then,' Sunil continued, 'as her mother is not here to give her a name, I think she should be named after the person whose hands brought her into the world, don't you?'

The midwife blinked, and was surprised to feel tears in her eyes. She turned back to the incubator. 'Charity,' she breathed, and then shook her head. No. It wasn't right. 'I don't think so,' she told the doctor. 'This little girl will need enough charity in her life as it is.'

The doctor shrugged. 'That's true,' he said. 'But she needs a name. I think you should choose it.'

Charity's eyes misted over. 'I was pregnant once,' she said. 'Oh, I lost the child. But that didn't stop me giving it a name.' She smiled. 'Dani. That's what we'll call her.'

Sunil put his hand on her shoulder, and then left the observation room. The midwife knew that she too should leave soon, but she allowed herself a couple more minutes with the little girl. It didn't seem right just to leave her. On a whim, she stepped out of the observation room and, checking to see that no one was watching, walked into the Special Care ward itself and up to the little girl's Perspex cot. She lay the soft toy she had bought on the clear cover – no doubt it would be removed by a doctor, but she didn't know what else to do with it. It lay there as floppy and seemingly lifeless as the baby herself.

'Just get through this, my little love,' she found herself whispering to the child. 'Just get through this. Nothing you'll ever have to do in your life will be nearly as hard if you can just get through this.'

She drew a deep breath and did her best to steady the emotion that was suddenly threatening to overcome her.

'Keep fighting, little Dani,' she breathed.

She did her best to smile at the baby, who didn't even know she was there; then she turned and left the ward, closing the door quietly behind her.

Chapter One

Twelve years later

Dani Sinclair heard the bell go for morning break. All around her, her classmates scuffed their chairs back and started talking. The teacher at the front of the class – Mr Wynn – called out something, but it was lost in the hubbub of noise as everyone hurried out excitedly for breaktime.

Everybody except Dani.

Nobody stopped to run out to the playground with her. Nobody called to her, or smiled at her, or paid her any attention at all. And for that, Dani was pleased. When the other children did pay attention to her, it wasn't the kind of attention she wanted.

She was the last to leave the classroom, and Mr Wynn hurried her on. 'Come on, Dani,' he said impatiently. 'Outside for break-time, please.'

Dani nodded timidly and left the classroom; Mr Wynn followed her out into the playground.

It was a clear winter's day, cold enough for the raw chill of the air to burn Dani's bare legs. Her school skirt was short, not as a fashion statement, but because her mum – her foster mum, actually – had not bought her any new clothes for ages. All her school mates seemed to have new trainers every other week, and they certainly noticed that Dani was not as well dressed as them. It was one of the many things that they used to pick on her.

She skirted round the edge of the playground, trying to make it look as if she was busy doing something when in fact she was just wandering aimlessly. As she passed certain groups of kids, they shouted names at her, but she was so used to them doing so that she hardly heard them.

Dani had been wandering for perhaps five minutes when they stopped her. Ashley and Tammy were the two most popular girls in the class. They had long hair and wore perfume and make-up, even though you weren't supposed to at school. It made them look much older than their twelve years, and it also put them on a different side of the playground to Dani, who never had anything to make her look pretty. Ashley and Tammy were mean girls. They were always picking on Dani, always teasing her for being so quiet, always trying to get her to say dirty words she didn't want to say. They made her cry on an almost daily basis, and she hated it when they turned their attention to her.

Dani tried to carry on walking, to get away from the potential confrontation, but they weren't having it. Tammy wolf-whistled at her, and Ashley stepped forwards and grabbed hold of the hem of her skirt, pulling it up and down so that it billowed. From somewhere else, Dani heard the sound of other children laughing, and she felt blood rise to the skin of her face.

'What you doing, Sinclair? Going on the pull?' Ashley called.

Embarrassed, Dani looked down at the ground and carried on trying to walk away; but the girls kept following her.

'Don't think there's anyone fancies you much round here,' Tammy added.

'Shut up,' Dani retorted from behind clenched teeth.

It wasn't like her to answer back. The other girls knew it and they jeered. Ashley went for the skirt again. This time, Dani swung round and lashed out at the other girl. It was a pitiful sight – Dani was no fighter, and the other two were good at it. Immediately they piled in, pushing Dani to the ground and pulling at her hair. Dani wanted to fight back, but she was not good at this sort of thing, and she curled up into a little ball as a crowd gathered round to watch the entertainment. There were shouts of encouragement as the girls started punching her curled-up body. Dani was in no doubt about who they all wanted to win the fight.

'Fucking cry-baby,' Ashley shouted gleefully when she noticed the hot tears that had suddenly started to stream down Dani's face. And then again, in a sing-song voice, slightly babyish but all the more aggressive for that: '*Fucking cry-baby* …'

'All right, you three. That's enough!' a man's voice barked from nearby. Dani looked up to see Mr Wynn, his green eyes flashing angrily. 'I said, *that's enough!*'

The scratching and clawing stopped. Humiliated at being the only one still on the ground, Dani pushed herself up.

'That's not the first time I've seen you three fighting,' Mr Wynn said severely. 'I don't expect to see it happening again.'

Dani looked wide-eyed at him, smarting from the injustice of it.

'Don't look at me like that, Miss Sinclair,' Mr Wynn snapped. 'I won't have any fighting in the playground while I'm on duty. Is that understood?'

Dani felt herself nodding. 'Yes, sir,' she said quietly.

'Ashley? Tammy?'

'Yes, sir,' they replied in unison, their voices chanting almost sarcastically.

'Good.' Mr Wynn nodded his head decisively, and then turned and walked to the other end of the playground. With his back to them, he did not see the spiteful little smile that Ashley and Tammy cast in Dani's direction.

It was late on Friday evening, and there were three people in the meeting: Kate Swinton, a tall, curly-haired social worker with a thin face and kind eyes; Andy Martin, also a social worker – a young man with a shaved head to hide the fact that he was balding; and Alice Gray, a fair bit older than the other two, their line manager. It had been a long afternoon, and their meeting had overrun. All three of them were looking forward to getting out of the bland room in the council offices and going home. But there was a final case to get through before that could happen.

'All right,' Alice said with a sigh of relief. 'Last one.' She looked at the agenda on the table in front of her. 'One of yours, I think, Kate?'

Kate Swinton nodded. 'Dani Sinclair. Twelve years old. I've mentioned her to you once or twice before.'

Alice smiled. 'Sorry, Kate,' she said. 'Heavy caseload. You'll have to refresh my memory.'

Kate pulled a file out from a little pile by her side. 'She's only come my way in the last couple of years. Before that we had no reason to become involved. She was placed with a foster family at birth, a couple in south-west London. Two younger siblings, but neither of them fostered.'

'Unusual,' Andy butted in.

'Mmm,' Kate replied. 'I spoke to the mother about it. They tried to conceive naturally for a long time before they fostered, and she fell pregnant soon afterwards.'

'Sod's law.'

'Quite.'

'Come on,' their line manager said briskly. 'Let's wrap this up. What's the problem with the child?'

'Difficult to say,' Kate told her. 'On the surface of it, nothing – at least nothing that I can detect. She's very quiet, and by all accounts finds it difficult to make friends. Young for her age, I'd say – not as streetwise as a lot of the kids we see nowadays. But that's really nothing out of the ordinary – nothing that would require our intervention. It's the mother who's more of a worry. Her husband left the family home two years ago as a result of an affair, and he hasn't been back since. Divorce is only just coming through now, but he's not paying any maintenance, and the CSA being what it is …'

Alice rolled her eyes.

'Exactly,' Kate said. 'Anyway, unusually it was the mother who got in touch with us. Her husband leaving hit her pretty hard, I think. She told me that it was getting more and more difficult to look after the three children, and she didn't think she could continue fostering Dani.'

Both Alice and Andy blinked. 'How old did you say the girl was again?'

'Twelve.'

'And she's lived with the foster mother all her life?'

Kate nodded.

Alice shook her head. 'Some people—' she muttered. 'Are you trying to tell me she's requesting that the girl be reassigned?'

'I'm afraid so.'

'Has she given you any reason, other than not being able to cope? Any *real* reason, I mean?'

'Yes. She's complaining that the child is showing signs of becoming violent.'

'Violent?'

'Getting into fights at school, attacking the other two children at home.'

'Have you spoken to the school about it?'

'Yes.' Kate pulled a piece of paper out of her file and glanced at it. 'I spoke to a Gina Sawyer, her class teacher. She seemed very surprised by the suggestion that Dani was aggressive. My understanding is that Dani Sinclair does get into scrapes, but they're not of her own making.'

'Bullying?'

Kate shrugged slightly. 'Her teacher didn't use that word, but that's what it sounded like to me.'

Alice frowned. 'Poor little thing. What's your take on it?'

Kate took a deep breath. 'Well,' she said, 'the mother's approached us, so we have to follow it up. I don't think there's any doubt that she's finding things tough. Money's obviously tighter than it used to be, which doesn't help matters. But in my view, moving the child from her family home would be deeply traumatic, especially if she's having difficulty at school. I think it should be avoided.'

'I'm assuming you have no reason to believe the child is in danger. No signs of abuse?'

Kate shook her head. 'As I say, she's a very retiring kind of girl. It's difficult to get much out of her. I wouldn't say she's the happiest child I've ever met, but no, I wouldn't say she's demonstrating any of the warning signs.'

'Do you think we need a supervision order?'

'I'd say it's early days for that.'

'OK.' Alice looked at Kate and Andy. 'Kate, you need to keep tabs on the family – keep an eye out for any deterioration. But are we agreed that it's in the child's best interest for her to stay where she is?'

'Absolutely,' the two social workers said in unison.

'Good.' Alice smiled at them. 'Well, I guess that wraps everything up.' She scraped her chair back and stood up. 'Have a good weekend, you two. I'll see you both on Monday.'

Dani Sinclair had dark brown hair, pale skin and clear brown eyes. She was small for her age, though close up you could tell that she was almost a teenager. When she cried, the tears would collect in her lower lids like water swelling against a dam; but the dam would eventually break, and the tears would suddenly wet her cheeks profusely. It happened a lot. Dani was a tearful little girl, not robust like some children, and she found it difficult to stop herself from crying when she started to feel the tears coming.

She felt them coming now as she sat at the meal table with the two younger ones. It was fish fingers for tea.

Dani didn't really like fish fingers – didn't like the way the fish oozed a kind of milky sap against the orange bread-crumbs when they were warm. But she never said so because the other two – James and Rebecca – loved them. Instead, she pushed the little pieces around her plate, occasionally summoning up the courage to eat a mouthful. She knew that they just got worse as they grew colder, but that didn't make it any easier to eat them up when they were hot.

At the other side of the small kitchen, their mum clat-tered around at the sink. Dani would be in trouble when her mum saw that she had barely eaten any of the food, and that thought spurred her on a bit. She stuck her fork into a piece of fish finger, put it in her mouth, chewed and swal-lowed. She shivered as the food went down.

'Finished!' Rebecca shouted loudly.

'Me too!' James chimed in.

Their mum turned from the sink, suds dripping from the yellow washing-up gloves she was wearing. She walked to the table and picked up the two empty plates, before looking down at Dani's.

Dani returned the look and steeled herself for what was to come.

'You're a fussy little beggar, Dani,' she snapped. 'Why can't you eat the food I give you? Why can't you be more like your brother and sister?'

Dani kept quiet, and endured the smug stares coming from the younger children.

'Go on,' her mum said waspishly. 'I'm sick of the sight of you. Go to your room.'

Silently Dani got down from the table, left the kitchen and trudged up the stairs. 'And when your Auntie Rose comes round, you make sure you don't have that surly bloody look on your face!' Mum's voice carried up the stairs.

'Dani never eats her dinner, does she, Mum?' she heard Rebecca saying from the kitchen.

'Shut up, Rebecca,' the little girl was told.

Mum wasn't her real mum. Dani had known that for as long as she could remember. But she hadn't always been like this. In Dani's earliest memories, things had been happier. There had been a man in the house, for one thing – the man she called Daddy. He had been kind to the children, and to Dani in particular. One day, however, he wasn't there any more. Dani asked any number of times where her Daddy had gone, but she never received a straight answer from her mum. It was left to her to piece things together from half-heard conversations between grown-ups not intended for her ears. Conversations about things she didn't really understand.

Dani opened the door to her bedroom. The other two children shared a room, but having a room to herself was not intended as a treat for Dani – she knew that well enough. It was because Rebecca would rather share with James than with her. Their room was nice and big; Dani's was tiny, with room for only a small single bed and an old chest of drawers. But she didn't mind. No one ever really disturbed her in here. It was the one place she could go and be sure of being by herself. She sat on the bed, hugged her knees and rested her head against the wall. The wallpaper was pink; her dad had put it up for her before he left and nowit was looking a bit old and tatty – in one corner it was coming away from the wall. There wasn't any point mentioning it to Mum, of course, any more than it was worth mentioning the trouble she'd had at school that day. She would probably just shout at her, so she kept quiet about it.

Downstairs, she heard the television being switched on. Dani would have liked to have gone down to watch it with the others, but she chose not to – not with Mum in the mood she was in. Much better, she had learned, to keep herself to herself. She put her thumb in her mouth, closed her eyes and gently rocked herself. It would be bedtime soon. Bedtime was all right. When the lights were out, she could lose herself in her own little world and pretend things were better than they really were.

In truth, she knew, they could hardly be worse.

It had been several months ago that Mum had first told her she didn't want Dani to live with them any more. Her words rang in the little girl's head more clearly than anything anyone had ever said to her. At first she had persuaded herself that it was just a joke, that she didn't really mean it; but when she kept repeating it in moments of anger, Dani wasn't so sure. The arrival of the social worker had confirmed it for her. She was a nice lady called Kate, who had come to talk first to Mum and then to Dani herself. The grown-ups didn't know that Dani had listened in on their conversation, however; they didn't know she had heard her mum beg the social worker to take her away. 'I can't cope with her any more,' Mum had said. 'She's going off the rails, always fighting other kids and bullying her brother and sister.'

Dani had blinked. She didn't recognise herself in that description at all. But she knew that she would have to try very hard to make her mum want her again. It was difficult, though. Dani never seemed to be able to do anything right. Anything at all. She was always being shouted at, complained about. One time, Mum had even hit her – not hard, but hard enough to bring those tears to her eyes that always seemed to enrage her mother even more.

The very thought of it made her want to cry now.

She was woken from her reverie by the ringing of the doorbell and a little fluttering of apprehension in her stomach. That would be Auntie Rose. Dani couldn't decide what to do. If she stayed here in her bedroom, she would be told off and accused of being unfriendly; but if she went downstairs, no doubt they would find something to complain about. Dani sat still, paralysed by indecision for a few minutes, before finally deciding to leave the safety of her bedroom and venture back downstairs. She grabbed the little pink and blue teddy bear – the one that had been hers ever since she was a baby, which was now worn and tatty and was still deeply loved – and went down.

At first, nobody noticed her standing in the doorway of the front room. Mum was in the kitchen, for a start, while James and Rebecca stood around Auntie Rose. Dani's aunt – her mum's sister – was a chubby lady. In her private moments, Dani had always thought that she looked a bit like a toad – a fat, poisonous toad with jowly cheeks and flat eyes that would sit there, hardly moving, waiting to be fed. She looked particularly toad-like today, sitting on the comfortable sofa with a wide, indulgent smile on her face. In her hands there was a large, dark green plastic bag. Not the sort of plastic bag Mum brought back from the supermarket: this was thicker and altogether more exciting – you could tell just by looking at it that it contained something more fun than food shopping. James and Rebecca could tell that too. They stood excitedly on tiptoes, waiting to see what their aunt had brought them.

James's present came out first – a shiny metal car in a bright yellow box. 'Thank you, Auntie Rose,' he gabbled automatically, before taking his gift off to a corner of the room to unwrap it further. Meanwhile, Auntie Rose was removing something else from the bag. Rebecca looked a little crestfallen when she saw what it was: a magic wand, with a star at one end and a little button at the other. She pressed the button and the wand lit up, a sparkling golden colour. There was a tiara too, which Auntie Rose placed on Rebecca's head before pinching her affectionately on the cheek.

'Auntie Rose,' Rebecca said in a quiet, whingey voice. 'I'm too old for toys like that. I'm not a baby.'

Auntie Rose bristled slightly, and looked as if she was about to tell Rebecca off for her ingratitude; but at that moment she noticed Dani, and the indulgent smile fell from her face. 'Dani,' she said abruptly, as though greeting a grown-up she didn't like very much. Her voice was lower than that of most of the women Dani knew.

'Hello, Auntie Rose,' Dani replied politely. She glanced at Rebecca's glowing wand and the plastic bag. She didn't really expect there to be anything in it for her, but she couldn't help feeling a whisper of hope.

Auntie Rose looked away. 'You're too old for toys like that, Dani,' she said by way of explanation that the bag was empty.

Dani felt a tiny crush of disappointment. In her mind she searched for the words to explain that Rebecca was only a year younger than her; but it wasn't in her nature to answer back, and anyway, before she could say anything, she felt her mum pushing past her into the front room.

'You spoil them, Rose,' she said perfunctorily. 'They've got enough toys as it is.' She handed her sister one of the glasses of wine she was carrying, and then took a hearty swig from her own.

'I *like* to spoil them, Tess,' Auntie Rose replied. She also took a sip from her wine, and the awkwardness with Dani seemed to be immediately forgotten as they started chatting. Unobserved, Dani took a step backwards, and then silently climbed back upstairs to the refuge of her bedroom.

It had always been like this. Even before Dad left, Dani had always felt second best. Mum made no secret about it – about the fact that after Rebecca and James came along, she had wanted Dani to move somewhere else. It was Dad who had insisted on her staying, but now he had left. 'Run off' was the phrase everyone used. And since then, Mum had seemed increasingly bitter towards the little girl, as though she had been left with a burden she had long since lost interest in but couldn't get rid of.

It was just the way things were. But that didn't stop it hurting every time she was left out. It didn't stop the little surge of embarrassment and shame coming to her cheeks. It didn't stop her from almost crying. She was almost crying now, as she sat once more on her bed, waiting for night-time to come.

Half an hour later, perhaps a little more, she heard James and Rebecca traipsing upstairs. There was a time when Dani would be in charge of making sure they brushed their teeth and washed their faces, but that time was long gone – there was no way her siblings would ever put up with being bossed around by Dani now. And so she waited, listening for the sounds of them getting ready for bed to die away. Eventually she heard footsteps up the stairs – not the fast, impatient footsteps of her mum but the more plodding gait of Auntie Rose. She listened as the footsteps went into James and Rebecca's room. It sounded as if she was going to read them a story. Stories were a bit babyish, she knew. Still, for a moment Dani considered knocking on their door and asking if she could listen too, just for a bit of company. Just to feel as if she was part of things. But she soon discarded that thought. They probably wouldn't say no, but it would still be clear to everyone – her included – that she wasn't really welcome there. No, there wouldn't be a story for Dani tonight. There hadn't been a story for her since the night her dad had left.

A few minutes passed, and eventually Dani heard Auntie Rose going back downstairs again. She would be staying until late in the evening, drinking wine with Mum until they both became drunk and noisy. Dad never liked Mum drinking alcohol, but she did it more and more now, as if she was punishing him for going off like that, proving that she could have a nice time without him. But it never really seemed to Dani that she *was* having a nice time – not if the way her mood got even worse the morning after was anything to go by.

Dani gave it a few more minutes before deciding to go and brush her teeth and get ready for bed herself.

It was dark outside now, and the landing light had been switched off. Rebecca's wand caught Dani's eye the moment she stepped out of her bedroom door. It was lying on the floor, discarded but still switched on, its glow bathing the landing in a soft, golden light. To Dani's young eyes, it looked like some kind of treasure, and she found herself walking almost automatically towards it. She knelt down and gingerly picked it up.

It was such a beautiful thing, she thought. She couldn't understand why Rebecca hadn't liked it, why she had just left it lying there. If it had been Dani's, she would have taken better care of it; she would have put it somewhere special in her room and made sure it could not get damaged by accident. She longed to take it to bed with her, keeping it switched on under the covers so that everything would be suffused with its magical light.

Gently, Dani switched if off and then on again; off and on. She waved it in the air, drawing an elegant curve as she whispered something under her breath – a magic spell in an invented language. How the others in her class at school would laugh at her if they saw her doing this – Dani was always going off in her own little world, and being teased for doing so.

'What you doing with my toy?'

Dani jumped, and looked guiltily over her shoulder. Rebecca was standing there in her nightdress, an accusing look on her face.

'Nothing. Nothing … I was just—'

'Give it here.' Dani's foster sister lashed her arm out and grabbed the other end of the wand. It happened in a split second – the golden star at the end broke off in Rebecca's hand, and the light was immediately extinguished, plunging the landing into a semi-darkness that was broken only by the light from the hallway downstairs. For a moment the two girls looked in silent horror at the broken toy, and Dani felt a twist of apprehension in the pit of her stomach.

She knew what was coming.

Sure enough, her ears were suddenly filled with the sound of Rebecca's wailing scream. 'Mum! *Mum!* Look what she's done now, Mum!' Then she threw the piece of the wand that was in her hand down to where Dani was kneeling.

Dani froze as she heard the sound of footsteps rushing up the stairs. The landing light was turned on and there she was, Dani's foster mother, looking down on her as she held half the broken toy in her hand.

In her little mind, time seemed to stand still.

Then the air was full of screaming. *'What the hell do you think you're doing?'*

Dani's tongue seemed to stick in her throat, and her body started to shake as she tried to catch her breath. 'I didn't …' she whispered.

Then Rebecca was screaming too. 'She broke it! She broke my wand! It was her – I saw her do it!'

Suddenly Auntie Rose was there, wrapping Rebecca in her arms and whispering soothing words to her. Dani's mum, however, had grabbed Dani by the arm and pulled her to her feet. 'Get to your room,' she hissed, and she pushed the little girl along the landing and through the door, slamming it closed so that the two of them were shut in there. Dani thought she could smell wine on her.

'I'm sick of you!' her mum blazed. 'You haven't got a fucking idea, have you? What it's like.'

Dani was sobbing uncontrollably, great heaving sobs shaking through her whole body. She desperately wanted to explain to her mum that she hadn't broken Rebecca's toy, that she *wouldn't*, but the words would not form in her mouth.

The little girl's sobs seemed only to enrage her foster mother even more. 'What have you got to say for yourself? *What have you got to say for yourself?*'

She didn't answer, and her silence seemed to push the woman over the edge. It seemed to happen in slow motion as she raised her hand and brought it down with a surprising, shocking force against the side of Dani's face. She started to fall towards her bed, and as she did so, her ankle twisted, as did her body. With a sharp, sickening bang, her face fell against the corner of her chest of drawers. The thud seemed to go all through her as she continued falling to the floor, and within a few seconds she felt a burning, stinging sensation creep over her skin. She looked up at her mum, who was standing above her, eyes blazing. She seemed surprised by what she had just done, but not, Dani thought, sorry.

'I wish we'd never set eyes on you,' her mum hissed, and Dani thought she could detect a slurring in her voice. 'It was *him* that insisted on taking you in. *Him.* Twelve years, and never a word of thanks for what I've done. And how dare you go around breaking my daughter's toys? How fucking *dare* you?'

Dani just stared at her, wide-eyed.

'You're an arrogant little cow,' her mum said, delivering a parting shot before turning round, leaving the room and slamming the door behind her.

Dani stayed on the floor for several minutes, her hand pressed painfully to the side of her face that her mum had hit with such sudden violence, tears welling in her eyes. There was the murmur of voices on the landing – Auntie Rose calming Mum down – but no one came to Dani's room. Noone came to check that she was all right.

Dani didn't clean her teeth that night or wash her face. She just removed her clothes, switched off the light and climbed into bed. She wept for a long time, being sure not to make too much noise about it.

After all, she had created enough trouble for one day.

Chapter Two

The following morning was Sunday, and everything was unusually quiet in the house.

Dani woke with a throbbing pain on the side of her face. In her chest of drawers was a hand mirror. She took it out and had a look at herself. The bruising was a mottled purple-black. It surrounded her left eye and went down the side of her face. Gently she touched her skin with her fingertips and winced. It was terribly sore, even to the lightest touch. Her arm was sore too, where Mum had grabbed it to drag her into the room. Dani peeled away the material of her nightie and saw bruising there too.

She gazed at herself in the mirror for what seemed like an age before mustering the courage to go downstairs.

James and Rebecca were already there, watching television in the front room. They knew not to have it on too loud in case it woke Mum up. As Dani appeared in the door, they both turned to look at her.

Their stares said it all.

'You all right?' James said in a small voice.

Dani nodded, and gave the boy a little smile. He looked frightened, and she didn't want him to be. Then she turned to Rebecca.

'I never broke your toy,' she said, doing her best not to let herself cry.

Rebecca didn't reply. Her lips went a little bit thin, her eyes narrowed and she turned resolutely back to the television, as if she was doing her best to pretend Dani wasn't even there.

Dani left them to it and went to the kitchen.

The place was a mess. There were two empty bottles of wine on the side, and an overflowing ashtray that smelled so bad it made Dani want to be sick. Dani took the cardboard wrappers from the microwave meals Mum and Auntie Rose had obviously had for their dinner and tried to put them in the bin; but it was full to overflowing, and she couldn't get them in, even by pushing the other rubbish down hard. So she left it where it was, her attempt to stop her mum being even more angry with her ending before it had really begun, and went back up to her bedroom.

It was at least an hour before she heard her mum getting up. Dani didn't know whether she was scared that she might come into her room, or whether she hoped she would. Either way, it didn't matter. She listened to the sound of her getting ready in the bathroom and stomping down the stairs. Minutes later the front door slammed shut.

By lunchtime she hadn't returned, so Dani made sandwiches for them all. James and Rebecca seemed unable to look at her bruised face as she handed them over, and she took her own lunch up to her room and ate it there.

All afternoon, Dani stayed in her room, occasionally looking at herself in the mirror. Mum didn't return until evening. She didn't come and see Dani, who went without any dinner and spent a broken, fitful night worrying about what people would say when they saw her at school the next day.

Miss Sawyer was late, and she broke her own rule by running down the corridor towards her classroom, her register and other school books clasped tightly to her chest. God only knows, she thought to herself, what bedlam the kids were creating. She knew from experience that the lesson would be a write-off – let them run riot in the first few minutes and they'd never calm down. What a way to start Monday morning!

She glanced at her watch. Five past nine. 'Shit,' she muttered, and she upped her pace slightly.

Gina Sawyer's classroom was at the far corner of the school, so it took a while to get there. It was a big school, with a huge catchment area that covered some of the biggest, most sprawling estates in the area as well as more well-to-do parts of town. She had worked there getting on for ten years now, and although some days seemed like a struggle, she was honest enough with herself to admit that she thrived on it. That said, there was no doubt that things were getting tougher nowadays. Some of the kids they had to deal with barely seemed like kids at all: they were so full of anger, so well versed in the world of adults. More than once, children who Miss Sawyer knew when they were only small had been excluded for carrying knives; and she'd lost count of the number of teenage pregnancies she'd had to deal with in her additional role as child support officer. By rights she was an English teacher, but the truth was that the teaching bit of the job was something that she seldom got to do.

Miss Sawyer was out of breath as she turned into the corridor where her classroom was located, so she slowed her run down to a brisk walk. Just ahead of her, walking a good deal more slowly in the same direction, was a pupil. Miss Sawyer recognised her immediately, even from behind – recognised the long, black hair and the slightly battered book bag that was slung sloppily over her shoulder.

'Come on, Dani,' she said, doing her best to hide her breathlessness. 'Chop chop. The bell went five minutes ago.'

Little Dani Sinclair was a funny one. Twelve years old, but to look at her you wouldn't think she was more than nine or ten. The teacher supposed that the girl had a working vocabulary, but if she did then it was seldom given an outing. In all her years teaching she had never come across such a quiet child. Hardly surprising that she was often picked on, because she never fought back. She just wasn't that kind of girl.

It had only been a few days earlier that a social worker had come into the school to talk about Dani. There had been reports, the woman had said, of the little girl starting fights. Had the social worker not been so earnest, Miss Sawyer would have found the idea almost comical. Dani Sinclair would no more be involved in that sort of thing than stand in the middle of the playground reciting Shakespeare. She had respectfully put the social worker's mind at rest and promised she would keep a special eye on Dani.

The little girl stopped walking, and Miss Sawyer noticed from behind that she appeared to lower her head and move her hand up to the side of her face, as though hiding it.

'Dani?' she asked. 'Are you all right? What's the matter?'

The little girl didn't answer.

Miss Sawyer took a couple of steps towards her; then she bent over so that she was more on Dani's level and put a gentle hand on her shoulder. The girl immediately shrugged her away, suddenly, as though she had been burned. She walked towards the wall and kept her face covered.

'Dani Sinclair,' Miss Sawyer said a bit more sharply than she intended. 'I really don't think it's at all appropriate for you to behave towards your teach—'

She stopped. The moment she had raised her voice, the little girl had seemed to jump. Her arm fell limply to her side and she slowly turned round and faced the teacher. It was that look that had stopped Miss Sawyer in her tracks.

One of Dani's eyes was almost closed. The lids were swollen and black, and the bruising extended all the way down one side of her face. A twitch of embarrassment flickered over the side of her face that wasn't bruised, and Miss Sawyer noticed that she avoided looking her teacher in the eye.

'Oh my God,' she whispered. 'Dani, what happened to you?'

Dani's face twitched again, but she didn't say anything.

From down the corridor, Miss Sawyer became aware of the sound of her class, boisterous as she expected. She looked over in that direction, slightly panicking that if she didn't go now and sort them out, they'd just go from bad to worse. But another quick look at Dani's face reminded her that she had a more important duty now.

'Come with me, Dani, love,' she said, as kindly as she could. She offered the child her hand, but Dani declined to take it. She just followed slowly, her feet dragging, as Miss Sawyer led her to the office where she dealt with child protection issues.

It was a small office, cosy in its way. There was a wooden desk and a comfortable chair, which seemed to dwarf Dani as she sat in it.

'Would you like a glass of orange, Dani?' Miss Sawyer offered.

Dani shook her head.

'What about a biscuit? I think I've got some chocolate ones somewhere.'

Another shake of the head.

'OK,' Miss Sawyer said quietly as she took her seat behind the desk. She couldn't remember a pupil ever turning down drinks and biscuits during school hours, but then she had to remind herself that Dani had always been a bit more timid than most. 'Now then, Dani, why don't you tell me how you got the black eye?'

The child didn't answer. She just looked down at the floor.

'Dani, love, you won't get into trouble for just telling me who it was. We can make sure it doesn't happen again.'

'No one did it,' the girl replied quickly. She looked scared.

Miss Sawyer narrowed her eyes. 'What do you mean, no one did it?'

Dani looked around the office, confusion in her face. 'I mean – I mean … It was me.'

'You?'

'I got in a fight. On the way to school.' Still she refused to catch Miss Sawyer's eyes.

'A fight? When?'

'This morning.'

'Who with?'

'Some boys.'

'Which boys, Dani? Why don't you tell me?'

A look of desperate concentration passed across Dani's bruised face, and she shook her head.

Miss Sawyer sighed. It was so often the way: kids getting beaten up and refusing to admit who it was. The unwritten code of silence was stronger in the school than she imagined it was in any prison. Even so, something wasn't right. It took a while for bruises to come up like that. Whatever had happened to the little girl hadn't happened just this morning.

'Are you sure you're telling the truth, Dani? You can tell me, you know. You won't get in trouble.'

'*I am!*' The girl's voice was uncharacteristically firm.

Miss Sawyer sighed. She knew there was more to this than met the eye, but what could she do? 'All right, Dani,' she said in a resigned tone of voice. 'I can't make you tell me. But if you decide you want to, you only have to say.'

Dani remained tight-lipped and looking at the floor.

'In the meantime, I don't think you need to be at school today. You wait here and I'll call your mum. She can come and get you and take you home. You can stay there until your face gets better, if you like.'

As she spoke, Miss Sawyer saw something change in Dani's expression. She almost looked as if she was about to say something, but the moment soon passed, and she went back to staring at the floor.

'I'll be back in a few minutes,' Miss Sawyer said. 'Are you sure you wouldn't like some orange while you wait?'

'What did you tell her?'

They were alone in the kitchen. Mum had arrived at school quickly with a dangerous kind of look in her face. Her eyes widened slightly when she saw the extent of the damage to her face: this was the first time she had looked at her foster daughter since the night it had happened, Dani having crept out of the house early for school that morning. She rushed Dani out of Miss Sawyer's office, despite the fact that the teacher seemed to want to talk. They hadn't spoken a word on the way home, Mum walking briskly and Dani struggling to keep up with her. Now she was looking accusingly down at her foster daughter, her eyes cold.

'*What the hell did you tell her?*'

'Nothing,' Dani replied.

'You just said you'd got in a fight?'

Dani nodded her head.

Mum seemed slightly mollified. 'Good,' she muttered. 'She wouldn't have believed you anyway.' She sounded to Dani as if she was trying to persuade herself, but the little girl didn't know why, because it was true. No one would *ever* believe her if she told them what really happened.

Mum turned away from her and took a packet of cigarettes from her bag. She lit one and sucked in deeply as the acrid smell hit Dani's nose. She felt the familiar sensation of tears welling in her; she did her best to suppress it, but she never could. The others at school called her a cry baby, and they were right. She always seemed to be crying.

'I didn't break Rebecca's toy,' she whispered, her voice cracking.

It was as if something snapped in her mum. She turned round and there was a look in her eyes that terrified Dani to the very core. Her mum looked crazy. She stepped towards Dani, and as she did so she raised the hand that held her cigarette. As if by reflex, Dani cowered, falling to her knees and automatically raising her arms to cover the bruised side of her face as she waited for the blow. 'Please don't hit me,' she cried.

But the blow didn't come; instead, there was a torrent of words. 'Just get out of my sight, Dani. You're always causing trouble. You should count yourself lucky you don't get punished more often. Go on, go to your room. I don't want to see you any more. I'm sick and tired of having you under this roof. Sick and tired of it, you ungrateful little—' And there her words deserted her.

Dani looked up to see that her mum had lowered her arm and was dragging again on the cigarette, fiercely, as though the smoke was the only thing that could stop her from going over the edge. In the sudden silence that followed the outburst, she could hear the ash crackling as a good third of the cigarette burned down in one puff. Dani knew when to take her chance. She stood up, steadied herself on legs that felt suddenly very weak and ran up the stairs to her bedroom.

Downstairs, she heard something crash, but she couldn't tell what it was.

Miss Sawyer had been distracted all morning. Little Dani Sinclair's bruises were terrible, and something hadn't been quite right when her mother had turned up. Mrs Sinclair had seemed worried, certainly. Concerned. But not affectionate. There had been no kind words or hugs, just a vague impression that this was all a bit of an inconvenience.

It wasn't just the mother. Miss Sawyer didn't believe for a minute that it was Dani who had started the so-called fight – she was clearly just scared, protecting whoever the real culprits were. And in the wake of the social worker's warning the previous week, it all seemed as if there was something more going on. So, come morning break, instead of joining her colleagues for a cup of coffee, she made her way to her office and phoned social services. Short of going round to the Sinclair house and getting to the bottom of this herself, it was all she could do.

Gina Sawyer just hoped she was doing the right thing.

It was mid-afternoon when the doorbell rang. Dani hadn't dared venture out of her room all day. She was hungry, but not hungry enough to risk a trip to the kitchen. Curiosity, however, got the better of her now, and she pulled back a corner of the curtains that she had kept shut all day and took a peek to see who it was.

Her heart stopped when she saw the social worker, Kate. She was a nice lady, but her very presence scared Dani.

She had shoulder-length curly hair and was wearing a skirt with a smart matching jacket. Under her arm she had a leather case. Through the window Dani could tell that the door had been opened, and Kate spoke for quite a long time before she was finally allowed into the house. Butterflies fluttered in Dani's stomach. What was she here for? What did she want? *Please, God*, she whispered in her mind. *Don't let her be here to take me away.*

Walking as softly as she could, Dani crept out of her bedroom and tiptoed down the stairs, avoiding the third one from the top, which she knew creaked loudly when it was trodden upon. The door to the sitting room was ajar, and from inside she could hear voices. Her heart in her throat, she approached the door and stood outside, listening carefully.

Mum was crying. It was a strange sound to Dani's ears, because Mum never cried. The little girl felt a sudden hot rush of shame. Was it her fault that Mum was so upset? She strained her ears to hear what her foster mother was saying between sobs.

'I just can't cope with her any more,' she whimpered. 'She's gone off the rails and I can't control her … not by myself. She's always fighting, always bullying the little ones. We try to get her to behave and be part of the family, but she won't do it. I'm at my wits' end … I just don't know what to do.'

Dani blinked furiously as she listened. She felt embarrassed by what she heard.

The social worker started to speak. Her voice was calm and gentle. 'Mrs Sinclair,' she said. 'You have to understand how disruptive it would be for Dani to be taken out of the home environment she's known all her life—'

But as she spoke, a fresh wave of sobbing drowned her words. 'What about my children? My *real* children? It's affecting them too.' She dissolved once more into those strange-sounding tears.

'Mrs Sinclair,' the social worker asked, 'may I talk to Dani, please? Is she in the house?'

Panic surged through the little girl. She stepped away from the door and hurried up the stairs, doing her best to stay light-footed despite the sudden rush. Back in her bedroom, she sat on the bed, aware that her breathing was a bit heavier than it should have been and unable to stop her face looking guilty.

There was a knock on her bedroom door. 'Dani.' Kate's voice came softly. 'Can I come in?'

Dani shrank against the wall of her bedroom and didn't reply.

The door opened slowly and Kate appeared in the room. She had kind eyes, which Dani remembered from the last time she had been here; but those eyes suddenly widened when they saw the state of Dani's face.

'Mind if I sit down? Do you remember me?'

Dani nodded.

Kate gave her a smile. 'You look as if you've been in the wars. Want to tell me about it?'

Dani looked down at her bedclothes, feeling suddenly uncomfortable under the glare of the social worker's stare. Downstairs she heard the front door opening again – James and Rebecca coming back home from school. Having the whole family in the house, being the centre of attention when all she wanted to do was disappear into the background, made her feel even worse.

'Your teacher told me you got into a fight,' Kate persisted. '*Did* you get into a fight, Dani?'

She looked up, wide-eyed, and tried to put as much honesty in her face as possible; then she nodded her head. The moment she saw a look of suspicion in Kate's eyes, however, she looked away.

'I want you to know, Dani, that you can tell me anything you want without worrying that I'm going to tell anyone else. Do you understand that?'

Dani nodded her head again, still looking away.

'Miss Sawyer said you started the fight, but you know what I think? I think you're not the sort of girl who goes round picking fights with people.' The social worker stretched out her arm and squeezed the little girl's hand. 'You're not, are you?'

Dani shook her head.

A silence fell between them. It was broken only by the sound of Dani's mum downstairs, shouting something at James and Rebecca. The noise of her voice made Dani start, and she looked guiltily up at Kate.

The social worker's eyes narrowed, as if something had just made sense.

'Is there anything you want to tell me about your mum, Dani?'

She shook her head again, quickly and emphatically.

Another silence. When Kate spoke again, it was almost in a whisper. 'Dani,' she said. 'I want you to listen to me very carefully. Sometimes grown-ups do things that make children very sad. And sometimes, when that happens, children think it's their fault. But it's *not* their fault, Dani. If any grown-ups have done anything to make you feel sad, you *must* tell me. You won't be in trouble, I promise, and we can try and make sure it doesn't happen again. Ever.'

Dani clenched her teeth. Half of her wanted to tell Kate about what had happened; but the other half of her wanted to clam up, to keep it secret. If she told, it would only make things worse.

Kate squeezed her hand for a third time. 'I can't do anything if you don't tell me what happened, Dani,' she said quietly. 'Who did this to you?'

It happened so quickly. Just a single word that seemed to escape Dani's lips before she even knew she had said it. A single word that she never intended to say, but which was teased out of her by the kind eyes of the well-meaning woman in her room.

'Mum.'

Then, astonished by her confession, Dani covered her mouth with her hand and she felt the tears coming again. She shook her head, as if a sudden denial would somehow take back the word she had spoken, but it didn't. Kate's eyes narrowed slightly, and she sat there in silence for what seemed to Dani an age, though in truth it was little more than a minute.

'I want you to wait here, Dani,' the social worker said finally. There was something steely in her voice.

'You … you won't tell, will you? You won't say I told you?'

To Dani's horror, Kate didn't give a straight answer. 'Just wait here, Dani. I'll be straight back.' She stood up and left the room.

Dani found herself holding her breath. Holding her breath and waiting for the shouts.

They didn't take long to come.

'*She's a little fucking liar! Don't you see what I have to put up with!*' Dani felt herself cringing inside as she heard the unmistakable sound of footsteps coming up the stairs. Moments later, her mum was there in the room, the madness having returned to her eyes.

'What have you been saying? What lies have you been saying, you stupid little girl?'

'Nothing,' Dani whimpered. 'I never said anything. I promise.' But she could tell her mum didn't believe her. Her mum never believed her – why should she start now?

Suddenly she heard the social worker's voice again. 'Mrs Sinclair, please. This isn't in anyone's interest—'

'Oh, shut up!' Dani's mum shouted. 'What's it got to do with you anyway?'

'Mrs Sinclair.' The social worker's voice was suddenly startlingly firm. 'Your foster daughter has just made a full disclosure of substantial physical abuse. First thing tomorrow morning I'm going to apply to the courts for an Emergency Protection Order, but in the meantime, I intend to remove Dani to a place of safety. You can either let me do my job or you can obstruct me, in which case I will call the police.'

Kate's ultimatum hung in the air as Tess Sinclair looked between her foster daughter and the social worker, her lips thin and her eyes flashing. 'All right, all right!' she spat finally. She cast a poisoned look in Dani's direction, and then stamped back down the stairs.

Everything seemed to be a blur as the social worker walked back into Dani's room. 'Now listen to me, Dani,' she said. 'I'm going to take you somewhere else, so we need to pack a few things.'

Dani felt sick. 'I don't want to. Where are we going?'

'Somewhere safe. Just for a little bit, until things settle down here.'

'But I don't want to go anywhere else.'

'As I say, it's just for a little bit. You'll be able to come back home soon.'

'I was only joking,' Dani tried desperately. 'It wasn't really my mum. It was these boys, on the way to school—'

But the social worker gave her such a piercing look that there was no way she could maintain her lie, and she simply dissolved into a flood of tears. Kate took her in her arms and held her gently.

'Will I see my brother and sister again?' she asked weakly.

'Course you will, Dani. Just as soon as we've sorted everything out. Come on. I'll help you pack a few clothes.'

Ten minutes later, Dani had packed a small bag. There wasn't much in it – some underwear, a couple of tops, a pair of trousers and some pyjamas – but she made sure that her teddy bear, the one that had seen her through so many tearful nights, was safely stowed away. Then, with an encouraging look from the social worker, she followed Kate downstairs.

Mum was in the kitchen, smoking a cigarette and looking steadfastly out of the window.

'We'll be in touch, Mrs Sinclair. Would you like to say goodbye to Dani?'

Dani's mum glanced over her shoulder at them. She curled her lip spitefully and almost looked as if she was going to say something; but in the end she just took another drag on her cigarette and looked back out of the window.

Dani felt her face crumple into a confused frown as her foster mother's indifference stung her like little darts.

'Come on, Dani,' Kate said quietly. 'Let's go.' She took the girl's hand. As they left the kitchen, Dani looked back over her shoulder, hoping that her foster mother would have a change of heart and at least give her a goodbye cuddle. But Tess Sinclair remained where she was, cigarette in hand, facing resolutely in the other direction.

James and Rebecca were in the front room. They sat quietly, side by side, on the sofa, their faces a picture of incomprehension.

'Where you going, Dani?' James asked.

'Don't know,' Dani replied.

'Are you coming back?'

'Of course she's coming back, James,' the social worker butted in. 'Just as soon as she can.'

James's eyes grew wide, and he didn't seem to know what else to say. He shuffled a bit closer to his sister. Rebecca said nothing. She just watched in silence as Dani approached them and gave them both a kiss on the cheek.

'Bye, James,' Dani whispered. 'Bye, Rebecca. I'm sorry your wand got broke.' Rebecca looked down at the ground.

'Come on, Dani,' Kate said gently. 'You'll see your brother and sister soon.'

And with that, they left the house.

The social worker's small red car was waiting outside. Kate opened the boot and put Dani's clothes inside; then she opened the back door and waited for her to climb in. Dani, however, found herself rooted to the spot. This little house was where she had spent all her life – at least, all of it that she could remember. Suddenly she was being taken away, and it gave her a horrible feeling. A cold feeling. Somehow what her foster mother had done to her didn't matter – she wanted to go back. If only she had the words to explain it.

Whether or not the social worker could tell what she was feeling, Dani didn't know. But as she stood there looking back at the house, she felt Kate take her gently by the shoulders and manoeuvre her into the car. Had she been less timid, Dani would have struggled. But she didn't. She strapped herself in and let Kate close the door. There was something ominous about the way it banged shut.

As Kate walked round to the driver's entrance, Dani looked back towards the house. Through the glass, she could see the silhouettes of two children, their faces pressed against the living room window, watching them depart. Then another figure, taller than the others, appeared behind them, pulling them away and closing the curtains.

The engine started, and the car moved off.

From her seat in the back, Dani could see herself in the rear-view mirror. As she stared at her reflection, she hardly recognised the face – bruised, battered and totally terrified – that was staring back at her.

Dani Sinclair looked like a stranger, even to herself.

Chapter Three

As they drove, the social worker made some phone calls, jabbering away on her mobile, clearly talking about Dani and making arrangements but saying things that the little girl didn't understand. Not that she was listening much. She just stared out of the window of the moving car, the shock of what had just happened seeming to numb her.

'How are you doing, Dani?' Kate called after a while, a sense of forced cheerfulness in her voice.

'Where are we going?' Dani asked. She knew she sounded sulky, but she couldn't help it.

'Not far from here now. I think you'll like it.'

'Where am I going to sleep?' Dani persisted.

'It's called Linden Lodge.'

'Is it a home?'

Kate fell silent for a moment. 'That's not really a word we use, Dani.'

'Is it a home, though?'

'It's residential care. There are fourteen or fifteen other children there, some of them the same age as you. And plenty of grown-ups to look after you. You'll like it there.'

Dani wasn't so sure. The idea of being forced into a place with other children she didn't know filled her with apprehension.

'Is my mum going to be in trouble?' she asked meekly.

Again that silence. 'Your mum needs some help, Dani. That's all. We're going to try to give it to her. We're going to try to make things so that you can go back there very soon. Does that sound all right?'

Dani didn't know what to say. The idea of spending just one night away from home was horrible; the prospect of more than that didn't bear thinking about. 'My face hurts,' she said in a quiet voice.

'I know,' Kate replied. 'I know.'

It took forty-five minutes through the rush-hour traffic to reach their destination. Dani, of course, had no idea where they were driving – it had been ages since she had ventured this far from home. As they drove down a busy high street, Dani saw a bus stop. There were some girls her own age waiting for a bus without any grown-ups, and Dani remembered the one time she had tried to do that. Some of the kids from school had seen her and started to make fun of her, and she had realised she was standing on the wrong side of the road, waiting for the wrong bus. The embarrassment she had felt came back even now, and she cringed at how naïve she must have seemed.

As they carried on driving, the traffic thinned. It grew darker outside and the area seemed to grow less populated, and greener. They were still in London, Dani thought, but further out, away from the centre.

Suddenly Kate slowed down and turned right, through some big iron gates and up a long driveway. She came to a stop in a small car-parking area in front of a large house.

'Here we are,' Kate said as she turned the ignition off. She got out of the car, opened Dani's door and helped her out; then she took the bag out of the boot and held Dani's hand.

The house she led them to was large and detached, constructed from an imposing brown-grey stone. It had tall bay windows from which light spilled out to the front, casting a shadow of the window frames onto the ground. Craning her neck to look up, Dani saw that the house had lots of chimneys, and there were some tall oval windows jutting out from the roof. This was an old house, and Dani didn't like the look of it.

Together they walked up the steps, and the social worker rang the doorbell.

'Where are we?' Dani asked quietly as they waited for someone to answer the door.

'Near Sutton. Have you heard of Sutton?'

Dani shook her head, but before Kate could explain any further, the door opened and a man appeared. As soon as he saw Kate and Dani standing at the doorway, his face broke into a broad, friendly smile – the kind of smile that seemed to crease all his skin. He was in his fifties, and had neatly cut blond-grey hair. He nodded at Kate, and then bent down so that his eyes were at Dani's level. His smile grew even broader, but she could tell that his eyes kept flickering involuntarily to the bruises on her face.

'You must be Dani,' he said in a soft voice. He extended his hand, and coyly Dani did the same. 'I'm Christian,' the man said, wrapping his warm palm around Dani's little hand and shaking it politely. 'Welcome to Linden Lodge, my love.'

Dani looked at Christian, and then up at Kate, who was smiling down at her, and a wave of weakness crashed over her. 'I want to go home,' she said.

Christian let go of her hand. 'Well, Dani. With a bit of luck and a fair wind, you'll start to think of Linden Lodge as your home before too long. We're like a big family here, and we're always pleased when new people come along. I'm going to be your key worker here, and that means we'll be seeing a lot of each other. Tell you what – why don't I show you where you're going to sleep, and then you can come and meet some of the others.'

He stood up and gestured with one hand that Kate and Dani should come into the house. Kate stepped forward, and as she was still holding the social worker's hand, Dani had no option but to follow her.

The main hallway into which they walked was long and high-ceilinged. It had a chequered floor, and at the far end there was a wide, winding staircase that led upstairs. Once she was inside the house, Dani became aware of a smell not unlike that which came from the kitchens at her school – the smell of food being cooked for a lot of people. As they walked along the hallway towards the stairs a couple of boys crossed their paths. They were older than Dani, and they looked at her with interest; but it was in Dani's nature to feel embarrassed by unwanted attention, and she hung her head as soon as their gazes crossed.

'Your room's just along here,' Christian said as they reached the top of the stairs. They were in a long corridor, lit by strip lighting, with several rooms leading off it. Christian knocked on the second door on the right; when there was no response, he opened it and ushered Dani and Kate inside.

It was a comfortable room. There was a thick red carpet on the floor, and a couple of snug-looking armchairs. The walls were covered with posters of pop stars that she didn't recognise. Along one side of the room there was a bunk bed, and there was a further single bed positioned at right angles to it. It had a pink duvet cover, and was neatly made.

Christian pointed to it. 'That'll be your bed, my love,' he said. 'Look all right for you?'

But Dani barely heard him. She was too busy looking at the bunks. 'Who else sleeps in here?' she asked.

'Ah,' Christian smiled. 'You'll be sharing with two others. Both girls, about your age. Vicki and Kaz. Nice girls. I'm sure you'll all get on like a house on fire.'

Dani had never shared a bedroom with anyone before, and the idea made her nervous. She tugged on the social worker's arms and looked up at her. 'Please can I go home?' she begged. '*Please?*'

This time it was Kate's turn to crouch down to her level. 'Dani, I promise you, it's just for a little bit. We have to put you somewhere where you're going to be safe. Once your mum is feeling better, we'll talk about you going home. But everyone here's really nice, and Christian's going to look after you. Aren't you, Christian?'

The man took a step towards them and placed his hand on Dani's shoulder. He squeezed ever so gently. 'Of course I am, my love,' he said. 'We all are.'

Dani looked up at the two concerned faces smiling at her. She didn't know why, but she thought there was something odd about the way they spoke, almost as if they were trying to convince themselves.

'Dani,' Kate said as she started to rummage inside her bag. 'I need to take a photograph of your face. Do you mind if I do that?' She pulled out a small digital camera.

The little girl shook her head. She did mind. She didn't like people seeing her in this state, and she certainly didn't want anyone taking photographs of her.

'It's just one picture, Dani. No one will see it unless it's necessary, I promise.'

Dani wasn't born to argue. Despite her misgivings, she stood up straight and stared flatly at the camera as Kate took her picture. As soon as it was done, she put her hand to her bruises, trying to hide them.

'I've got to go now, Dani,' Kate said gently. 'But I'll come back tomorrow and see how you're getting on.'

'Do you promise?' Dani asked.

Kate smiled. 'I promise.'

'Do I have to go to school?'

'Not tomorrow,' Kate replied. 'We'll work out something called a care plan for you over the next few days, but in the meantime I just want you to get used to living here.' She gave the little girl the bag of clothes they had packed.

'What about my brother and sister? Can they come and see me?'

'We'll see about that,' Kate said in a tone of voice that didn't give Dani much hope. She stood up. 'I'll see you tomorrow,' she said, before turning and leaving the room.

Dani watched as the door closed, and there was an awkward moment before Christian broke the silence that had suddenly descended on the room.

'Shall we put your things away, my love?' he asked. 'Look, you've got some drawers here, and a little bedside table of your own.'

The little girl did as she was told in a kind of trance. When her few belongings were packed away – all except the teddy bear, which she clung on tightly to – Christian spoke again. 'Why don't you stay here for a while and get used to the room? Tea'll be ready in a bit – I'll ask Vicki or Kaz to come and get you, shall I?'

Dani squeezed her teddy bear a little tighter and nodded her head.

She felt a bit better once Christian had left the room and she was alone, but only a bit. It all seemed so unreal: this morning she had been going to school as normal, and this evening she had been taken into care, away from everything she knew. It had been like one body blow after another, and more than anything, she missed her own home. It didn't matter that her mum had hit her; it didn't matter that Rebecca had been mean. Right now, she would even be happy to see Auntie Rose. All she wanted was her family.

Dani looked at herself in a mirror that hung on the wall. The familiar bruised face looked back at her. She touched the skin – it was a bit less sore than it had been yesterday – and for an idle moment she wondered if the other children in this place would look anything like her, beaten and battered. Then she remembered the two boys she had seen in the hallway. They had looked perfectly normal. No, she knew with a horrible certainty that she was going to be the different one here.

Just as that thought went through her head, the door opened, and she started. For a moment she didn't turn round, choosing instead to look at the reflection of the room in the mirror. There were two girls standing and looking at her. They were dressed in trendy clothes, nothing like Dani's. One of them, who had long hair and an Alice band, stood with her hands on her hips – a strangely adult stance – while the other, whose hair was straight but only shoulder-length, had hers firmly in the pockets of her trousers. They both had slightly pursed lips.

Slowly, Dani turned round to look at them properly. 'Hello,' she said.

The girl with the Alice band spoke first. 'I wouldn't spend so much time looking in the mirror,' she said, 'if I looked like that.'

Automatically, Dani's hand touched her bruise again. 'I was just—'

'Yeah, we know what you were doing,' the girl interrupted her. She strode over to Dani's bed, sat on it and gave her a combative stare.

'I thought that was my bed,' Dani said, doing her best to sound polite.

But the girl wasn't listening to her. She had found Dani's teddy bear, lying there on the pillow. She picked it up by one ear and held it dangling in the air. 'This yours?' she asked with a sneer in her voice.

Dani nodded.

Suddenly the two of them burst out laughing. The girl holding the teddy bear threw it to her friend, who acted as if it was too hot to touch and threw it back.

As quickly as she had picked it up, the girl on the bed threw the teddy on the floor. Dani rushed to pick it up, but before she could get to it the girl kicked it out of her way. Dani turned to grab it again, and this time managed to. She held the soft toy close to her, but that only seemed to amuse the girls more.

'You got any sweets?' the second girl asked her.

'No,' Dani replied.

'Ciggies? Money?'

She shook her head.

'How old are you, anyway?'

'Twelve.'

'You don't look like twelve to me. Look more like ten.' She turned to her friend. 'Looks more like ten, doesn't she, Kaz?'

'Yeah,' Kaz replied.

'How old are you?' Dani asked.

Kaz tapped herself on the chest. 'I'm thirteen, Vicki's twelve. But you're nearly thirteen, aren't you?'

'Yeah,' said Vicki. 'So you're the youngest. Least, you act the youngest with your stupid cuddly toy.'

'I'm not staying here for long.' Dani tried to say it defiantly, but it ended up sounding a bit apologetic.

The two girls started laughing. 'Yeah,' Kaz snorted. 'That's what they tell everyone. I've been here since I was ten.'

Dani blinked, and she felt the familiar wave of sickness in her stomach. 'Yeah,' she said. 'Well, I'm not you, and I'm going home soon.'

Kaz shrugged. 'Whatever. Creepy Christian says you've got to come down to tea, and we're supposed to take you.'

'Why do you call him that?' Dani asked.

The girls smirked elusively. 'You coming or what?' Vicki asked.

Dani looked down at her teddy bear, not knowing what to do with it. Just then, Vicki stood up from the bed and walked to the door, leaving Dani free to rest the soft toy on her pillow. She tried to do it nonchalantly, but when she turned round again she saw that the two girls were still sneering at her from the doorway.

They left the room, leaving Dani to run after them. She followed them back down the stairs and into the hallway, where other children were passing through. Dani recognised one of the boys she had seen on her arrival. 'Who's that?' he shouted out to Vicki and Kaz.

The two girls looked back over their shoulders at Dani, and then over at the boy. Kaz made some kind of gesture with her hands that she couldn't make out; whatever it was, it made the boy laugh as they walked through a door off the hallway, down a small corridor and into a dining room at the end.

There were two long tables here, positioned parallel to each other, and one shorter one. Against one wall there was a serving hatch where two chubby, red-faced women stood serving food to the line of children and a few adults who were queuing up for it. Some of them had already been given their food and were sitting down – the children at one of the two long tables, the grown-ups at the shorter one. There were perhaps twenty people in the room – five adults to fifteen children – but to Dani's ears they made enough noise for fifty.

She stood in the doorway, watching everything happen. Not everybody had noticed her, but those who did cast curi-

ous glances in her direction; she felt her face flushing as she
tried to avoid their eyes.

Then she felt a hand on her shoulder.

'Hi, Dani.' She recognised Christian's upbeat voice
almost immediately, and felt a small surge of relief that he
was there. 'Met Kaz and Vicki, have you, my love? Come
on, let's queue up. I'll show you what to do.'

Dani's key worker handed her a plastic tray from a pile
next to the serving hatch and they waited their turn in
silence. When they came to be served, Dani looked unenthusiastically at the spoonfuls of rice and something else that
was served on to Christian's plate.

'Chicken curry,' he said with a smile. 'My favourite.'

Dani didn't like the look of it at all, but she said nothing
as the serving ladies filled her plate.

'New girl?' one of them asked with a smile, and again
she could tell that the woman's eyes kept flickering to the
bruise on her face.

Dani nodded.

'Ah,' she commiserated, her voice dripping with sympathy. 'Never mind. You'll soon settle in.'

'Come on, Dani,' Christian interrupted. 'Let's find you a
place to sit.'

Christian led her to one of the long tables and found
her a place next to Kaz and opposite a boy she didn't
recognise. Neither of them looked particularly thrilled to
have Dani sitting with them, but they kept quiet. 'Look
after Dani for me now,' Christian said brightly. He put his
hand back on her shoulder. 'We'll have a little chat after
dinner, my love, and I'll introduce you to some of the
staff.'

Dani ate in silence. She didn't like the food, but she didn't want to make a fuss about it, so she held it down while the children around her made a special effort not to talk to her. She kept trying to think of things to say to break the ice, but nothing would pop into her head, so she sat there with a frown on her face as she concentrated on eating her dinner.

Gradually, the others in the room finished their food. She saw them all took their plates up to the serving hatch, scrape the remains of any food into a large bucket and then leave in twos or threes, talking noisily. Before long, Dani was the only person left at her table.

A couple of the grown-ups had left, too; there were three remaining now, and once Dani had pushed her plate away, Christian came up to her and suggested she come and sit at their table. Dani did as she was told, aware of the intrigued looks from the few children who remained in the dining room, and Christian introduced the other grown-ups.

They were both women, both of them about the same age as her mum, and they smiled at Dani with the same look of sympathy that the lady who had served her dinner had given her. One of them had blonde hair in a short bob, with brown eyes. She wore a blue V-neck sweater, and was introduced as Rachel. The other woman, Tanya, reminded Dani a bit of Miss Sawyer at school, with her curly brown hair and chunky beige cardigan. They both shook Dani's hand, and assured her in words that the little girl forgot as soon as she heard them that if she needed anything, she could always come to them, day or night.

'That's what we're here for,' Christian concluded. 'I know everything feels very strange at the moment, Dani, and I know you've been through a lot. But we really do want you to think of this place as your home, so if you have any problems – anything at all – you *must* come to us.'

The two women nodded their agreement. 'It's what we're here for,' Tanya said, echoing Christian.

Dani's key worker looked at his watch. 'It's nearly seven,' he said. 'We like you to be in bed by eight-thirty. Does that sound OK, Dani?'

Dani nodded.

'Good. So you've got an hour and a half. Did Vicki and Kaz show you where the day room is?'

'No,' Dani answered.

'Ah, well, it's where most of the others will be. Shall I take you there?'

Dani blinked. The idea of having to be with everyone else – with Kaz and Vicki and all the other children who had either ignored her or stared at her as if she was some sort of unwelcome curiosity – made her hands shake. She clenched her fingers to hide the tremor from the grown-ups before answering. 'I want to go to my bedroom,' she said.

Christian cast a worried look at the two women before allowing his face to break into another smile. 'It's been a long day, hasn't it, my love?' he sympathised. 'Go on, then. We'll introduce you to some more of the children tomorrow.' He looked over to where Dani had been eating. 'Scrape your plate before you go, there's a good girl.'

Dani got down from the table, took her plate to the serving hatch and left the room.

To her relief, the hallway was empty again, and she hurried up the stairs before anyone could see her. She just wanted to be by herself, under the bedclothes. Once she was covered, in the dark, she could pretend she was anywhere. She could pretend she was back at home. This place, Linden Lodge, seemed so strange and huge and unfriendly. She knew from experience that those girls were the type who would carry on being mean to her, no matter what she did to try to make friends with them. All she wanted – and she wanted it with every ounce of her being – was to go home. It didn't matter to her that Mum had hit her. It wouldn't happen again. Mum would be sorry, wouldn't she?

With these thoughts going round in her head, she approached the door of her bedroom and opened it. It took a while to take in the sight that met her.

Dani's duvet was no longer on the bed. She looked around the room to try to find it, but it was nowhere to be seen. Her few clothes – the ones that Kate had helped her unpack into the drawers – had been removed and were slung all over the floor.

She found herself breathing heavily, panicking at the sight. Everything she owned was on the floor, strewn carelessly, spitefully, all over the place. She took a step into the room and started to gather everything in her arms in a bundle.

Then she stopped.

Not quite everything had been accounted for in her brief scan of the room. One thing was missing: the one thing she cared about more than any of the others. She stood in the centre of the room, dropped the clothes from her arms and spun around, desperately trying to find it.

It didn't take long to locate her teddy bear. The first she saw of it was its foot, peeping out from under her pillow.

She tripped slightly over her clothes as she stumbled towards the bed and lifted the pillow up. Then she stopped, completely still, as though she had been turned to stone.

The bear's belly had been slit open, and most of the stuffing – a yellow, spongy substance – had been pulled out and was now by its side. The bear's head had been removed, and for a moment Dani couldn't see it, until finally she realised it had been partially stuffed down the side of the bed.

She dropped the pillow on the floor and sat next to the teddy bear.

It was only a toy, she knew. She knew she was too old for it really. But that didn't make her feel any better.

Her hands were trembling even more now as she delicately picked up some of the stuffing and tried to push it back into the bear's carcass. But it was too spongy and kept springing out again, so in the end she had to give up. She gathered all the bits together, neatly placed them on the bed and then went around the room picking up the rest of her clothes.

Once they were all put away again, she climbed on to her bed. No doubt they would let her know where the duvet was sooner or later, but until then she could think of nothing to do but lie on the bed, foetus-like, with the remains of her teddy's body close to her skin. She put her thumb in her mouth, closed her eyes and wished – harder than she had ever wished anything before – that she could be anywhere but here.

Chapter Four

Morning came all too quickly.

When Kaz and Vicki had returned to the room the previous night, Dani had pretended to be asleep. From the nasty comments they made, it was clear they didn't believe her, but it was easier to lie there with her eyes shut than to have to face them, to talk to them. A few minutes later, one of them had fetched the duvet and slung it on top of Dani; and soon the lights were turned out.

'We know you're awake,' Kaz said after a couple of minutes.

Dani said nothing.

'We're not idiots,' Vicki added.

Still nothing. Dani lay there, unnaturally still, her muscles tense, praying for them to fall asleep.

In the darkness it was impossible for her to tell how long it was until she was sure, from the sound of their heavy, regular breathing, that the two girls were truly asleep. An hour, maybe. It was only when she *was* sure that she silently moved her duvet from where it had been slung over her and sat up. She quietly took off her shoes, and then the rest of her clothes, folding them neatly and putting them in her drawer before removing a pair of pyjamas, making her bed and then climbing back into it. She pulled the duvet over her head and took refuge in her little cocoon of darkness.

More than anything, Dani wanted to stay awake. Night-time, she knew, passed slowly. She liked that. It put off the coming of the dawn. Darkness was like a refuge, protecting her from having to face a new day. But she was tired, and it wasn't long before she felt her eyelids become heavy. She did her best to keep them open, but the events of the day were catching up with her and she soon fell into a deep, troubled sleep.

Dani was woken the following morning by the sound of voices. As she tried to shake off the blanket of sleep, she felt momentarily confused. Where was she? What was this strange room, this strange place? Then it all came flooding back, and she felt as though she had received the terrible blow all over again.

By the time she had sat up, her room-mates were already dressed. Kaz was standing in front of the mirror, brushing her hair, while Vicki applied some lipstick. Dani had never used make-up; she tried not to stare as Vicki did it with such ease, but she couldn't help watching.

'What you looking at?' Vicki demanded when she realised Dani's eyes were on her.

Dani looked away quickly and blushed. 'Nothing,' she replied.

'Yeah, right.' She went back to her make-up.

Dani climbed out of bed and retrieved some clothes from her drawer. But as she stood there in her pyjamas, she was suddenly overcome with embarrassment. At home she was able to dress and undress in privacy; now, if she wanted to put her clothes on, she had to take her pyjamas off in front of these two girls. Timidly, she turned round and shuffled to the end of the bed, where she would be slightly out of their view. She tried to get changed quickly, but it only meant that she got herself tangled up.

'Don't worry,' Kaz said. 'We're not eyeing you up.'

The two girls laughed and left the room.

Dani wished she could go back to bed and stay under the duvet for the rest of the day; but she was hungry, and she knew that if she didn't go down to breakfast she would only have someone come and get her, so she mustered all the courage she could. As she left the room, she caught a glimpse of herself in the mirror. The bruising had gone down – just a little bit, but enough to give her a tiny amount more confidence than she had had yesterday.

She needed to find the bathroom first, but no one had told her where it was, so it was up to her to wander up and down the corridor until she found a door with a little stick picture of a woman. Like everywhere else in this place, the girls' bathroom was lit by a flickering striplight. There were square white tiles on the floor and walls, which were splattered with puddles from that morning's use. There was a row of four sinks, and behind a partition there were three baths, lined up next to each other without any privacy. On the other side of the room were three cubicles. Dani splashed water on her face, and then steeled herself to go downstairs.

She avoided her room-mates at breakfast, choosing instead to sit next to an unfamiliar face – a sturdy boy with broad shoulders, strawberry blond hair and freckles. He seemed a bit older than Dani, and for some reason sitting next to him made her feel happier. The moment she took her seat, however, she regretted it.

'Looks like you pulled, Dingo,' a voice called from somewhere further along the table, and the boy turned to look at her with an unpleasant leer. There was giggling all around, and Dani felt as though all eyes were suddenly on her. A hot blush rose to the surface of her skin as she pretended not to notice what was going on.

Dani wolfed down her breakfast, and was just about to leave the room when she sensed someone walking up to her.

'Dani, Dingo,' Christian's voice said brightly. 'I'm glad you two have met. I'm sure you'll be very good friends. Dingo, you'll look after Dani, won't you? See to it that she's all right. Make her feel at home.'

Dingo sucked his lips in, as though he was trying not to smile; Dani could tell that Christian wasn't even vaguely aware of it. He shrugged archly. 'Yeah,' he said. 'Course.'

Christian nodded with satisfaction. 'Good lad,' he said. 'Good lad.' And with that he walked back to the staff table.

Dingo glanced at Dani, and then snorted contemptuously before turning back to his breakfast and ignoring her as studiously as possible. She stood up and prepared to take her tray with her; but as she did so she heard her name being called.

'Dani!'

It was Christian again. His voice rose above the hubbub, and for a brief moment the noise in the dining room quietened. 'Just pop over here for a minute, would you, my love?'

Dani cringed, knowing that the other children would be looking at her and smirking at Christian's term of endearment. She did as she was told, though, and walked to where all the grown-ups were sitting.

'And how did we sleep?' Christian asked her.

Dani shrugged. 'All right,' she muttered.

'Excellent,' Christian replied. 'Now then, everyone else will be going to school today, but not you. We have to sort you out with a place somewhere, but there are things we need to arrange before then. So that means you've got the run of the place. That'll be nice, won't it?' He smiled at her, a broad, well-meaning smile that lit up his eyes. She did her best to smile back, and although she knew it must have looked forced, it seemed to please Christian, who reached out and gave her another of his trademark squeezes on the shoulder. 'Good girl,' he said. 'I'll come and find you later.'

Over the course of the next ten minutes, all the children in the home disappeared, running out of the front door with shouts and schoolbags. Dani couldn't quite face going back to her room yet, so she spent some time exploring.

The day room, which Christian had mentioned the night before, was on the opposite side of the hall to the dining room. It was a large space, with a snooker table and table-tennis table. Checking over her shoulders to ensure noone was looking, Dani rolled one of the red snooker balls against a cushion. A snooker cue was propped up against one of the walls, and she would have liked to have had a go with it; but she was too timid for that, so she made do with an idle couple of minutes of rolling the ball back and forth with her hand. There were a few armchairs dotted around, and several tables which had childish graffiti scrawled on them in pencil – though not as much as the ones she was used to using at her school. On one of the tables was a little pile of newspapers, but they didn't look as if they had been opened. At one end of the room were some wide windows that looked out on to a fairly large back garden. There were some swings and slides, and a couple of football posts; but it was grey and drizzling outside, so she didn't venture any further.

Dani wandered around the room for a further few minutes before she felt she had exhausted the possibilities of the day room. She wandered out, back into the hallway, just in time to see Kate, the social worker, coming in through the front door. She was wearing smart clothes and looked hurried and harassed. At first she didn't see Dani, standing quietly at the other end of the hallway; when she did, she seemed surprised, but she soon regained her composure.

'Dani,' she said brightly. 'How was last night?'

Dani shrugged.

'Did you meet anyone? Make any friends?'

Dani ignored her question. 'When can I go home?' she asked.

Kate's eyes looked away. 'Why don't we go to your room?' she suggested, her voice suddenly a little more subdued. 'We can talk about it there.'

Dani could tell from the way she spoke that she had bad news, and she led the way up to her room nervously. Once inside, they sat together on Dani's bed, and the girl was glad that her vandalised teddy was hidden under the duvet. Kate looked her straight in the eye.

'I want you to know exactly what's happening, Dani. I don't want there to be any secrets, OK?'

'OK,' Dani replied quietly.

'We've been granted something called an Emergency Protection Order. That's something we ask for if we want to take a child away from their home when we think they're in danger.'

'But I'm not in danger,' Dani complained. 'Mum was just cross, that's all. I was being naughty.'

'No, Dani,' Kate told her firmly. 'Grown-ups should never do that to you. Never. The Emergency Protection Order only lasts a few days, so in the meantime we are going to apply for a Care Order. That means that the people here, at Linden Lodge, will take on the responsibility of looking after you instead of your mum. Does that make sense?'

Dani shook her head. Nothing made sense – nothing at all. 'I just want to go home.'

Kate took Dani's hands in hers. 'I know,' she said. 'I know. But that may not be possible for a while. Your mum has told us that she's had difficulty coping, and for the moment she's asked that …' Her voice trailed off and she looked at Dani with sympathetic eyes.

Dani's face fell. 'She doesn't want me back, does she?'

'She might change her mind, Dani,' Kate said hopefully. 'People *do* change their minds. It just might take a little while, that's all.'

Dani was breathing heavily now. 'The girls here,' she said, 'the ones I'm sharing with – they said everyone gets told they're going home soon, but they never do.'

'Don't listen to them, Dani. Everyone's going to do their best for you, and you'll be looked after properly here.'

Dani suddenly felt cold. She removed her hand from Kate's grip and wrapped her arms around her own body.

She wished Kate would go, just leave her room – leave her life and never come back. Every time she saw her, she acted as though she was there to make things better for her; and yet every time she made things a little bit worse. Dani was not prone to hatred, yet in that moment she felt she hated the social worker, sitting there and pretending she was performing acts of kindness.

'I think I'd like to be left on my own now,' Dani said.

Kate nodded. 'All right, Dani. I'll come and see you again soon. I'll go and explain to Christian everything that's going on.' She stood and looked as if she was about to say something else; but at the last moment she appeared to think better of it, and left the room.

Dani didn't know how long it was that she sat there, hugging herself, staring into space and feeling as though her heart would break, but it was a long time and she barely moved. Wild thoughts went through her head – thoughts that she had never entertained before. Perhaps she could run away, run back home. If her mum saw her on the doorstep, perhaps she would have a change of heart. Deep down, though, she knew that probably wasn't the case, and the sting of that rejection pierced her to the core.

She just wanted something to hold on to. Something familiar. Comfortable. Gently she pulled back the duvet to see the tattered remains of her teddy bear – the one thing she had with her that reminded her of home. And now that too was spoiled.

Just then there was a knock on the door; it was opened without Dani giving a reply, and Christian was there. Quickly Dani threw the duvet back over the bed.

'Ah, Dani,' Christian announced. 'There you are. How is everything, my love? Settling in?'

Dani looked down at the floor, but didn't answer. Christian seemed to consider that for a moment before he spoke again. 'I've never met a girl,' he said with a smile, 'who doesn't like hot chocolate. Do you like hot chocolate, my love?'

Dani nodded.

'Come on, then,' Christian smiled. 'Come to my room and we'll see what we can find.'

Christian's quarters were scrupulously neat, if a little shabby. The walls were covered with books, and there was a modern stereo player and a TV in the corner, as well as a sofa and a couple of other comfy chairs. Her eyes were immediately caught by a pile of comics at about her height on one of the bookshelves.

Christian noted her interest. 'Help yourself,' he said, but Dani immediately looked away.

At one end of the room there was a door, which Dani presumed led to his bedroom, but it was firmly shut. He indicated a place on the sofa. 'Sit down, my love,' he said as he switched on a kettle that was sitting on a low table. He spooned some brown powder into a mug, poured on the boiling water and handed the mug to Dani. Then he sat down next to her.

Neither of them spoke for a little while. Christian just watched her intently as she sipped the steaming hot drink. It made her feel a bit uncomfortable.

'Thank you,' she said diffidently after a couple of minutes, more to break the silence than anything else.

'That's all right, my love,' Christian replied. 'You can come here any time, day or night. I mean that, my love. *Any time.*'

Dani nodded and went back to sipping her hot chocolate.

'If you feel like a cuddle,' he persisted, his voice much quieter now. 'Or anything else.' He carried on staring at her.

As Dani took another sip of her hot chocolate, she felt his fingers brush lightly against her bruised face. They were fat and sausage-like, the skin strangely dry. Instinctively, Dani moved her head away, and she became immediately aware that the atmosphere had turned awkward.

Christian stood up. 'I wondered if it still hurt,' he said by way of explanation as he walked back to the kettle and screwed the lid of the hot chocolate powder back on. He looked over at Dani. 'Nearly finished?' he asked.

Dani hadn't, but she understood the tone of his voice and quickly put the cup down on a coffee table and stood up.

'Lunch at one o'clock,' he told her. 'I'll see you there.'

Dani nodded, and quickly left.

At lunch it was only her and the grown-ups. She was invited to sit at their table, but she didn't speak to them, and Christian barely even looked in her direction. For Dani, it couldn't end quickly enough, and she was grateful to be able to go back to her room and sit on the bed, where she listened to the persistent rain falling outside. She willed the afternoon to pass slowly, but time flew and soon she heard the sound of the other children coming back from school. She was still sitting on the bed when Kaz and Vicki burst in.

They were shouting at someone down the corridor, and as they fell into the room, they laughed boisterously. At first they seemed not even to notice Dani, but when they realised that she was sitting there watching them, their smiles fell from their faces.

'Still here?' Vicki asked spitefully. 'Not gone home to Mummy yet?'

'Surprise surprise,' Kaz added.

'I wish you hadn't ruined my bear,' Dani said.

The two girls looked at each other. 'Who said it was us?'

Dani shrugged.

Vicki stepped up to her. 'Anyway,' she said, 'you go telling anyone things like that, and we'll give you a bruise on the other side of your face. So you'd better shut it.'

Dani clamped her lips tightly shut. As she did so, Vicki tapped her three times on the bruised side of her face with the flat of her hand. Dani winced, but that just made Vicki and Kaz giggle. They continued giggling as they left the room.

The evening passed slowly. Dani remained in her room, apart from at dinnertime, when, as before, nobody spoke to her. Even Christian refrained from coming up and offering her a cheerful word, though he cast the occasional glance in her direction while they were eating. After dinner, part of Dani longed to go into the day room and watch the others playing snooker and table tennis, to try to chat to someone or maybe even just look at a magazine; but no one asked her, and she was too unsure of herself to brave being with the others of her own accord. So she went back to her bedroom. Her little prison. It seemed to her that she would spend the rest of her life sitting on that bed.

She brushed her teeth and washed her face before anyone else started getting ready for bed – that way, she would be able to avoid any encounters in the bathroom. She would have liked a bath, but the lack of privacy prevented her. Maybe tomorrow, when everyone else was at school, she'd be able to; but just now the idea of taking her clothes off in front of the other girls sent a shiver down her spine. Once she had washed, she got into her pyjamas, climbed into bed and waited for the inevitable onslaught from her two room-mates as soon as they arrived.

It was gone eight o'clock when Kaz and Vicki sauntered into the room. For once they were silent, and although they cast the occasional scornful look over at Dani as she lay beneath her duvet, they didn't make any of the comments that she was expecting. They just got ready for bed, turned the lights out and fell silent.

As soon as the lights went out, Dani pulled her covers over her head and retreated once more into her little cave of darkness, and for the first time that day, she felt a moment of comfort.

It didn't last long.

It couldn't have been more than twenty minutes before they charged into the room. In the darkness, Dani couldn't tell how many of them there were – five, maybe six. Someone ripped off her duvet. She was already in a foetus-like position, but she clamped up even closer when she realised what was happening.

There was laughter as they pushed her and poked her. They called her names that she didn't even understand. Dani cried out – in little more than a pathetic whisper.

'Shut up,' a voice hissed, and she recognised it at once. It was Dingo, the boy she had met at breakfast: the boy who was supposed to be looking after her.

She whimpered again; someone punched her and hissed once more. Then she lost control. A scream, loud and desperate, escaped from her lips; and once she started, she couldn't stop. Startled by the sound, by the vehemence of it, everyone around her instantly melted away, disappearing from the room as quickly as they had appeared. But Dani still didn't stop screaming. She just couldn't.

Kaz and Vicki said nothing as Dani lay there, still scrunched up, her duvet on the floor. Tears seemed to take over her whole body. She was shaking with them. And still the screams came.

The lights were turned on. Panicked by the sudden thought of being seen by anyone in this state, she jumped out of bed and grabbed her duvet. She was back on the mattress before she saw who it was in the room. Tanya, the care worker she had met at tea the previous night, was standing in the doorway.

'What's going on here?' she demanded.

Kaz and Vicki said nothing. Dani looked over in their direction and she saw that now it was their turn to pretend to be asleep. Tanya was looking angrily at them, but then she turned to Dani and saw the state she was in. Immediately her face softened.

'What's the matter, Dani?' she asked, coming over and sitting on the edge of the bed.

Dani shook her head, and it was an effort to speak. 'Nothing,' she managed.

'It doesn't look like nothing.'

'I just want to go home,' she stuttered, and then she bit her lip. She knew Kaz and Vicki weren't really asleep; and she knew comments like that would give them ammunition with which to tease her.

For a minute Tanya didn't reply. She just sat there, gently stroking Dani's hair, as the little girl struggled to get her emotions under control. Finally she spoke. 'Come with me,' she said, and she stood up.

Mutely, Dani did as she was told and, wearing only her pyjamas, followed Tanya out into the corridor. 'Where are we going?' she asked when they were out of earshot of the bedroom.

'We'll go and see Christian,' she replied. 'He's your key worker. If anything's wrong, you really need to talk to him about it.'

Dani's brow creased, but she didn't say anything.

Christian was in his room, sitting on the sofa reading a magazine, a chunky tumbler of whisky on the coffee table in front of him. The overhead lights were off, and there were just a couple of dim lamps illuminating the room. As they stepped inside, Dani heard the sound of classical music playing on the stereo, just a little too softly for it to be properly heard. Christian looked up from his reading, and for a split second Dani thought she could detect a flicker of annoyance in his face. But if that was the case, he soon mastered it and allowed his features to spread into the familiar broad smile.

'Good evening, Tanya,' he said quietly. 'Good evening, Dani. What can I do for you?'

Tanya looked down at Dani, as though expecting her to speak, but when she didn't, the care worker spoke for her.

'Dani's a little bit upset,' she said. 'I thought you might like to talk to her about it.' She stroked Dani's hair. 'A problem shared and all that.'

Christian closed his magazine, placed it on the coffee table and patted the seat next to him. 'Come and sit down, Dani,' he offered. 'Come and tell me all about it.'

'There's nothing to tell,' Dani mumbled.

'I'll leave you to it,' Tanya interrupted tactfully, before exiting the room and quietly shutting the door behind her.

Dani stood by the door. It suddenly seemed to her very inappropriate to be wearing just her pyjamas, but she didn't know why. There was a silence between them, filled only by the quiet music. Dani found herself concentrating on the sound of the piano, tinkling in the background. She felt that her face was scrunched up and serious.

'Please sit down, Dani,' Christian asked her.

Timidly she shuffled towards the sofa and took a seat at the opposite side to Christian. He waited a moment before he spoke again. 'So what's the matter, Dani?' he asked softly.

Dani closed her eyes. She knew what would happen if she told. She knew how the other children would react if they found out. But all of a sudden she couldn't hold in any longer. She had to tell someone. To speak. 'They all just came into my room,' she said. 'Loads of them. They took my duvet and they pushed me around and they told me to shut up ...' Her voice trailed off.

Christian's brow furrowed, and he pursed his lips. 'Who did, Dani?'

Her breath was shaky now. 'I don't know,' she whispered. Then, even more quietly. 'I think Dingo was one of them.'

Christian raised an eyebrow. 'Dingo?' he asked, his voice betraying his surprise. 'I'm sure Dingo wouldn't do a thing like that, my love. He's a good lad.'

Dani looked up at him, and she could instantly see from the look on his face that he didn't believe her.

'It's true,' she said.

Christian surveyed her for a moment and then smiled – an indulgent smile, sympathetic yet disbelieving. He leaned forward, resting his elbows on his knees and twisting his body slightly to the side so that he was face to face with her. 'Dani,' he said softly. 'I know how difficult it is for you to be here. It's a dreadful shock, and everything seems different and strange. But they're nice children here, and you'll all soon be friends. I know you want to go home, but making up stories like this really isn't the way to go about it.'

Dani blinked. 'I'm not making it up,' she said breathlessly.

Christian inclined his head and thought for a moment. 'OK,' he said finally. 'OK, Dani. Here's what we're going to do. Tomorrow afternoon, when all the others have come back from school, you, me and Dingo are going to have a little chat.'

She looked at him in horror. 'No,' she breathed.

But Christian talked over her. 'Dingo's an honest lad,' he continued. 'If there's anything to tell me—'

'No, but you *can't*,' Dani interrupted. They'd think she was a sneak, and that would make things a million times worse.

'Dani, Dani,' Christian said in a mollifying tone of voice. 'Come along now. If you're telling me the truth, there's nothing to worry about, is there?'

But Dani couldn't reply. An absolute terror had seized her heart, and she knew that what would happen if anyone found out she had gone to the grown-ups didn't bear thinking about. She wanted to explain, to beg him not to speak to Dingo, but the words froze in her mouth.

Before she knew it, Christian was standing up. He put his hand on her shoulder and squeezed gently in that way of his, before wandering over to the door and opening it. 'Come on now,' he said with a smile. 'Time for bed.'

Dani stood up and walked, somewhat dazed, to the door. 'Sleep tight, my love,' Christian called after her as she padded barefoot away from the room. The door clicked shut behind her, and she suddenly felt the solitude of the corridor horribly keenly. With every step she expected to see someone jump out at her. She was scared to be alone out here; and she was scared to go back to her bedroom.

It was pitch black in there. She closed the door of the bedroom behind her and, her eyes unaccustomed to the dark, groped blindly towards her bed. Before she got there, however, she heard a voice.

'If you told anyone about that, they'll fucking do you.'

Dani couldn't tell if it was Vicki or Kaz speaking.

'Dingo's Creepy Christian's favourite,' the voice taunted, in a sing-song tone. Dani found the bed and hurriedly bundled herself inside the duvet.

'He'll never believe you.'

Dani scrunched her eyes up, as though doing so would somehow shut out all the awfulness.

'And *we're* not going to say it happened.'

Silence.

She expected more taunts. More mean words. Her muscles tensed in preparation for those verbal blows. But they didn't come. Gradually Dani became aware of the steady, rhythmical breathing that indicated that Vicki and Kaz were asleep. She knew, however, that sleep would not come to her. Not yet. Not for a long time.

What if they came back? Maybe not tonight, but tomorrow. Or the day after. Or the day after that. Dani knew when she was despised; she recognised the signs. Things weren't going to get any easier here. They were going to get worse.

As Dani prepared to endure the rest of the night, one thing became abundantly clear to her. She could not stay in this place. She could not wait for Christian to reveal to the whole home that she was a sneak, that she had told. She could not wait for the torment, or the teasing, or the fighting.

Dani Sinclair didn't belong here.

It was called a home, but it wasn't a home.

She didn't have a home. She didn't have anywhere. But she couldn't stay here.

There was only one thing she could do. She saw that quite clearly.

She had to leave. She had to get away from these people. And she had to do it tomorrow.

Chapter Five

Dani had never stolen anything in her life. It wasn't just that she knew it was wrong: it was that she would be far too terrified of being found out.

That was about to change.

The sun had risen, its grey light creeping into the room as she lay there, her eyes wide open. Vicki and Kaz were breathing heavily, but she had lain there in terror, knowing it would not be long until they awoke. Until everyone awoke. Then the day would start again. The prospect had made her feel numb. Linden Lodge, this strange, horrible place in which she had been put against her will, seemed to close in on her. Every corner seemed to house some new misery.

Dani was not a decisive girl; nor was she brave. But as she lay there that morning, waiting for her torment to begin again, she knew she couldn't stay here. Not when everyone was being so mean to her. Not when nobody believed a word she said. If the social workers wouldn't let her leave, she would have to do so by herself. She had no idea where she would go, or sleep, or what she would eat. She would have to work all that out later. She just had to get out of there.

She had washed and brushed her teeth early, before the others had woken up. Then she had crept out of the bedroom and waited downstairs in the hallway so that she didn't have to put up with the girls' comments. By the time the dining room was finally opened, a few of the other children from the home had also congregated outside it. No one spoke to Dani, but a couple of them cast sly, amused looks in her direction. Apart from Dingo, she didn't know who it was who had beaten her up the previous night, but from those looks, she could guess.

As always, she ate her meal in silence. This time, no one sat close to her, but that was fine with Dani. Not long now and she would never see these people again.

Dani finished her breakfast before anyone else, and she was the first to leave the dining room. She went up to the bedroom and hurriedly stuffed her clothes in the bag she had brought from home; then she placed the whole lot back in a drawer, out of sight. The last thing she wanted to do was raise anyone's suspicions, so she sat back down on the bed, wrapped her arms around her knee, and waited for her room-mates to come back.

She didn't have to wait long. Vicki and Kaz came bursting in a couple of minutes later. They looked archly at Dani before getting their things together in silence. No one mentioned last night's bullying, but their whispered threats still rang in Dani's ears and she was well aware that her two room-mates knew all about it – that they had been expecting it, even. As they got their things together and left the room, she hoped it would be the last time she ever saw them.

The first place she looked was the drawer where Vicki kept her make-up. Any other time, she would have lingered over the tempting, colourful boxes of powder, the grown-up tubes of lipstick. But this morning she knew she had to be quick. There was nothing in the make-up drawer, so she moved to the one below it. This was where Vicki kept some of her clothes – underwear, mostly, and a few T-shirts. Dani rummaged through it, not bothering to keep it neat. There was nothing, so she turned her attention to the white wardrobe that the two girls seemed to share. Hurriedly she rifled through the pockets of the trousers and dresses that hung there. Still nothing.

It was only by chance that she found the first hiding place. One of the pairs of trousers slipped off its hanger and fell to the ground. Instinctively Dani picked it up; and as she did she heard the jingling of coins. She had already checked the pockets, so now she examined the trousers in more detail. It didn't take long for her to work out that the money – two ten-pound notes, a five-pound note and a sprinkling of change – had been hidden in the turn-up of one of the legs. She grabbed the money and stuffed it into her own pockets, before shoving the trousers back into the wardrobe.

Kaz's pocket money was easier to find, hidden between two T-shirts in her drawer. It was a similar amount to Vicki's – Dani didn't count it exactly but just put it in her pocket with the rest. She went to her own drawer, grabbed the bag, put on her coat and took a deep breath. She was slightly surprised by this new determination, and she knew she couldn't stop to think about it too carefully because if she did, she would never go through with her plan. She strode towards the door and left that hated bedroom without a second glance.

The corridors were empty. In a way, that made it more difficult – more nerve-racking – because Dani knew that if she bumped into anyone she might have to answer awkward questions. She walked quickly and decisively. It wasn't far to the exit, and before long she was there. Dani slung her bag over her shoulder, opened the front door and walked confidently out.

It was the first time she had been outside since she had arrived at Linden Lodge. Thankfully the rain from yesterday had let up, leaving a clear, sunny day in its wake. But it could have been a monsoon for all Dani cared – nothing was going to stop her from leaving that place. She blinked in the sunlight and looked away from the house. It had been dark when she arrived, and she hadn't noticed the tall trees that lined the driveway up to the building. She decided that walking under the trees would give her a better chance of not being seen; once she was out of the main gates, she knew she would be able to just melt away.

It was cold, and as she walked along the tree-lined driveway she pulled her coat tightly around her. *Walk quickly*, she told herself. *It'll keep you warm.* That was what grown-ups always said. She upped her pace, and soon she was on the street.

Dani had no idea which way to turn; she had no idea where she was going. Home wasn't an option, even if she knew which way it was. Her mum had made it brutally clear that she wasn't wanted there, and despite the fact that she longed to see her family, she knew that going back to them would only end in her being sent back to Linden Lodge. She shuddered at the thought.

As Dani walked, she tried to make it look as if she knew where she was going and what she was doing. She knew that as soon as they found out she was missing from the home, the police would be called, so she didn't want to raise anyone's attention by looking lost and confused. Leaving Linden Lodge felt almost like going on holiday, and for a short while she felt liberated, as though she was enjoying herself. She walked into a newsagent's and bought a can of fizzy drink and a chocolate bar – something she had barely ever had the money to do before – and then sat on a wall and gorged on her treats.

It was colder sitting still, however, so when she had eaten her fill she carefully found a litter bin in which to dispose of her wrappers; then she continued walking, and as she walked, in her childish mind she formulated the beginnings of a plan.

Kate had told her when they arrived that they were near Sutton, but Dani had already decided that she had to leave that town. Sutton was where the kids in the home lived, and despite the frisson of excitement she felt at her reckless behaviour, she still could not shake the expectation – the dread – that one of them would be waiting for her just around the corner. So it was that when, as she walked, she saw a signpost to the train station, she headed in that direction. She had no idea how much a train ticket cost, but she hoped she would have enough.

By the time Dani reached Sutton station, it was the middle of the day. She was relieved to see a ticket machine, which meant she didn't have to speak to the grown-up at the ticket booth. It took her a while to work out which buttons she was supposed to press, as she had never done anything like this before; and she panicked a bit when the machine kept spitting out the ten-pound note she put in. Fortunately, however, the station was not crowded at that time of day with a long line of impatient commuters to start tut-tutting behind her; and when the machine finally accepted her note before dispensing a ticket and a handful of change, she felt a small surge of exhilaration. Acting like a grown-up was not so difficult, she thought to herself.

Soon she was on the train heading towards London.

The ticket collector gave her a strange look as she handed over her ticket. Ordinarily, under a stare like that, Dani would have withered, but not today. Today she felt braver. She was small for her age, but despite what Vicki and Kaz had said, she was not so baby-faced that people would be completely surprised to see her travelling alone. She returned his stare with a confidence she almost felt, and the man moved on.

It took about half an hour for the train to pull into Victoria, a vast, busy space filled with men in suits talking loudly into their mobile phones. As the doors hissed open, Dani felt her confidence waning slightly, but then she remembered the previous evening. It was enough to get her moving again, and she jumped off the train and on to the platform. Once she was out on the street, she looked around in confusion – it was all so unfamiliar – before remembering that if she was going to avoid anyone's attention she had to look as if she knew what she was doing. So, not knowing which way she was going, she started to walk.

It was busier here than anywhere she had been before – busier than Sutton, busier than home. The roads were grid-locked with traffic, and all the pedestrians on the street

seemed in a dreadful hurry. If she had worried about being
seen by anyone, she needn't have been; nobody paid her any
attention whatsoever as she wandered along the busy, fume-
filled roads. She walked and walked, not knowing where
she was headed, for some reason preferring the busy, open
streets to the smaller ones with fewer people on them.

For an hour or two Dani wandered, finally approaching
the West End. It was even busier here – vibrant; and as the
daylight began to fail, she felt a thrill at the sight of the
lights outside the theatres and the happy crowds of people
congregating in restaurants and pubs. It grew colder, and
her feet became sore; but for a while she didn't mind. She
was too busy walking, drinking in the sights and enjoying
this strange, slightly scary freedom.

By Covent Garden station there was a man with a metal
stove selling hot dogs and fried onions. The smell perme-
ated the air, and Dani was drawn towards it, reminded that
she was hungry again. There was a delicious warmth
coming from the stove, and she stood a couple of metres
away from it, transfixed by the way the man in his black
woolly hat and rainproof overcoat flipped the onions over
with a metal spatula.

She must have been standing there for a long time, because
after a while the man noticed her. 'Looking to buy a hotdog,
missie?' he asked, his voice gruff and far from welcoming.

Dani would have liked to say yes, but she found herself
tongue-tied. Besides, she had already spent a lot of her
money today. It would be silly to spend any more. So she
shook her head.

The hotdog man grunted, clearly unimpressed. 'Move
on then,' he said, turning his attention back to the food.

'You're putting the punters off, standing there looking like a charity case. Where's your mum and dad, anyway?'

Dani blinked. 'They're, er ...' she started to say, but it was clear that the man wasn't really listening, so she stepped backwards, turned on her heel and walked down a side street, blushing furiously.

As the evening wore on, Dani grew colder. Her pace, which had been brisk for most of the day, started to slow down; and as she passed restaurants, their golden glow shining out on to the street, she started to think longingly of the warmth that they offered. She gritted her teeth and tried to carry on with the same determination; whenever she felt it flagging, she thought back to Linden Lodge. The thought gave her a bit of courage to go on.

At about eleven o'clock, she stopped, removed her coat and took another top out of her bag. As she pulled it over her head, she heard the sound of someone wolf-whistling at her from the other side of the road. She blushed for the second time that night, and scrambled to get her coat back on again. She heard some laughter, but didn't hang around to see where it was coming from, choosing instead to pick up her pace and walk away. She had no idea where she was – it was a dense network of streets, full of cafés and vagrants, drunk people and shops with things in the front window that made her embarrassed. She walked around in circles, and as she did so she felt panicked, for the first time that day. Where was she? Where would she sleep? What was she going to do? The setting of the sun seemed to have taken all her confidence with it, and she felt, all of a sudden, the needle-like pain of her solitude.

There would come a point, Dani knew, when she couldn't walk any more; when she would have to find a place to stay. She stopped, recognising that she had already walked down this street several times before. Her instinct now was to get away from the crowds, to avoid unwanted attention, so she took a left-hand turn and then a right, into a little side road that she knew was practically deserted. There were some large metal bins along one pavement – twice Dani's height – and they were surrounded by full black carrier bags. There was a pungent smell about them, but at least it kept people away. Dani chose a doorway that had a big iron lock on it – nobody would be walking out of here – and she placed her bag on the doorstep before sitting down next to it.

Only when she had taken the weight off her feet did she realise that her legs were trembling. She had walked a long way today, and on very little food; and now that she had stopped walking her tummy started growling. Trying her best to ignore it, she lay down on the cold concrete of the doorstep, her head on the bag, and closed her eyes.

It was freezing now, and the concrete seemed to draw any remaining warmth out of her. Her bony hip ground uncomfortably into the doorstep, but she didn't move because she knew that whichever position she chose would be equally hard. She preferred to pull the hood of her coat tight over her head so that it covered her eyes. In the darkness, she could once more pretend she was anywhere.

Resolutely, she told herself that she had not been stupid; that she had done the right thing; that this was better than whatever the children at Linden Lodge had in store for her. And with those thoughts buzzing around in her brain, she patiently waited for sleep to relieve her of the overwhelming tiredness that seemed to be in her very blood.

The rubbish lorry roused her at dawn from her half-sleep. When she awoke, her body seemed to have fused with the step; it was as cold and hard as the concrete. The bin men shouted boisterously at each other as they collected the vast containers of waste, but if they noticed Dani, they didn't mention it. The little girl's head ached from tiredness, and although she was now fully awake, she lay still for nearly an hour, unable to face the day ahead.

It was hunger that finally made her sit up. As she did so, the side of her body felt bruised. She winced as she pushed herself up to her feet, and then again as she bent down to pick up her bag. Her legs were stiff from walking, her feet swollen and sore. Any sense of freedom she had felt on leaving the home the previous morning had long since deserted her.

As she walked out of the back street and into one of the main roads of Soho, Dani felt dirty. Her fingernails were black and her clothes seemed to cling greasily to her. The early-morning roads were filled with rubbish waiting to be collected, and its pungent smell filled the air, making her feel bilious and even more unclean. She wandered randomly on to Shaftesbury Avenue and then up to Piccadilly Circus. On one corner there was a large fast-food restaurant, one of the only places open at this early hour. Dani walked, zombie-like, towards it. There would be somewhere to wash there, and then she could buy some breakfast.

The restaurant was gratifyingly warm as she pushed the heavy doors open. There weren't many customers in the brightly lit seating area, but there was a bustle of noise from the kitchen as the restaurant workers shouted good-naturedly at each other. A smell of fried food hung in the air, which made Dani even more ravenous. She shuffled across the floor towards the toilets, pushing the door open with her shoulder and looking forward to the feeling of hot water against her face.

To her surprise, she wasn't the only person in there. Two other women stood at the sink, and as Dani entered a third came out of one of the cubicles lined along the wall to her left, accompanied by the sound of a flushing chain. One of the women was quite young – in her early twenties, perhaps – and she stood there, brushing her teeth as naturally as if she was in a fine hotel. The other two were much older – Dani couldn't really tell how old, because they both wore heavy woollen hats that disguised much of their features. Their clothes were patched and threadbare, but they seemed to be wearing plenty of layers to keep them warm.

The two older women stared at Dani as she entered. Uncomfortable in the heat of their gaze, the little girl walked straight into one of the cubicles. She had to flush it before she could use it, and she stayed in there for longer than she needed to, listening for the swinging of the main door and hoping that the others had all left. When she emerged, the two older women had indeed gone, but the younger one was still there. She was perched on the edge of one of the basins, noisily sucking her teeth. Her eyes did not leave Dani as the girl approached another basin and turned the tap on.

'Sleeping rough?' The woman's voice was low and gravelly, as though ravaged by a lifetime of cigarettes.

Dani looked at her and shook her head.

'No one washes in these places if they're not sleeping rough,' the woman insisted.

Dani turned back to the basin, cupped her hand under the running water and splashed it onto her face.

'Got money?' the woman asked. She was invading Dani's personal space now, and the girl felt it keenly.

'Not much,' she replied without looking up.

'Lend us a fiver.'

'I haven't got much,' Dani replied, turning and making her way to the door. Before she could get there, however, she felt a hand digging into her arm. The woman had grabbed her, and now she was pulling her back towards the basin end of the room and up against the wall. Her other hand pinched Dani's still-wet cheeks, and her face closed in. The woman's breath stank, and it was all Dani could do not to gag. Looking into the woman's eyes, she saw that they were bloodshot and watery, the pupils astonishingly large. The skin around her nose was pimpled, red and sore.

'Where's your money?' she hissed.

Dani's tongue seemed to freeze. Before today, she would never have thought of doing anything other than handing something over in a situation like this; but the few pounds she had in her pocket were everything to her now, and she stayed silent.

'Where's your fucking money, you bitch?' the woman repeated.

Dani felt herself trembling. 'I could buy you something to eat,' she whispered.

The woman sneered, as though Dani had just said something hilariously funny but she wasn't going to deign to laugh. Instead, she removed her hand from Dani's arm and, still pinching her face, plunged it into the pockets of her jeans. The money was all there, of course, and she emptied the pockets with hunger in her eyes. Only when she appeared sure she had got everything did she let Dani go, casting her away like an unwanted piece of debris. She cupped the money in her hands as though she was carrying a huge haul of treasure; then she stuffed it into her own trousers before leaving the room without even a glance back at Dani.

Dani stood, alone and shocked. In another life she might have cried, but she felt as if all the tears had been squeezed out of her. She staggered out of the toilets and into the restaurant. Now there were a few more people, queuing up to buy their breakfast. Dani scanned the customers, but the woman who had stolen her money was nowhere to be seen. Maybe, the little girl thought to herself, she didn't want the money for food. Maybe she wanted it for something else.

She stared at the people and their plastic trays of food. She stared at the way they bit hungrily into their breakfast burgers and gingerly slurped steaming hot paper cups of tea and coffee. She thought about asking someone for some money, but her natural timidity stopped here. Moreover, she didn't want anyone asking questions. It would only take one curious person to put two and two together and she would be on her way back to Linden Lodge.

'You buying?' A voice spoke from behind her and she spun round to see who it was. A member of the restaurant staff – a young man with his hands placed sternly on his hips – looked down at her.

'Toilets for customers only,' he said officiously. 'You buying?'

Dani cast her eyes down to the floor, and she shook her head.

'Then you've got to leave,' the young man said.

But he needn't have: Dani was already turning and heading for the door.

Hunger.

Dani didn't just feel it in her belly: she felt it all over her body. Her limbs were weak and she trembled, not because of the cold but because her body was crying out for food. By the middle of the day she found she could no longer tramp the streets because all the energy had been sapped from her body. So she sat on the pavement, against the wall of a boarded-up Soho shop, hugging her knees and desperately wondering what on earth she was going to do.

She had seen a number of people begging on the streets that morning. They seemed to feel no embarrassment as they sat on the pavement – much as Dani was now – shouting out for spare change. Some of them even walked up to people, hand outstretched, and asked them for money. So far she had not seen any passers-by hand over so much as a coin, but she supposed it must happen sometimes – otherwise the beggars would not bother.

Dani could not quite bring herself to ask for money. It would bring too much attention to her, and that was the one thing she didn't want. But as the hunger pangs became more severe, she knew it was only a matter of time. She had to eat, and soon.

The afternoon passed. At about three o'clock she noticed a policeman approaching her. Despite her hunger, Dani sprang to her feet and sprinted round the corner, losing herself again before emerging on Soho Square. She walked past the railings into the square itself and collapsed onto a park bench, waiting for—

In truth, she didn't know *what* she was waiting for.

Evening came, and the temperature dropped once more. She watched office workers, warmly bundled up in heavy coats, hurrying through the square back to whatever awaited them at home. Idly she daydreamed about approaching one of them, asking for shelter for the night, but she knew she never would. Instead, she prepared herself for another night in the cold, another night of enduring the discomfort of a concrete mattress and an empty stomach. Reluctantly she hauled herself up from the bench. It was too out in the open here – she would attract attention. Instead, she would try to find her way back to the place where she had slept last night. Somehow, in this unfamiliar world, she thought she might find some comfort from that strange element of routine.

Dani did not see the man following her. She didn't realise that he had been watching her in the square for nearly an hour, and as she trudged down Carlisle Street she didn't notice him, only a few metres behind, doggedly making sure he didn't lose her. Only when she was approaching the bins where she had slept last night did she become vaguely aware of something: a prickling sensation on the back of her neck. She stopped and turned.

The tiny side street was empty apart from Dani and the man, who, quite calmly, crossed the road and continued walking slowly along the other side. Dani hurried towards the bins. Quite why it was that she thought she would be safer there she didn't know – maybe it was the fact that the large metal containers offered some sort of protection from the passing world; and when she sat down on the metal step she did feel a moment of relief. It soon passed, however, when she realised that the man had stopped on the other side of the street and was looking over at her.

Dani lowered her head, pretending that she hadn't seen him; pretending – in some futile way – that she belonged where she was. She could sense him drawing nearer, however, and when he came and sat down next to her on the step, she could hardly pretend not to have noticed him.

'You look freezing, lassie,' he said in a broad Scottish accent.

He was a well-dressed man. His jeans were a very dark blue, and seemed new; he wore a thick black polo-neck and a black leather jacket. His head was shaved close and he had a long, aquiline nose. Although it looked as if it had been broken at some point in the past, it didn't give him a threatening look because his eyes, which were dark brown and seemed more deeply set than most people's, were kind and full of concern. She could smell his aftershave. It was warm and musty.

'I'm all right,' Dani replied. She didn't feel comfortable talking to anyone.

The man nodded his head, and for a little while they sat in silence. She wondered if she should get up and leave, but she didn't.

'Sleeping rough?' he asked.

'No.'

'It's all right,' the man said. 'Don't worry. I'm not going to tell anyone.'

Another silence.

'Got any money?' he asked lightly.

Dani felt her muscles tensing. If she'd learned one thing today, it was that that question could lead to something nasty.

'No,' she said firmly, hoping it would make him lose interest. When he didn't move, she heard herself speaking a bit more forcefully. 'No good trying to nick it off me,' she said. 'Someone already did that.'

'So you *are* on the streets, lassie,' the man replied softly. 'Run away, did you?'

Dani looked down. 'I didn't say that.'

'You didn't have to. What's your name?'

She sniffed. 'Dani,' she said, her voice cracking.

He smiled. 'That's a nice name,' he told her. 'What's it short for? Danielle?'

Dani shook her head. 'No,' she said. 'Just Dani.'

'You must be starving, Dani, if you haven't got any money.'

There was no way she could pretend that wasn't true. She looked up at him and nodded her head.

'Tell you what,' he said. 'There's a place round the corner where they sell big slices of pizza. I'll get you one, if you like.'

The offer of food quickly got Dani's attention and made her instantly forget any nervousness she had. She nodded again, eagerly, and even allowed the man to take her by the hand. 'Come on, then,' he said, and together they walked down the street and out into the evening bustle of the West End.

The pizza counter he took her to was situated under a covered walkway at the end of Shaftesbury Avenue. The man didn't ask her which flavour she wanted – they all looked the same, anyway – and just ordered her a slice. It came sandwiched between two shiny paper napkins and was steaming hot. Dani bit into it hungrily, and greedily tried to swallow the doughy food so that she could take another bite quickly. Within minutes, she had devoured the whole lot while standing there in the street, the man watching over her.

'Would you like another one?' he asked.

Dani nodded.

By the time she had eaten two of the huge slices of pizza, she felt less chilled and more able to cope with another night in the doorway. She sucked the grease from her fingers, aware that the man was watching her every movement as she did so.

'Thank you very much,' she said politely. 'I'd better go now.'

The man shrugged slightly without taking his eyes from her. As she stepped away, he walked with her. 'You're not going to sleep the night in that doorway, I hope, lassie,' he said as they wove their way through crowds of people, most of whom seemed to be walking in the opposite direction.

'No,' Dani lied.

'Where you sleeping, then?'

Now it was Dani's turn to shrug. 'Haven't decided yet,' she said, aware that it sounded rather pitiful.

'I can get you a bed for the night, if you like.'

Dani stopped and looked up at him; then she shook her head and bashfully continued walking. 'No thanks,' she mumbled.

'Don't worry, lassie,' he laughed. 'I won't be there myself. Just other ladies, like yourself. It's up to you, but there's a spare bed there, and it's warm.' They continued walking. Suddenly, though, he grabbed her by the arm and bent down to her level. 'No police, either,' he said with a glint in his eye. 'No one to ask any questions if you don't want to answer them. Safe. You can stay as long as you like.'

Dani looked nervously around her. They were being tutted by passers-by in whose way they were standing, but none of them seemed to see anything strange in the sight of the two of them. That was reassuring, she decided. Although she had steeled herself to spend another night in the doorway, the opportunity of a roof over her head was tempting. And as if to reinforce that thought, it suddenly started to rain – cold, heavy droplets that would soon soak her to the skin.

'Where is it?' she asked.

The man smiled. 'Just round the corner from here,' he said. 'We can walk there.'

Dani thinned her lips, trying to make herself look as if she was considering the offer, though in truth she knew that the choice had pretty much made itself. For although there were alarm bells in her head – well-remembered warnings never to go off with strangers – she couldn't see how taking this man up on his offer could possibly be worse than another night on the street. In any case, he had been kind to her. He had bought her food when she was hungry. It was the most real kindness anyone had shown her in a long time.

'I don't know your name,' she said. Somehow it seemed impossible to go off with someone when she didn't know what he was called.

The man smiled. She saw that one of his teeth was entombed in gold.

'My name's Baxter,' he said, and he offered her his hand to shake.

Dani took it. It was cold and rather clammy, but she liked the way he treated her as a grown-up.

'Shall we go, lassie?' he asked her.

Dani nodded, and together they walked hand in hand further up Shaftesbury Avenue, and back into the high-sided maze of Soho that Dani was beginning to feel she knew so well.

Chapter Six

They stopped outside a black door. Dani didn't know the name of the street, but it was high-sided, very narrow and not as crowded as the others that surrounded it. The door itself had neither a letterbox nor any indication of what number it was. There was a large lock on the door, and it took Baxter a little while to unlock it.

He pushed the door. It seemed heavy to Dani, and creaked open slowly to reveal a long hallway. There was no light there, and as she stood in the doorway, peering into the gloom, she couldn't see where the hallway led. A twinge of doubt passed through her: it looked spooky through the door, and it didn't seem much warmer in the house than it did outside. Almost as a reflex action, she stepped backwards.

But Baxter was there. He put his hand on her back and gently encouraged her through the door frame. 'Don't worry about the dark, lassie,' he said. 'There's a light switch here somewhere.' He hustled in behind her, and then shut the door. The two of them were plunged into absolute darkness.

Dani froze and a sense of panic started to rise in her. All of a sudden she didn't like it here. The noise outside had receded the moment the door had shut, and there was an unpleasant smell of damp, musty and thick. Somewhere in the blackness she heard the sound of Baxter moving about – looking for the light switch, she presumed, but it seemed to be taking him a long time to find it. She stepped back and pressed herself against the door, feeling gingerly for the handle. Just as she touched it, however, the light came on, dazzling her slightly; Baxter grabbed her hand and gently pulled her further down the hallway.

It seemed very dingy to her. The ceiling was high and yellowing, with a single light bulb hanging from a bare wire. On the floorboards there was a rug of sorts, so old that the pattern had disappeared in the centre, leaving nothing but a brown patchwork of threads. At the end of the hallway were some stairs, and to the left of these, under the stairs, there was a door. It was firmly shut.

Baxter pushed past Dani and locked the main door from the inside. 'Up the stairs, lassie,' he said, and he stood there, his arms folded, waiting for her to do as he told her to.

'Why do you have to keep the door locked?' she asked.

'Can't be too careful,' he said blandly. 'Middle of London – lots of bad types about. That's why we don't want you sleeping on the streets, isn't it?' He smiled at her.

Dani glanced up the stairs. They led up to a little landing, where they turned back on themselves. On the landing itself there was a small window. It had three metal bars running top to bottom and the grey paint around its frame was peeling away.

'Go on, lassie,' the man encouraged her in his soft Scottish accent. 'Your room's up there.'

Nervously, Dani started to climb the stairs.

They walked silently up three storeys. At each level of this tall, thin townhouse there were two doors, but none of them was open, so Dani couldn't tell what was behind them. She had the impression, however, that they led to separate rooms. On the second floor there was a toilet. As she passed it, Dani managed to glance inside. The walls were old and stained, the floor damp. A terrible stench emerged from the place, and it did not look like the sort of toilet Dani would like to use.

The layout of the third floor was slightly different. Here there was nothing other than a single door, flush against the top of the stairs. Baxter pushed it open and stepped into a flat, followed by an anxious Dani.

It wasn't much brighter in the top-floor flat than it had been downstairs, though the carpet in the hallway was less threadbare. At the end of the hallway there was an open door, through which Dani could just make out a bathroom; to her right was a sparse kitchen, about the size of the one at home but a good deal less full. There were three other doors off the main hallway, all shut.

However, it was not the carpets or the rooms or the doors that had grabbed Dani's attention the moment they walked in; nor was it the dim lighting or an acrid smell she didn't recognise, and which seemed to be woven into the very fabric of the place. It was the woman standing there in front of them, looking for all the world as if two strangers had just walked into her private space. She had obviously just come out of the bathroom, because her long, dark hair was wet and combed back from her face. She wore a pair of skinny jeans and a tight, low-cut top, but no shoes. Her face was haughty and suspicious, and she had three piercings along the length of her left ear.

She looked from Baxter to Dani and then back again.

'Who the fuck's that?' she demanded in a harsh, Eastern European accent.

Dani felt her skin burn with embarrassment, and she looked down to the floor.

At first Baxter didn't answer. He stepped over to one of the other doors and peered inside. While he was doing this, the woman didn't take her eyes from Dani; nor did she bother to hide the loathing that she obviously felt for her.

'I said, who the fuck's she, Baxter?'

Baxter turned to look at her, and as he did Dani saw a change in his expression. Until now he had seemed almost benevolent, providing her with food and a place to sleep – almost like a guardian angel. There was nothing angelic about the look he gave the woman, however. 'Shut the fuck up, Kris,' he told her as he stepped back towards Dani. 'Where's Ellie?'

'With a John,' Kris replied. She gave Dani another meaningful, unpleasant look, and then disappeared behind one of the doors that led off the hallway.

By now, Dani's whole body had gone cold and she wanted to get out of there. 'Who was she?' she asked in a small voice, but the man didn't reply. Instead, he held open one of the doors and indicated brusquely that Dani should walk into the room beyond.

It was a small space. There was a mattress on the floor in one corner, with a couple of brown blankets strewn over it. Against one of the walls was a dressing table, with two drawers and a mirror that was old and spotted. On the dressing table was an old-fashioned lamp, the only source of light in the room. There was no carpet on the floor, just rough floorboards, and the room was windowless.

'You can sleep here,' Baxter said. As he spoke, he opened the drawers, checking to see if there was anything in them. Dani didn't see what it was that Baxter removed from one of them and put into his pocket.

She stood in the doorway. 'I think I might go now,' she said.

Baxter shook his head. 'No,' he said shortly without even looking at her. And then, after a few seconds' pause, 'You'll get used to it.'

She stepped back from the doorway and into the hall, feeling her lower lip start to tremble. When Baxter noticed this, his own lip curled in a dismissive sneer, and instantly Dani wondered how she could possibly have seen anything friendly in this man's face. He strode towards her, grabbed her firmly by the arm and then yanked her into the room and over on to the mattress. Dani fell, dropping her bag beside her, and looked up in fear at him. 'Just stay the fuck there, shut the fuck up and don't make a fucking nuisance of yourself,' he told her abruptly, before walking out of the room and closing the door behind him.

Dani sat statue-still, shocked by Baxter's sudden change of temperament. She felt bruised, as if she had been punched by more than just unkind words. From behind the door she heard things – the hurried sound of someone leaving, and then voices. A man's – Baxter's, obviously; but if she listened carefully she thought that maybe she could also make out two different women. Although she couldn't hear what they were saying, it was clear that they were arguing, and it didn't take much intuition to work out that they were arguing about her. That woman – Kris – had obviously not wanted her to be here. Dani wanted to creep up to the door and listen to what they were saying, but she didn't dare. The change in the man's attitude had been so extreme that she had gone in an instant from trusting him to fearing him, and she didn't know what he would do if he caught her listening to their conversation.

Suddenly Baxter shouted something, and the other two fell silent. Then there was a slamming of what sounded like the front door, followed by a deep, ominous silence.

Still Dani didn't move off the mattress. She looked around the room, taking in the old, patterned wallpaper and noticing thin, silvery lines of cobwebs in the corners of the high ceiling. The blankets on the mattress were coarse and uncomfortable; and as she moved them away from her, she noticed a couple of large, stains on the mattress, and an aroma coming from it that was not pleasant. Her flesh naturally crept away from those patches, but it soon became apparent to her that the whole thing was stained. Forgetting her fear for a moment, she jumped up, not wanting to be anywhere near those stains.

Now she was on her feet, she summoned the courage to approach the door and put her ear to it.

She listened carefully.

Nothing.

No voices. No sound of footsteps.

Her trembling hand felt for the door handle; with her breath sounding loudly in her ears, she pressed down on it and lightly opened the door.

There was no one in the hallway to see the little girl creep silently to the main door. When a floorboard creaked underneath her feet, it sounded to her ears as loud as a foghorn; she stood still, her breath held, but nobody seemed to have been disturbed by the sound, so she continued towards the door. She stretched out her hand to the circular door knob, twisted it and pulled.

Nothing happened. The door was locked.

She pulled again, as though a second tug would make a difference. Of course it didn't, and as another hot wave of panic crashed over her, she started shaking the door with all her vigour, ignoring the noise she was making. All thoughts of stealth had left her; she just wanted to get out.

When it became clear that the door simply wasn't going to open, Dani banged on it in frustration, and then slumped on the floor, her body shaking and her back to the hallway, little more than a crumpled pile. She buried her head in her hands and started rocking back and forth, as though that soothing, babyish motion would do something to make things better. But it didn't.

Dani knew she was trapped. She didn't know why, but it was suddenly obvious to her how stupid she had been to go with this man she didn't know. Why would he be kind to her? When had *anyone* been kind to her? Dani grew angry with herself. She deserved this. She deserved it for being such a stupid little girl.

'You going to sit there all night?'

The voice came from the other end of the hallway. It was smoky, though not as gruff as Kris's had been, and it made Dani jump. Still crouching on the floor, she spun round and looked at the woman to whom the voice belonged.

She was tall with long, platinum blonde hair, and she wore a white towelling dressing gown. In her right hand was a burning cigarette, which she moved up to her lips and dragged on deeply. As she sucked, her cheeks became more sunken, accentuating the startling thinness of her face. There were black rings around her deep green eyes, which stared directly at Dani. The little girl could detect no emotion on her face.

'I want to go,' Dani said.

The woman's eyes tightened slightly. 'Not going to happen,' she said, looking away from the girl. 'Might as well forget about that.'

'Why not?' Dani asked, feeling her voice going. 'Why do I have to stay here?'

The woman shrugged; then she stepped towards Dani, her left arm outstretched. 'Might as well stand up,' she said. 'No point sitting on the floor. No point not being comfortable.'

Dani cast her a hateful look and pushed herself up to her feet without grabbing the woman's hand. She shrugged a second time. 'Suit yourself,' she said, turning to walk into the kitchen. 'Brewing up, if you fancy one,' she called.

The girl didn't understand what she meant, but she followed the woman into the kitchen. Like the rest of the house, it was dimly lit. A yellowing blind covered the window, and there was a table with rickety metal legs and a full ashtray placed almost exactly in the centre of the square room. Apart from a toaster, a plastic kettle and an old portable television that wasn't even plugged into the wall, there was nothing on the short length of work surface against the left-hand wall; and the stand-alone stove looked as if it was older than Dani herself.

'So do you, titch?'

'What?'

'Fancy a brew?'

'What's a brew?'

A flicker of a smile played across the woman's face. 'A *brew*,' she replied insistently. 'A cuppa. Cup of tea. You're a bit green, aren't you? How old are you, anyway?'

Dani looked away. 'I don't really drink tea,' she said.

The woman watched her thoughtfully for a moment. 'I'll make you one anyway,' she said finally, flicking the switch of the kettle. 'I'm Ellie, by the way.' She smiled briefly, perfunctorily, at Dani, who didn't reply. 'You got a name, have you?' the woman persisted. 'Or you not going to tell me that, neither?'

'Dani,' the girl replied. 'And I really do want to leave now, please.'

'What happened to your face?' Ellie asked, ignoring her request.

Dani touched her cheek with her fingers. With everything else, she had forgotten about the bruising. It must have been going down, she thought, because it didn't hurt any more; but clearly it was still visible. 'Nothing,' she said quietly.

Ellie nodded knowingly. 'Boyfriend, was it? Bastards some of them.' She poured boiling water into two cups. 'Total bastards.' She bent down in front of the fridge and opened it. Dani saw that it was empty, apart from a carton of milk, which she removed and sloshed into the cups of tea. She squeezed out the teabags, discarded them in the sink and then shovelled a couple of teaspoons of sugar into each cup. 'I had this one bloke, didn't like me being on—'

'It wasn't a boyfriend,' Dani interrupted her. 'I haven't got a boyfriend.' She cast her eyes down to the floor. 'It was my mum.'

A flicker of surprise crossed Ellie's face, but she soon mastered it. 'Your mum, eh?' she asked lightly, putting the cups of tea on the table. 'Best out of that, then.' She pulled a chair from under the table, sat down and took a packet of cigarettes and a lighter from the pocket of her dressing gown, which she laid on the table. She lit a cigarette, dragged deeply and then pushed Dani's cup of tea towards her. 'Might as well sit down,' she said.

Not knowing what else to do, Dani took a seat and sipped the tea. It was hot and sweet, and strangely nanny-ing. She took another sip.

'So …' Ellie said after a minute or so. 'Never had a boyfriend?' She sounded to Dani as if she was asking a question other than the one on her lips, but the little girl didn't know what it was. She blushed a little as she shook her head. Ellie's lips thinned, but she kept quiet.

Dani sipped her tea again. 'Who's the other lady?' she asked. 'The one I saw.'

Ellie took another deep drag on her cigarette and her eyes flickered towards the door, as if she was checking nobody was listening. 'Kris,' she said quietly. 'Another of Baxter's girls.'

Dani's brow furrowed. 'Does Baxter have lots of girl-friends?' she asked.

As she spoke, Ellie was watching her; she didn't take her eyes off the little girl, but neither did she reply, choosing instead to stub out her cigarette in the ashtray and light another one. Dani sensed she had asked a silly question, but she didn't know why.

The awkward silence between them was broken by the sound of a buzzer. It was loud and seemed to fill the whole flat. Ellie looked at her watch, and then back at Dani. 'Best go off to your room now,' she told her.

'Why?' Dani asked, the thought of that horrible stained mattress making her feel nauseous. 'Couldn't you just let me out?'

Ellie looked away. 'Can't do that,' she said tersely. 'Best go to your room now. Only for twenty minutes. Won't take long.'

'What won't take long?' Dani asked, but Ellie had already scraped her chair back and was walking to the kitchen door. She stood there and, rather severely, gestured to Dani to get out. The little girl did as she was told. As she passed the front door, she had to suppress the desire to bang on it, to shout for help. But she didn't. She walked obediently to her room and closed the door behind her.

Dani couldn't bear to be near the mattress, so she crouched in the opposite corner and sat on the hard floor. From the hallway she heard the door open and a brief murmur of voices, followed by footsteps, and then silence.

On the streets it had been noisy, and that noise had seemed threatening and scary to Dani. It wasn't as bad as the silence, however. Thick, all-pervading. A silence that seemed to stick to her; a silence that made it impossible to tell how much time was passing; a silence that seemed to be an ominous prelude to something, but she didn't know what. Dani stood up and started to walk around the room, drawing some sort of comfort from the sound of her own footsteps. Occasionally she put her ear to the door and strained to see if she could hear something. But no – just the silence.

She had to get out of there. She had to escape.

Perhaps the door was unlocked now. If it was, she could just slip outside and make her way down the stairs. Once she was at the front door, she could make some noise, to let people know she was there. It was a bold idea, but this place scared her and she was desperate to get away.

Dani opened her bedroom door and crept out for the second time in less than an hour. It didn't take long, however, for her to establish that the door to the flat was still locked. No doubt she had been stupid to think otherwise.

Then she heard a sound behind her.

She spun round to see one of the other doors off the hallway open. A man stepped out. He was clearly surprised to see Dani standing there, because for a split second he stopped doing up his tie. Ellie appeared behind him, still in her dressing gown, and he turned back to look at her.

'Who's she?' he asked.

'No one,' Ellie replied. 'She won't be here long.'

The man looked back at Dani and continued doing up his tie. He had a curiously square face, she noticed, with short, curly brown hair, and looked about the same age as Christian – about fifty. He wore a grey, single-breasted suit and a plain white shirt. As he did up his tie, Dani noticed a gold wedding band on his left hand. He stepped forward towards her, seemingly unable to take his eyes from Dani.

'Welcome to the party,' he said gruffly. His voice seemed quite posh to Dani, and out of place in this run-down flat. 'Maybe I'll see you again.' He smiled, a thin, self-satisfied smile that had no humour or pleasure in it.

Dani didn't reply. She just stepped out of his way as he walked towards her.

'Forgotten something, have you?' Ellie asked in a clear voice.

The man stopped and turned around. 'Of course,' he said without embarrassment, and he drew his wallet from inside his jacket. He pulled out a couple of notes, which he handed over to Ellie. She tucked them into the pocket of her dressing gown, and then nodded towards Dani.

'Forget about her, eh?' she said quietly.

The man smiled again, and then walked over to where Dani had pressed herself against the wall by her bedroom door. 'Oh, I don't think I'll forget about *her*,' he whispered. 'I don't think I'll forget about a pretty little thing like *her*.' He stroked the back of his fingers against her cheek. Dani moved her head away, but that only seemed to please him the more.

'Time to go,' Ellie announced abruptly. She strode over to the door and took a key from a piece of string round her neck. Once the door was unlocked, she stood by it and arched a single eyebrow – a look that clearly indicated to the man that he should leave now.

Dani grabbed her chance. She scurried round the man and ran to the door; she might even have got through it, had she not tripped at the last minute and fallen flat on to the hard floor. Instantly she felt strong hands clutch her arms;

hauled up to her feet, she was flung by the man back into the hallway, where she fell to the floor again.

The man sneered at her. 'Night night,' he said; then he turned and left as Ellie locked the door behind him.

Tears fell down Dani's cheeks. 'Why don't you let me go?' she wailed. 'Why do I have to stay here? I don't under-stand – why can't I just leave?'

Ellie looked down at the girl, her expression unreadable. For a moment, the only sound in the flat was that of Dani's uncontrollable sobbing – a desperate, pitiful sound. Ellie stepped forward. 'Come on,' she said quietly in her husky voice. 'I'll make you another cuppa.'

'I don't want another cup of tea!' Dani shouted. *'I just want to go home!'* And with that, she stood up and stormed tear-fully into her bedroom – not because she wanted to be there, but because it was the only place to go.

Once she was alone again, Dani collapsed to the floor and allowed the huge, shuddering sobs to overwhelm her. She felt as if she would never stop crying, as if something had been unleashed inside her and now all the fear she felt was bursting forth.

How long she crouched there, crushed and broken, she couldn't have said. It was the sound of someone entering the room that made her look up again, and the acrid smell of smoke. Looking up through the blur of tears, she saw Ellie in the doorway, burning cigarette in hand.

'That man,' the blonde woman said shortly. 'Do you know what he was here for? Do you know why he came to see me?'

Dani shook her head.

'You got no idea?'

'I don't know, all right? I just don't know. I want to go home.'

Then Ellie was there, down on the floor with her. She stretched out her hand and gently stroked Dani's hair. The little girl was too exhausted to move away, and so she let the woman carry on, gently stroking. It calmed her a little, and after a short while the tears stopped.

Dani looked up at her. Ellie's face was beautiful, she realised now that it was close up, despite the bloodshot eyes and dark rings. And it was tinged with an unmistakable look of sadness and sympathy.

'Please let me go,' she begged.

'I can't, titch,' Ellie replied hoarsely. 'I just can't.'

Dani bowed her head. 'Do you live here?' she asked.

'Could say that,' Ellie answered. 'Live here. Work here. Same thing really.'

'If you live here, you're in charge. You can let me go.'

Ellie took a deep, shaky breath. 'Yeah, but it's not as easy as that, is it? Things are never as easy as they should be.'

They sat there in silence. As the woman continued to stroke Dani's head, the little girl noticed that her hands were shaking slightly.

'What *was* he here for?' she asked after a while. 'That man.'

'Doesn't matter.' Ellie's voice was little more than a whisper, barely audible.

'I didn't like how he looked at me.'

'It doesn't matter,' Ellie repeated, as though she was trying to persuade herself as well as Dani. 'I'll speak to Baxter. Make sure he doesn't …' Her words petered out.

'Doesn't what?' Dani asked timidly.

Ellie avoided her question. 'You should get some rest,' she said instead. 'Go to sleep, if you can.' She stood up and moved back towards the door. 'Things'll seem better in the morning. Always do, don't they?'

And with that she departed, leaving Dani still crouching on the ground, terror piercing her like a knife.

Chapter Seven

Somehow, she slept.

Dani avoided the mattress, and lay on one of the brown blankets on the floor, using the second to cover herself. It was hard and uncomfortable, but at least the warmth wasn't being sapped from her as it had been the previous night when she had lain on the cold concrete of the doorway. With the lamp switched off and her head buried under the cover, she could pretend she was somewhere else – anywhere but here. The skin on her face was sore from crying, but despite that, she dozed off.

It was the voices that awoke her. Loud voices. Angry. Dani blinked in the darkness, momentarily confused as she tried to work out where she was. When it all came flooding back to her, she felt sick.

She heard Ellie's voice first, but she couldn't work out what was being said. Throwing the cover off her body, she groped in the pitch black towards the door; it took her a few clumsy seconds to find it, but once she was there she pressed her ear against the wood to hear what was going on.

'It's sick,' Ellie was complaining. 'You're fucking sick. I've got a mind just to let her out of here, when you're not around.'

There was a scuffling noise, and then the sound of blows. Ellie whimpered, and then started to shout again. 'Get off … all right, Baxter, all right … I'm not going to do anything.'

Dani had to strain to hear his reply. 'Too fucking right you're not,' he hissed. 'Do something like that, you stupid bitch, and you know what'll happen.'

More scuffling, followed by another whimper.

'You *know* what'll happen,' Baxter repeated.

'Yeah, all right,' Ellie spat. 'All right, I know. Just hand it over.'

'Maybe I won't,' Baxter taunted, a malicious tone in his voice. 'Maybe I'll take it with me, make you wait till tomorrow.'

A silence. Then Ellie spoke again. This time her voice had changed entirely. It was humble. Frightened, almost. 'No, but don't piss around, Baxter,' she said. 'I'm not going to do nothing stupid.'

'You're fucking pathetic,' Baxter told her. 'All right, here it is. But you mess me around again and the supply fucking dries up. Got it?'

'Yeah,' Ellie replied, almost sulkily.

'Good. Where's Kris?'

'I'm here.' The dark, hoarse tones of the other woman suddenly came into the mix. 'What the hell's going on, Baxter? I'm trying to sleep.'

'Just explaining a few things to Ellie,' Baxter growled. 'I hope you're not thinking of doing anything stupid about your new flatmate.'

'She here to steal our tricks?' Kris asked.

'*Your* tricks,' Baxter pronounced the words slowly and clearly in his strong Scottish accent, 'are *my* tricks, and don't you fucking forget it.'

A pause.

'Course,' Kris replied. 'Not a problem.'

'Good,' said Baxter. 'Kris, you're coming with me tonight. If you're lucky, there might be a few quid in it for you. *You*' – it sounded to Dani as though he was addressing Ellie – 'don't forget what I just said. I fucking mean it.'

Dani hadn't understood what was going on, but she didn't have to be that clever to realise that it sounded bad for her. She couldn't listen to any more, so she crept away from the door, back to where the blankets were lying. They were a bit more crumpled than when she had first laid them out, but she didn't want to alert anyone to the fact that she was awake, so she made do.

There was no way of telling what time it was in that dark, windowless room. Dani heard the front door slamming shut, and then she just lay there, sleep now a distant possibility.

The only way Dani could tell that morning had arrived was by the thin line of grey light that appeared underneath the doorway. She was hungry again now, and thirsty; but more than that she was cold. The blankets had not been enough to keep her warm as the night turned to morning. She stood up, her head stuffy with lack of sleep, switched on her lamp, and then silently walked out into the hallway and through to the kitchen.

There was nothing in the fridge other than a half-full pint of milk. Dani located a few plates, pots and pans, but no food. If there was any, she decided, it would be hidden away in one of the high cupboards that were out of her reach. It didn't occur to her to stand on one of the chairs to get up there. Instead, she went to the bathroom.

There was a big white bath against the far wall. Inside it was covered with thick, yellow scum marks. Along one side was a frayed shower curtain that was spotted with mildew; the shower itself was encrusted with limescale. There was no soap; there was not even any paper by the toilet with an old-fashioned, high-level cistern above it. Dani felt an over-whelming desire to clean herself. She shut the door behind her and locked it with the little hook lock, before remov-ing her clothes.

Dani shivered as she stood naked by the bath with the showerhead in one hand, trying both to regulate the temperature and to stop herself from thinking about the dirt of the bath itself. It seemed there were only two temper-atures – ice cold or scalding hot – so she was forced to climb into the bath and let the freezing water sluice over her. Rubbing her skin hard with the palm of her hand, she tried to get the grime of the street off her; it was difficult without any soap, but she did the best she could to get clean before turning the shower off.

As she stood dripping on the floor, she realised she had nothing with which to dry herself. She could use the blan-kets, she thought, but she was too ashamed of herself to risk rushing naked to her room. Instead, she took her jumper and used that to wipe off the water, before pulling her dirty clothes back on to her still clammy body. Even when she was fully dressed, she was still shivering; but at least she didn't feel so dirty.

The voices from the previous night had not left her. Those strange things they were saying. Dani was worried about Ellie, worried about what had been said to her. Done to her. As she left the bathroom, she lingered outside the woman's room. There was no sound from inside. Gently, Dani tapped on the door.

She waited. Nothing.

Another tap.

Nothing.

Dani pushed the door open and peered inside.

The acrid smell that hung around the flat was stronger in here, but Dani couldn't tell why. Ellie's room had a window, but it was barred on the outside and only looked out on to a blank brick wall. It was covered with a large thick blanket, so it let little light in. Enough, however, for Dani to see that this was a neatly kept room. There was a dressing table and an armchair; even a cupboard. There was also a double bed. And lying on the bed, splayed out, was Ellie. She was still wearing her dressing gown, but she looked as though she had fallen on to the covers and lost consciousness the minute she hit them. One of her sleeves was rolled up, and her hand clutched something, though Dani couldn't see what.

The little girl sensed that she shouldn't be in there.

She stepped back, and as she did so she stumbled clumsily and clattered against the wall. Ellie stirred and looked up groggily. '*Get out,*' she hissed when she saw that someone was in the room.

Dani turned and left, running back into her own room and banging the door behind her, hot with the shame of being caught doing something she shouldn't. She crouched in the corner of the room again, and gathered up her blankets as though they would give her some sort of comfort.

A few minutes later, the door opened and Ellie walked in. She still looked groggy and tired, but she wore an apologetic smile. The sleeve of her dressing gown was rolled back down now, and she carried a plate in one hand and a cigarette in the other. 'I brought you some toast,' she said quietly.

Dani looked up at her. In the dim light of Ellie's room, she hadn't been able to see the woman's face; but now that it was illuminated by Dani's lamp, the little girl was shocked by what she saw. The skin around her right eye was purple and swollen, and her lip was split and bloodied. Ellie's face seemed paler than it had the night before, and she noticed that the hand that was holding the plate was trembling. The woman stepped further into the room and placed the plate on the floor in front of Dani.

There was a single piece of toast on the plate, with a thin scraping of jam. Dani looked gratefully up at Ellie before devouring it quickly. Only then did she speak.

'What happened to your face?' she asked.

Ellie shrugged. 'Make a right pair now, don't we?'

'Was it Baxter?' Dani asked. 'I heard you arguing.'

A look of suspicion passed across Ellie's face. 'What did you hear?'

'Nothing much,' Dani lied, but Ellie didn't really seem to believe her.

'Doesn't matter.' Ellie seemed to brush it away. 'Not the first time I've had a black eye. Probably not the last either.'

'I hope he doesn't hit me,' Dani said.

Ellie's brow furrowed slightly. 'Just have to do what he says, titch,' she told her. 'Do what he says, and you'll be all right.'

'But I don't know what he wants me to do. I don't know why I'm here and why I'm not allowed to leave.'

Ellie looked away. She seemed to be deciding whether to say something or not, but apparently she soon decided against it. Her hand still trembling, she took the plate and stood up. 'You'll need a few things if you're going to stay here,' she said, as though she was talking to someone who had just checked into a hotel. 'Towel, toothbrush, clothes. Some food. You got any money?'

Dani shook her head. 'Someone stole it.'

Ellie didn't look surprised at that. 'Haven't got much myself,' she said. 'I'll see what I can do, though.' She headed towards the door.

'Ellie,' Dani said before she could leave, and the woman turned round.

'Yeah?'

Dani hesitated. She had only spoken because she didn't want to be left alone, and now she had to think of something to say. 'Thank you for the toast,' she mumbled.

Ellie nodded, and then left.

Dani stayed in her room. When she heard the front door closing, she slipped out to try the handle; but sure enough it was locked.

It was an hour or so before Ellie returned. The woman came straight back into Dani's room. She had changed out of her dressing gown into a pair of jeans and a green jumper – a tight one that accentuated the curves of her body – and had applied some make-up to the bruises on her face. She carried two shopping bags. Placing them on the floor, she brought out a toothbrush and toothpaste, some soap and a small white towel. 'Not much,' she said a bit apologetically.

'All I could afford, really. Wanted to get you a pillow, but didn't have the cash. Borrow one of mine if you like, though.'

Dani felt she should thank Ellie, but somehow the words wouldn't form on her lips. The woman had been kind, there was no doubt about that; but it had not escaped the little girl's notice that these items seemed to seal the reality of her imprisonment. You don't buy toothbrushes, she thought to herself, for someone you don't expect to stay.

The lack of thanks didn't seem to worry Ellie, who was busy pulling something else out of the bag. She held up a tin of baked beans. 'Food,' she said shortly. 'Not a big eater, me. Didn't really know what to buy for chil—' She stopped herself. 'For other people,' she concluded a bit weakly. She put the beans back in the bag. 'Don't talk much, do you?' she commented.

Dani looked down at the floor.

'S'all right,' Ellie said. 'Look, sorry I shouted at you earlier on. In my room. It's just … you should knock on my door before you come in, that's all. And if I don't answer, leave it for a bit, all right?'

'All right,' Dani replied.

'Come on, then.' Ellie did her best to sound bright. 'Let's go and have a brew.' She smiled. 'Remember what a brew is, do you?'

Dani stood up and looked at the woman seriously. 'Yes,' she said. 'I remember.' And she followed her into the kitchen.

They ate beans on toast and drank tea in silence. When they had finished, Ellie took the plates and placed them in the sink. Occasionally she tried to make conversation with

Dani, but the girl found it difficult to answer and so she just kept quiet. At intervals the older woman disappeared to her room. When that happened, Dani stayed put, as she didn't feel inclined to return to her own. Ellie always came back after an hour or so, however, to check on her.

And so the day wore slowly on.

Evening approached. As it grew darker outside, Dani noticed that Ellie's manner had started to change. She had become twitchy, nervous, and was flitting in and out of the kitchen more frequently. Looking at her watch. When she spoke, she sounded distracted, as though her mind was on something else; after a while she stopped speaking at all, and began acting almost as if Dani wasn't there.

When the bell rang, Ellie was pacing around the kitchen, and Dani noticed the way she dug her nails into the palm of her hand. The woman shot straight out into the hallway and lingered by the door, clearly waiting for it to open.

That happened soon enough.

Dani watched from the kitchen as Baxter entered; instantly a cloud seemed to descend on her. Before he said anything, he handed something to Ellie. She grabbed it hungrily. As she did so, a second person entered the room. From where Dani was sitting, she couldn't tell who it was, because he stood on the other side of Baxter.

'Back again?' Ellie said to this other person.

'Just fuck off to your room,' Baxter told her. 'It's not your trick this time.'

Ellie looked as if she was going to say something; but she thought better of it. Instead, she glanced towards Dani. Their eyes met, and Ellie quickly looked away, as if embarrassed. Then she turned and disappeared into her room.

Baxter walked into the kitchen, followed by the other person. As soon as Dani saw his face, she recognised him. It was the man from yesterday – the one who had come to see Ellie and who had stroked Dani on the cheek. He lurked in the doorway while Baxter approached Dani.

'This is Mr Morgan,' he said, without any kind of preamble. 'You do what he tells you. Understand?'

Dani looked at Mr Morgan. He wore the same grey suit as yesterday, and his tie was smartly done up. His square face was fixed in a bland smile, but his eyes seemed to shine.

'I said, do you understand?'

Dani nodded.

'Good.' Baxter turned to the other man. 'All yours,' he said, almost dismissively. 'Hope it's worth it. You know where to go.'

Morgan nodded. He pointed at Dani, and then towards her bedroom. 'In there,' he said, his voice little more than a whisper. 'Now.'

She shook her head – a timorous little movement, but all she had the courage for. As she did so, Baxter gave her a look. Its meaning was clear; he didn't have to say anything. Anxiety burning in her stomach, Dani pushed back her chair and stood up; then she walked past the two men into her bedroom. She tried to close the door behind her, but something got in her way. There was really no point in looking back to see who or what it was, because she could sense that Mr Morgan was following her into the room. He shut the door behind him.

For a minute, neither of them said anything. They stood in silence looking at each other.

'Come here,' Morgan broke the silence. His voice had a slight tremble of excitement in it.

Dani stepped towards him.

As he reached out his hand, she flinched. 'Don't worry,' the man said, sounding like a parent comforting their child. 'I'm not going to hit you.' Dani kept looking to one side, but she couldn't stop his hand brushing against her cheek as it had the night before.

Morgan started to breathe heavily. 'You're a pretty girl,' he said.

Her skin tingled with revulsion, and she cast her eyes down to the floor.

'Don't be so shy,' he whispered. 'It won't hurt. You'll probably like it. You'll probably want it to happen again.'

'Leave me alone,' Dani whimpered. 'Please leave me alone.'

'In a bit,' Morgan replied. 'I'll leave you alone in a bit. But you have to do something for me first. You know what it is, don't you?'

She shook her head as tears splashed on to her cheek.

Morgan chuckled. 'Well,' he said. 'We'll soon teach you. I'm sure you're a fast learner.'

Slowly, Morgan moved his hands away from her face and then started undoing his tie. His hands were shaking, Dani noticed, and when their eyes met his mouth twitched slightly. The light from the lamp illuminated a thin covering of sweat on his upper lip. He slid the undone tie from under his collar, and it made a smooth hissing sound, like a snake. Then he took off his jacket and slung it on to the dressing table.

'Take your clothes off,' he instructed.

Dani's mouth went dry and she stepped back. Shaking her head, she tried to whisper the word 'no', but nothing came out.

Morgan sneered. He approached her and cupped his trembling hand round her throat. He squeezed – not hard enough to hurt, but easily hard enough to scare. 'I said, take them off.'

He tightened his grip slightly.

Dani's body seemed to go into spasm. Short, jerky movements shot down her legs like little electric shocks of panic, and her breathing became heavy; but even though Morgan was squeezing her neck harder and harder, she still managed to shake her head.

Eventually, he threw her on to the mattress in anger. 'Stupid little cow,' he muttered, before leaving the room, slamming the door behind him.

Dani lay with her face against the stained fabric. It smelled, but though she wanted to move away from it, her body was shaking too much for her to gain control of it. Her breath came in short gasps, and she was too scared even to try. The man might have left the room, but she knew that was not going to be an end to it.

Sure enough, barely a minute later, the door opened again.

It was not Morgan this time but Baxter. Dani didn't know who she feared the most. Baxter stood by the mattress, his face a thundercloud, and looked down at her.

'Get to your feet,' he instructed.

Dani stayed where she was, still shivering. Immediately she felt a strong hand grab her around the top of her arm, and she let out a short gasp as Baxter pulled her to her feet as easily as if he was picking up a rag doll. She stumbled off the mattress and tried to retreat into the corner, but his grip was too strong. Dani wasn't going anywhere.

Baxter bent down so that his face was inches from hers.

'Listen to me,' he said in his thick Scottish accent, 'and listen well, because I'm nae going to say this twice. You work for me now, and you do what I say. When that man comes back into this room, you're going to do exactly what he tells you to. You're his for as long as it takes. And if I have to come back in here to speak to you again—'

His other hand slipped into his inside jacket pocket and he withdrew something. To start with, Dani couldn't tell what it was; it was only when he touched a little lever and a blade flicked up, shining and sharp, that she realised it was a knife.

'If I have to come back in here to speak to you again, I'll cut your pretty little face to ribbons.'

Ever so gently, he pressed the tip of the knife into the flesh just below Dani's eye. Her terrified breathing became shorter, sharper, but she did not dare move for fear that the blade would slice into her skin. Baxter kept it there for what seemed like an age, all the while staring implacably at her. Dani was in no doubt, no doubt whatsoever, that he meant what he said.

When Baxter removed the knife from her face and loosened his grip on her arm, there was no sense of relief. Just a different quality of fear. He stood up again, and without another word he left the room.

There was a murmur of voices outside, and then Mr Morgan appeared. He had a smug, satisfied look on his face as he closed the door.

'Do it,' he told her. 'Or you know what'll happen.'

And so it was that a curious numbness fell over Dani. Slowly, awkwardly, she started to peel off her clothes. For some reason – maybe because it took a few extra seconds – she felt the need to fold them neatly before placing them in a pile on the floor. Morgan watched patiently; the gleam in his eyes even suggested that he enjoyed the process. When Dani was down to her pants and vest, she stopped and looked at him, her arms crossed over her abdomen as if in some small way that protected a little bit of her modesty.

'Them too,' he said.

'Please don't make me,' Dani begged. '*Please.*'

As she spoke, however, Morgan looked meaningfully towards the door. Dani knew what that look meant, and the fear of Baxter's knife overcame the fear of being naked in the presence of this man. She removed the rest of her clothes; then she stood there, her hands still attempting to cover herself.

Morgan surveyed her approvingly, before undressing himself. Dani averted her eyes, unable to watch, unable to look at him. Her skin was covered in goosebumps, and her limbs were shaking. Her breath was now so short and sharp that it was becoming difficult to breathe, and she felt faint as he approached. It barely took anything for him to push her on to the stained mattress; and she lay there in crucified terror as he lowered his heavy body on to hers.

It hurt when he forced her legs open; but that didn't hurt nearly as much as what followed.

Morgan hardly made any noise throughout. The only sounds in the room were whimpers of pain from Dani's anguished throat. She felt his hot breath against the skin of her face, and when she dared to open her eyes, she saw sweat emerging from the pores of his skin. She had never known pain like it. It was as if the knife that Baxter had shown her was being thrust inside her, hot and relentless. The little girl squirmed, but it did no good as the weight of Morgan's body kept her pinned to the mattress. There was no escape until he had finished what he had come here to do.

The process was mercifully short. When he withdrew sharply, the girl called out in pain.

Morgan barely seemed to notice.

He barely acknowledged that she was there.

The gleam in his eye had gone, replaced by a flatness – an anger almost. The lips that had been so close to her face had curled into a sneer. Somehow that look suited his face.

As Dani curled up, foetus-like, into a little ball, a fire burning in her belly, Mr Morgan simply dressed as though he was getting ready for work in the morning. He ignored her sobs. He ignored her very presence. There was not a word for her as he approached the door.

Dani Sinclair had provided a service to him. Now that it was finished, he was going to leave.

Chapter Eight

Mr Morgan walked out of the door, but he didn't shut it.

Baxter was waiting for him, standing by the main door, his arms folded. 'You'll be wanting to pay,' he said curtly.

There was a shuffling as Mr Morgan removed his wallet. Crouching on the mattress, Dani couldn't see how much money he handed over, but she heard their conversation.

'Five hundred, we said,' Morgan stated blandly.

'Aye,' replied Baxter. 'Five hundred.'

Morgan glanced back into the room. 'It'll be less next time, now she's no longer ...' He failed to finish his sentence.

Baxter shrugged. 'It's a risk for me, keeping her here. I won't be doing it for peanuts.'

'Just don't forget what I bring to the table, Baxter. Don't forget that.'

'Seems to me, *Mr Morgan*' — he pronounced the words ironically, as though he knew it was not a real name — 'that both of us have something to lose from this arrangement going wrong.'

Mr Morgan didn't have a reply to that. 'Are you going to let me out, Baxter? Or am *I* going to be one of your little prisoners too?'

'No,' Baxter said. 'I don't see why you should stay around here any more than you need to.' He took a key from his pocket and unlocked the door. In an instant, Morgan was gone.

Baxter locked the door again and then approached Dani's bedroom. 'Put your clothes on,' he instructed; then he turned away and walked into the kitchen.

Dani did not want to move. The pain in her tummy hadn't subsided with the end of the rape, and she feared that standing up would just make it worse. The memory of Baxter's flick knife had not deserted her, however. She knew beyond doubt that he would do what he had said he would if she didn't obey him. So slowly, painfully, she uncurled her body and moved to a sitting position.

It was almost with a sense of detachment that she saw the blood on the mattress. It was on her skin too, down the inside of her thighs. Almost immediately the detachment turned to alarm. Wincing, she stood up and grabbed the clean white towel that Ellie had bought her. The blood was stubborn, and try though she might she could not remove all of it from her body – sticky patches remained that she simply could not clean up without soap and water. Nevertheless, by the time she had finished, the towel looked more like an old bandage.

Almost stumbling over herself, Dani pulled her clothes over her soiled skin. Just as she had finished dressing, Baxter appeared in the doorway. His face was severe, and he looked at her with undisguised aggression as he pointed in her direction. 'You give me trouble like that again, my girl,' he hissed, 'and I swear to God I'll kill you.'

The threat echoed around the room, and around Dani's head. Baxter stared piercingly at her for a few seconds; then he turned and let himself out of the flat. Dani could not help but listen for the sound of the lock turning.

As soon as she was alone, she doubled over in pain, clutching her belly. How long she remained like that, standing bent over in the middle of the room, she couldn't have said; time suddenly meant nothing to her. When she finally straightened up, she took her bloodied towel and the toiletries that Ellie had bought her, and headed straight for the bathroom.

Earlier that day, she had been repelled by the dirt around the bath; now she hardly noticed it. She turned on the shower, and instead of allowing it to run cold, she turned the dial so that it was scalding hot. No matter that the water would burn her: she craved the heat against her soiled skin, her soiled body. If it was hot enough, maybe it would wash away the sense that she still carried of Mr Morgan's bulk, heavy against her. She stripped off, unwrapped her bar of soap and stepped into the dirty bathtub.

The hot water brought tears to her eyes, but she weathered the pain as she worked the soap into a lather and started to scrub her skin. At first she used the palm of her hands, but it did not feel as though that was doing any good, so she started scraping herself with the ends of her nails. Her skin shrieked, but still she carried on, burning and scratching it, doing whatever it took to rid herself of that filthy sensation. The more she scrubbed, the more it hurt and the faster flowed her tears, until she resembled a frenzied, weeping shadow of herself.

Eventually, she collapsed into the bath, sobbing frantically and allowing the burning water to spray over her skin. And when, finally, her tears would come no more, she climbed out and roughly rubbed the bloodied towel against herself.

Raw, but dry and relatively clean, Dani Sinclair stood in the bathroom and realised that suddenly she was seeing the world through new eyes. No longer through the eyes of a child.

She understood now where she was.

She understood what was happening.

She understood that this nightmare, that seemed somehow to be of her own foolish making, would never, ever end.

Several hours later Ellie re-emerged.

Dani was sitting in her own room, her back against the wall, staring at the bloodstained mattress where it had all happened. No tears – like a wet flannel that had been vigorously wrung out, she had cried herself dry. Her red eyes were pinned open, despite the fact that it was the small hours of the morning, and the numbness that surrounded her prevented her even from noticing the woman standing in the doorway.

'You all right?' Ellie asked.

Dani jumped, and like a frightened animal looked up at her. Ellie's face was pallid. It made the bruise that Baxter had inflicted upon her seem even more severe. More alarming, however, was the look in her eyes. Haunted. Full of loathing, though for what it was impossible to say.

Dani turned her gaze back to the mattress. 'You knew, didn't you?' she asked.

'What?' Ellie demanded, her shaky voice defensive.

'What he was going to do.'

Ellie took a step inside the room. 'It's what we're here for,' she said abruptly. 'It's what we do.' Then, a little more quietly, 'It's what we *are*.'

They fell silent.

'It hurt,' Dani said after a minute. '*Really* hurt.' She looked up at Ellie. 'Does it always hurt like that?'

'Not always,' Ellie whispered. 'You get used to it.' She stepped further into the room, and then sat on the floor next to Dani. Ellie took the little girl's hand, but Dani didn't react to the silent gesture. 'Best not to fight them, titch,' she said. 'Best just to let it happen.'

Dani didn't reply.

'Did he use anything?' Ellie asked.

'What do you mean?'

'You know, any—' But as she spoke, her face reflected her realisation that Dani didn't know what she was talking about. Ellie stood up and shuffled out of the room. A minute later she returned with a box. She put it on the table and pulled out a small, foil-wrapped object. 'Next time,' she said, 'tell them they need to use one of these.'

Dani blinked, her eyes stinging as she did so. She stared at the thing Ellie was holding up, but she didn't register what it was, nor even much of what the woman had said. Instead, two of Ellie's words rang in her head.

Next time.

Next time.

'I don't want to do it again,' Dani whispered. 'I never want that to happen to me again.'

Ellie returned the object to its box. 'Best just to let it happen.' She repeated the phrase like some kind of mantra, her voice flat and emotionless.

Something snapped deep inside Dani as she stood up suddenly and started screaming. 'I don't want to do it again!' she yelled. '*I don't want to do it again! I hate it!*'

Ellie looked around fearfully, as though Dani's screams were going to disturb someone she was scared of. But there was no one here. No one to listen to the screams, apart from Ellie and Dani. The little girl knew that well enough.

'Just let me out of here!' she begged, her voice sore from the sudden screaming. 'Why can't you just let me out of here? *Why can't you just do it?*'

As she spoke, a transformation came over Ellie's face. It might have looked haunted before, but now it morphed into an expression of such wretchedness that it almost made Dani take a step back.

'I just can't, all right?' the woman shouted back. '*I just fucking can't!*'

'Why not?' Dani railed. 'Why can't you go to the police?'

A look of scorn crossed Ellie's face. 'The *police*?' she scoffed. 'You got to be fucking joking. Wouldn't do any good anyway. Baxter's too smart for that. Got the police stitched up good and proper. Got them in his pockets. No, don't worry about that – you won't see the police round here any time soon.' She turned and walked to the door. 'I'm trying to help you, you know?' Her voice was shaking now, as though she was barely keeping control of it. 'I'm doing what I can.' She touched the bruises on her face. 'You've seen what he does to me,' she continued. 'And you've seen—'

She faltered, and momentarily bit her bottom lip.

'Forget it,' she whispered, almost to herself, and she walked away.

Moments later, Dani heard Ellie's bedroom door slam. She ran out into the hallway, to the main door, and started banging and kicking on it. 'Let me out!' she yelled – to whom, she didn't know. 'Let me out! Please! Someone let me out!'

But there was no one to hear her.

Once again, she slumped to the floor and waited for time to pass.

Baxter returned the following day. Kris was with him. She had a haughty, superior look, and she kept touching his arm in an affectionate way that suggested their relationship had changed. From her doorway, Dani watched as Kris gathered some things from her room. It was clear she was leaving. They left without speaking a word to Dani.

When a customer arrived that evening for Ellie, Dani hid in her room. She didn't want to be seen – didn't want to be preyed upon by someone who, like Mr Morgan, might be attracted by her youth. She listened for the sound of the customer leaving, and a few minutes later heard Ellie clattering around in the kitchen. Starving hungry, she walked across the hallway and stood by the kitchen door.

'Making beans on toast.' Ellie didn't turn to look at her, but she was clearly trying to pretend that the argument of the night before had never happened. 'Want some?'

'Yes please,' Dani said.

They ate their meal in silence, and then went separately to their rooms.

It was late when the front door opened again. Dani held her breath as she listened to the footsteps and a murmur of voices. An ice-cold tingle shivered through her veins, and she found herself whispering a half-remembered prayer, begging baby Jesus not to let whoever had just arrived in the flat walk into her room.

Her prayer was not answered.

The door opened, and Baxter appeared. He fixed her with a serious kind of glare – a glare that she could tell was intended to warn Dani not to put a foot wrong. Then he stepped aside.

Dani had been half expecting to see Mr Morgan; she couldn't tell whether she felt relief or disappointment when she didn't recognise the man Baxter ushered in. He was smaller than Morgan, not a tall man at all, and he wore a heavy beige overcoat and an old-fashioned kind of hat. The water dripping from his clothes suggested to Dani that it was raining outside. It made Dani momentarily wonder how long she had been trapped indoors, but there was no way she could calculate that – not with this sudden new and sinister presence. The stranger didn't look at her, choosing instead to keep his gaze aimed at the floor. Dani just felt sick.

Baxter closed the door.

The man didn't say anything. Not at first. He seemed embarrassed, and the way he kept his gaze averted suggested that he didn't want Dani to see his face. He shuffled in, and quickly removed his hat, placing it over the top of the lamp; immediately the room dimmed to a gloomy half-light. Only then did Dani get a chance to look at his face. He had a short, stubby nose, a fat, blotchy face and thin pink lips. His brow was furrowed, making him look as if he didn't know why he was there or what he had come to do. And though he still refused to look directly at her, he couldn't help his eyes flickering greedily in her direction.

He gestured to her that she should move over to the mattress.

Dani looked towards the door, and for a brief moment she considered running. The idea flitted away almost as soon as it had come as Baxter's words, so deeply meant, rang in her head.

If I have to come back in here to speak to you again, I'll cut your pretty little face to ribbons.

You give me trouble like that again, my girl, and I swear to God I'll kill you.

And she knew he would. She could almost feel the sensation of the knife pressed against her skin.

In a kind of daze, she stepped towards the mattress.

The man started undressing. Dani couldn't look at him; instead, she indicated the box on the dressing table that Ellie had supplied her with. 'You have to use one of them,' she said weakly, not knowing what it was she was telling him to do.

The man looked round, saw the box and obediently took one of the little foil packages out of it. He stood there, wearing nothing but his shirt as he unwrapped it; then, lightly holding the little piece of plastic it contained, he took a few steps towards her.

'You need to get undressed now,' he whispered. His voice was reedy and nasal, and it had a little tremor of excitement in it.

Dani's limbs went weak with dread; she felt as if all the strength was suddenly being drained out of her. She wanted to run – she wanted to run so desperately. But she couldn't. There was nowhere to go. There was nothing to do, other than obey. Shivering from both cold and fear, she started to undress.

Best not to fight them, Ellie had said. *Best just to let it happen.*

She lowered herself on to the mattress, closed her eyes and waited for it to be over.

As the days passed, Dani fell into a kind of routine. A twisted, dark, nightmarish routine, but a routine nevertheless. The men who Baxter brought to the flat never came during the day. It was as if they were scared away by the sun. That was not to say, however, that they never received daytime visitors. People would call for Ellie at any time of the day or night. She always referred to the men who came to see her as tricks, but Dani could not bring herself to use that word. To her, a trick sounded like something fun. Something happy. There was nothing happy about what these men came to do.

Each morning, Dani would stay in her room until hunger drove her out. Every couple of days Ellie would go out and buy tins of food, to which Dani would help herself. The woman barely ever surfaced until midday. Invariably she would come into the kitchen to find Dani eating; but the girl seldom saw her eat anything herself. Instead, Ellie would light a cigarette and make sweet, milky tea. Sometimes they would talk; other times not. It rather depended on what Dani had had to endure the night before.

There were regulars. Mr Morgan was one of them. He would come two or three nights a week. Whenever she saw him, he would always be wearing the same clothes – that suit and tie Dani had learned to loathe – and she had grown to recognise his smell. There was an aftershave that he wore that seemed to precede him as he walked into the room. The moment that smell hit her nose, Dani would be overcome by dread. He barely ever spoke as he walked in; he would just look at her with a sense of expectation on his face. *You know what I'm here for*, he seemed to say. *You know what to do.*

There were others, too. She never knew their names, or anything else about them. Mostly, when they arrived, there was a sense of nervous excitement about them; when they had done what they came to do, however, their mood would change. They would seem angry, blunt. Without exception they just wanted to get out of there, and they never looked back as they left the room.

When it was over, she would overhear Baxter discussing money, and as a result of those conversations, she started to get an idea of her worth. The five hundred pounds Mr Morgan had paid the first time was a one-off. Normally Baxter would demand between a hundred and hundred-and-fifty pounds, depending on who it was. The only exception was Mr Morgan, who seemed to have secured a preferential rate. Fifty pounds, normally; on one occasion she even heard Baxter jocularly tell him, 'This one's on the house,' and the man left without paying. But no one else was afforded that kind of treatment. There were never any grumbles, never any complaints. The men always just paid up and left. Dani sometimes wondered if they were scared of Baxter – she wouldn't have blamed them if they were – of if, like her, they just wanted to be out of that place. Whatever the reason, Dani's visitors never stayed around after they had finished with her.

Very occasionally, once the client had left, Baxter would appear at the door and wordlessly drop a ten-pound note on the floor. Dani would have found it humiliating enough, even if she had been able to spend it, but she wasn't. Kept under lock and key day and night, she gave her money to Ellie. The older woman would use it to buy food and things for Dani to keep herself clean on one of her infrequent trips to the shops. Occasionally Dani would ask her to take her blankets to the laundrette, and the woman would oblige without a word.

Baxter almost never spoke to Dani, a fact for which the little girl was very grateful, because when he did, his words were like poison in her ears. 'You're a worthless little bitch,' he told her in his broad Scottish accent after the second time Mr Morgan had paid a visit. 'No one cares about you. I could kill you now, and no one would even know.'

Dani had winced as she heard the words, which she knew to be true.

'So just remember, lassie, what will happen if you mess up. Don't ever forget that you do what I say, or else you pay the price.'

After each client's visit, she would wait to hear the door closing, followed by the inevitable sound of the key turning in the lock. When she was sure that no one was going to return, she would tramp sadly to the bathroom and undergo what had now become a ritual of cleansing herself with scalding hot water and rough soap. She would rub herself until her skin was sore, until it squeaked, before going back to her bedroom.

Nothing in the world would make her lie on the mattress if she didn't have to. She could have taken the one from the bed in Kris's old room, but she knew what had gone on in that room, so it was almost as distasteful to her as her own. Instead, she slept on the floor, between the two rough, brown blankets. Before – at home, at Linden Lodge – she had preferred the dark, preferred the way she could hide under the blankets and pretend she was somewhere else, somewhere happy. Now, however, even that source of release had been taken from her. In her head, there was no longer a difference between light and dark, day and night.

It was all dark. All night.

Dani started to lose count of the days, and then of the weeks. She lost count of how many men visited her, and how often they did so. Each wretched, sordid encounter became much like another – a short period of horror punctuating the blanket of misery that had descended upon her.

The little girl could not have said how long it was into her time of imprisonment that the snow started to fall. A month, maybe two. She was sitting in the kitchen when it happened. There was a small window there, looking out onto a brick wall a few metres away. The window had bars across it, and it was too far up for Dani to see what there was on the street below. The snowflakes started to fall softly at first, but within minutes there was a flurry of white dots, like little fairies flying manically around. It reminded Dani of the time when, their differences dissolved by the excitement of snow on the ground, she and Rebecca had made a snowman together. How long ago that seemed! She had been a different person then.

As these thoughts danced through her head like the snow dancing in the air, Ellie walked into the room. She lit a cigarette, as she always did; then she leaned against the side and smoked it in three or four deep breaths.

Ellie was a mystery to Dani. The little girl had long since given up begging her to let her leave: it was clear that wasn't going to happen. Why that was, Dani didn't know. Maybe Ellie was as scared of Baxter as she was; maybe it was something else. Yet she seemed – not affectionate, exactly, but caring. She would inexpertly prepare meals for Dani when she could, and sometimes she would come back from her shopping trips with a little treat – a bar of chocolate, maybe, or a magazine. They were treasures for Dani, these tokens from the outside world, and she found that rather than hating this woman for continuing her imprisonment, she grew fond of her. She grew to trust her. To depend on her.

'Snowing,' the woman said in her characteristically curt manner as she looked out of the window. As she often did when she first emerged from her bedroom, she looked haggard. As the day wore on, her complexion would start to improve; but by evening she would become twitchy again. Snappy. The only thing that seemed to make her less anxious was the arrival of Baxter. It didn't make any sense to Dani.

The little girl nodded. 'I wish I could go out and play in it,' she said in a small voice.

'Don't start, Dani,' Ellie said wearily.

'No,' she replied quickly. 'I wasn't. I was just—' She shrugged. 'I was just saying.'

A pause.

'I know what you were saying,' Ellie conceded by way of an apology. She lit another cigarette and switched the kettle on.

That evening, Baxter brought a new client to the flat. As always, Dani was holed away in her room, praying that the sound of someone at the door was not a prelude to something. The moment she heard her own door opening, however, that now familiar hot wave of sickness crashed over her as she saw Baxter's face, and saw him step aside in his usual way to allow the visitor to enter.

Dani squinted in the gloomy light to see who it was. Some of them were rougher than others, and in a perverse kind of way she sometimes felt relieved to see that it was one of the less aggressive clients. But she didn't recognise this man's face. Baxter closed the door and left the two of them together in the room.

This new client had black skin. He was tall and bulky, and his hair was cropped short with three neatly defined razor lines along one side. Despite the snow outside, he wore just a T-shirt under the raincoat that he removed and slung on the floor. He smiled at Dani to reveal a single gold tooth. Down the left-hand side of his face there was a line of pale scar tissue.

Dani closed her eyes and tried to shut out any feeling. She knew what was going to happen, and she knew she could only weather it by cancelling out any emotions.

When she opened her eyes again, however, the man had stepped nearer. All these people frightened Dani, but there was a look in this man's eyes that sent an extra tremor of terror down her. He must have seen that, because his lips curled into a sneer as he took another step nearer and stretched out his hand to take her by the neck. The man pulled Dani towards him and squeezed a little harder before throwing her onto the mattress.

She landed with a thump and then looked up in fear. Where it had come from she didn't know, but the man held a knife in his hand.

'Get to your feet,' he growled. He had a low voice, with a pronounced London accent.

Dani started to hyperventilate.

'I'm not going to tell you again. Get to your feet.'

Slowly, she pushed herself up.

The knife was long and thin, and Dani couldn't take her eyes off it. Nor did she know what to do. None of the men who came to her had ever been violent like this before. Rough, sometimes, but not vicious. Remembering the last time a knife had been pulled on her, she thought that perhaps she was doing something wrong, so in a desperate effort to make amends she started awkwardly removing her clothes.

'I didn't fucking tell you to get undressed,' the man hissed, and as he did so, he raised the knife in the air, as though preparing to slash it down. It was too much for Dani, and instantly she started to scream – three sharp, ear-piercing bursts that surprised even her with their ferocity.

It happened in a blur. Almost the moment the scream left her throat, the door opened and Baxter was there.

Within seconds he had taken in the scene. 'What the fuck?' he spat, and he strode towards the client.

The beating Dani's pimp imposed on the much larger man was swift and brutal. He grabbed the knife hand and sharply kneed him in the groin. The man doubled over, and Baxter used the same knee to supply a second blow to his chin. He grabbed the knife out of the man's hand; then he pushed him to the wall and, with a swift, vicious slice, cut into his cheek. Dani watched in horror as blood started to dribble down his face; she was only too aware that had it not been for Baxter's intervention, the same could have happened to her.

'You touch one of my girls again, you piece of shit, and I'll put a knife in your fucking guts. Got it?'

The man didn't reply. He had his hand to his cheek now, trying to stem the flow of blood. But when Baxter had finished speaking, he stumbled to the door, out into the hallway, and left the flat.

A silence followed the man's departure. Baxter looked at his bloodied hands in annoyance, seemingly quite unperturbed by the wound he had just inflicted, and then round at Dani, as though she was the cause of all this. Dani herself, almost weak with relief that she had avoided the man's knife, felt a curious gratitude towards Baxter.

'Thank you,' she murmured.

Baxter took a few paces in her direction. He was still holding the knife, and as he approached, he held it up towards her face. Dani recoiled as much from the blood as from the blade: she didn't want it anywhere near her skin. Little by little, however, Baxter moved the knife closer to her, until eventually it was resting against her cheek. The blood was still slightly warm, and it felt sticky.

'Don't flatter yourself,' Baxter whispered. 'Any of these bastards put a mark on you, your price goes down. Simple as that. There's only one person allowed to take a blade to you, or a fist for that matter, and that's me. I'll do it if I have to, so don't think I've had a sudden change of heart.'

Dani shook her head fractionally as Baxter's eyes bored in to her. Then he nodded, satisfied that his point had been made. Lowering the knife, he turned and left the room.

As for Dani, she fell to the ground. There were still spots of the man's blood spattered on the floor, but for now she didn't notice them.

She buried her head in her hands, and for the first time ever she found herself wondering if it might not be better to be dead.

Chapter Nine

Hayley Carter looked out of the office of her workplace. The snow had been falling for a few hours now, and it would be a cold, difficult journey back home through the rush hour. Not that she would be going home any time soon. There were still three crime scene reports to be typed up, and the DCI wanted them on his desk first thing in the morning. She sighed and turned back to her screen.

She had been working at this central London police station for six years now, and she was part of the furniture. Most people didn't stick at being a police secretary for much more than a year – indeed most of her colleagues were temps, here for a few weeks at the most before moving on to something else – and Hayley would be the first to admit that it was a boring, repetitive job. But for some reason she didn't mind that. When she had first come here, at the age of twenty-one, it had seemed like the answer to all her prayers. A place where she could be treated like an adult. A place where she could earn enough money to rent a little one-bedroom flat, at the opposite end of London from the parents who she never wanted to see again. The first thing she had done when she left that hated flat in that hated council estate was change her name from Clark to Carter. A break with the past, and a way of making it a bit more difficult for her parents to track her down.

It was a large open-plan office, brightly lit by strip lighting, each person's desk delineated by a couple of textured brown screens. There was the usual hum of activity all around, a noise that Hayley had learned to ignore in her years of working here. She took a report from the pile and started to type.

'Can't get enough of the place, eh, Hayley?' a cheerful voice said from behind. Hayley turned to see Ryan, a new sergeant who had been paying her quite a lot of attention. He was a nice-looking boy, and seemed like fun. But he was barking up the wrong tree. Hayley hadn't been in a relationship since – well, since she'd been an adult, certainly. And there was no way she intended to change that. But it made her feel good to be noticed, even if she knew she was never going to reciprocate Ryan's attention.

'Sucker for punishment,' she replied.

'Maybe I can sweeten the pill a bit,' Ryan suggested. 'I've got a pay cheque burning a hole in my pocket, and there's that new pub opened round the corner.'

Hayley smiled. 'It's sweet of you, Ryan,' she declined, 'but I've got to—'

'—get back,' Ryan finished her sentence. 'Yeah, yeah. You can't blame me for asking.' And with a wink he was on his way.

Hayley turned her swivel chair back round to her screen and continued typing.

The one thing about this job was that you got to know what really went on out there, on the streets of London.

Maybe if she was a secretary in a more provincial station she'd see a different side of life; but as it was there weren't many days when she didn't find herself a bit surprised by something she read in one of these reports. The one she was typing out at the moment was a perfect example. An officer had been called to an incident in a room above a shop in Old Compton Street, having been alerted to shouting by a member of the public. When the officer arrived, the door had been opened by a ten-year-old kid. The mother was there, but she had passed out on the floor, surrounded by all the paraphernalia required for smoking crack cocaine.

Hayley found herself shaking her head as she typed. The way people treated their kids these days – it just wasn't right.

That thought made her falter. She cursed as she mistyped several words in a row; then she pushed herself dramatically away from her desk, allowing the wheels on the swivel chair to roll back. She was all too familiar with the little lightning shock of anguish that raced through her whenever she thought of a child in distress. Who did she think she was, criticising how other people brought up their children? And as that thought popped into her head, a thousand others rushed to follow. Images. Half-remembered words. They all jostled for space in her mind, crowding her consciousness.

It had been so long ago, that rainy night when she had walked away from the hospital, walked away from her responsibilities. She had been a different person. No more than a child herself. Yet her actions had stayed with her, shaped her, moulded her into what she was. For years she had told herself that she had done the right thing – the *only* thing she could. But lately her opinion of herself and her actions had changed. Maybe it was her time of life. The biological clock she kept reading about in magazines. Whatever the reason, these days Hayley Carter found herself thinking more and more of her abandoned baby.

There was no one to talk to about it, of course, because no one knew. Not a single soul. When the pangs of guilt and distress crept up on her unawares, there was noone to turn to or share them with. They just had to be dealt with. Mastered. Buried.

With a sigh, Hayley pulled herself back towards the desk and carried on with her work. It took an hour and a half to finish typing the reports, by which time it was seven o'clock. All the rest of the secretarial staff had gone home, though there were still plenty of police officers around. She glanced over to the glass-fronted office of DCI Barker, Hayley's immediate boss. He'd been in the job for a couple of years and was pretty much universally loathed, not least by Hayley, who hated the dismissive way in which he talked to her, and the brutish comments. How he had ever got so far up the greasy pole she'd never know. Quickly she gathered up her things. It would be just like him to find something for her to do just as she was leaving, so she bowed her head, grabbed her bag and coat from under her desk, and left.

She was right about the journey home. It took another hour and a half to get from the West End out to the eastern end of the Central line where she lived. By the time she had walked from the tube station to her little flat on the eighth floor, she was shivering with the cold, and the sludgy snow had seeped through her boots. It was with relief that she closed the door behind her.

The flat was immaculate, as always. Everything in its place. The front door opened on to a living room with a small kitchenette area; directly adjoining that room was the bedroom, off which there was a small bathroom. There were no corridors between the rooms, and little scope for privacy. That didn't matter. There would only ever be one person living in this place: Hayley had no emotional room in her life for company. No pictures hung on her wall; no family portraits, or friends. There was no clue in this little space to anything in her past, and that was how Hayley liked it. The past was too painful, and she had trained herself to block it out.

She had a hot bath and fixed herself some food, which she ate in front of the television. Almost as soon as she had finished it, however, she started to nod off. So she left her dirty plate by the sink and headed for the warmth of her bed.

Sleep came quickly. And with it the dream.

Hayley didn't have this dream every night, or even every week. It was not regular, or persistent. But it was familiar. She had been having it ever since, well, ever since she became a mother.

It always started with the screaming – the weak, help-less wail of a newborn child. At first it seemed to come from nowhere, from the darkness. Hayley was in a room, a dark room, groping around trying to find the source of the sound. She fumbled blindly until her fingers touched a pane of glass. She pressed against it, and tried to see through.

Her eyes were getting accustomed to the darkness now, and little by little she could see around her. It was a small room, with no windows or doors, divided in two by that large pane of glass. On the other side of the glass was a tiny bundle. It was so close to her, and yet so far because she could not reach it. She pressed longingly against the glass, and as she did so, the crying became more intense. More frenzied. Locked in the dream, Hayley started to bang against the glass, trying to shatter it with her fists. But she couldn't.

She could see the child's face now, and she recognised it as her own. Every ounce of her being longed to gather it in her arms, to cuddle it. To make things all right again. She could see perfectly clearly now, even though there did not seem to be any source of light in the room. And as it always did, every time she had this dream, the blankets fell away from the child, leaving her exposed, naked and still screaming.

Suddenly, however, the screaming stopped, and Hayley ceased banging against the wall. The child, tiny though it was, slowly sat up. Its face seemed to change. It was still the face of a baby, but somehow its eyes were different. Older. Eyes that understood. They fixed Hayley with a desperate stare, a stare that was full of need and which seemed to drive a corkscrew into her heart. Then, just as Hayley felt she could bear no more of this, the child's mouth opened and it emitted a scream of bloodcurdling horror.

It was at this stage of the dream that Hayley always woke up.

She did so now, trembling and sweating. For a confused moment she thought she was still in the room of her dream, and she looked all around, trying to see the baby. Then reality kicked in again, and she realised there was no baby to be found. The child was long gone. Hayley would never be able to gather her up in her arms.

Quietly she slipped out of bed, removed her dressing gown from the peg on the back of her door, put it on and walked into the main room. It was dark, but she had not closed the curtains, and she was attracted towards the window. The snow had stopped, and it was a clear night. From high up on the sixth floor she could see quite a distance. London was spread out in front of her, a vast, impenetrable maze, filling the night sky with the glow of its artificial light.

London. It was where Hayley had left her daughter. Left her for the possibility of a better life. Was she still here, she wondered? Was she happy? Did she know that her birth mother was out there somewhere, thinking of her? Or did she know nothing of Hayley's existence? And maybe it was better that way.

Hayley stood at that window for a long time, simply gazing out and wondering. After a while, however, she shivered. It was cold. Her duvet beckoned. She padded back into the bedroom, covered herself up and fell into a fitful, disturbed sleep.

Ever since she had been brought to the flat, Dani had avoided looking in the mirror. At first it had been because she couldn't bear to see the reflection of her bruised face; but now the bruises had cleared up it was something else. Shame, guilt – she wasn't sure she knew the words for the emotions she was feeling.

The morning after Baxter had attacked his client, however, something had changed, and as the sun rose, Dani found herself sitting at the little dressing table and staring into the blotchy, spotted mirror against the wall.

What she saw was horrifying, yet she could not turn away.

Her skin, which had always been pale, was practically white, with a ghostly pallor that she assumed was due to lack of sunshine. Her face was thin, her cheeks sunken; and she looked as if she had two bulging black eyes, so dark were the rings around them.

She stared and stared. The face looking back at her seemed almost like a stranger's.

For hours she gazed in the mirror, touching her fingers to her face, like a blind person familiarising themselves with a new person. It must have been nearly midday when she heard Ellie moving about. The woman went into the bathroom and stayed there for a long time – nearly an hour – before coming out again and tapping on Dani's door.

'Yeah?' Dani said quietly.

The door opened. If anything, Ellie looked worse than Dani. She was scratching at her nose and sniffing badly; and of course she had the ever-present cigarette in her hand.

'Got a trick in a couple of hours. Going shopping now, though,' she said in a hoarse voice. 'Want anything?'

Dani shook her head, and then turned back to examining her face in the mirror.

Ellie took a deep drag on her cigarette. 'Right, then,' she croaked. 'See you in a bit.'

Dani didn't answer, but a moment later she heard the front door open and shut. Obviously Ellie had locked her in the flat, and she knew from experience that the woman would be gone for at least an hour.

Where the idea came from, Dani didn't know. After Ellie had told her off for walking into her room there had been a tacit agreement that it was out of bounds for the girl. But today she felt different. Maybe last night's encounter had had an effect on her. Maybe something had changed in her. If she carried on being timid, being scared, one day someone would try to attack her again. And next time, Baxter might not be there so quickly. She had to stop being so trodden upon. She couldn't stop these men doing what they came here to do; but maybe she could do something to protect herself.

Courage was not something that Dani Sinclair was used to feeling; but she started to feel the stirrings of it now.

Quite why this new attitude led her to do what she did next, she couldn't have said. Perhaps there was no other means of rebellion. Whatever the reason, she surprised herself entirely as she crept towards Ellie's room and slowly looked inside.

It was much as she remembered it. A thick blanket still covered the window, blocking the bright sunlight that illuminated the metal bars. There were very few belongings, and the place was neatly kept. Dani stood in the centre of the room for a couple of minutes, just looking around. There were a couple of photographs on the dressing table: one of Ellie, clearly taken a few years ago, the other of an older couple – her parents, maybe. Dani felt a flicker of nervousness in her tummy as she opened Ellie's wardrobe and saw the small collection of clothes and shoes that she had already seen the woman wearing. Somehow it was a disappointment not to find anything more interesting, although she didn't really know what she was looking for.

Closing the cupboard doors, she turned her attention to the dressing table. It was much like the one she had in her own room – a bit newer perhaps, the mirror a little brighter. Tentatively she pulled out one of the drawers.

There was a plastic bag in there, scrupulously sealed. Dani pulled it out and saw that it contained five needles, like the ones they had in hospitals and doctors' surgeries. She stared at the needles for a few seconds, shocked by what she saw; then she turned her attention to the other objects in the drawer. There was the base of an old Coke can, like a little dish with razor-sharp sides. The rest of the can had clearly been roughly cut away with a pair of scissors. Next to it was a little bag of cotton-wool balls. A large brown bottle had a label saying 'Citric Acid', and there were three cigarette lighters – cheap plastic ones, all of them about half full. Nestled in one corner was a long shoelace.

Dani felt a wave of hotness prickle through her. Her mouth went dry. Gingerly she returned the bag of needles to the drawer and then swiftly shut it, somehow embarrassed by what she had just seen. There was no doubt in Dani's mind that she had just located something she was never supposed to find: Ellie's darkest secret. And though she was not streetwise, she had some notion of what those needles were for. A man had come to her school once, telling everyone about the dangers of drugs. Lots of the other children had laughed about it in the playground afterwards, but the stories the man told, the warnings he gave, had frightened Dani to her core.

She shuddered to think what Ellie would say or do if she knew Dani had discovered her secret. For a moment she panicked that the woman would know that the things in her drawer had been moved around; but she realised she couldn't do anything about that. She had to get out of there, quickly. If Ellie came back and found her there ...

Dani hurried through the door and back into her own room, shutting herself inside as she tried to come to terms with what she had just learned.

When Ellie returned, Dani stayed where she was. Her face would give her away, she thought. Guilt would be written all over it. Much better to stay hidden. Out of the way. Dani listened instead to the sound of Ellie's client arriving and leaving. Then she waited for her own.

It was about eight o'clock when she heard Baxter letting himself into the flat. She had learned to loathe that sound, because she knew what it meant. Any minute now, her door would open and one of those horrible men would be there. Maybe it would be Mr Morgan; maybe it would be one of the others. It could even be somebody new. Dani held her breath and waited for it to happen.

Sure enough, her door clicked open. To her surprise, however, Baxter was unaccompanied. He looked at her as if sizing up a piece of meat. 'Night off,' he said unenthusiastically. 'Got nothing for you.' He didn't sound at all pleased about it, and he turned back into the hallway without another word, leaving Dani's door wide open.

Ellie was waiting for him there; and as she had done so many times before, Dani watched as Baxter handed over a little packet, which Ellie grabbed hungrily. Without another word, he left, and Ellie hurried into her room, shutting the door behind them.

Silence descended on the flat. A still, unnatural silence. Dani found that she was holding her breath. Now she knew what the little packets were that Baxter had been handing over to Ellie, she found herself horrified and intrigued at the same time. Something compelled her to try to find out more; to see what was involved. She was scared of Ellie catching her, certainly, but she was so used to fear by now that she barely noticed the sensation.

As quietly as she could, she tiptoed out of her room, across the hallway and up to the door of Ellie's room. If Ellie came out, Dani told herself, she would simply say that she was making her way to the bathroom.

She crept up to the door, put an ear to it and listened.

At first there was nothing; then, as she strained to hear better, she picked up the almost imperceptible sound of movement.

Slowly, carefully, Dani bent down to her knees. There was a keyhole in Ellie's door; she shut one eye and peered through, barely daring to breathe.

Through the keyhole, she saw everything.

The drawer of Ellie's dressing table was open, and all its contents were laid out in a line on the surface. Ellie herself sat at the end of the bed, facing them. With trembling hands she unwrapped the paper pouch that Baxter had given her and carefully poured the contents into the makeshift metal dish. From where Dani was watching it was difficult to see clearly, but it looked to her like a dark brown powder. Ellie then turned her attention to the needle. She unscrewed the syringe and used it to measure a quantity of water from a glass on the dressing table, which she then squirted into the dish. She did the same with the brown bottle of citric acid.

Once that was done, she picked up the dish and held it a few centimetres above the table. With her other hand she sparked a lighter. It took three or four goes to get a flame, but once it was burning, she held it under the metal dish and waited. Her eyes looked greedily down at the liquid she was boiling up, and Dani thought she could even make out her lips twitching slightly.

A minute or so later, she extinguished the lighter and put the dish down on the table. She tore a piece off one of the balls of cotton wool, rolled it between her fingers so that it became tiny and compact, and then dropped it into the dish. The cotton wool swelled, absorbing the liquid. She took the syringe and placed the nozzle into the heart of the cotton wool, before sucking the liquid out of it and up into the body of the syringe.

Then she attached the needle.

Ellie's hands were shaking even more now, but she took the time to collect up the accumulated paraphernalia and shove it back in the drawer, before taking the shoelace. She rolled up the sleeve of her top, and then tied the shoelace to the upper part of her arm, pulling so tightly that she winced momentarily. She gazed at her arm for a dreamy moment; then she slapped the skin a few times.

It was all Dani could do to stop herself from gasping when she saw Ellie pick up the needle and, with a little flick of her wrist, jab it into her flesh. She felt her blood pumping though her veins as the woman slowly squeezed the end of the syringe. Ellie took a deep intake of breath as the liquid decanted itself into her blood; moments later, her eyes rolled in her head. She seemed to be struggling to stay sitting upright as she squeezed the last drop from the syringe; when it was empty, she cast it carelessly on to the dressing table, and then fell heavily on to the bed.

Dani stayed crouching by the door for a full minute, but Ellie didn't move. So she stood up and quietly walked back to her room.

It should have been a good night, without any visitors. After what she had just seen, however, there was no chance of peace. The little girl didn't know exactly what it was that Ellie had just injected into her arm. But that didn't matter. So many things had just fallen into place. So many things made sense. Like why she was so obedient to Baxter. Why she became so anxious as evening approached.

And why she wouldn't let Dani out of the house.

Not now.

Not ever.

No matter how much Dani asked. Begged. Ellie would never crumble. Because her life was not her own. Dani hardly knew anything about drugs, but she could tell that Ellie was not the master of her own actions.

She was a slave. They were both slaves. And there didn't seem to be any way out.

Chapter Ten

When Hayley Carter awoke, she found that the dream had stayed with her.

It didn't normally. Normally she could put the image of the wailing child to the back of her mind, as she had done for so many years. But lately, that had not been the case. Lately the lost child, so fleetingly glimpsed and so easily left, had been more on her mind than she had for a long time. Demanded more of her attention. Of her sadness. As she lay in bed, listening to the gentle hum of the radio, which had woken her up, she found she could not shake that uncomfortable feeling of distress. She couldn't get the memory of her abandoned daughter out of her head.

It was a struggle to get out of bed, and she sat on the edge of her mattress for a long while, trying to settle herself. A glance at her clock. Nearly eight. She was going to be late.

Damn it, she thought to herself. Throw a sickie. How many times had she done that in the six years she'd been working at the station? She reckoned she could count them on one hand. Her hand fumbled for the telephone and she made the call, taking care to make her voice sound weak and unwell.

Maybe a shower would wash away the uneasiness the dream had left her with. Hayley tramped into the bathroom, removed her nightclothes and dumped them in a pile on the floor; then she stepped into the shower and turned the heat right up.

It was no good. When she got out again she felt just as displaced and disconsolate. Getting dressed in sloppy, everyday clothes, she went to make herself some coffee.

Why was it, Hayley thought to herself as the kettle boiled, that illicit days off were never quite as liberating as you thought they were going to be? Having made the call, she now felt guilty; and although it was nice to have a day to herself, all of a sudden she didn't know how to fill it.

Or rather, she knew how to fill it, but she didn't know how to start. Or if she should.

Hayley had been thinking about trying to trace her daughter for a while now. The idea had started off as an idle daydream – one that she had had ever since the child had been born, really. But in the last few months – quite why, she couldn't say – she had been thinking about it more and more. Something was missing in Hayley's life, and she thought she knew what it was.

She had even written down a number – of an agency that helped reunite parents and children. It was a couple of months ago now that she had scrawled it down and then put the piece of paper in a box on a shelf in her bedroom. It had felt at the time as if she had taken a giant step forward; but since then the piece of paper had stayed exactly where she had put it. On a few occasions Hayley had thought about taking it out and phoning the number; but whenever she considered it, her palms went cold and clammy and her muscles seemed to shut down. She was, she understood only too well, scared to make the call.

She was scared now, too. Sipping her coffee, she glanced over the rim of the mug through the door that led into her bedroom. By chance she could see the box from here, an ornate little thing that she had picked up in a junk shop long ago. For a while she stared at it, in deadlock, trying to pluck up the courage to open it and call the number that was held inside.

You've got to do it, Hayley, she told herself. *Unless you want to live with this feeling for the rest of your life, you've got to do it.*

She stood up resolutely, plonked the coffee cup down in the kitchen area and then went to retrieve the box.

The piece of paper was still there, just the corner of a notepad with a number scrawled hastily on it. She pulled it out and held it delicately between her fingers. Just a short string of digits, but Hayley couldn't help wondering whether dialling those numbers would change her life.

She closed her eyes, took a deep breath and picked up the phone.

The woman she spoke to was friendly enough, in an overly sympathetic kind of way. She took some details, and then asked Hayley how, precisely, she could help.

'I, er … It's for a friend,' Hayley stuttered.

'I see,' the woman replied blandly. *Yes,* Hayley imagined her thinking, *it often is …*

'She … she wanted to trace her child, who she thinks was adopted.'

'She *thinks* was adopted?'

'Um … yes.' Hayley started tripping up over her words. 'You see … the child was abandoned.'

The word sounded harsh.

'Abandoned?'

'At the hospital.'

'I see.' Was that a note of disapproval Hayley could hear in the woman's voice?

'She, er … she didn't tell the hospital her name. The mother that is.'

'I see,' the woman repeated.

An awkward silence.

'Well, I'm sorry, Miss Carter,' the woman told her. 'There isn't very much to go on. Without an idea of the name of either the mother or the child, there really isn't very much we can do to trace the current carers.'

'But surely,' Hayley insisted, 'there would be some sort of record? Of the baby having been, you know, abandoned.'

'I'm afraid it's not the sort of information we would have. It's really more a matter for the police, although …'

'What?'

'Well, Miss Carter, I'm no expert, but there are laws against abandoning children. Your, er, *friend* would need to bear that in mind if she were to go to the police.'

Hayley fell silent. 'Is there really nothing you can do?' she said after a while.

'I'm sorry, Miss Carter.' The woman suddenly sounded genuinely regretful. 'I'd like to say yes, but …' Her voice trailed off apologetically.

Hayley closed her eyes. 'I understand,' she said. 'Thank you for your help.'

'You're welcome, Miss Carter.'

The woman hung up.

Hayley sat on the edge of her bed, the phone hanging listlessly in her hand. She couldn't help feeling as if she had been thumped in the stomach. For so long she had been mustering the courage to make that call; she hadn't even considered that there was nothing that could be done. It didn't seem right that a mother couldn't get in touch with her daughter, no matter how much water had flowed under the bridge. It didn't seem right that her craving could not be satisfied.

A curious numbness descended on her: the realisation that everything suddenly seemed a bit meaningless. This flat. The job. Hayley might have broken away from her abusive parents, but now that was not enough. She wanted to see her daughter. Even if it was just once, she wanted to look into her eyes, to drink in the sight of her face.

To tell her she was sorry.

A matter for the police. Well, she didn't wear the uniform. She didn't have the ID. But she worked in the right place. It would probably break a million rules, but all of a sudden Hayley didn't care. If there was a police record, somewhere, of what had happened to her little girl, she was ideally placed to find it.

And find it she would, if it was the last thing she did.

Ellie had three tricks the next day. Dani wondered if they knew that she was on drugs. Or if they would even care.

Her own clients – there were two of them that day – arrived at night-time, as usual. The first was a new man, as timid and embarrassed as they always were initially; and a couple of hours later, after Ellie had retreated into her room, Mr Morgan arrived. He seemed angrier than usual, and was rough with her. After he had left – around midnight – the smell of his aftershave seemed to cling to her skin, and she wanted to wash herself down even more thoroughly than usual in order to get rid of it. But Baxter was still there – quite why, she didn't know – and she didn't like the idea of being naked with that man in the house any more than she had to.

She waited. Baxter didn't leave. He sat at the kitchen table, silently, smoking cigarettes and looking thoughtfully out of the window. There were no unpleasant glances in Dani's direction; no aggressive words. Just a silence that covered the flat like a blanket.

As she wondered why Baxter was sticking around, Dani's newfound brazenness – the same brazenness that had urged her to poke around in Ellie's room – propelled her into the kitchen. Baxter didn't notice her standing in the doorway, so she coughed slightly, as she had seen grown-ups doing on the television, to attract his attention. He turned round to look at her, cigarette smoke billowing out of his nostrils. He raised an eyebrow.

'Mr Baxter?' Dani asked, looking at him with wide eyes.

'Aye?'

'I've been here for a long time now. I've lost count of how long, but maybe five or six weeks.'

Baxter shrugged. 'So?'

'I was just wondering if, you know, maybe one time I could go out for a bit.'

The man widened his eyes, an expression that confused Dani. 'Outside, you mean?'

She nodded.

'What, outside to *play*?' He put a curious emphasis on the last word.

'Yeah,' Dani replied. 'Sort of.'

'And I suppose you'd promise,' Baxter stood up as he spoke, 'not to run away. To come straight back here.'

Dani felt suddenly breathless. It sounded as if he was on side, as if he was open to the idea. 'Of course I'd promise, Mr Baxter,' she said with as much honesty as she could fake. 'I'd come straight back.'

His eyes widened even more. 'Do you swear?' he asked. 'On your mother's life?'

Dani nodded again.

Baxter smiled. He walked round the table and approached Dani until he was standing right in front of her. He knelt down, eye to eye, and then suddenly grabbed her by the throat. 'Don't be so fucking stupid?' he hissed. 'What do you think I am – an idiot? You're a good little earner for me, and if you think I'm going to let you run away …' He turned his head and spat on the floor. 'Swear on your mother's life?' he said mockingly. 'What good would that do, hey? No one fucking cares about you – you're lucky to have a roof over your head.'

Baxter cast her aside, and she fell heavily against the wall and then on to the floor. He straightened up and walked over her, as though stepping over a piece of rubbish, before letting himself out of the flat and locking the door behind him.

Dani lay on the floor, stunned and shivering until the sound of his footsteps disappeared down the stairs.

She didn't even wash that night. It was a relief finally to get between the two blankets on the hard floor of her bedroom. A relief to know that there were nearly twenty-four hours before she had to see Baxter, and whichever hated customer he brought with him, again.

The following morning, Dani awoke from an uncomfortable sleep in a state of panic. All night she had heard Baxter's words ringing in her head. *If you think I'm going to let you run away … No one fucking cares about you …* And when she emerged from her muddled, confused sleep, everything seemed worse, not better. More than she ever had, she felt overwhelmed by the need to get out of there.

Dani stood up and strode to the front door. She banged on it. 'Let me out!' she cried to no one in particular. She banged again. 'Let me out!'

She ran into the kitchen and started shaking the bars on the windows. *'Let me out!'*

The little girl was screaming now, louder and more frenziedly than she ever had before. *'Let me out! Let me out!'* The bars rattled, but of course she was not strong enough to dislodge them in any way.

Her breath came in short, sharp gasps, and tears blurred her vision. She didn't care what it took – she had to be heard. Someone *had* to pay attention to her. If only she could break through the glass – perhaps someone would be walking below, perhaps someone would notice her shouts and bring help. She fitted her little wrist through the bars and started banging on the window pane with her fist – gently at first, but then with increasing vigour. The glass shook slightly in its fittings.

'Let me out! Let me out!'

More tears. More anger and desperation.

Then the one thump that shattered the glass. It barely made a sound – just the faintest of tinklings – but it stopped Dani in her tracks. The instant her fist went through the window pane, the skin around her hand and wrist became streaked with scarlet blood. She gasped, with surprise at first, and then with sharp, needling pain as she realised she had lacerated herself.

The area of the window around the punch hole was surprisingly unaffected by the breakage – just a small network of cracks. But the edge of the hole itself was surrounded by sharp, treacherous shards, and as Dani gingerly pulled her now trembling hand back through the window, she caught it against a particularly ugly shard, and it dug deeply into her flesh.

The blood flowed freely. As Dani looked at her injured hand in horror, it dripped down her arm and splashed onto the kitchen floor. Coldness embraced her, and the rest of her body felt like an ice statue as she watched the blood oozing from the many cuts on her hand and wrist. Her breath shook as she looked at it.

Then she started to scream again.

Her screaming was louder this time, louder than when she had been banging on the door and shaking the window bars. It didn't even really sound like her; it was more like the sound of an animal in pain. Dani stood alone in the middle of the kitchen, looking at her wounds, watching the blood drip off them and screaming horribly for a good few minutes before Ellie was roused.

Red-eyed and tousle-haired, the woman appeared in the doorway in her dressing gown. At first the look on her face was one of annoyance at the sound Dani was making, and she seemed barely awake, barely in control of her faculties. Looking at the little girl, however, she blinked; and from the depths of her stupor something seemed to stir.

'Oh, titch,' she whispered. 'What have you done?'

Dani didn't reply. She just looked in shock towards the broken window, and then back to her hand.

Ellie took a step nearer. She was unsteady on her feet, but the look of determination on her face suggested she was trying to master that. 'Come here, titch,' she breathed. 'Let me have a look at it.'

Still too stunned to say anything, Dani stumbled towards Ellie. The woman seemed reluctant to touch the bleeding hand, but she looked closely at it.

'Wait there,' she told Dani, before staggering uneasily out of the kitchen and returning a moment later with a towel. 'To stop the blood,' she explained curtly. 'Wrap it round.'

Dani's body was shaking even more now, but she did as she was told. The white material of the towel immediately turned red – just as it had done when Dani cleaned herself up the first time she was raped.

'Sit down,' Ellie told her, and she collapsed into a chair. The woman hovered nervously around her. 'You need a hospital,' she whispered almost to herself.

Dani looked up sharply. 'Take me,' she pleaded.

Ellie bit her lip, and an agony of indecision crossed her face. She turned around and looked towards the kitchen door. Dani's heart was in her throat, and for a moment she forgot about the sharp pain in her hand. 'I need a doctor,' she whispered, knowing that it could be her ticket out of here.

But when Ellie spoke again, she refused to look at her. 'Maybe we can patch you up here,' she muttered. 'I can talk to Baxter when he turns up.'

'No,' Dani breathed. 'Take me now. *I need to go now.*'

When Ellie turned to look at her again, her face was a picture of anguish. 'I'm sorry, titch,' she whispered, so quietly as to be almost unheard. 'I can't. I just can't. If I don't wait for him, he'll—'

She never finished her sentence. Dani doubled over as a sharp pain shot up her arm and into her chest.

The rest of the day passed in a blur. Ellie manoeuvred Dani into the bathroom and inexpertly washed her hand with cold water from the shower head. Dani gasped as she did so – the water felt like a thousand needles stabbing her skin, and the bath became filled with swirling red water like something from a horror film.

'There's bits of glass in there,' she heard the woman say, but she was too faint now to pay much attention. Ellie helped her into her bedroom and edged her towards the mattress; despite everything, however, Dani started shaking violently as they approached.

'Not there,' she shuddered. 'I'm not lying there.'

So Ellie moved her out again, into the room that Kris had used. It was completely bare, apart from the bed; Dani lay reluctantly on the mattress as Ellie wrapped another towel around her still bleeding hand. It was obvious from the way she was handling it that she did not have the faintest idea what she was doing.

She might not have let Dani out of the flat, but Ellie didn't leave her side all afternoon, a fact for which the little girl was extremely grateful. The blood from her hand flowed in fits and starts: sometimes it seemed to be slowing down, others it ran just as it had when she had first cut it. A customer arrived; Ellie sent him away. Dani could tell from the man's tone of voice that he wasn't impressed; and she knew that Ellie was risking Baxter's displeasure in refusing him.

'He'll understand, when he sees you,' Ellie muttered, though she sounded as if she was persuading herself more than anybody else.

Evening came, and Dani grew increasingly weak. Her hand throbbed agonisingly, and her body alternated between being worryingly hot and shiveringly cold; at times the room started to spin.

It was almost with relief that she heard the front door open.

Ellie got to her feet and laid a gentle hand on Dani's forehead. 'I'll speak to him,' she said. Even through her daze of illness, Dani could tell that she was on edge. It wasn't just because Dani had hurt herself; it wasn't just because she was nervous of Baxter. The little girl realised that Ellie needed the packet that he gave her every evening.

Ellie left the room, and Dani heard the murmur of voices outside the door. In an instant Baxter appeared, and behind him a man whom Dani vaguely recognised. Baxter's face was a sneer; the other man looked rather more shocked. 'Jesus,' he muttered; then he turned to the pimp. 'Look at her arm, mate, she's all fucked up. Think I'll leave it, eh?'

Baxter turned to him. 'Wait,' he said. 'Wait, I'll—'

But the man had already walked away, and Dani heard him letting himself out.

Baxter approached her, his lip curling nastily. He glanced down at Dani's bloodied arm, but it seemed barely to affect him. 'What the fuck you been playing at?' he hissed.

'She needs a doctor,' Ellie said from the doorway. 'You got to take her to a hospital.'

Baxter turned round slowly. '*I* got to take her to a hospital? Are you fucking joking?'

Ellie's voice was shaking now. 'You can't keep her here forever, Baxter,' she said.

Baxter turned on her, and from her bed Dani saw a look of sudden fear in Ellie's eyes. In one swift movement he stepped towards her and whacked the back of his fist against the side of his face. Ellie gasped from the blow, but stood firm. 'She's got glass in her, Baxter. She's all cut up. I can't deal with it – I don't know what to do.'

'Serves her fucking right,' Baxter shouted. He turned back to Dani. 'You scare any more Johns away with your fucking games, I'll ...'

In his anger, his words deserted him.

He stormed out, pushing roughly past Ellie, who followed him into the hallway and out of Dani's sight.

'Baxter!' she said urgently. 'Wait!'

Footsteps towards the door.

'*Wait*,' she said, desperate now. 'You forgot ...'

A silence. Then, from Baxter, a low growl. 'You're fucking pathetic,' he told her. There was a shuffling, and then Dani heard the door shut.

There was a pause before Ellie appeared again. She was clutching something in her right hand, and her eyes were haunted.

A shiver ran through Dani's body. 'Don't leave me,' she whispered. 'Please don't leave me alone. I don't feel well.'

Ellie's face twitched, and she clutched whatever she was holding a little tighter. At first she didn't reply. She didn't seem to know what to say, as if there was an argument going on in her head, an argument that only she could hear.

Finally she stepped back.

'I'm sorry,' she whispered hoarsely as her face disappeared into the darkness of the hallway. 'I just … I can't … I have to …'

Then she was gone, back into her room. Dani knew what she would be doing. She knew she would see nothing more of her that night.

Her hand hurt more than ever now; her whole body ached. She felt desperately weak.

Dani Sinclair laid her head heavily against the mattress, and prepared to face the night on her own.

Chapter Eleven

DCI Barker was already in the office when Hayley returned to work after her day off. Checking her watch, she saw that she was ten minutes late, and from the look he was giving her, it was clear that the fact wasn't lost on her boss. She tried to avoid his glance as she briskly removed her coat and hung it on the back of her seat; but even as she switched on her computer, she could sense him walking towards her.

'You're late,' he growled.

'Sorry, sir,' she said, not looking at him.

'Yeah,' Barker retorted. 'I'm sure you are. And I'm sure it's very stressful, sitting behind that desk all day doing the typing. But while the rest of us are doing some proper police work, it's not too much to ask that you grace us with your presence on time, is it?'

Hayley looked coolly up at him. 'If you don't need anything else, sir, I'd like to start work now.'

Barker's eyes narrowed. 'Thin ice, Miss Carter,' he threatened quietly. '*Very* thin ice.' And with that he turned and made his way back to his glass-fronted office. As he walked, he failed to see Ryan making an insulting gesture with his wrist. Hayley smiled, despite herself.

The morning passed slowly as Hayley typed up reports without even registering the words she read. Her attention was elsewhere. Barker wouldn't be in the office all day, she hoped; when he left, perhaps she could steal a few minutes at one of the station's terminals of the PNC – the Police National Computer, a database for, well, nearly everything.

Ten o'clock came and went. Eleven o'clock. It was gone twelve when Barker curtly stood up and left the office without a word to anyone else. His jacket remained on the back of his chair, but Hayley wasn't fooled by his little deception – he often did that when he wanted people to believe he was still in the station. She gave it a few minutes, just to convince herself that he wasn't coming back anytime soon, and then headed across the open-plan office.

There were two terminals in full view of everyone in the office, but Hayley couldn't use either of those. These were strictly for police use, and a mere secretary had no business accessing the databases. In fact, as far as she could guess, it would be a sacking offence. There was a briefing room, however, seldom used, which housed a third terminal, and it was here that she headed. As she expected, there was no one in there, so she took a seat at the terminal and faced the screen.

Hayley stared at it blankly. The truth was, she didn't know where to begin. She had a date of birth, but no name – no nothing. What was more, she had never used one of these terminals before, and—

'Found anything interesting, Miss Carter?'

Hayley's stomach lurched, and she spun round to see DCI Barker standing, arms folded, in the doorway.

'I … I was just—'

'I can see what you were doing,' Barker announced as he stepped further into the room. 'And there'd better be a bloody good explanation.'

As he spoke, however, Hayley became aware of another figure in the doorway. It was Ryan. His eyes were narrowed slightly as he took in the situation.

'Any luck, Hayley?' he asked brightly.

Barker looked round, his eyebrows furrowed.

'Not yet,' Hayley said a bit meekly, hoping that she had understood Ryan's game.

The DS looked at his boss. 'Bit snowed under,' he smiled. 'I asked Hayley to pull a couple of records for me.'

Barker didn't look convinced. 'I suggest, Detective Sergeant, that you do your own work in the future, and let Miss Carter get on with hers.'

Ryan bowed his head, and did a very good impression of looking chastened. 'Yes, boss,' he muttered.

'Get back to work, both of you,' Barker told them, before storming out of the room.

Ryan waited until he was well out of earshot before he turned back to Hayley with a boyish grin. Hayley felt embarrassed, but relieved. 'Thank you,' she murmured sheepishly.

'Anytime,' Ryan told her. He inclined his head. 'What *were* you doing at the PNC, anyway?'

Hayley looked up at the young sergeant. He was about her age, with a short, neat blond hair and a lack of stubble that made him look several years younger than she knew he must be. She liked him, but he liked her better – he'd made that perfectly clear before now. Maybe she could use that to her advantage. Maybe she could get him to help her.

'I was looking something up for a friend of mine.' She smiled at him as winsomely as she could.

'I wouldn't have thought you'd have been trained to use that thing, though.'

Hayley shrugged a little helplessly. 'I haven't,' she said.

Ryan looked over his shoulder again, double-checking that nobody was looking. 'Come on, then,' he said, stepping towards the terminal. 'What is it you need?'

Hayley stood up and allowed him to take the seat. 'I'm trying to locate a child,' she said. 'A girl. All I have is a date of birth – the eighteenth of December, nineteen ninety-six. She was born at Hammersmith Hospital, and the mother abandoned her less than an hour after the birth.'

As she spoke, she watched Ryan's face crease into an expression of disapproval. It stung.

'You got the mother's name?' Ryan asked.

Hayley shook her head. 'I promised,' she said, and as she spoke her voice cracked. 'I promised I wouldn't tell. But it wouldn't do any good – she never told the hospital staff who she was.'

Ryan pushed himself back from the computer terminal. 'Well,' he said seriously. 'It doesn't matter anyway. The PNC wouldn't hold this kind of information.'

'Oh,' Hayley replied in a small, crestfallen voice. There was a silence – an awkward one, and neither of them looked at each other. Finally, Ryan spoke.

'Eighteenth of December, nineteen ninety-six, you said?'

Hayley glanced at him and nodded.

'Leave it with me,' he muttered quietly; then he turned and left.

She didn't see him for the rest of the afternoon; but she saw Barker sure enough. He seemed to be watching her all the time, and Hayley couldn't help wondering how the guy found time to do his actual job. She had never understood Barker. No one in the office did. The guy didn't seem to have a friendly bone in his body. Middle-aged and – astonishingly – married, he seemed less interested in the business of policing than he did in keeping a firm grip on everyone under his command in the station. And on that particular afternoon his attention was firmly fixed on Hayley, and she could do little else other than sit at her desk and plough through the pile of reports that needed typing up.

Come five o'clock, Ryan still hadn't appeared. Hayley tidied her desk, closed down her computer and prepared to leave. Only then did she see him walking back into the office. He approached her casually.

'Think I might have what you're looking for,' he told her conspiratorially.

Hayley's eyes flickered over to Barker; sure enough, he was watching them.

'What did you find out?' she breathed. There was a sense of excited expectation in her chest.

Ryan smiled – that friendly, disarming smile he had directed at her so many times before. 'Tell you what,' he said. 'I don't get off duty till seven. Why don't you meet me in that new pub then? I'll buy you a drink and show you what I've got.' His face was beaming.

Hayley smiled, doing her best to hide the apprehension she felt. 'All right,' she said quietly. 'I'll see you then.'

It was cold outside. Hayley had two hours to kill before her rendezvous with Ryan, and she filled the time by tramping the streets. There was no way she could just sit still and wait, so, despite the freezing temperature, she preferred to do this. The two hours passed desperately slowly. Half of Hayley urgently wanted to hear what Ryan had discovered; the other half wanted to escape home, to hide under the duvet and pretend she hadn't opened this can of worms.

Despite her misgivings, it was with a certain relief that she opened the door of the pub just north of the Strand and felt the warm, beery fug hit her in the face; it was only when she stepped into the cosy interior that she realised just how cold she was. The pub was crowded with after-work drinkers, and as Hayley stood just inside the doorway, she scanned the throng nervously, looking for Ryan. He was sitting at a small table in the corner by himself, a pint of beer in front of him. The detective sergeant had changed out of his uniform and was now wearing a white T-shirt and a dark brown leather jacket. He looked good, Hayley conceded, and she smiled at him despite herself as she approached.

Ryan stood up. 'What can I get you?'

'Vodka and tonic, please,' Hayley said.

Minutes later, they were sitting together, their drinks in front of them. Hayley had taken a couple of hefty gulps to calm her nerves, and she couldn't help her eyes flickering down at a thin file that Ryan had in front of him.

'So?' she asked apprehensively.

'You know I could get fired for doing this, don't you?' Ryan told her seriously.

Hayley looked at him, tight-lipped and unable to say anything.

'Your friend,' Ryan continued, 'whoever she is, can't *do* anything with what I'm about to show you.'

'She won't,' Hayley said in a small voice.

He nodded. 'OK then. I've spoken to social services, and they've managed to track down the child in question. Want to know her name?'

Hayley nodded dumbly, unsure as to whether she really did or not.

'Dani Sinclair.'

She drew a deep breath as a cold, clammy feeling crept through her blood.

'*Dani*,' she whispered, almost to herself.

Ryan was looking at her, making no attempt to hide the suspicion in his face. 'You want me to go on?' he asked.

Again Hayley nodded.

He took a swig of his beer, opened the file and started to read. 'Born premature ... fostered at the age of six months by a Mr and Mrs Sinclair ... there's an address here, but I don't think you should give it to your friend. Wouldn't be a terribly good idea for her to go banging on the door.'

'No,' Hayley agreed quietly.

'Wouldn't do any good, anyway.'

Hayley looked up sharply. 'Why not?' she asked.

'Because she's not there any more. I spoke to the social worker in charge of her case. Seems she was removed from her foster parents under an Emergency Protection Order.'

She blinked. 'Why?'

Ryan's face grew even more serious. He removed a piece of A4 paper and handed it across the table. 'I think this might have something to do with it,' he said grimly.

Hayley noticed, as she stretched out her arm to take the paper, that her hands were trembling. She grabbed the sheet and then looked at it. It was a colour photocopy of a girl. She had long brown hair and brown, frightened eyes. But it was not the child's hair or her eyes that commanded Hayley's attention: it was the terrible bruising that spread over one side of her face. Blue and purple. Mottled. As she looked at the horrific details of that picture, Hayley felt herself going first hot, and then cold. Anger rose in her, directed firmly at whoever had inflicted these wounds. Then she felt a sensation that was at once familiar but also long forgotten: the desire, the overpowering need, to take this girl in her arms. To comfort her. To protect her.

As these thoughts went through her head, Hayley became aware that Ryan was speaking again. 'That picture was taken by the social worker after the girl was placed in a children's home in Sutton.'

'She's got a name,' Hayley snapped.

Ryan blinked. 'Sorry,' he replied mildly, and she instantly regretted her comment. 'It was taken after Dani was placed in a children's home. That was only a few weeks ago.'

'Do you have the details?'

'Yes,' Ryan nodded. 'But again, they won't do much good.'

'Why not?'

'Because she was only there for two days. She ran away. No one's heard of her since.'

His words were like arrows. Hayley found she could not drag her gaze away from the picture of the girl she held in her hands, and as Ryan spoke it was all she could do to prevent herself from bursting into tears.

When he had finished, he closed the file and pushed it across the table to her. 'Honestly, Hayley,' he said. 'I mean it. Your friend can't start trying to knock on doors. This stuff is confidential. I've only given it to you because … well, never mind.' He took another sip of his drink.

Hayley didn't reply at first. With all the self-restraint she could muster, she slipped the photograph into the file and turned her attention back to Ryan. 'She's twelve years old,' Hayley whispered. Then, realising that he hadn't heard her above the noise of the pub, she repeated herself, a bit louder this time. 'She's twelve years old. If she's gone missing, surely there are people out there looking for her?'

Ryan looked at her in sympathy. 'Hayley, we have thousands of reports of missing children every year. They don't all get the publicity that some of them do. Every case gets investigated, and most of the time the kids are found. But not all of them are. Seems that with Dani Sinclair, the trail just went cold.'

'But they're still looking, aren't they? They're still trying to find her?'

Ryan's face said it all.

'I'm not saying they don't want to, Hayley. But a lot of the time, these kids are trying *not* to be found.' He spread out the palms of his hands helplessly. 'And you know what it's like in the Job,' he added. 'Resources and all.'

A silence followed. The two of them sipped their drinks awkwardly, and Hayley held on tightly to the file Ryan had given her. After a couple of minutes, she spoke.

'I've got to go,' she said.

Ryan nodded. 'All right,' he replied quietly, politely. 'Look, Hayley, this wasn't quite what I wanted it to be. Maybe another time—'

'Maybe,' Hayley replied, a bit too quickly. Then, less harshly, an apology in her voice, 'Maybe. And thank you, Ryan. For this. It means a lot.'

'To your friend,' Ryan reminded her.

Hayley nodded. She stood up, put on her coat and, still firmly gripping the file – as tightly as though she was holding on to her daughter herself – she walked to the exit.

As she left the pub, she looked back to see Ryan watching her. Calmly. Thoughtfully.

It wasn't an unpleasant sensation. But it was buried in other emotions. Fear. Panic. And a blind determination that her daughter wasn't going to stay missing for long.

The night passed in a haze of delirium.

By the time the steely grey of dawn had started to light up the room, the mattress on which Dani lay, uncovered, was damp with sweat. Her body was burning, and she dipped in and out of consciousness. When she was awake she felt her hand pounding with agony, and there was a harsh dryness in the back of the throat. She longed for a glass of water, but there was no way she could go and get one: her body seemed to have been sapped of whatever strength it had. The little girl couldn't move.

Time had no meaning, so she couldn't tell when it was that she emerged sweating from a pool of unconsciousness to see Ellie standing over her. Had she been in any other state, the sight of the woman would have been a shock; as it was, Dani stared blankly at her face. It was grey and haunted, spectral almost. Both frightened and frightening – though Dani was in no position to be scared. She could do nothing other than focus on the pain in her hand and the heat of her body, and the way she both shivered and sweated at the same time.

Minutes later – or was it hours? – Dani felt something on her forehead. Something cold. She opened her eyes to see that Ellie was pressing a wet towel against her skin. The older woman's hands were trembling and her face still seemed thin and pallid. But the towel was cooling and pleasant. Dani tried to thank her, but the only sound that left her lips was an inhuman croak.

'Shhh,' she heard Ellie say, and then she felt the woman's fingertips brushing lightly against her cheek. Dani closed her eyes and breathed a deep, shaky breath. There was something soothing about Ellie's touch. It seemed like a million years since anyone had comforted her in that way. Now, whenever she was touched by another person, it sickened her; but Ellie's gentle stroking, and the whispering of her voice, was reassuring.

Darkness. Then another period of wakefulness. Ellie was unwrapping the material with which Dani's hand was bound. It hurt, but the little girl could not speak up to complain, nor move the hand away. Instead, she found herself breathing more heavily.

'I know.' Ellie's husky voice filled her senses. 'I know. But I got to clean it. Won't get better if I don't clean it.'

She felt the woman dabbing her wounds. Each time she touched her, it was as if a knife was being inserted into her flesh. Dani clenched her eyes shut and prayed for it to be over.

The next thing she knew, Ellie had put a glass of water to her lips. Dani propped herself up on her elbows with difficulty, and she was glad she did: the water was like honey, soothing her raging throat and bringing much-needed moisture to her dry mouth. She tried to smile at Ellie, but the smile soon turned to a wince as a lightning shock of pain shot through her arm and she slumped back down on to the mattress.

'I don't feel well,' she whispered.

'I know,' Ellie's voice cracked. 'We'll get you better, though, won't we?'

The next voice she heard was Baxter's. She didn't know what time he arrived, but it was darker in the room now; evening had clearly arrived. He appeared in the doorway, shadowy and indistinct – Dani might not have known it was Baxter had she not heard his familiar Scottish accent. 'The bitch is fucking costing me money,' he growled, before turning away.

And then night fell again. Another long, intolerable night. Ellie was no longer there, of course. Dani had no option other than to endure it alone.

The next day was Saturday. Ordinarily, Hayley would lie in, enjoying her lazy day off and recuperating from the week. Not today, though. Today she got up before six, having been awake long before that. It was still dark outside, and rain pounded steadily against the windows of her little flat.

The thin folder that Ryan had given her the previous night was still by her bed. She had fallen asleep reading and re-reading the scant information it contained and wondering what to do with it. Ryan had made her promise that she wouldn't go knocking on doors, but some promises were made to be broken. Nothing was going to stop Hayley from trying to find out more about her daughter; it was just a question of how to go about it. As she dressed and made herself some coffee, she finally made a decision. It was risky – illegal, even – but if she wanted people to talk …

It was a little after seven when she left the house and headed back to the police station with a large, empty bag slung over her shoulder and clutching the file. It took her half the time it usually did to get there during the week. As she arrived, the duty sergeant gave her a confused look.

'Left my purse here,' she said, smiling at him as she passed, and he rolled his eyes in a comradely way before turning back to his paperwork. He didn't appear to notice that Hayley headed not for the open-plan office where she worked but to the women's changing rooms at the back of the station. It was deserted in there, just as she had hoped it would be – shifts wouldn't change for another hour or so. Hayley hardly ever came in here. There was no need, as she didn't change into uniform as the WPCs did. She had been in here enough times, though, to know that there was a stash of spare police uniforms hanging on a rail at the end of the row of metal lockers. They weren't used very often, but they needed to be there just in case.

Hayley looked over her shoulder, double-checking that no one could see her, before grabbing a uniform that looked about her size and stuffing it into her bag. It seemed to take an age to do so, and every moment she expected someone to walk in and challenge her; but no one did, and barely a minute later she was walking back out of the station, giving the duty sergeant a cheery goodbye and hoping that her guilt wasn't too plain on her face.

As she ducked down into the tube station, Hayley couldn't help feeling that she was being followed; the sensation was still with her when she emerged at Victoria and scanned the departures board for the next train to Sutton. Ten minutes. That would get her in at ten o'clock. Perfect. She bought a ticket, and waited for the train to arrive.

At Sutton she took a taxi – not something she was used to doing on her tiny wage, but necessary today. She gave the driver the address of the children's home that Ryan had tracked down for her; he nodded wordlessly and drove off. It took fifteen minutes to get there. As the short journey progressed, Hayley started to feel more and more on edge. She could so easily be found out; awkward questions could so easily be asked. It wasn't like her at all to do this kind of thing; but she was being driven by a powerful urge, and in the battle between her nervousness and her need to find the little girl with the bruised face, that urge was winning.

The taxi pulled up alongside a large set of gates. On the wall outside was an old bronze plaque, stained and weather-beaten: 'Linden Lodge'. Hayley paid the driver, and then stepped out.

For a minute, she did nothing. She just stared at the gates, and at the imposing-looking house that stood at the end of a tree-lined drive. It gave her a curious feeling, a kind of tingling, to know that this was somewhere her daughter had actually once been. It was the same sort of feeling she had got on the few occasions when she had passed the hospital where Dani had been born.

Dani.

It felt strange to know her name. Made her feel at once closer to and more distant from her.

Hayley looked around her. She needed somewhere to change, but on this main road there were no clothes shops or restaurants. Further up the street, however, she saw a public toilet – the type that required a coin to enter. Inside it was cramped, but she managed to change and stuff her regular clothes back into the bag; and if any of the passers-by found it strange to see a uniformed police officer walking out, they showed no signs of it. Hayley took a deep breath and once again approached the children's home.

The drizzle started again as she walked with a confidence she didn't feel up the tree-lined driveway, stopping only to hide her bag behind one of the tree trunks. By the time she reached the heavy front door her clothes were uncomfortably damp. Through one of the large ground-floor windows, she saw the faces of a couple of children peering curiously out. She snapped her gaze away from them, and then immediately worried that she appeared nervous. That wouldn't do.

She needed to be confident.

She needed to be in control.

Hayley pressed the bell at the side of the door, stood up straight and waited for it to be answered.

It took a couple of minutes, though it seemed much longer to Hayley. When the door was finally opened, a kindly faced woman with curly brown hair appeared. She didn't seem overly surprised that a policewoman was standing at her door.

'Good morning,' she said calmly. 'Can I help you?'

Hayley smiled at her. 'WPC Jane Adams,' she said, trotting off the name she had been practising in her mind all morning. 'Metropolitan Police.' Hayley prayed she wouldn't ask her for ID.

The woman stepped aside. 'Come in, officer,' she replied. 'What can I do for you?'

'I'm here to ask you a few questions about a former resident,' Hayley told her. 'A Dani Sinclair. I have a photo here if you'd like to look at it.'

The woman shook her head. 'No,' she said, 'that's all right. I remember Dani. My name's Tanya, by the way.'

'Pleased to meet you,' Hayley replied, before realising that she sounded much too familiar, and not enough like a police officer making enquiries. Feeling her body stiffen, she prepared herself to start asking questions in a more official way, but Tanya spoke first.

'We've actually already given statements to the police about Dani,' Tanya observed.

'Just following up,' Hayley lied smoothly.

'Well, you'll probably want to speak to Christian. He was Dani's key worker – he had more to do with her than the rest of us in the short time she was here. Why don't I take you up to his room? I'm pretty sure he's in.'

Hayley nodded her agreement, and followed Tanya down the long hallway and up the stairs at the end, doing her best to ignore the glances from the few children who were passing through. Together they walked down the institutional corridors, with their thin carpets and cream-coloured walls and the smell of food from the kitchens heavy in the air. Eventually they came to a stop outside a bland wooden door. Tanya knocked, and they waited in silence.

The man who opened it had grey-blond curly hair that was flecked with grey. He appeared to be in his fifties, and was somewhat jowly. He looked at each woman in turn, and Hayley couldn't help noticing a flicker of annoyance cross his face.

'Christian Walker,' Tanya spoke first. 'This is DS—' The woman faltered.

'Adams,' Hayley supplied.

'What can I do for you, DS Adams?' Christian asked with a bland smile.

'I'd, er, I'd just like to ask you a few questions, if I may.'

'Dani Sinclair,' Tanya added helpfully.

Christian appeared to think about that for a moment. Finally he stepped back and gestured to Hayley that she should come in.

'I'll leave you to it, then,' Tanya said brightly. 'Let me know if you need anything.'

Christian's room was warm and musty. The curtains were closed, and the dull light that illuminated the place came from a couple of lamps. As the door clicked behind her, Hayley felt distinctly uncomfortable, and she struggled not to let that show in her face.

'Have a seat, officer,' Christian offered. He stood by a bookshelf, on which Hayley noticed a pile of comic books, and indicated the sofa. Hayley sat down, and it unnerved her slightly that Christian elected to remain standing. 'I should warn you that I've already told the police everything I can about Dani,' he advised.

'I'm sure that's true, Mr Walker. But if you wouldn't mind, I'd like you to go through it with me again.'

Christian shrugged. 'Of course. She arrived here on … I can't remember the date, but it was a good couple of months ago, maybe more. There had clearly been some domestic abuse.'

The image of Dani's bruised face flashed through Hayley's mind. *Some kind of domestic abuse*. You can say that again, she thought.

'How did she seem when she arrived?'

Christian shrugged. 'What do you mean?' he asked.

'Well,' Hayley said, flailing, 'did she seem at all upset?'

'She was just being brought into care. Certainly she seemed upset.'

Hayley felt herself blushing. 'But … anything out of the ordinary?' she suggested. All of a sudden she had become aware of the fact that she didn't really know what to ask, or indeed what she thought she was going to learn on this fool's errand.

For a moment Christian didn't reply. He walked across the room and lightly parted the curtains with a single finger. He looked out for a few seconds, and then let the curtain fall closed again before turning back to Hayley. His brow was furrowed. 'Dani Sinclair,' he said quietly, 'was quite a difficult little girl.'

Hayley blinked. The man's words were like thumps in the stomach.

'What do you mean?'

'It's not at all surprising,' Christian continued as though he hadn't heard her, 'what with her coming from that kind of background. We see it a lot. But there are certain things that we frown on at Linden Lodge. Lying is one. Stealing is another. Dani did both those things. She accused children that I know to be very good-natured of bullying her, and before she ran away she stole really quite a lot of money from her two room-mates.'

Hayley felt anger rising in her. This man's blithe criticism of her daughter sounded harsh and unfair, and she wanted to tell him so; but of course she couldn't.

'Surely you have systems in place?' she heard herself saying.

Christian raised an eyebrow. 'What do you mean?'

'Well,' Hayley said, faltering. 'When a child is unsettled ... when there's a risk that they might run away ...'

'Lock them up, you mean? No, officer, I'm afraid we don't do that. We just try to help them, to treat them kindly. But like I say, Dani didn't respond to that terribly well.'

'But do you have any idea *why* she left?'

'I'm afraid not, officer. If I'd had more time with her maybe ...' As he spoke, Christian's eyes narrowed. 'Shouldn't you be writing this down?' he asked.

Hayley felt a sudden shock of self-consciousness. 'What do you mean?' she asked.

'When they were here before, the police, they wrote everything I had to say down in their notebooks.'

His comment hung in the air like an accusation.

Abruptly, Hayley stood up. 'Thank you for your time, Mr Walker,' she found herself gabbling. 'If I need anything else—'

Christian inclined his head politely, but his eyes were still full of suspicion. 'Of course,' he murmured as he stepped towards the door and opened it.

'I'll see myself out,' Hayley told him, barely daring to glance in his direction as she headed out into the corridor.

She walked briskly away but somehow, without knowing how, she could tell that the care worker was standing at the door to his room, watching her go.

Suddenly she couldn't get out of there quickly enough. Christian suspected her; how long before someone else twigged that she was impersonating a police officer? She hurried down the stairs.

As she was crossing the hallway towards the front door, she saw two girls standing side by side. Hayley didn't glance at them long enough to take in their features, but as she passed she heard one of them speak.

'Pig,' the girl muttered, before starting to cough, clearly pretending that her insult had been nothing more than a clearing of the throat. Her friend started to giggle. Hayley blushed again, but by now she was at the front door. She opened it and stepped outside into the rain. Striding down the road, Hayley didn't look back, not even when she stopped to pick up her bag of clothes from its hiding place. It was relief when she emerged on the street and was able to lose herself in the anonymity of the London suburb.

Linden Lodge children's home had left her with a very uncomfortable feeling. Christian Walker's words had been like poison in her ear, and she couldn't help feeling that she too, as a child, would have wanted to run away from such a place. What if the care worker had been right, though? What if Hayley's daughter really was an unpleasant child, a thief and a trouble-maker? The thought was almost too much to bear.

Anyway, Hayley thought to herself as the rain continued to pour and her police uniform grew wetter and wetter, at the moment it didn't matter what kind of girl she was. The duplicitous trip to Linden Lodge had taught her nothing. She felt foolish. If the real police had not been able to learn anything about Dani's location, what the hell had made Hayley think she – a mere secretary – would be able to? For the third time that day she felt herself blushing, and now she realised that the rain on her face was mixed with tears.

Once they had started, they wouldn't stop. They blinded her. They stung. But they didn't sting as much as the only thing that Hayley felt she had brought away from the children's home.

The single fact.

The inescapable truth.

Dani Sinclair was still missing, and no one, not even her mother, had any idea how to find her.

Chapter Twelve

'I got something for you.'

Dani's eyes flickered open. It was light in the room, and though she didn't know whether it was morning or afternoon, she immediately noticed that she felt a little stronger than she had last time she had been awake. Ellie was standing over her, and the woman's face was kind and concerned.

'I got something for you,' she repeated. Proudly she held something up. It took a moment for Dani to be able to focus on it; when she did, it became clear that it was a small cuddly toy — not a bear, but some other animal that Dani couldn't quite make out — not much bigger than the woman's palm. Ellie handed it to her expectantly. 'Not much. Couldn't afford much. Thought it might cheer you up, though.'

'Thank you,' Dani managed to croak. She took the toy and forced her lips to smile at Ellie. Something approaching relief passed across the woman's face.

'How you feeling?' she asked gently.

'A bit better, I think,' Dani replied. She looked at her hand. It was still bandaged up.

'We need to clean it up again,' Ellie said.

Dani nodded, and allowed Ellie to unwrap the bandage. Even though she knew what to expect, it was a shock to see the state of her skin, ragged and glistening. At least she wasn't bleeding any more, though.

'What day is it?' she asked.

'Monday,' Ellie told her. 'It's been four days since you hurt yourself. You had me worried.'

'I should go and see a doctor,' Dani told her. 'I know I'm feeling a bit better and everything, but still …'

As she spoke, however, Ellie walked away from the bed and left the room. Dani pushed herself up to a sitting position – an action that took all her effort. By the time she had managed it, Ellie had returned with a clean bandage.

'No need for doctors,' she said without catching Dani's eye. 'Have you right as rain in no time.' She took the little girl's arm and started to apply the bandage gently, though with shaky hands. When she had finished, she brushed the back of her hand against Dani's cheek. 'I'm sorry, titch,' she whispered. 'You know I can't let you out. You know what he's like. But we'll be all right here, you and me, just the two of us. We will, won't we?'

Ellie's voice sounded so pleading that Dani felt she could do nothing but nod her head.

'Good girl,' Ellie said softly – gratefully, almost. 'Good girl. And don't go punching your way through no more windows. Hardly ladylike, is it?'

Now that she felt a little less weak, Dani managed to stagger into the kitchen. She fetched herself a glass of water and drank deeply from it, and Ellie made her a bowl of cereal with milk, which she ate greedily, not having realised how hungry she was. By the time she had eaten, however, she felt exhausted once more, so she staggered into her own room.

As she always did, Dani avoided the mattress; instead, she sat on the floor and gathered her brown blankets around her. It would have been more comfortable in the other room, but this was her own space, and to Dani's surprise she found she was craving it. In a horrible kind of way, it felt like home.

Her hand still hurt, but at least the fever was gone. And as she sat there, bundled up in her blankets, it almost felt as if life had gone back to normal. When she heard the doorbell ring, she knew it would be a man calling for Ellie; as she always did, Dani stayed put, out of sight, clutching the soft toy the woman had given her as she listened to the sounds of the man arriving and then, about twenty minutes later, departing.

She wondered how long it would be before Baxter had her working again.

In the end, she barely had to wait.

He arrived soon after dark. Dani held her breath as she heard the familiar sound of him locking the door and then walking into the spare room to see if she was there. In her head she pictured him viewing the empty bed; then she heard his footsteps crossing the hallway and approaching her own room.

And then Baxter was there, framed by the open door. He looked down at her, scowling. If he felt any sympathy for her recent illness, he didn't show it.

'Finished with your fucking malingering, have you?'

Dani didn't know what that word meant, so she kept quiet.

Baxter stepped inside. 'You're a sulky little cow, you know that, missie? You'd better not be so sulky tonight. You've cost me a lot of money with your stupid Houdini, through-the-glass tricks, and it's time you started earning it back. I'll be bringing you a customer later – you'd better have wiped that moaning look off your face. You'd better give him what he comes for. Do you understand?'

She remained silent and drew the blankets a bit tighter around her.

A dark look crossed Baxter's face. He strode towards her, bent down and pulled the blankets away. Dani tried to grab them back, but as she did so he took hold of her bandaged arm and squeezed.

The pain was indescribable, and so was the scream that escaped Dani's lips. She looked up in horror as the man raised his free arm, preparing to bring it down on her; at the last minute, however, he seemed to change his mind. 'You cause me any fucking trouble tonight …' he whispered.

The unspoken threat hung in the air as Baxter left.

There were moments when Dani wished she could slow time down. Now was one of those moments. Untold dread surged through her exhausted body, and she prayed that the evening would not come.

But it did. It had been dark a long time when the door opened again. Dani started to shiver as she heard the unmistakable sound of footsteps approaching her room. She had not moved since Baxter had left, and she didn't move now; she just looked up to the door and waited, heart in mouth, for it to open.

The hinges creaked, and the unmistakable figure of Mr Morgan appeared in the frame.

None of Dani's regular clients would have been welcome; but some would have been less welcome than others. Mr Morgan was least welcome of all. He was the last man she had been with, before the window and everything that followed. It seemed so desperately unfair that he was the first one back through her door now that she was feeling a little bit better. But Dani had long since decided that fairness was a myth, something for other people; it had no place in her warped little world.

Mr Morgan closed the door behind him, and the click of the latch seemed to echo round the room. His square face was unsmiling as he indicated with a flick of his hand that Dani was to move over to the mattress.

It wasn't stubbornness that stopped her doing what she was told: it was fear. There was something in Mr Morgan's eyes this evening, a look of such steely unpleasantness that it sapped Dani's limbs of what little strength they had. When it became clear that she wasn't going to move, he hurried towards her and grabbed her by her bandaged hand, pulling her to her feet.

Dani screamed as the pain surged through her. Morgan's free hand brutishly covered her mouth, but for an instant she expected to see Baxter storming in, protecting his property. Then she remembered: Mr Morgan was different. Baxter seemed to allow him to get away with more, and to pay less. Dani didn't know why it was, but she realised as he dragged her across the room and hurled her onto the bed that tonight was going to be one of the worst she had yet had to cope with.

She wasn't wrong. With some of the men she could switch off, pretend it wasn't happening; and it was normally over quickly, too. Not with Mr Morgan, and not tonight. It seemed to last forever; and whenever she shouted out in pain, far from subduing him, her shouts seemed to spur him on to new heights of viciousness. He hit her in the belly and round the top of her naked legs; he pulled her hair tightly; he abused her, not once, but several times.

By the time Mr Morgan had finished, Dani was beyond crying. Like a rag doll she lay, shivering listlessly, while the man put his clothes back on. Not even the greasy stains of the mattress could encourage her to move until he had wordlessly left the room; and even when she was alone it took a while for her to spark her numb, brutalised body into movement and cover herself with her clothes. Her hand still hurt; she ached where he had hit her. But it was nothing compared to the pain and shame that she felt inside.

Dani stood in the middle of the room, still shivering and slightly stooped from the pain in her belly. This would never stop, of that she was sure. But those few days of illness, of delirium, now seemed to her to be almost desirable. She wished there was a way that she could recapture that longed-for unconsciousness.

She wished there was a way she could forget.

Baxter was still there after Mr Morgan had left. Dani didn't know why, but she could hear him talking to Ellie. The little girl didn't want to see him, couldn't bear to look at his hated face; but her loathing of the man was overcome by her need to get to the bathroom, to scrub away the remnants of Mr Morgan's touch. So, unable to hold off any longer, she left her room.

Baxter was standing by the main door to the flat, Ellie lingering close to him. As Dani stepped out into the hallway, she saw him hand her the now-familiar small wrap of paper. Ellie grabbed it hungrily and kept her fist tightly clenched around it. Then, with a guilty glance at the little girl, she disappeared back into her own room, shutting the door firmly behind her.

Dani knew what was in that little wrap of paper now. She knew it was the drugs that she had seen Ellie injecting into her veins, even if she didn't know what kind of drug it was. An image of Ellie flashed through her mind. She was lying on her bed, splayed out, unconscious. Unaware. When Dani had seen her like that, it had been terrifying. But now she thought she understood. To be unconscious to all the horror around her ... somehow it was all she craved.

Dani stood there, watching Ellie's closed door. A moment later she became aware of Baxter staring at her. His eyes were narrowed, and he had a thoughtful look on his face. Dani couldn't bear to have him look at her like that, so she hurried to the bathroom to perform the ritual scrubbing of her body.

When she emerged a good twenty minutes later, her hair was wet and her skin sore, but at least the smell of Mr Morgan was gone, and the sensation of his hands on her body. With a sense of shock, she saw that Baxter was still there, standing just where he had been before. She lowered her head and walked towards her room, and as she did so, she noticed that Ellie's door was slightly ajar. It had definitely been shut a few minutes ago.

Once she was in her room, she shut her own door firmly, meaningfully. Seconds later, however, it clicked open again and Baxter was there. He still had that look in his eye – pensive and shrewd – and he was carrying a plastic bag that she hadn't noticed before. Baxter stepped inside and closed the door behind him.

'Thought we'd have a little chat,' he whispered.

Dani looked away. 'Don't want to,' she said.

Baxter ignored her. 'You saw what I gave to Ellie, didn't you, lassie? You know what it is?'

Dani looked up at him, but she didn't reply.

'Ever wondered why she doesn't want to share it with you? Ever wondered why you don't get to have any?'

'No.'

'It's because that's how much she likes it,' Baxter said quietly. 'It's because that's how good it makes her feel. Why would she give it to you, when she can have it all to herself?'

Dani shrugged.

'You've been a good girl,' Baxter continued, his voice insistent. 'You've worked hard. I can give you a bit, if you like. As a reward.' He held up the carrier bag. 'Just a little bit, mind. Just to see if you like it.'

He stepped towards her.

'It's only for grown-up girls, this, you know. You'd be very grown-up if you tried it. And you know what grown-up girls are allowed to do, don't you?'

Dani looked at him. 'No,' she mumbled.

'Grown-up girls,' he said, 'might be allowed to go out.'

He stood silently in front of her, allowing his words to sink in.

Dani looked at the bag in his hands, and again the image of Ellie laid out on the bed entered her mind. Was that all she had to do, she wondered? Did she simply have to fall asleep in order to earn her freedom? The memory of Mr Morgan's visit was still sticking to her, and the thought of unconsciousness was a precious one.

She looked at the bag. 'Is that it?' she asked Baxter.

Baxter nodded; then he turned to the dressing table and carefully laid out the contents of the bag. Dani recognised them, of course, from when she had taken a peek into Ellie's other world. She recognised the metal dish and the bootlace, the lighter and the little brown bottle. And the needle.

Dani was transfixed as she watched Baxter prepare it. He was not as skilful as Ellie had been, but he seemed to know what he was doing. 'It's important to cook it properly,' he said as he unfolded one of his paper parcels and poured some brown powder into the dish, before adding a drop of liquid from the brown bottle. 'If you don't cook it properly, it won't make you feel nice.' A thick smell hit Dani's nostrils as he sparked up the lighter and held the flame under the metal dish. When he was satisfied, he put the dish back down on the side; then he filled the syringe with the preparation and fitted the needle to it.

Baxter turned to Dani. 'You ready?' he asked.

Dani blinked. As though she had been woken from a state of hypnosis, she felt a sudden chill, and all the fear she had previously felt drained back into her. She took a step back. 'I don't really want to,' she said in a small voice.

Baxter stared at her, his flat eyes unemotional. He shrugged. 'Can't force you, lassie,' he said. 'Not without doing you harm, and I'm not inclined to do that to one of my best little earners.' He put the needle down and started packing the things away again. 'Guess you're not such a big girl after all.'

A silence followed, punctuated only by the sounds of Baxter dropping the paraphernalia into the plastic bag – all of it except the needle. Yet again, Dani found herself transfixed by the sight of it; yet again, the thought of Ellie reclining peacefully on her bed filled her mind. And Baxter's promise – it had been a promise, hadn't it? – that if she tried it he would let her go out.

He had picked up the needle now, and was heading to the door.

'Wait,' she said.

Baxter stopped; then he turned round, with one eyebrow raised. Dani didn't say anything else; she just felt herself nodding timidly at him.

What happened next hardly seemed real. Dani found that she was sitting on the floor, while Baxter tightened a bootlace round the top of her good arm. It hurt a bit, but she didn't say anything and soon a vein started to bulge through the skin above her elbow.

'Just a small fix for the first time,' she heard Baxter saying, but she didn't really understand what he meant. Her breath was heavy and shaking, and even though she knew she was being bad, she couldn't help feeling a small thrill of excitement as the needle drew closer to her arm.

She breathed in sharply as it punctured her skin, and then gasped as Baxter squeezed the syringe. Her arm felt icy cold. Numb.

Then Baxter was pulling out the needle, and observing her with a cold, clinical look on his face.

At first she felt nothing.

But then, a few seconds after he had removed the needle, a wave of intense nausea crashed over her.

'I'm going to be sick,' she breathed, before pushing herself unsteadily to her feet. She felt dizzy, but despite that managed to stagger to the bathroom, where she retched unproductively into the toilet bowl. How long she remained there, crouched over the bowl, she couldn't have said. A couple of minutes, perhaps, until the nausea passed.

Only then did it hit her.

She was still dizzy, but now that the nausea had passed, the dizziness wasn't unpleasant. As she stood up and wandered back to her room, unable to keep in a straight line, Dani felt, for the first time in she didn't know how long, entirely free of worry. As light as a feather. She almost felt that she could smile.

Baxter was still in her room when she returned.

He was a bad man.

He made her do bad things.

He kept her locked up when she didn't want to be.

She knew all that. But she didn't care.

As she sat down on the bed, she saw the stains, but they didn't revolt her. Drowsiness seeped from every pore of her body, and the only thing she wanted to do was fall asleep. She lay on the mattress, and felt the light from the lamp – visible only from the corner of her eye – dancing around.

Everything was all right.

Everything was good.

She closed her eyes, and fell into a deep, beautiful sleep.

* * *

When Dani awoke, Baxter was no longer there.

It took a while for her to open her eyes. They felt as if they had been glued shut, despite the fact that she could feel her eyeballs rolling in their sockets. Her limbs, too, were immobile, as though the joints had been stuffed with concrete and would creak and snap if she tried to bend them. Her head pounded, and the nausea that she had briefly felt the night before had returned with a vengeance. She felt that if she moved so much as a muscle, she would be sick; so she lay there on the mattress, eyes still closed, waiting for the feeling to pass.

It didn't.

Outside the room, she heard the familiar sound of Ellie moving about. Dani had never woken later than her, and she felt a sudden flash of panic. She was ashamed of what she had done last night. Ashamed and a little bit scared. If Ellie saw her in this state, she would suspect. She would know. Dani wanted to keep it a secret, so she tried to force her eyes open. The lids were heavy, like stones, and the dim, dusty light from her lamp burned into her retinas, causing a sharp pain to crack through her already sore head.

She needed to get up; even as she tried to move, however, the door opened and Ellie appeared, wearing her dressing gown and holding a half-smoked cigarette.

'You all right?' the woman asked, her voice that little bit huskier, as it always was in the morning.

Dani squinted at her. She saw the dark rings under her eyes and wondered if she looked like that herself. Painfully she pushed herself up to a sitting position and glanced over to the dressing table. To her relief, there was no sign of the paraphernalia Baxter had obviously stolen from Ellie's room.

'Yeah,' she replied weakly. 'I'm all right.' She closed her eyes again to suppress another wave of nausea.

'Want a brew?'

Dani shook her head. The smell of Ellie's cigarette wafted in front of her, and she wished the woman would leave her alone.

'Well, I'm putting one on, if you want one. Make you some breakfast, if you like.' A pause. 'You sure you're all right, Dani? Hand hurting again, is it?'

Dani nodded. 'Yeah,' she lied. She couldn't feel any pain in her hand whatsoever. 'Hand's hurting.' Her eyes flickered towards Ellie, who was taking a deep drag on her cigarette and looking at her curiously. She didn't say anything else, but turned and left.

She suspects. Dani pushed herself to her feet, and instantly regretted it. Staggering over to the dressing table, she grabbed hold of the side while her balance settled. She needed to get out there, to pretend to Ellie that everything was as normal. With a deep breath she staggered to the door, regained her balance once more and then headed to the kitchen.

Ellie was pouring hot water into a cup as Dani entered. The little girl did her best to put a smile on her face, but she was aware that it must look forced. Neither of them spoke, but as Dani sat at the table, Ellie poured some breakfast cereal into a bowl, sloshed some milk over it and placed it in front of the girl, along with a spoon.

Dani looked down at the food. The very sight of it nauseated her, and she knew there was no way she could eat it. Gently, she pushed the bowl away.

'Not really hungry,' she told Ellie, whose face now mirrored her concern. 'Think I'll go back to my room.'

She stood up and left. 'Tell me if you want something,' Ellie's voice called from behind. It sounded weak. Pathetic. And Dani knew why. The one thing Dani wanted was the one thing Ellie wouldn't give her. A way out.

As the morning passed, so did the nausea. Gradually Dani started to get some feeling back in her bad hand, but she barely noticed the pain. Her mind was full of the memory of last night. She kept seeing the little blue bulge of vein in her arm, the clean sharp needle as it entered her.

Most of all, she remembered the feeling it gave her.

It was as though her whole body was a wound, a piece of skin that had been painfully grazed. Ever since she had left home, the wound had been irritated and scratched, until it was an agonising open sore that would not stop hurting. But last night, the injection that Baxter had given her was like a soothing ointment. It took the pain away. It was soft, and calming. It made her feel better.

Now, though, the wound was as painful as it had ever been, and Dani longed for that balm to be applied to it once more. To take the pain and the horror away.

So what if it had made her sick? That was a small price to pay.

As the afternoon turned into evening, she found that she could think of nothing else. She would be polite to Baxter when he arrived. If there was a client, she would grit her teeth and wait obediently for it to be over. She would wait for Ellie to disappear into her room.

Then she would ask him.

For some reason, she felt absolutely sure that he would allow her to repeat what happened last night.

Chapter Thirteen

As the days turned into weeks, Dani began to look forward more and more to the little wraps of paper Baxter supplied.

On the second night, he showed her how to cook it herself. She did so with trembling hands, her tongue frequently moistening her lips as she waited impatiently for the syringe to be ready.

On the third night he told her what it was. Dani had heard of heroin, of course; she knew that it was something to be scared of. But by that stage she was beyond caring. She longed for the glorious numbness that it brought her, and she started to think about it every day.

Dani and Baxter fell into a kind of routine. A sinister, nightmarish routine, but a routine nonetheless. He would bring Dani a client, sometimes two. While they were in the room with her, he would give Ellie her wrap. Without fail, once it was handed over, Ellie would retreat into her own space; within twenty minutes she'd be unconscious. They never discussed the fact that Dani didn't want the older woman to know what was going on, but Baxter seemed to understand that, through some kind of intuition. When the clients had gone, he would enter her room and hand over Dani's reward. On the fourth night he had presented her with a bag containing everything she needed to prepare her own syringes. He cut a slit in the side of the mattress that was pushed up against the wall, and showed her how to secrete everything in the stuffing.

Sometimes she panicked that he wouldn't arrive; she even snapped at Ellie, who continued to do whatever little was in her power to make her feel better. Dani began to lose track of time passing, but it couldn't have been much more than five weeks after her first fix that she realised she couldn't do without Baxter's wraps.

The mornings were always the most difficult. While it hadn't been long before she could inject herself without being sick, the dizziness and nausea were always present when she woke up. If anything, her paranoia that Ellie would find out about her dirty little habit increased, so she made a special effort to appear brighter and less unwell than she really was when she emerged from her stupor. Nothing could make her touch food, however, and it took only a few days for her already thin face to become gaunt and ghostly.

Dani could sense Ellie looking at her with increasing desperation. The older woman started making an extra effort with her, bringing little treats back more often on the occasions when she left the house. They were sweets, mostly, handed over with a nervous smile and a kind look. Dani hadn't the heart to say that she couldn't bear even to think about eating, and so she hid the sweets in the mattress, along with the secret implements that had usurped the sweets' position in Dani's life. At times she felt bad for Ellie, for what she was putting her through; but that feeling didn't last long.

No feelings lasted long. They were just supplanted by the overwhelming need, which increased in intensity day by day, for what Baxter had started calling her 'fix'.

Each time she had a fix, Baxter was there, watching over her almost solicitously. At first it made her feel uncomfortable; but after a few nights, she was past caring who watched her.

One night perhaps a week after her first fix, however, Dani noticed a change in Baxter. He appeared at about the usual time, with Mr Morgan, who dealt with her as brutally as he normally did. Dani tried to switch off while it happened, focusing instead on the oblivion that would be hers after the man had left. She didn't even bother to shower once the time came. Her hands were shaking, and all she could think about was the fix to come.

Baxter re-appeared in her room. From the silence in the flat she could tell that Ellie was out of it, and she looked up at him expectantly, waiting for what she had come to think of as her payment to be handed over.

But Baxter shook his head.

'Not tonight, lassie,' he told her with a bland smile.

Dani blinked. 'What do you mean?' she asked.

'What I said. Not tonight.'

'But …' She felt a rising sense of panic which she didn't know how to articulate.

Baxter stepped into the room, approaching her with a vicious look in his eyes. It was all she could do to keep standing – the prospect of Baxter leaving without giving her anything was too much to bear. He stood in front of her and grabbed her face with one hand, squeezing so tightly that she could feel his nails digging into her cheeks.

'Tonight,' he whispered, 'you go without. Just to see what it's like. Just so that you know what will happen if you *ever* do anything to piss me off.'

With a sharp jerk of his arm, he pushed Dani backwards. She tripped and fell heavily on to the mattress, and then watched in horror as he turned and left the room.

'Don't go,' she whispered.

Then, with a voice that didn't even sound like hers, she started to shriek. 'Don't go! Please don't go! I did what you wanted! Please! *Please!*'

But her tortured words fell on deaf ears. Baxter left the flat and locked the door behind him.

It was a night of torment.

Less than an hour after Baxter had left, Dani found herself retching in the bathroom. Back in her bedroom she lay on the mattress. Her legs started to twitch violently and she seemed to have no control over them. Goosebumps came out all over her skin, which felt desperately tender and raw to the touch, and her eyes began to water uncontrollably. Towards morning she started to sneeze, and her body felt as if it was riddled with the flu, only a hundred times worse. She started to hunt desperately through the stuffing of her mattress, fooling herself that there might be some of the precious brown powder stashed away along with the gear. But there was nothing – just the bars of chocolate that Ellie had bought her and which she could never face eating, especially now that she was feeling terrible cramps in her stomach and all over her body.

Impossible thoughts went through her mind. Perhaps Baxter hadn't locked the door properly – she tried it, shaking the handle violently. Of course it didn't open. Maybe there was another way of getting out of here, of finding someone who would give her a fix. She staggered towards the kitchen window, but the memory of her accident there made her arm, still bandaged, sting with pain. And as a wave of horrible nausea passed over her, she realised that it would be stupid to try to get out of the flat anyway. The only way she was going to get her next fix was to wait for Baxter. To do what he said. To do what he wanted.

Unless …

As Dani walked out of the kitchen and into the hallway, she bent double with a cramping pain in her abdomen, a pain that she knew would be relieved by only one thing. Straightening up again, her eyes fell on Ellie's door.

Ellie.

They were both in the same boat now, Dani realised; she knew now why Ellie would not let her out. Dani was prepared to do anything to make the withdrawal symptoms go away; and in the absence of Baxter, the woman with whom she shared this flat was her only other option. She was just going to have to wait until Ellie woke up, and hope that she went out that morning.

The seconds ticked painfully by. At times Dani wanted to scream with the pain of it all, but her last scrap of self-control prevented that from happening. From time to time her nails started to dig into the cheap wallpaper on the wall, leaving little white streaks in their wake. She trembled, she twitched and she cried. She chewed on her lip until it was wet and sore. She went from sweating to shivering in a matter of minutes; but every minute seemed like an hour as she waited for the sound of Ellie stirring.

Finally it came. The moment Dani heard footsteps in the hallway, she sat bolt upright. The sudden movement made her feel dizzy, and she took a moment to steady herself. It was important that Ellie didn't think there was anything wrong. If she was worried about her, she wouldn't leave the flat; and Dani needed her out of here. She *desperately* needed her out of here. Somewhere in the back of her mind there was a half-remembered twinge of guilt – something she knew she should feel, but which she somehow couldn't. Like a hungry person at a table of food, she could focus on nothing other than feeding her desire.

Standing up, Dani brushed herself down with her hands, as if that was likely to make her look any better. She straightened her hair slightly, and forced her lips into a smile as she prepared to leave the room and face Ellie.

Ellie was standing in the kitchen, facing the sink and filling the kettle. A cigarette hung from her mouth. The smell made Dani feel particularly unwell, but she did her best not to let it show in her face. She didn't look round as Dani walked in, but she spoke, hoarsely.

'Brew?'

'Yeah,' Dani replied. 'Thanks.' Her fingers nervously clutched the cuffs of her jumper as Ellie clumsily went about the business of making tea, hot water sloshing on to the side as she poured it into the cups.It was only when she handed one of them to Dani that she looked at her.

Her eyes narrowed and she took a deep pull on her cigarette. 'Christ, titch,' she said. 'You look awful.'

Dani clenched her jaw. 'Didn't sleep well,' she muttered. Her voice was wavering, and she struggled to keep it under control. She was feeling dizzy again and needed to sit down, so she pulled a chair from under the table and took a seat.

'You sure you're all right?' Ellie asked.

Dani avoided her gaze, but nodded and took a sip of her tea, just for show. 'Fine,' she said. Then, as nonchalantly as she could manage, 'You going out today? This morning?'

Ellie sniffed and looked out of the window. 'Suppose,' she said. 'We need a few things. I can buy you some sweets if you like. Got a bit extra last night.'

Dani smiled thinly. 'Thanks,' she said. She tried to sound keen, but it didn't happen.

Ellie dragged on her cigarette and then carried her tea to the door. Before she left the room, however, she turned round and looked at Dani. She opened her mouth to say something, but before she could speak Dani interrupted her.

'I'm fine, all right,' she snapped.

Ellie frowned in confusion at Dani's sudden outburst. She looked hurt, but rather than feeling bad about it, Dani just found herself getting more angry, and it was all she could do to keep that anger from boiling over. She turned around, and resolutely faced the other way.

Five minutes later, Ellie left the flat, making a lot of noise about it.

Finally Dani was alone.

She only gave it a minute – a scant minute to make sure that Ellie wasn't coming back. It would be safer to give it a bit longer, she knew. But there was no way she could. Scraping her chair back from under the kitchen table, she hurried through the hallway and opened the door to Ellie's room.

Dani never went in here. In all the weeks since she had been imprisoned in this dingy flat, Ellie's room had always seemed out of bounds. Despite everything, despite the fact that the woman had helped Baxter keep Dani locked up in here, she had been kind to her. Somehow Dani knew that invading her little space would be a terrible betrayal in Ellie's eyes; but there was nothing she could do to stop herself. Nothing at all. If there was anything in here, anything that would relieve the pain and the desperate need for a fix, Dani had to find it. And now.

The room was just as she remembered it. A thick blanket still hung over the window, making it dim and dusky in there. A thick, acrid odour filled the air. Dani knew what the smell was now, of course. It was both foul and sweet to her at the same time.

She made no attempt to cover her tracks as she started rummaging through the drawers and cupboards. As Ellie's clothes fell on the floor, she didn't bother to pick them up. Her hands were shaking in desperate anticipation; her body was numb with sickness and pain. It was almost blinding.

There was nothing in the cupboard, nothing in the drawers – apart from a bag of needles and the cooking instruments. Tears sprang to Dani's eyes as she desperately tugged the duvet off the double bed. Nothing. It took all her strength – and there wasn't much of that – to tug the mattress from its frame, but that didn't yield anything either.

Sobs of desperation racked through her. She started looking back through places she had already searched, in the folds of clothes and under corners of the carpet. But there weren't that many hiding places in this little room, and as it became increasingly clear that she wasn't going to find what she was looking for, her sense of panic became worse. She ripped the blanket from the window – she wasn't sure why – and as it fell to the floor, she found herself blinded by the sudden stream of daylight that flooded into the room. She clapped her hands to her eyes and fell to the ground, the debris of her frantic search scattered all around her.

Then she heard Ellie's voice.

'Dani?'

She sounded shocked. Breathless.

'Dani, what the—'

Ellie didn't finish her sentence. Dani had stood up and, like a fox cornered by a hound, was looking all around her, trying to find a way out. Her vision was still blotchy from the way the sunlight had dazzled her, and she had only the vaguest sense of Ellie approaching. She felt her, sure enough, though, when the woman grabbed her by the wrists. Her hands felt bony, but her grip was surprisingly strong.

'Dani,' she hissed. 'What's going on? What have you—'

It was only then that Dani saw Ellie's face clearly. It surprised her. Dani expected to see anger. Fury. But she didn't. Ellie's eyes, those red, watery, drug-addict eyes, had filled with tears, and a look of total horror had filled her face.

'No,' Ellie whispered.

Then again. '*No.*'

Dani looked away, and tried to struggle, tried to break away from Ellie's vice-like grasp. But she couldn't. Either the little girl was too weak or Ellie was too strong – Dani couldn't tell which. She started to struggle even more as

Ellie let go of one wrist and slowly pushed her jumper up the length of her arm. With her free hand Dani swung out and hit Ellie across the side of the face; but Ellie ignored it and continued pushing her jumper up. Dani clawed at the fabric, not wanting to let Ellie see her skin. But the woman was insistent. Relentless.

And once her bare arm was revealed, they both looked at it in horror.

The area around Dani's inner elbow was bruised and mottled – like the bruising on her face when she had left home, but somehow worse than that. There were a number of tiny red dots around the veins, where the needles had been injected; but the veins themselves could not be seen. Already Dani was having difficulty getting them to protrude, even with the use of a belt or a bootlace.

Ellie let go of Dani's wrist, and the little girl instantly pushed the sleeve back down. But it was too late: Ellie had seen, and there was no way she would not realise what the bruising meant; no way she would be fooled as to why Dani – timid, undemonstrative Dani – had just ransacked her room.

'Not that,' Ellie practically croaked. 'Please, don't say it. Not that.' She took a step backwards, and then another. If her face had shown horror before, now it was etched with indescribable self-loathing.

Dani found herself rooted to the spot. The physical symptoms had not left her, but something had chipped away at the emotional numbness she had been experiencing; and there was something shocking about the sight of Ellie, about the riot of conflicting emotions that now streaked across her face.

'How long?' she asked.

Dani shrugged, and then winced as another of those waves of pain surged through her abdomen.

'It was him, wasn't it?' Ellie pressed. 'Baxter? *He* gave it to you.'

Dani nodded.

Ellie's thin face screwed up as she closed her eyes and started beating her clenched fists against her forehead. An inhuman sound escaped her throat – not a cry, exactly, or even a shout. More a wail, a long, low wail, full of anxiety and helplessness.

'He wouldn't give me any last night,' Dani finally managed to speak. 'He told me … he told me …' But she couldn't get the words out. She couldn't speak.

Then Ellie was there again, holding her hands – not firmly this time, but gently. Tenderly, almost. Dani looked into her eyes again, those tired, frightened, addled eyes. It was like looking in a mirror that showed the future.

'You have to stop,' Ellie said, her voice cracking. 'You have to stop, now. If you carry on, you'll—' She paused. 'You can't end up like me, Dani. He'll control you. You'll never leave.'

As Ellie said these words, Dani felt the anger and irritation suddenly rise up in her again. She couldn't control it. 'What do you mean I'll never leave?' she hissed. 'I'll never leave anyway. I'll never leave because of *you*. It's *your* fault as well as his. It's *your* fault I'm like this. It's *your* fault I'm here.'

Ellie's breath started to come in fits and starts. 'I've tried to look after you,' she said weakly, but she didn't even sound as if she was convincing herself. Dani rushed past her, out of the room, full of devastation. She slammed the door behind her and rushed into her own room, where she collapsed on the mattress in a small, feral ball, shaking, retching, weeping and wishing this could all be over.

Wishing she could die.

Ellie stood in the middle of her room, numb and dumbfounded.

Dani's words had been like thumps in the stomach. Like bullets. She felt wounded by them. And they were all the more morbid because they were true.

She closed her eyes. Her head was thick, confused – and not just because of the hangover from last night's fix. Ellie didn't know what to think, what to do. It was as though she was torn in two.

She knew what she had done. It didn't matter how many times she told herself that she had been doing her best to help the little girl in the room next to her; it didn't matter how many ill-afforded presents she bought to salve her conscience; it didn't matter how many hours she had sat by Dani's bedside when she was ill and delirious. In her few moments of honesty, of sobriety, Ellie knew that she was the one person who stood between that poor little girl and the terrible life Baxter had imposed on her.

Baxter.

The very thought of his name made her lip curl. Her hatred of her bastard pimp had long been dulled by the little packets of brown he brought her every evening; for years now she had ignored his true nature. She had even felt grateful to him, whenever he handed over the wrap. But now just thinking about him, thinking about what he had done to Dani, made her feel ill.

The image of Dani, startled and desperate in Ellie's room, flashed though her head. Ellie knew what she was doing in there, of course. She could see it in her eyes and on her face. She knew the urgency, the overpowering need for junk when you didn't have any. You'd do anything, try anything, search anywhere just for a hint of the stuff.

But Christ! Ellie didn't know how old Dani was. Something had always stopped her from asking – she just didn't want to know. Too young to be on the game, certainly. Far too young for that. But somewhere, somehow, Ellie had supposed that it would end. Baxter couldn't keep her locked up in this flat forever.

But he had been clever. He had been sly. He was doing to Dani just what he had done to Ellie. He had taken control of her. He was seeing to it that he didn't *need* to keep the little girl under lock and key. He was placing her in a prison far worse than the one she had endured for the past few weeks since she had arrived here.

The thought of it made her shiver. In her mind's eye, she pictured Dani cooking the junk, shooting up. It made her feel ill just to think about it.

She couldn't let it happen.

But what could she do? Baxter had made it quite clear: if Dani left the flat, if Ellie let it happen, the consequences would be unthinkable.

Baxter was a violent man. He would think nothing of laying into her. Beating her. Badly.

But he wouldn't need to.

All he would need to do was what he had just done to Dani. He only had to withhold that precious little wrap of brown powder and Ellie's life would become intolerable.

The very thought of it made her shake. It made her scowl even more. Why should she put herself through that? She wasn't Dani's friend. She wasn't her mother. She had no responsibility towards her. Why should she go through hell just because that stupid little girl wasn't street-wise enough to avoid getting into this situation in the first place?

What was it to her?

She started storming around the room, picking up items of clothing and making half-hearted attempts at putting them back where they should be. It made no difference to the state of the place. The thought of everything that was happening had just made her angry, and she found herself spinning round in the middle of the room, as though looking for a way out.

But there was no way out.

Not for either of them.

They had to continue the way they were. Servicing Johns. Doing Baxter's bidding. And waiting for the little rewards that came at the end of the day.

There was no other option.

Her fingers went to the chain around her neck, the one on which the key to the flat was hanging. Out of Dani's reach, even when Ellie was asleep. Unconscious.

She let her hand fall.

It wasn't going to happen. Ellie had herself to think about. Her own needs.

She and Dani were going to stay as they were.

There was no other option.

Dani's blood ran hot and cold.

She was scrunched up in a little ball, her knees tucked in under her arms. She found that if she squeezed herself tightly, it made the sickness and the pain go away, just for a few seconds; and as she stared blankly into the middle distance, she was unaware of the passing of time. Vaguely she heard sounds from Ellie's room next door – the stamping of feet, the slamming of doors – but these barely registered in her brain. Dani could think of nothing but the agony of her withdrawal, and the one thing she knew would relieve it.

The little girl closed her eyes and started rocking gently to and fro. To distract herself, she started to sing, a tuneless little song with no words, rendered in a weak, crackling voice. In her ears, it sounded as though someone else was singing, as though there was somebody else in her room, a ghost. It brought her no comfort, yet she continued to sing.

The door opened. Dani didn't turn to look at it. She just carried on rocking, and humming tunelessly.

'Dani.'

Ellie's voice was quiet and wavering. But serious. There was something in it that made Dani stop rocking and turn to look at her.

The woman was standing in the door frame. She was pale – paler than usual – and her eyes were haunted, her lips almost indistinguishable from the rest of her skin.

'Get up,' she said.

Dani didn't move.

'Get up,' Ellie hissed. '*Get up now.*' She stormed into the room and grabbed Dani by the upper part of one of her arms, pulling her to her feet as easily as if she was a soft toy. The room span.

'What are you doing?' Dani asked.

Ellie didn't answer. Instead, she wordlessly pulled Dani towards the door of the bedroom and out into the hallway.

'*Get off me!*' Dani screamed. '*What are you doing?*'

Ellie stopped, and in the dim light of the hallway she looked straight into Dani's eyes.

'Listen to me,' Ellie hissed breathlessly. 'We're leaving. Now. We have to go quickly. Who knows when he's going to be back? It could be any minute.'

It took a moment for the words to register.

We're leaving. Now.

She blinked, stunned.

Then she looked around her. Every ounce of her being wanted to go with Ellie. To be rid of this place. But something held her back.

If she left now, she didn't know where her next fix would come from. The pain would never end.

'I can't,' she whispered.

Her quiet words seemed to echo in the air.

Ellie's grip on her arm loosened, and ever so slowly the older woman turned to face her. Dani could see that she was shaking, torn.

'Listen to me, Dani,' she breathed. 'You know what will happen to me when he finds out I've done this. You *know* what will happen, don't you?'

Fearfully, Dani nodded her head.

Ellie took a deep breath. 'Look at me, Dani,' she whispered. '*Look at me.*' Her red, raw eyes were intense. 'If you don't leave now, you'll never leave. You'll never be *able* to leave and you'll never *want* to leave. Don't you see what he's doing to you? Don't you understand?'

Dani nodded again as Ellie continued.

'There's a place I know,' she said. 'A place for … for people like you. They'll help you – help you off the junk. It won't hurt, and they'll do it gently. But *please*, Dani. We *have* to go now. If he finds us both trying to leave …'

Her eyes were darting about nervously, and Dani could suddenly sense the fear emanating from her. She shared it.

'My things,' she muttered.

'There's no time,' Ellie stated flatly. Then, inclining her head slightly, 'Quickly, Dani. Quickly before I change my mind.' As she spoke, all the fear she felt came flooding out in her voice, and Dani understood in a moment of sudden clarity just what it was that Ellie was doing for her. Just what it would cost.

'If you're coming, Dani, now's the time to say so.'

Dani closed her eyes, and felt all the muscles in her face cramp up.

Then, slowly, she nodded her head.

Ellie let out an explosive breath. 'Good girl,' she said. 'Let's go.'

Then she took the key from around her neck, placed it in the lock of the door to the flat, and then opened it.

For the first time in Dani did not know how long, she stepped out into the landing beyond.

Chapter Fourteen

The stairs were as dark as Dani remembered. As dark and as steep. They were precarious for her as she weakly stumbled down them, stopped from falling only by Ellie's careful hand on her shoulder. As they turned the corner of the landing below the flat, Dani fully expected to find Baxter standing there, waiting for them. She fully expected to see the harsh lines of his face; to feel his hard fist against her skin. She could almost see one of her clients, the men he brought to visit her, lurking behind him. Maybe Mr Morgan; maybe one of the others.

But he wasn't on the second floor, and staggering down to the first floor she could see that he wasn't there either. The only obstacle that remained was the main entrance, and in the blinking of an eye Ellie had opened that too, and they stepped outside into the street.

When Dani was little, she sometimes used to lift up rocks or old bricks in the small garden of their house. There would be insects underneath – earwigs and the like – and they would crawl manically, driven to distraction by the sudden sunlight, which they weren't used to. That was how Dani felt now. The bright light – a light that she hadn't seen for weeks or months – blinded her, and the fresh air was like ice in her lungs.

'Come on,' Ellie urged her. 'We have to get away, off his turf. If anyone sees us here …'

She pulled Dani away from the door, down the side street in which the flat was situated, and round a corner into a main road.

There were people here, lots of them, and cars too. Dani felt herself shrinking from them all, panic rising in her breast. They were looking at her – all of them were looking at her.

They knew what she was doing.

They knew what she was.

They knew her secrets.

The sickness was still surging through her as she stumbled blindly along the streets. Ellie had her hand now, and was holding it tightly. Dani noticed that she had her head bowed, as though she did not want to be recognised, as though she *would* be recognised. She was tugging Dani, urging her to walk more quickly than she felt she could. Her legs, she realised, were weak from lack of exercise.

The more her eyes grew used to the daylight, the more people she saw; and the more people she saw, the more paranoid she became, until suddenly, without quite knowing why she was doing it, she stopped and started to scream.

'It's all right, Dani.' Ellie's soothing voice floated into her consciousness. 'It's not far now. It's going to be all right.' Dani stopped screaming, but her breath still came in short, sharp, frightened gasps.

Then there was another voice. A woman. 'You all right, dear?' it asked, concerned.

'It's fine,' Ellie snapped. 'She's fine. We'll be OK.'

A hubbub. More voices. She was aware of a little crowd of people around them.

'Come on, Dani,' she heard Ellie say. 'Nearly there. Let's go.'

Dani nodded her head and, looking fearfully at the crowd, which seemed to have appeared from nowhere, she allowed Ellie to pull her away.

'Where we going?' she gasped after a while.

Ellie didn't stop to answer. 'It's not far,' she repeated. 'Come on, we'll soon be there.'

Despite what Ellie had said, it seemed to take an age for them to get wherever it was they were headed. The traffic seemed to swarm around them, and every time Dani heard a car horn, or the frightening roar of a bus's engine, or the shout of a passer-by, she felt as if an electric shock was surging through her body. As they walked, she looked around her, wild-eyed, constantly expecting to see Baxter or one of the men. Constantly expecting to be stopped and dragged away. Yet, at the same time, it was as if she was connected to that hated flat by some sinister elastic band, pulling her back to the promise of another fix. The further they moved away from it, the thinner the band became. If it snapped, Dani thought she might die, and it took every ounce of her determination and control not to break away from Ellie and run back. Not that she would have known the way.

By the time they stopped, Dani's ravaged body was aching with exhaustion and seemed to be screaming at her. Though she didn't know where they were, she could sense that this was a very different part of London, away from the bright lights of the West End. A poorer part. More run down.

'This is it,' Ellie told her tersely. 'This is where you have to go.'

Dani looked up. The buildings on both sides of the street were high, and they were stained with the black marks of many years of pollution. They were big, imposing brick buildings – unfriendly, if a building could be said to be so – and they seemed to cast a shadow that blocked out the bright, chilly sun. The door outside which they had stopped was painted a pale green, but the paint was peeling slightly.

'Where are we?' Dani asked.

Ellie took a deep breath. 'It's a refuge,' she said. 'Kind of. It's for people like you …' She smiled a bit sadly. 'Like us, I suppose. People who need help with, you know … People who want to come off.'

Dani felt her eyes darting around. She wasn't sure she wanted to be here. There was no cure for the illness she was feeling; of that she could be sure.

'What do they do?' she asked nervously.

'Methadone,' Ellie said, and then, seeing that Dani didn't understand, she continued. 'It makes you feel better. Takes the sickness away.'

Dani cast her gaze down to the floor. The tremors were worse than ever now. She felt as if she would do anything to make herself feel better.

'Are you coming with me?' she asked in a small voice.

Ellie closed her eyes momentarily. 'No,' she whispered. 'I have to go back.'

'Why? Why can't you come? We can both get better together.'

All of a sudden, Ellie looked as though she might burst into tears. 'Oh, Dani,' she breathed. 'You don't understand. It's too late for me. I'm too far gone. I don't even know if I *want* to get better any more. Even if I did, what would I do? But you're young. Too young for this. Too young for Baxter and too young to be near me and people like me.'

There was a silence. A horrible, pregnant silence.

'What will he do?' Dani asked finally.

Ellie looked away. 'I do good work for him,' she said, almost as though she was trying to convince herself of something. 'He'll be cross, but I do good work ...'

She took a deep, wavering breath.

'Will you come in with me?' Dani asked. 'Just for a bit?'

Ellie shook her head and took a step backwards. 'I've got to go, titch,' she said. 'You'll be all right. They'll take care of you here. You'll be all right.' She tried to smile, but that one smile obviously contained in it more emotions than Ellie wanted to convey, or even knew she was feeling.

'I'll miss you,' Dani said. The words surprised her, not least because they were true.

A furrowed look of confusion crossed Ellie's face. 'Just do one thing for me,' she whispered. 'Don't tell the police. About me. If they take me away, away from Baxter, I'll ...'

She couldn't finish her sentence. The two of them looked awkwardly into each other's eyes.

'Good luck, sweetheart,' Ellie managed finally. And without another word, she turned and walked briskly away.

Dani wanted to follow her, to run after her. It was almost as though Ellie could read her mind, however, because she suddenly stopped, looked back and shook her head in warning. *Don't follow me*, she seemed to say. *Don't ever follow me.*

With that stark and honest – but silent – warning, she turned a corner and was gone.

And with her disappearance, Dani was alone again.

A burning pain flowed through her veins. The sickness that had been with her all night reached a new height of intensity. Suddenly she became overcome with dizziness. There was a great rushing sound in her head and she tottered and fell, exhausted, to the floor.

And as if the lights had suddenly been extinguished, Dani Sinclair became unconscious, nothing more than a crumpled, sorry heap on the pavement.

When Dani awoke, she was lying in bed.

For a brief moment she thought she was dreaming. The room was small, but bright – a far cry from the musty darkness of the place she had woken up in every day recently. The walls were painted white; the bed linen was crisp and clean, and smelled of laundry – a smell Dani thought she had forgotten. Beside her was a small bedside table with a lamp, and next to that there was an empty armchair.

It was clean.

It was comfortable.

Dani *had* to get out of there.

She had not been awake for more than a few seconds when the withdrawal symptoms hit, a violent crunch in her stomach and a terrible, overpowering nausea. She looked around her, dry-lipped and desperate, and barely noticed the relative comfort of the place she was in. The only thing she could focus on was the door. Climbing weakly out of bed, she didn't even bother to remove the clean nightdress she was wearing. She just put on her old clothes,which were slung over the back of the armchair. Reaching for the door handle, she opened it and prepared to leave.

'You're up!'

The voice made Dani's heart jump. She looked up and saw an unfamiliar woman wearing a starched nurse's uniform and carrying a tray. Dani backed away nervously, into the room, her eyes darting around.The nurse walked briskly in and placed the tray – which carried a jug of water and a selection of pills – on the bedside table; then she turned and smiled at Dani.

'How are you feeling, dear?

Dani didn't answer. She just looked edgily at the door.

The nurse's eyes narrowed slightly. 'Do you know where you are, dear?' she asked.

Dani shook her head. As she did so, the withdrawal pain came into her abdomen again, and flashed all through her body. She doubled over. The nurse was there immediately, holding her firmly and edging her back to the bed. 'Wait there,' she instructed. 'I'll get a doctor.'

It was all such a blur. There were people – three, maybe four – rushing in and out, taking her temperature, examining her eyes, asking questions that she couldn't answer because all she could focus on was the agony of her withdrawal. She sweated and she shivered. She coughed and she retched. With every second that passed, she wanted more and more to rush out of that door; but at the moment she couldn't even summon up the strength to get out of bed again.

It was only when one of the people around her – a man with short blond hair who told her he was a doctor – said the word 'heroin' that her attention was grabbed. Dani didn't know what question he had asked her, so she didn't answer it. She didn't have to, though. Her reaction said it all.

The doctor nodded to the nurse. 'Fifty milligrams,' he said curtly. 'Now.'

The nurse nodded and disappeared.

'Now listen to me,' the doctor said. His voice was calm and kind, and as Dani lay on the bed he looked down at her with an intense expression. 'I'm going to give you some medicine. It's a small dose to start with, just for us to check that it doesn't make you ill. If you seem all right, we'll give you a bit more, and it'll stop you feeling so unwell. Does that sound OK?'

Dani nodded. There wasn't much else she could do.

When the nurse returned, she was carrying a small paper cup. The doctor handed it to Dani. 'Drink it,' he said.

There was a small puddle of green liquid in the cup. Dani tried to put it to her lips, but her hand was shaking too much, so the doctor had to help her. The liquid tasted astringent, and Dani struggled to get it down.

'Good girl,' the doctor told her. 'Now it's going to take a couple of hours for us to check for side effects.' He looked towards the door. 'Do you want to tell me your name?'

Dani shook her head.

The doctor didn't seem surprised. 'All right, then. But you have to listen to me. If you want to make the with-drawal symptoms go away, you have to stay. Running away won't do you any good. You've no money, and you've no means of finding any drugs. We're going to have someone in here all the time, and if you need anything, you only have to ask. Does that sound OK?'

She nodded.

'Good. I'll see you in a bit.' And with that the doctor turned and left.

The two hours passed slowly and painfully. The nurse remained with Dani, but they barely spoke as she looked on with a kind of determined sympathy. When it became clear that Dani's symptoms, though severe, were not getting any worse, she was given a larger cupful of the green liquid, and then told to wait once more.

The effect crept over her slowly. At first it was barely perceptible, but gradually Dani felt as though someone had rubbed a soothing balm over a particularly spiteful wound. The tremors calmed down; the pain in her abdomen stopped. She would not have said that she felt fine, but at least she didn't feel wretched. At least she didn't feel an overwhelming need for one of Baxter's needles, for one of his insidious little wraps of brown powder.

The improvement clearly showed on her face. The nurse smiled at her and, as though she was talking to a little child who had just bumped her head and been comforted, she asked, 'Better now?'

Dani nodded. She even managed a little smile.

'Good,' the nurse said kindly. 'Good. Now then, I think it would be a good idea if we got you something to eat, don't you?'

It was dark when Ellie returned to the flat. She had been putting it off. Avoiding it. Walking the streets, blindly and aimlessly, too scared to return and too scared to stay away.

She had wept as she had left Dani. Ellie could not remember the last time tears had moistened her face, and she had scrunched up her eyes as she walked in an attempt to make them go away. Who the hell was she crying for, she wondered as she hurried away from the hostel? For Dani, and everything she had been through, thanks to Ellie's own inaction? Or for herself? For what was going to happen when Baxter learned that she had crossed him?

As the afternoon waned, and the cravings started gradually to kick in again, the foolishness of her actions started to become apparent to her. What had she done, she asked herself as she walked slowly along Shaftesbury Avenue, the menacing hunger creeping up on her? What the *hell* had she done? Baxter would go crazy. He'd beat her up, of course. But worse than that, he'd withhold the junk. The very idea made her sweat. She thought about trying to get some herself, but that would be impossible. She didn't have enough money, for a start, and none of the other girls she knew, the ones who were using, would dream of sharing their stash. It was too precious to them.

Maybe she could go back to the hostel. Get Dani back. But when she thought of it, thought of the little girl's big eyes and imagined the impossible, gruesome sight of her cooking up, she knew that could never happen.

No. She was going to have to face Baxter. Maybe she could persuade him. Lie to him.

Something.

Anything.

As she turned into the street where the flat was situated, Ellie felt as though she was walking to her own execution.

The flat seemed strangely empty without Dani. No one could have said that the kid was much fun, but she had been company, of a sort. Ellie knew the whole thing was fucked up, but in a weird kind of way she had liked having her there. She'd liked having someone to look after. To care for. The little gifts of sweets and chocolate that she'd brought home – Ellie had pretended they were for Dani. In truth, they were as much for her benefit as the child's.

She'd missed two appointments that day. Two tricks. That meant Baxter would already know that something was up. He would have been here, and found the flat empty. Ellie had half expected him to be here when she arrived, nervous, trembling, desperate for her fix. But the place was empty. Empty, dark and quiet.

She was just going to have to wait.

Wait for whatever it was he had in store for her.

She didn't have to wait long.

Ellie was sitting on the edge of her bed when she heard the door to the flat open and then close again. From the sound of his footsteps, she could tell that the first thing Baxter did was check Dani's room; that was followed by an abrupt slamming of the door, and then another burst of footsteps as he approached Ellie's room.

Then he was there. Short. Squat. Framed by the doorway. Ellie had never seen such fury on a face before. His eyes were half closed, his lips curled. Behind him, she saw the unmistakable figure of the man who liked to call himself Mr Morgan. But it was not Ellie's former client, the man in whose affections she had been replaced by little Dani, who worried her: it was her pimp. Baxter oozed anger.

'*Where ... the fuck ... is she?*' he hissed, speaking every word slowly and meaningfully.

Ellie stared back at him. Guilt was written all over her face, she knew; but like a terrified schoolgirl put on the spot by a furious teacher, she couldn't answer him.

Baxter wasn't playing around, though. He strode into the room and with one swift movement grabbed Ellie by the neck. His fingernails dug harshly into the soft flesh of her jugular, and she found herself gasping for breath.

'*I said, where is she?*'

Her whole body was shaking now. 'Please, Baxter,' she pleaded hoarsely. 'Please let go of me.'

'Listen to me, you worthless little whore.' Somehow his Scottish accent was more pronounced, thanks to his fury. 'I'm going to ask you one more time. I swear to you that if you don't answer me, you won't need to worry about where your next fix is coming from. You won't need to worry about anything ever again. Do I make myself plain?'

He squeezed her neck harder. She could barely breathe.

'I let her go,' she gasped apprehensively. 'I'm sorry, Baxter. I let her go.'

Baxter roared incoherently, and with a brutal swipe he hurled Ellie by her neck, off the bed and on to the floor, where she fell heavily on to her side. Then, almost as if it was part of the same furious movement, he kicked her in the stomach with one of his big, heavy boots.

'What the *fuck* do you mean, you let her go?' he yelled apoplectically.

Mr Morgan had entered the room now. He stood just by the door, surveying the scene with a somewhat cool detachment.

'You need to get on top of this, Baxter,' he said, his voice edgy with a tone of warning. 'You hear what I'm saying. You need to get on top of it.'

'Do I look like a fucking idiot?' Baxter screamed, and he booted Ellie in the stomach once more.

From the corner of her eye, Ellie saw Mr Morgan step further into the room, cold and calculating, ice to Baxter's fire. 'You look,' he said quietly, 'like someone in a whole heap of trouble. If that girl grasses you up, there won't be anything *I* can do to keep you out of the fucking clink. I'll fucking well be in there with you.' He turned away; then he continued more quietly, more threateningly. 'You've got to find her, Baxter. I don't care what it takes. You've got to find her, and you've got to shut her up. I'll do what I can from my end, but at the moment the only lead you've got is lying on the floor in front of you.'

Morgan's words seemed to echo around the room. Ellie, curled up and shaking on the floor, closed her eyes, expecting another attack from Baxter. But it didn't come. Instead, there was a horrible, ominous silence. Then Morgan left the room, and she heard him letting himself out of the flat.

She was alone now with Baxter.

Just the two of them.

Now it was really going to begin.

Ellie felt herself clenching her bruised stomach muscles, ready for the next bout of kicking. But the kicking didn't come. Instead, the silence remained. Timorously, she half opened her eyes. Baxter wasn't even looking at her. He was pacing the room, his head bowed, chewing his lower lip. His eyes seemed lost in thought.

Painfully, Ellie pushed herself up to a sitting position. She knew it was ridiculous, but she had to ask. 'You got something for me, then, Baxter?'

Baxter stopped and looked incredulously at her. His lower jaw moved, as though he was chewing on a piece of invisible gum.

'Got something for you?' he asked. 'Are you fucking joking?'

Ellie swallowed. 'Come on, Baxter,' she said feebly. 'You weren't going to keep her here for ever, now, were you? You was going to have to let her go some time.'

'Oh really?' Baxter asked softly. His head seemed to nod hypnotically from side to side.

'She's just a kid, Baxter,' Ellie continued, emboldened by the fact that he hadn't flown off the handle, hadn't attacked her again.

'Aye,' Baxter repeated. 'Just a kid.'

A pause.

'I couldn't bear it, Baxter. I couldn't bear the sight of it. Not any more. She's a good girl, though. I asked her not to go to the police. I don't think she will.'

'You don't think so, eh?'

'She was running away from something, Baxter. If she goes to the police, they'll catch up with her. Send her back. She won't want that.'

Baxter didn't take his gaze off her, surveying her through his hard, half-closed eyes as if he was weighing her up. But he didn't contradict her. She felt that she was talking him round. It excited her. It meant she was that bit closer to persuading him to hand over her next fix.

'So have you?'

'Have I what?'

'Got something for me?' She couldn't stop her voice from shaking as she asked.

'Aye,' Baxter said slowly. 'Aye, I've got something for you.'

Ellie was still sitting on the floor. Baxter stepped forward until he was only inches away from her. He bent down slowly. Then, with a sudden, cruel swiftness, he grabbed a handful of Ellie's long hair.

She gasped in pain, but that didn't deter him. He squeezed the clump of hair harder, and then twisted it round slowly. Ellie shouted out.

'Shut the fuck up,' Baxter hissed, and he pulled her by the hair so that she staggered up to her feet. Ellie was slightly taller than her pimp, and as he held her by the hair he resembled an executioner holding up a severed head.

With his spare hand, he grabbed her once more by the neck. His face was close to hers now – so close that she could smell his breath and see the pores on his nose.

'You don't get a fucking thing from me until I know where she is,' he told her through clenched teeth. 'If you think I'm going to go to prison because of your stupid games, you've got another think coming.'

Tears of pain sprang to Ellie's eyes. 'Please, Baxter,' she whimpered. But Baxter's face alone made it clear that he was in no mood for pleading.

'Shut up,' he told her, and then he flung her down on to the bed again. Ellie's hands quickly moved up to her sore scalp, but she almost forgot about the pain he had inflicted when she saw him moving towards the door.

'Baxter,' she whispered. 'Baxter, you got to give it to me—'

Baxter's lip curled once more. 'You tell me where she is, I give you the fix. Simple as that. You going to tell me?'

Ellie's face screwed up. The choice was impossible.

'I can't, Baxter,' she whimpered. 'She's just a little girl.'

Baxter shrugged nastily. 'Fine,' he said. He stepped towards her again, and stretched his arm out towards her neck. She flinched, but he didn't strangle her this time. Instead, he grabbed the necklace that hung there – the necklace on which she held the key to the door. He pulled, and the chain snapped, digging into her flesh as it did so. Once he had the key in his fist, he stormed out.

'You're not going anywhere,' he warned as he went. 'I promise you, you're not going anywhere.'

Ellie pushed herself up from the bed and ran after him, but she was too late. Baxter had left the flat and closed the door behind him. She heard the unmistakable sound of the key turning in the lock.

'Baxter!' she screamed as she flung herself against the wall and started banging on it with clenched, desperate fists. *'Baxter!'*

But there was no reply. No reply, because there was no one there.

Ellie was alone and trapped. Just her, her addiction and the threat of a terrible choice hanging over her like a blade.

Chapter Fifteen

Morning came.

Dani's sleep had not been entirely uninterrupted, but it had been less haunted than of late. The methadone had made her woozy, and she still felt strangely detached from the real world when there was a knock on the door and a person she didn't recognise entered. She was a young woman, perhaps in her twenties, and though she was far from pretty there was something appealing about her face. Her dark hair was tied behind her head in tight dreadlocks, and she wore a brightly coloured woollen jumper. Her nose was pierced in two places, her ears in several.

She carried a tray with her. There was toast and orange juice. Dani realised how hungry she was. It was a sensation she had not felt for a long time, and she sat up eagerly.

'Morning,' the woman said brightly, in a husky smoker's voice, as she placed the tray on the bedside table.

Dani nodded at her. She was more interested in the tray of food than anything else. The woman must have sensed this, because she handed her a plate of toast, and then stood back as Dani devoured it, before taking the orange juice and drinking it in three thirsty gulps.

'Better?' she asked.

'Much,' Dani replied.

The woman smiled at her again. 'My name's Anabella,' she said. 'What's yours?'

Dani looked away.

'Aren't you going to tell me?' Anabella asked. 'I'm hoping we can be friends, but that's going to be difficult if I don't even know your name.'

Dani sniffed. Her head still felt as if she had a cold, and as she desperately tried to think of a name, she had the sensation that her brain was not working as it should. It was working fast enough, though, for her to realise that she didn't want anyone to know who she was. For the first time in ages, she felt safe; but if the truth was revealed about her, she might be sent away.

'Ellie,' she said finally. 'My name's Ellie.' It was the first name that came to mind.

Anabella nodded, her face expressionless. Dani couldn't tell whether she believed her or not.

'How old are you, Ellie?'

'Sixteen,' Dani lied. It didn't seem to surprise Anabella, and for a moment Dani wondered if the ravages of the recent weeks had had such an effect on her features that she appeared to be that age.

'So, Ellie,' Anabella continued, her voice suddenly a little bit more serious. 'Do you want to tell me what's been happening?'

'What do you mean?' Dani asked guiltily.

Anabella stared thoughtfully at Dani for quite a long while, and the little girl felt suddenly uncomfortable. It wasn't an unpleasant glare; but there was something unnerving about it. Dani looked away.

Eventually, Anabella spoke. 'I'll be back in a second, Ellie,' she told her, before standing up and leaving the room. When she returned, she was carrying something: a piece of paper, though Dani could not see what it was. Anabella sat on the edge of the bed. Close up, the woman smelled faintly of cigarettes. But the smell wasn't unpleasant. It reminded Dani slightly of the real Ellie.

'Do you know where you are?' the woman asked.

'A hostel,' Dani replied. She didn't really know what a hostel was, but that was the word Ellie had used.

Anabella nodded. 'It's a rehabilitation centre for drug users. Do you understand what that means?'

Timidly, Dani nodded.

'I'm your case worker,' Anabella continued. 'Everything you tell me – and I mean *everything* – is confidential. I don't care what you've done. I just want you to get better. OK?'

Dani listened to what the woman had to say, but she was unmoved by the words. She'd heard them before, after all, in what seemed like another life. A life before Baxter. She glanced at the paper in Anabella's hand. 'What's that?' she asked.

With a little tilt of her head, Anabella turned it over and handed it to Dani.

The picture was grainy and in black and white, but there was no mistaking what it was: a photograph of Ellie and Dani, standing outside the hostel yesterday. Both their faces were clear, and Dani looked at her own features with a pang. So thin and drawn. She hardly recognised herself. And the sight of Ellie, too, brought a lump to her throat. There was something in her eyes – a look of such mystified fear.

'How long have you been using heroin, Ellie?' Anabella asked quietly.

The question knocked Dani off kilter. 'I don't know,' she muttered 'Probably a few weeks.'

Anabella took one of her hands. 'Why did you start? What made you do it?' Clearly seeing Dani's reluctance to talk, she continued speaking. 'It's all right,' she said. 'I've been there myself. I used to use. I know what it's like.'

Dani hung her head. 'They kept me locked up,' she whispered. 'And they made me do things. You know, with men.'

Anabella blinked, disbelief written across her face. 'You mean …'

Dani looked away again, and she felt a hot flush of shame rising from her neck. She wished she hadn't said anything. It was so obvious what Anabella thought of her now.

There was an uncomfortable silence.

Anabella broke it with another question. 'Where?' she asked. 'Where did they keep you locked up?'

Dani closed her eyes. 'In a flat,' she said. 'I don't know where – near Piccadilly, I think.'

The woman nodded intently. 'Who were they, Ellie?' she asked. 'Who's the woman in the picture?'

For a moment, Dani didn't answer. 'She's my friend,' she said finally.

'Your friend?'

'She brought me here. She let me out.'

'Was she in the flat with you, Ellie?'

Slowly Dani nodded her head. 'She lived there. Men came to see her, too. You know, for …' Her voice trailed off.

'What's her name, Ellie?'

But Dani shook her head to indicate that she wasn't going to say any more.

Anabella persisted. 'Who did this to you, Ellie? You can tell me.'

But Dani shook her head again. She had made a promise to Ellie and somehow, despite everything, she couldn't break it. Besides, she was too embarrassed to say any more.

When it became clear that Dani wasn't going to say anything else, Anabella squeezed her hand gently. 'We'll have another chat later,' she said gently, and then she stood up. She made to take the picture from the girl, but as she did so Dani held it towards her chest.

'I … I'd like to keep it,' she said. 'Please.'

A confused look crossed Anabella's brow. 'All right,' she said hesitantly.

'Thank you,' Dani replied.

And as the woman walked out of the room, Dani found herself staring intently at that photograph. Not at the picture of herself, but at Ellie, and wondering where she was now.

As the grey light of the same dawn crept into Ellie's room, it seemed to burn her eyes – eyes that had been wide open and staring all night long. They hurt. She wanted to scratch at them. To rip them out. The blanket that normally covered her window was still on the floor; she would have liked to have put it back up, but that was not possible. Nothing was possible. All she could do was lie on her bed, sweating, suffering. It felt as though things were crawling over her skin, like insects.

The withdrawal pains were like nothing she had ever known. They seemed to burn through her whole body, making the bruises that Baxter had inflicted on her stomach the night before seem like childish little grazes. She felt like howling. At times throughout the night she thought maybe she had cried out, but she couldn't be sure.

At moments she had started to hallucinate. It had been so frightening. Around midnight, she thought she had seen Dani, standing in the doorway to her room. The little girl's face was white, like a corpse, apart from around her eyes, which were a deep scarlet. Ellie had tried to say something to her, but instantly the vision had disappeared, leaving her alone with her agony.

It was still early when Baxter returned. She didn't hear him come in; he just seemed to be there, like another hallucination, standing over her, his face set in an expression of menace. He grabbed her hair again and pulled her to her feet. Ellie was hyperventilating now, nausea oozing through her veins.

'Where is she?' Baxter asked.

Ellie closed her eyes. 'Please, Baxter,' she stammered. 'Please just give it to me.'

'*Where is she?*' he hissed.

Ellie wanted to tell him. Every ounce of her being was telling her to reveal where Dani was. She even found herself opening her mouth. But then something flashed through her mind. It was a picture of Dani, thin and bedraggled. Her arms were bare, and the skin around her veins was bruised and punctured, just like Ellie's.

She couldn't do it. She couldn't hand that little girl back to this man. Almost involuntarily, she shook her head.

Baxter started to shake with anger. He squeezed the clump of hair harder and then threw her down on to the bed again. 'Stupid fucking whore,' he muttered, before turning and leaving the room.

'Baxter!' Ellie shouted, her voice dripping with desperation. '*Baxter!*'

It was no good. He had left the flat. Ellie started to retch violently, but nothing came up.

She had no idea when he would be back. She had no idea how much longer she would have to endure this living hell.

That afternoon, Dani was allowed to shower and given a set of fresh clothes. In the evening the nice doctor from the day before gave her another dose of methadone, and she was told that she could go into the dayroom and watch some television if she wanted. Dani preferred not to. There would be other people there, and she wasn't ready to see them. Not yet.

Anabella kept popping into her room to see how she was. She wore that expression of resolute sympathy that Dani had got used to seeing on people's faces before she had arrived at Baxter's flat; and though Dani could tell she wanted to ask her lots of questions, she refrained. Dani was glad. She wasn't going to say anything to get Ellie into trouble, but she found it so difficult disappointing Anabella in this way. Much better that no one asked her about her ordeal.

It was over now, that was the main thing. She never needed to speak about it again. To anyone. What would happen in the future was not clear to her, but at the moment that didn't matter. At the moment she was out of harm's way.

An hour after her methadone dose she became sleepy and climbed back into bed. Anabella came and checked on her a final time. She stroked Dani's head almost maternally, just as Ellie had done when Dani had been ill. It felt nice. Warm, somehow. She closed her eyes and was soon asleep.

The next morning Dani awoke gently, not brutally as had been her habit in the flat. She was still bleary from the methadone, and hardly a picture of health. But she was better already. Much better. Anabella brought her breakfast in for her again, and stayed while she ate it. She glanced occasionally at the picture of Dani and Ellie, which was propped up on the bedside table, but still she refrained from asking questions.

When Dani had finished eating, she spoke. 'We could go for a little walk, Ellie,' she said.

Dani shrank back. The idea of leaving the safety of these walls made her nervous. 'No thanks,' she murmured.

Anabella smiled. 'Come on,' she encouraged softly. 'I'll be with you. Just round the block. It'll be good for you, a bit of fresh air, get some sun on your skin.' And then, even more softly, she repeated herself. 'I'll be with you,' she said.

Dani glanced around the room. 'All right,' she heard herself saying, more to be obedient to this woman who said she wanted to be her friend than anything else.

She dressed slowly, as though trying to put off the inevitable. It was strange, wearing these new clothes, after having to wear the same old ones for such a long time.

Just as she was putting her shoes on Anabella knocked on the door again. 'Ready?' she heard her call.

Dani took a shaky breath. She felt like curling up into a little ball and hiding. Hiding from everyone. From the world.

Implacably there was another knock on the door. 'Ready, Ellie?' Anabella's voice called.

There was no putting it off, Dani realised. Nervously, she went to meet her.

As they stepped outside the hostel, Dani found herself breathing heavily. 'It's all right,' her companion murmured, folding her hand over Dani's in a gesture of companionship. 'There's nothing to worry about. Just a quick stroll, remember. That's all.'

It *was* just a quick stroll, but it seemed to Dani to take an eternity. Every time they passed someone in the street, she thought they were staring at her; and more than once she saw a man from the corner of her eye and thought she recognised him from the flat. From the mattress. One of her endless succession of faceless tormentors. Each time that happened, she felt as though her heart was in her throat. Anabella seemed to sense it, and she squeezed the right hand that she was holding solicitously.

It was a relief when they got back to the hostel. Dani went straight back to her room and sat in her chair, her arms hugging her body as she recuperated from the ordeal of going outside. Anabella watched her for a while, but didn't say anything. Then she left, closing the door softly behind her.

* * *

Anabella stood for a quiet moment with her back to the door of the girl who called herself Ellie, but who was no doubt lying. They always lied at first, these people. Until they learned that they could trust her. Even then, many of them kept up the pretence of being who they weren't. And that was just the ones who stayed. Lots of the addicts who were lucky enough to end up in this place simply weren't cut out for sobriety. The methadone didn't give them the right kind of kick, and they soon left, hitting the streets in search of a better high. The staff in the hostel were powerless to do anything about it.

Something told her, though, that Ellie wouldn't be doing that. She was different from the others. More fragile, somehow. And if what the girl had hinted at was true ... Anabella shuddered. It didn't bear thinking about. But it just added substance to her inkling that she wouldn't be hitting the streets any time soon.

Anabella took a deep breath and started to walk away from the room, down the corridor to the tiny cupboard that she laughingly referred to as her office. She sat down, and though there was a pile of paperwork to get through, she remained deep in thought. Absent-mindedly she reached for her packet of slim cigarettes, before silently cursing the fact that she wasn't allowed to smoke indoors. She was on edge, and she needed something to settle her nerves.

Something was nagging her. Anabella knew the rules. She knew that they promised the addicts who ended up here anonymity; she knew that they promised not to tell anyone that they were here, or why. It was the only way a place like this could work. Drug users, almost without exception, were terrified of the police. If they thought the hostel staff would report them, they would never come. Already the work they were doing was like emptying the ocean teaspoon by teaspoon. If they lost their integrity among the junkies, they might as well not be here.

But this was different. Little Ellie, so scared and timid. Even if half the tiny amount Anabella had gleaned from her was true, she had undergone a nightmare of unimaginable proportions. The girl *said* she was sixteen, but there was no way of telling if that was true. Her ravaged face was horribly ageless. If she was sixteen, she was small for her age. And if she wasn't ...

The argument chased itself around in her head for what seemed like an age. In the end it came down to trust. Little Ellie was trusting her to keep quiet about her predicament. She was trusting her to do what she had said. To be her friend.

But a crime had been committed. A terrible one, from all Anabella could tell. And the girl had been the victim, not the perpetrator. If that was the case, there was someone out there, maybe more than one person, willing to do terrible things. She didn't know who the woman in the picture taken from the CCTV was, the one who had brought the girl here; but she must have known something. She must have been involved in some way. And if Anabella didn't do something about it, whoever had done these terrible things would be free to do them again.

It was that thought which made her mind up. The girl would be cross. She would see it as a betrayal of trust. But there were bigger issues at stake here, and the police would be sensitive. She would ask them to give it a couple of days, and not to come to the hostel itself – that would cause panic among the inmates. When the time was right, she would take Dani to them. Gently persuade her that she had done nothing wrong; and to tell her, and then them, everything that had happened.

She nodded to herself, as though to affirm that she had made the right decision. Then she reached into a drawer below her desk and pulled out a black folder. Opening it at the first page, she found what she was looking for: a list of numbers protected by a see-through polythene wallet. With her index finger she scanned down them until she found the one she wanted.

Then, with a breath that was as deep as her sense of misgiving, she picked up the phone and dialled.

When Baxter returned, he wasn't alone: Mr Morgan was with him. As always, Ellie's former client was wearing a suit, but the tie was undone slightly and he looked more dishevelled than usual. Tired. Stressed. It was written all over his square face, which was unusually grim. It seemed odd to Ellie that he should be there, but she was in no state to think about it.

The two men stood by the doorway, staring at her as though they were looking at a caged animal in a zoo. Their faces bore expressions of disgust, and Ellie felt she knew why. No doubt she was a disgusting sight. She sat on the edge of her bed, as she had done for she didn't know how long, her breath coming in short, desperate gasps, like sobs.

It seemed an age before anyone spoke.

'You didn't need to come,' Baxter said. 'I've got it sorted.' At first, Ellie thought he was talking to her, and she was confused; but it was Morgan who answered.

'You have *not*,' the man replied slowly, almost contemptuously, 'got it sorted, Baxter. If you had it sorted, the girl would be here now.' They were speaking to each other almost as if Ellie wasn't there.

Baxter's face turned sour. 'I don't see why you can't do more to help,' he replied. 'It's your neck on the line as much as mine. If the girl sings, you—'

'If the girl sings,' Morgan interrupted, 'it'll be your blood they're after. Trust me, Baxter. I'm on top of it. I've got a lot less to worry about than you have.'

'If you've got nothing to worry about,' Baxter spat, 'what the hell are you doing here?'

Morgan didn't seem to have an answer for that.

'You've done fuck all,' Baxter continued, his face turning slightly red now. 'Fuck all since she disappeared.'

'There's nothing I *can* do,' Morgan snapped. 'I can get the police to turn a blind eye to this place, Baxter. But if she goes to them, if she makes a statement, that's it. Out of my hands. You need another plan. You know what they do with people like you in jail?'

'People like *me*?' Baxter scoffed. 'I never touched her – not like that, anyway.' He looked meaningfully at Morgan.

'Try telling them that in Strangeways, Baxter,' Morgan replied blandly. 'You need to get this one to tell you where the girl is, and you need to do it now.'

Baxter turned his attention back to Ellie. 'Oh, I will,' he said quietly. 'I will. I'm not doing bird on anyone's account, least of all hers.' His lips twitched aggressively.

Ellie turned to face him. Her whole body was racked with pain, as though fire was pumping through her veins instead of blood; but despite all that she felt a surge of overwhelming loathing for Baxter. She sneered at him, and though she found herself unable to speak, it was clear from Baxter's face that he understood everything that sneer was intended to convey.

Morgan sniffed. 'Why don't you leave her with me?' he said. 'You're obviously not as persuasive as you think.'

Baxter's eyes narrowed as he looked from Morgan to Ellie and then back again. 'Fine,' he muttered, before turning and leaving the room.

An ominous silence filled the space between Ellie and Mr Morgan, a silence punctuated only by her heavy breathing as he stood there and continued to stare at her. He seemed unnaturally calm, as though he was considering something, weighing things up, deciding on a plan of action. Then, equally calmly, he walked towards Ellie and sat next to her on the bed. For all the world he seemed like a friend coming to comfort someone in distress.

Ellie refused to look at him.

'You have to tell Baxter where she is,' the man told her.

Ellie shut her eyes and shivered. 'What's it to you?' she hissed.

For a moment Morgan didn't reply. When he did, his voice was barely audible. 'It's not as much to me,' he breathed, 'as it is to you.'

Slowly, he stretched out his hand and took her by the chin, turning her head to look at him. 'Baxter's holding back your smack, right?'

Ellie winced.

'You think that's bad?' he continued relentlessly. 'You think that's the only thing he's got up his sleeve? Baxter's a bastard, Ellie. I'm no Mother Teresa, but even *I* think he's a nasty bastard. And he's desperate. If you don't tell him where the girl is, what do you think he's going to do? Leave it at that?'

Ellie didn't reply.

'You think he'll just put up with it?' He squeezed her face a little bit harder. 'Well, do you?'

She was forced to shake her head.

'No,' Morgan whispered. 'I don't think so either. He won't kill you, of course. Not yet. Not while you still know where she is. But you'll probably wish you were dead. Know what I mean?'

His eyes were little more than slits now, gazing coldly at her.

'I said, do you know what I mean?'

His nails were digging into her skin now.

'*Get out of here*,' Ellie hissed. 'Just get the hell out of here.'

Morgan didn't move, for a moment. Then he gently let his hand drop, stood up and, without looking back, left the room. The door remained open, however, and Ellie could see him standing in the hallway and just hear what he said to Baxter, his voice dripping with warning and menace.

'Find out where the girl is, Baxter,' he hissed, glancing back into the room at her. 'Do whatever it takes, but find out where she is. This has gone on too long already.'

And without another word, he left.

Baxter didn't return immediately. Ellie was left alone with a sharp taste of anticipation in her mouth. Her body was screaming out for a fix; but through the mist of her addiction, she could sense that things were about to go badly for her.

She just prayed she could deal with it.

When Baxter returned, he seemed to be carrying something, but he cradled his hands in such a way that Ellie couldn't quite tell what it was.

She found out soon enough.

Baxter's knife gleamed momentarily as he swung it towards her. It sliced her cheek with remarkable ease, the flesh offering no resistance to the razor-sharp blade. Ellie gasped, not out of pain – not at first – but out of surprise. It had been totally unexpected, and it took a few seconds for her sluggish brain to register what had happened. Then the sensation came, jagged and piercing. She felt it not only in her cheek but all the way down that side of her body. It was only as her hand moved involuntarily up to the wound that she realised how suddenly and heavily she was bleeding.

Ellie started to panic. She had never liked the sight of her own blood, and now it was oozing over her hand and down her wrist. Baxter stood back, eyeing her clinically, almost as though he was surveying a picture he had just painted. He still held his knife slightly in the air; in a brief moment of detachment, Ellie could see a faint streak of red on it.

'Please, Baxter,' she whimpered, terror almost pushing away the horrible feelings of withdrawal. '*Please*.'

But she didn't even know what she was begging him for.

As her breathing became heavier, Baxter approached her again. Using his free hand, he grabbed her by the throat, seemingly ignoring the way her freely flowing blood oozed over his own hand now. Clutching her firmly in a stranglehold that made her breathing rasp, he held the blade of the knife gently against that part of her neck that was not entwined by his rough, coarse fingers.

Ellie had never known such fear; she had never known her stomach to freeze like this, never known the sensation of her blood stopping pumping in her veins. Her face was a sticky mess of warm moisture, and the cut on her cheek shrieked angrily. But worse than that, worse than any of it – worse even than the withdrawal symptoms that she had been suffering over the past twenty-four hours – was the look on Baxter's face.

It was not angry.

It was not mad.

It was just resolute. Calm.

'If you don't tell me where she is,' he whispered, 'I'll cut you up so bad you'll wish you were dead.'

And he would. She knew it. His eyes were flat and hard, his breathing deep and measured. He would do what he said.

The gash on her cheek kept bleeding – her hand was obviously not enough to stem the tide. Her body, which had been uncomfortably hot before, was now horribly cold. Baxter's eyes narrowed slightly, then widened again; and she felt the knife press slightly harder against the flesh of her neck. Her eyes darted around. She looked into his face, and then down at the wrist that was holding the knife. Just one flick – that was all it would take. A single flick, a movement of a couple of inches. His hand was perfectly still, perfectly steady. He was in control of it. If it happened, it wouldn't be an accident. It would be just what he meant.

Ellie found she was holding her breath through terror, doing her best to remain absolutely still.

She tried not to think of the blissful oblivion a syringe-ful of junk would bring.

She tried not to think of her own corpse, lifeless, lying on the floor of that room. Unwanted and unloved. Unfound for days.

But the more she tried to put these images from her mind, the more they flashed in front of her.

'If you don't tell me where she is right now,' Baxter whispered, 'I'll do it. You'll bleed to death in this room, and no one will be here to help you.'

She was almost too afraid to speak, in case the movement caused her skin to slice against the blade. But she had to. 'Please, Baxter,' she whispered. 'She's just a little girl. She promised me she wouldn't say nothing. *She promised me.*'

Silence.

No movement.

Then he moved his hands away.

Relief crashed over her. She moved her free hand up to that part of her neck against which the knife had been pressed, and delicately touched the skin. As she did so, however, she saw Baxter raise the knife. His faced tensed into an expression of bitter fury, and with a sudden brutality he started to swing the blade back down towards her.

Ellie screamed and threw her body to one side – a final, desperate attempt to save her skin. She fell heavily to the floor, moving her arms over her head to shield it from the blow to come. And as she curled up to protect herself, she heard herself shouting.

It was as if there was someone else's voice in her mouth, as if her words – words that shocked her, but which she knew were true – were being controlled by some force other than her own.

'Stop!' she yelled. 'Baxter, stop! I'll tell you where she is. Please don't! I can't take it any more. I'll tell you where she is, all right? *I'll tell you where she is!*'

Chapter Sixteen

Anabella walked hand in hand with Ellie, or whatever her name really was.

It was their second walk, on the second full morning since the girl's arrival at the hostel. She seemed a little less nervous this time, but still desperately frail, jumping at the slightest thing. Her eyes were everywhere, Anabella noticed, but they rested on nothing, as if she did not want to draw attention to herself by staring at anyone or anything too hard.

The hostel was just off Brick Lane, and for their first walk Anabella had avoided that road. It was too busy, too full of pedestrians, too full of restaurant owners calling out to passers-by and trying to cajole them into their premises. It would have been a bit much for the girl on her first excursion; but today Anabella thought she would try it. If Ellie grew too fearful, they could always turn into one of the many side streets, much like the one they were in now, away from the crowds.

Suddenly, Anabella stopped.

She didn't know what it was, but something made her look back over her shoulder.

'What's the matter?' Ellie asked.

Anabella paused. There were a few people in the street, most of them heading in the same direction towards Brick Lane, all of them nondescript. One man stopped and looked in a shop window; another pulled a packet of cigarettes from his pocket and lowered his face as he was walking to light the fag. Nothing out of the ordinary. Anabella shook her head in vague annoyance with herself. She'd had a strange feeling, as though someone was watching them. Following them. But it was stupid. She was probably just on edge, made nervous by Ellie's anxiety.

'Come on,' she said, pointing towards the bustle of Brick Lane. 'Let's go this way.'

As they turned on to the main street, she felt Ellie's hand clutch hers a little more tightly, and the girl's pace slowed down somewhat. 'It's all right,' Anabella murmured, stepping confidently forward and smiling down at her. 'It's all right.'

They meandered slowly up Brick Lane. Anabella liked it here. With her dreadlocks and ethnic clothing she felt she blended in, not as in some other parts of London, where she was definitely considered a curiosity. It was slightly strange that Ellie didn't seem to be concerned too much by her appearance; but then, if the snippets the girl had told her held any truth whatsoever, she probably had ways of judging people unconnected to what sort of haircut they had.

Now and then Anabella would stop outside the window of some shop or other, pointing out the contents to Ellie in a bright voice that they both knew was slightly forced. Ellie did her best to look interested, but it was clear that her attention was fixed elsewhere: on the people all around her, the people she obviously found so threatening. All the while, she clung tightly to Anabella, as though her life depended on it. When the older woman slipped into a newsagent's to buy cigarettes, she considered leaving Ellie on the pavement, but on second thoughts she decided that her charge wouldn't welcome that suggestion, and so she took her into the cramped little shop anyway.

'You want some chocolate?' she asked as they approached the counter.

Ellie shook her head – rather emphatically, Anabella thought. She considered asking her why, but at the last minute decided not to. Instead, she paid quickly for her cigarettes and took her outside again.

They had been wandering for perhaps twenty minutes when she heard the girl gasp.

'What's the matter, Ellie?' Anabella looked down at Ellie. She seemed frozen to the spot, and her face was the colour of one of the white cotton sheets back at the hostel. She didn't speak.

'What is it?' Anabella pressed.

Still the girl didn't speak. Her head was moving about, scanning the street, and her eyes were darting all over the place like flies round a campfire. Her breathing was heavy and shaky.

Anabella bent down to her height and took her gently by the shoulders. 'Ellie,' she urged. 'Look at me.'

Ellie did so. Her face was full of fear.

'What is it?' Anabella repeated her question.

'I thought I saw someone,' the girl muttered.

'Saw someone? Who?' There was something about her claim that made Anabella feel deeply uncomfortable.

Maybe it was the sensation she herself had experienced in the side street. Maybe it was something else.

Ellie's forehead furrowed. 'I don't know,' she replied weakly, unconvincingly. She looked around again, and then her tense body seemed to crumple slightly. 'Sorry,' she said in a quiet voice. 'I keep thinking I see people. People from ...' Her voice trailed away. 'It doesn't matter,' she concluded feebly.

Anabella surveyed the girl's face, not knowing what to say. There was so much wrong with this little girl. Not just the drugs – though she knew heroin made you paranoid – but other stuff. Stuff Anabella thought she could never fathom.

'There's no one,' she whispered. 'Just you and me. It's OK.'

Ellie's eyes fell to the floor. 'Can we go back now?' she asked, her eyes wide.

Anabella smiled. 'Of course we can,' she said, as kindly as she could make her voice sound. 'Of course we can.'

Hayley Carter processed her pile of papers almost unthinkingly.

There was a buzz all around the station. It was one of those days. Busy. Impossibly busy. Officers running round like headless chickens, people shouting across the open-plan office and files landing heavily on Hayley's desk. It was like this sometimes – something to do with the fact that the sun had started shining recently. Criminals generally seemed to be busier in the sunshine. Made sense, Hayley always thought, that they didn't want to go out to work when it was raining. Made life busier for the police, though. And busier for her.

It wasn't helped, of course, by the fact that DCI Barker hardly seemed to have been in the office over the past few days. Under ordinary circumstances, that would have been quite to Hayley's liking; but at the moment, when the station could do with a bit of organisation from the top down, it seemed pretty irresponsible to her. But he was here today, biting the heads off anyone who dared to try to speak to him. He was more aggressive than usual – everyone could see that, and nobody knew why – so Hayley just kept her head down and ploughed through her secretarial work. The last thing she wanted was to be at the sharp end of Barker's tongue. Not today.

Ryan was across the room, busy like all the others. Occasionally their eyes would meet, and when that happened Hayley would immediately pull her gaze away, feeling awkward. They had barely spoken since that night when he had bought her a drink and handed her the details of her daughter. He had tried to, but she'd been cold, hard and unreceptive. Each time she brushed him off, his honest face looked confused and a bit embarrassed. Hayley knew she was treating him badly; she knew her behaviour demanded an explanation. But the truth was that she didn't have one – she just had the vague sense that she too was embarrassed to tell him what she had been up to. Embarrassed by her ridiculous attempt to dress up like a policewoman; embarrassed by her belief that somehow she would be able to track down the little girl she abandoned all those years ago. It made her face burn just to think about it now. Hayley was a secretary, not a cop. She should stick to what she was good at. She took another file, opened it and started inputting the information it contained on to her computer.

About mid-morning she stopped to make herself a cup of coffee. Carrying it back from the small kitchenette that serviced everyone in the station, she caught another glimpse of Barker. He was square faced, with a dark expression; his tie was already undone. There was no one else in the glass-walled cubicle that served as his office, and he was standing up, one thumb in his mouth as he chewed nervously at the cuticle. He seemed a million miles away. As Hayley passed the office, their eyes met; just as she had with Ryan, she pulled her gaze instantly away. She didn't want to get into any kind of discussion with Barker, not when he was in the mood he was so obviously in today.

She took her seat, sipped her drink and picked up the next file from her pile.

Opening it, she skim-read the report. An Anabella Reese had called the station yesterday. It seemed she was a care-worker at a hostel near Aldgate for recovering drug addicts. A sixteen-year-old girl had made a disclosure to her, and she had felt beholden to report this. A duty officer had met her away from the hostel – the sight of police was likely to worry the recovering addicts – to take her statement. It had been requested that no further action be taken until the girl in question was in a better state of health.

Hayley found it difficult not to raise a cynical eyebrow. The way everything was in the station at the moment, they'd be lucky to get someone over to them this side of Christmas. She sighed and started to key the details into her machine.

It was only when she turned the page that she saw the photograph.

Her blood ran cold in her veins.

It was grainy and indistinct. Hayley had seen enough CCTV images to realise that this was one. There were two people in it: a tall woman with long hair and a gaunt face, and a girl. Her features were sallow and thin, and there were huge dark rings around her wide eyes. If you were looking at this girl for the first time, Hayley thought, you wouldn't know how old she was. She seemed somehow ageless. But Hayley wasn't looking at her for the first time. Indeed, that face – or at least a less thin, less bedraggled version of it – had been etched on her mind for the past few weeks. She would know it anywhere.

'Dani,' she breathed, so quietly that she barely heard herself speak. The bustle all around her seemed to have dissolved, so that she was barely aware of it. All there was was her and the picture. The picture of Dani. The picture of her little girl.

Hayley felt a momentary pang as her eyes flickered to the image of the other woman in the picture. A pang of jealousy. Who was she? What was she doing with her daughter? What had she done to her?

Her mouth was dry.

Her stomach was lurching.

'Hayley!'

She heard the voice, but it didn't puncture the bubble that surrounded her.

'*Hayley!*' Sharper now. She blinked and looked up.

It was Ryan. He was standing over her, his brow furrowed in an expression of concern. 'Are you all right?

You look like …' His voice trailed away – clearly he didn't know *what* she looked like.

Hayley looked up at him. Her face, she was aware, must have been betraying the myriad emotions that were now coursing through her. As nonchalantly as she could, she closed the file on her desk. Ryan didn't seem to notice – all his attention seemed to be on Hayley herself. That was good. She couldn't say why, but for some reason she didn't want anyone looking at the picture. Anyone knowing what she knew.

Hayley looked down, placed the file to one side and then turned her attention back to Ryan.

She smiled, the action taking all her effort.

'I'm fine,' she said.

Her voice cracked as she spoke, so she tried again.

'It's nothing. Nothing at all. I'm fine.'

It had taken Dani all of the previous day to recover from her walk with Anabella.

She knew, deep down, that she had been foolish. She knew that the men she kept seeing from the corner of her eye, the ones who looked like the clients who used to visit her in the flat, were not really who they seemed to be. She knew it was her mind playing tricks on her.

But he had seemed so real. The hair. The smart clothes. The eyes. Especially the eyes. The figure in the street yesterday had looked so much like Baxter that the briefest glimpse of him had caused her body to drain through terror. He had been barely twenty metres away from them, walking in the same direction. Dani had moved her horrified head round so that he wouldn't see her face; but somehow she was drawn to the sight of him, and she had looked around again.

When she did, he was gone. Just another trick of the mind. A walking hallucination.

But it had affected her badly. Upset her. It wasn't really him, she knew, but it brought it all back. The relentless, unending horror. It made her live it all again. That was why she had acted like that in front of Anabella; that was why, even once she got back to the safety of the hostel, her nerves were frayed and the hostel workers kept looking in on her, every half hour, to check she was all right. When her nightly dose of methadone came it was a relief, not because she knew it would stave off the feelings of withdrawal – feelings that she sensed were becoming less intense as the days passed – but because she knew it would make her drowsy. Sleep had seemed very welcome.

Now it was the next morning, and Anabella had just knocked on her door, wanting to take her out again. Their daily walk. Dani didn't want to go; but she wanted to please her caseworker. The strange-looking woman with the dreadlocked hair and the colourful clothes had been so kind to her – kinder almost than anyone had ever been – that she didn't want to let her down. So she had done her best to smile and agreed to go out.

It would only be for a few minutes. Then she could come back again, and sit alone in her little room, where she felt the most comfortable.

The sun was bright again today. It made Dani's eyes squint as she stepped outside, like a little mole that had taken a wrong turning. Anabella clutched her hand, and they walked for a while in companionable silence, along the same route as the one they had taken yesterday, towards the busy street that she had said was called Brick Lane.

'I need to tell you something, Ellie,' Anabella said in her husky voice after they had been strolling for about five minutes. She sounded kind of serious, and Dani looked up at her expectantly.

'You know when you first got here, a few days ago?'

Dani nodded.

'You told me something then, didn't you? About someone keeping you locked up. About someone making you do things.'

Dani looked away, embarrassed. She didn't know why, but she wished she had kept quiet.

'I don't want you to think I went behind your back, Ellie. I don't want you to think you can't trust me.'

Dani stopped. A chill went through her. Slowly she turned to look up at Anabella, who returned that look with a serious gaze, almost a frown. And when she spoke, it was in little more than a whisper.

'You told,' she breathed. 'You told someone.'

Anabella bent down to her level. 'I had to, Ellie. I had to tell the police. If there's someone out there—'

'The *police*?' Dani was aghast. Terrified. 'But they'll—' She stopped herself in mid-sentence. There was so much she hadn't told Anabella, so much she wanted to keep secret. If the police came, they would find out who she was. They would take her away, put her in places she didn't want to be. She shivered at the thought. She could say nothing. But her face, she realised, said it all.

'It's all right,' Anabella insisted quietly. 'I've told them not to come and talk to you until you're ready. And you won't be in trouble – because of the drugs, I mean. That's not what they'll be interested in. But you need to tell them the truth, Ellie, when they do come.'

Dani didn't know what to say. Her face fell to the ground.

'Come on,' Anabella said with forced enthusiasm. 'Let's keep walking.'

They continued, but the silence between them was now awkward rather than companionable. Dani was almost pleased when they turned into the bustle of Brick Lane, although the remnants of yesterday's hallucinations were still with her, and it was unnerving to be in the same place where the ghost of Baxter had haunted her.

It was noisy in the road, but Dani barely heard the sounds around her as they walked past the now familiar shops and cafés. When they came to the newsagent's where Anabella had bought cigarettes yesterday, they stopped again.

'Need some fags,' Anabella said shortly. 'You coming in?'

Dani hesitated. There was so much going round in her head that for some reason she felt she wanted to be by herself, even if it was just for a couple of minutes. She smiled weakly at Anabella. 'Think I'll stay out here,' she said simply.

Anabella inclined her head in agreement and then disappeared, leaving Dani to wait in the street with her back pressed against the brick wall by the shop. Passers-by sauntered past, but none of them paid her any attention; Dani felt comfortably anonymous among the crowds.

That comfortable anonymity did not last for long.

She seemed to appear out of nowhere. At first Dani thought it was another hallucination, another trick of the mind. It was like a dream as she walked towards her, her unmistakable platinum hair blowing slightly in the breeze, and Dani felt inclined to dismiss it as such. But as she grew closer, walking across the street against the flow of people hurrying up and down, it became quite clear that this was no dream.

'*Ellie*,' Dani gasped.

The closer she got, the more nightmarish the vision became. Ellie's face was paler than Dani had ever seen it, and across one of the cheeks there was an angry scar, glistening slightly in the sun. Wet. It was a new scar – that much was obvious. Her eyes were sunken and bloodshot, and her lips were strangely colourless. She smiled, and it clearly took all her effort.

'Dani,' she rasped.

Dani looked nervously around her. 'What are you doing here?'

Ellie's face twitched slightly. 'Wanted to see how you were doing, didn't I?'

Silence. Ellie was standing right by her now, looking down.

'Come with me,' Ellie said abruptly. 'I want to show you something.'

Dani glanced into the shop. 'I'd better—' she started to say.

'It won't take a minute. You'll be right back.' She grabbed Dani's hand and pulled her away from the newsagent's, off the pavement and on to the road.

'Wait!' Dani whimpered, but as she did so, Ellie looked at her with a hurt expression.

'It's only me, Dani,' she said. She looked left and right, and there was something nervous about her demeanour. 'I just wanted to see you. Come on, it won't take a minute.'

It all happened so quickly, and Dani seemed to have no control over it. A man with a beard bumped into them as they crossed the street, and as Ellie pulled Dani along the pavement back down the way they came, they seemed to be swimming against the tide, dodging people coming the other way.

'Where we going?' Dani asked breathlessly, but Ellie didn't answer.

Within seconds they came to a side street. It was deserted – a stark contrast to the bustle of Brick Lane. The buildings, made of old, brown brick, were high on either side and seemed imposing, threatening. Looking back over her shoulder, Dani could still just see the newsagent's, but it disappeared from sight as Ellie continued tugging her along.

At the end of the road there was a car park – a large, grey space about half filled with vehicles. There was barely anybody around: just a few bored-looking workmen in bright yellow coats standing by a hole in the ground that had been cordoned off with orange tape. The quiet seemed suddenly sinister, and Dani started to struggle more violently. Ellie's bony hands, however, gripped her tightly, and there was nothing the little girl could do to get away. She opened her mouth and screamed, but the noise that came out was barely audible – certainly not loud enough to attract the attention of the workmen.

They were in the car park now, surrounded by vehicles. Ellie stopped and, still clutching Dani's hand, turned to look at her. Dani gasped when she saw her face. It had looked bad before, but not like this: ravaged, tormented. Tears were streaming from her reddened eyes, and her mouth was fixed in a kind of inhuman grimace. She seemed to be trying to speak, but she was momentarily unable to get the words out. Finally, though, Dani understood what she was trying to say.

'I'm sorry,' she whimpered. *'I'm sorry, titch. I'm so sorry.'*

And as she spoke, she suddenly stood upright and seemed to be looking beyond Dani. The tears stopped, but the look of agonised torment didn't go away. If anything, it got worse. Ellie loosened her grip on Dani and took a step back.

A cold dread crept over the little girl. There was someone standing behind her. She could sense it. Slowly, she turned around, her eyes half closed, as though she knew she was going to see a monster but was too scared to look it fully in the face.

She was half expecting to see him, but still it was a jolt when his features filled her vision. Baxter's face was unsmiling, his lips set in a foul expression of hatred.

Dani stepped back. Every muscle in her body shrieked at her to run, and she looked round to see what her escape routes were. Her limbs would not move, however; like in a dream she sometimes had when she knew she had to escape some unknown danger but was unable to do so. This danger, though, was far from unknown. It was real. In front of her. He had come. He had tracked her down. And now that he had found her, she knew he wouldn't let her escape again.

A whimper escaped her throat as Baxter stepped forward and grabbed the hand that Ellie had held so firmly. Only then did he speak.

'Thought you'd go for a little holiday, did you, lassie?' he asked. His voice dripped contempt and seemed to Dani to promise all the horrors that were in store for her.

Baxter looked at Ellie. 'Get in the car,' he spat.

Ellie nodded fearfully, and turned towards an old brown saloon car that was parked nearby. Opening the front passenger door, she climbed inside. Baxter roughly pushed Dani in the direction of the vehicle, his strong, rough hands still clutching her wrist.

Panic overcame her. She had to get away. As though they had been suddenly freed from a coil of tight chains, Dani's limbs started to flail violently as she tried to escape. Anabella was nearby. If only she could get to her, run the few metres that separated them, she would be safe.

But Baxter's grip tightened, and he used his other hand to cover her mouth and stifle the screams she had barely realised she was making. He let go only temporarily when, having pushed her towards the car, he needed one hand to open the back door. He pushed Dani brutally inside, and the door slammed behind her.

She tried to open it again as Baxter hurried round to the driver's side, but it was locked from the inside. Ellie sat silently, her face shocked, as Dani banged ferociously against the window, filling the car with the sound of her desperate yelling.

It didn't do any good. Baxter climbed into the car, turned on the engine and calmly drove away.

Chapter Seventeen

As Anabella stepped out of the newsagent's, she was already unwrapping the cellophane from around the cigarette packet.

'I'm gasping,' she said huskily to Ellie, looking round to smile ruefully at the girl. Her brow furrowed slightly. Ellie wasn't where she had been a minute ago. Anabella looked over her shoulder, and then all around. A sinister, empty feeling washed over her stomach: a feeling of panic.

'Ellie,' she whispered. Then, more loudly, '*Ellie!*'

Where was she? Where the hell was she? Anabella realised that her fingers were crushing the cigarette packet as her eyes darted helplessly all around. She felt she should run – run and search – but she didn't know which way to go and instead found herself rooted to the spot. Desperately she looked into the crowds, hoping to see Ellie's troubled face, hoping to see those wide eyes and that serious expression. But she couldn't.

Anabella stepped on to the pavement. Maybe Ellie had gone into another shop, wandering off as kids do. Briskly she stepped into the shop next door – a jumbled place selling trinkets and smelling of joss sticks. She scanned the faces of the few customers, but there was no sign of her. No sign, either, in the next shop. Or the next. And with each passing second, Anabella's panic increased. She started to curse herself. How stupid she had been, telling Ellie while they were out and about that she had gone to the police! She should have done it back at the hostel – somewhere safe and familiar, where Ellie would have fewer opportunities to run away. There was no doubt in her mind that that was what she had done – run away. It happened so often with these young people. They got halfway down the path to recovery, and then …

'Damn it,' she spat suddenly. '*Damn it, damn it.*' A couple of passers-by gave her strange looks, but she barely noticed them. Anabella saw a nearby side street. If she had been trying to run away, that's where she would have gone. She rushed down there, finding herself in a half-empty car park. But there was no sign of Ellie – just an old brown saloon car leaving the car park and driving back up the side street towards Brick Lane.

'Shit,' Anabella hissed. It was useless. There was no way she was going to find the girl. She closed her eyes, opened them again and then strode back up the side street and on to Brick Lane, heading quickly back to the hostel to tell the others what had happened.

She arrived there soon enough, out of breath and still panicking. Rushing in through the main entrance, she practically crashed in to Amber, one of her colleagues.

'Anabella,' she exclaimed. 'What's the matter?'

Anabella caught her breath for a moment before answering. 'Ellie,' she replied. 'Have you seen her?'

Amber's eyes narrowed. 'Funny you should say that,' she said.

A surge of hope rose in Anabella's breast. 'What do you mean?' she demanded. 'Is she here? Did she come back here? Where is she?'

But Amber was shaking her head. 'I haven't seen her,' she said, stretching out one arm and placing it on Anabella's shoulder. 'Calm down, love,' she told her colleague and Anabella nodded. She took several deep breaths before looking back expectantly at Amber, wanting to hear what she had to say. 'Someone's just arrived,' she said. 'A woman. Mid-twenties, maybe. She had a copy of that CCTV picture. To be honest, she was gabbling a bit. She said she knew the girl. I was just coming to look for you, actually.'

A chill seemed to surround Anabella. Who was this woman? How was she going to explain what had happened – that Ellie had run away while in her care? 'Where is she?' the care worker asked her colleague.

'In the day room,' Amber replied. 'There was no one in there and I thought it would be more comfortable than, well, anywhere else. Are you all right, Anabella? What's happened?'

'Ellie's run away.'

Amber sighed and rolled her eyes slightly. When she spoke again it was in hushed, comforting tones. 'We can only help them if they *want* to be helped,' she said, repeating the mantra that they had all spoken at some time in the past.

Anabella nodded sadly. 'I know,' she said. 'I suppose I'd better go and talk to this woman. Did you get her name?'

'Yeah,' Amber replied. 'Yeah, I did. She said her name was Hayley something. Hayley Carter.' She smiled in solidarity. 'Good luck,' she said, before turning and leaving Anabella alone and still somewhat breathless in the hallway.

* * *

Hayley sat alone and nervous, looking around the small, strange room in which she had been placed by the hostel worker, who was clearly rather taken aback by her hysterical arrival. In her right hand, she clutched the picture that she had taken from the file back at the station, holding on to it as if it were Dani herself.

It was a cheaply furnished room. The walls were a grubby magnolia and there were five or six uncomfortable-looking armchairs, with a coffee table in the middle, on which a few old magazines had been scattered. Hayley glanced at the photo again and as her eyes fell once more upon the picture of the little girl, her glance turned into a stare. As she stared, the door opened and a woman appeared. To Hayley she looked rather forbidding, with her dreadlocked hair pulled tightly back across her scalp, and her piercings and ethnic clothes. She stood up nervously, but the look that this woman returned her seemed equally anxious.

'Hello,' Hayley said weakly. 'I, er … They said I could talk to someone about this.' She held up the picture.

The dreadlocked woman stepped inside. 'Are you Hayley Carter?' she asked. Her voice was throaty and it seemed to have a slight quiver in it.

Hayley nodded mutely.

'I'm Anabella.' She pointed at the photograph. 'Where did you get that?'

Hayley's eyes fell to the floor. 'I'd rather not say,' she replied.

'Do you know something about Ellie?' There was a hint of accusation in the woman's voice now. 'Do you know something about—'

'Her name's not Ellie,' Hayley interrupted.

A silence.

'How do you know?'

'I just – I just know.'

'What's her name, then?'

Hayley bit her lip. For some reason she didn't want to say. 'Is she here?'

They locked gazes. Anabella shook her head. There was something in her demeanour that made Hayley's blood run cold.

'I was told she was here. The woman I just spoke to, she said she was here.'

Now it was Anabella's turn to bow her head. 'She was,' she said. 'But she isn't any more.'

'Why? What have you done with her?'

Anabella suddenly raised her head. '*Done with her*? I haven't *done* anything with her. I've been trying to help her. But clearly not trying enough. She ran away from me, just now when we were out walking.'

Cold dread filled Hayley's veins. 'What do you mean, she ran away?'

'I mean what I said. Who are you, anyway? What's it to you? Why have you got that picture?' But as Anabella fired her questions at her, Hayley was already stepping forward. She grabbed the woman by her hands and looked appealingly, desperately into her eyes.

'You have to help,' Hayley pleaded quietly. 'You have to help me find her.'

Again there was a silence, and Hayley felt that this woman was sizing her up. 'Ellie had a bad past,' Anabella said finally. 'How do I know you're not trying to find her to hurt her? How do I know you have her best interests at heart?'

Hayley took a step back. 'Please,' she whispered. '*Please*. I've seen the police report – I work at the police station. You can't tell anyone that I came here, but please tell me what you know?'

As she spoke, she saw something change in the woman's face, as if Hayley's reaction had been enough to make her question her scepticism.

Anabella blinked and then spoke quietly. 'Why don't we sit down?' she suggested.

They took seats next to each other. Hayley continued to grip the picture, as if doing so would somehow relieve the churning of her stomach.

'When Ellie arrived,' Anabella said, 'she had an addiction to heroin.'

Hayley closed her eyes. Somehow, having this information confirmed by a real person made it a hundred times worse. Unbidden, the words that the man at the children's home had said to her popped into her head. *Dani Sinclair was quite a difficult little girl.* It sounded as if she was more than difficult. Was she just a junkie, like the kids she heard the officers back at the station talk about? Was that why she had stolen money from the children's home? Yet, glancing down once more at the picture, Hayley couldn't quite believe she knew the whole story. A mother's instinct? Sheer bloody-mindedness? Call it what you like, the truth was that the little girl needed her help.

'You said she told you things.'

Anabella nodded. 'If you've read the report, then surely you must know.'

Hayley took a deep breath. 'The abuse?'

'She said she was locked up. That men used to visit her. It's why I went to the police. She begged me not to, but …' Anabella spread her hands out in a gesture of hopelessness and Hayley felt her skin prickle at the thought of what this woman was saying.

'Why did she run away?'

Anabella looked at her with undisguised sympathy. 'They often do,' she said.

'They? What do you mean, they?'

'Addicts.'

The word seemed to echo round the room.

'I'll inform the relevant people,' Anabella said, breaking the silence. 'But she's sixteen, so if my experience is anything to go by, she'll just join a long list of missing persons.' She suddenly looked abashed. 'It's my fault,' she continued. 'I told her I'd informed the police about her. I told her just now, before she went. It was stupid of me. It makes them nervous, the idea of the police. And when heroin users don't want to be found …'

Hayley barely seemed to be listening. 'She said she was sixteen?' she interrupted.

Anabella nodded.

Hayley looked away. 'You have to tell me everything,' she insisted with uncharacteristic robustness. 'Everything she said. Anything that might give me a clue where to find her.'

Anabella looked at her helplessly. 'There isn't much,' she whispered. 'She was so quiet.'

'*Anything*,' Hayley begged.

Anabella closed her eyes, as though concentrating. 'All she said was that they kept her locked up, and that they made her do things.'

'Did she say where?'

Anabella opened her eyes. 'Yes,' she said slowly. 'Yes, now you mention it, she did. Piccadilly. But she seemed a bit vague. I didn't really get the impression she knew one part of London from another.'

'Piccadilly,' Hayley whispered almost to herself. A busy place for a little girl. 'Is that it?' she asked the hostel worker. 'Was there anything else? Anything at all? Did she say who the other person in the picture was?'

Anabella shook her head. 'She didn't say her name. I think, though, from what she said, that she was a prostitute.'

'A prostitute?' Hayley breathed.

'Ellie said she lived in the flat with her. The flat where they locked her up. She said men used to come and visit her.'

The two women sat there wordlessly. The implications of what Anabella was saying made horrific visions appear in Hayley's mind, visions that she had no choice but to expel. The idea of her little girl keeping the company of prostitutes, being locked up, using drugs and being sexually abused – it was all too much. She had to find her. She *had* to.

Suddenly she stood up. 'I have to go,' she said.

Anabella looked momentarily startled, but quickly recovered herself as Hayley walked to the door.

'Hayley,' she said sharply. Hayley turned. 'You will let me know, won't you? If you find her, I mean.'

Slowly Hayley nodded her head. 'Yes,' she said. 'I'll let you know.'

'And Hayley?' Anabella's voice had a distinct tremble in it.

'Yes?'

'What's her name? Her real name, I mean.'

Hayley blinked. 'Dani,' she said shortly, before turning around once more and leaving Anabella in the room.

'Get up there.'

Baxter's voice was quiet and all the more terrifying for that. He had grabbed Dani by her arm – the bad one, the one she had cut – and she felt the tips of his fingers dig harshly into her skin as he pulled her from the car, which he had parked up on the kerb just outside the door she recognised so well even though she had only seen it twice. The door to the flat. He didn't have to tell her not to scream; it went without saying that if she did that, she could expect something brutal. Dani wasn't sure she'd have been able to scream anyway: she was too scared.

She stumbled as she climbed the stairs, Baxter still holding on to her arm, pulling her up as if she was a rag doll. The smell of the place, so familiar, made her feel sick with dread. Behind her she was vaguely aware of Ellie climbing the stairs too. There might have been the sound of an occasional sob from her; or maybe that was just Dani's imagination. In any case, as she saw the door to the flat approaching, she couldn't really concentrate on anything else.

The flat was just as it had been when she left. Dani knew that, but it seemed worse somehow, a stark contrast to the clean, sterile surroundings of the hostel. Baxter pushed her roughly inside and she fell heavily to the floor of the hallway. To her left, the door to her bedroom was slightly ajar. Dani couldn't bring herself to look at it. If ever there was a room she had hoped never to see again, that was it. It seemed to ooze all the horrible things that had happened in there. She clenched her eyes shut, as if that would somehow make the room feel more distant; and as she did so, she was aware of Ellie being pushed into the flat. The woman didn't fall, but she staggered to the right of Dani as the little girl heard the sound that she knew would haunt the dreams of whatever was left of her life: the sound of the door to the flat being locked.

Dani stayed on the floor, her eyes shut. There was silence. She knew Baxter must be standing by the door, because she hadn't heard any footsteps. In her mind's eye, she pictured him staring at her, his eyes cold and dead. Surveying her. Wondering what to do with her. Wondering how to hurt her.

They seemed to stay like that for ages, like waxworks in a museum. It was Baxter who finally broke the silence, with his footsteps rather than his voice. Dani heard him walk in to the kitchen and, as if freed by the removal of his cold stare, she dared to open her eyes slowly.

Ellie was there, just where Dani expected her to be. Her back was pressed against the wall, and she looked down at Dani with bloodshot eyes, her face a picture of shock. Her body was trembling and a strand of her platinum blonde hair, greasy now and dark at the roots, hung over the front of her face. It didn't seem to bother her; in fact, she barely seemed to notice it.

They stared at each other and there was a world of meaning in that stare. The thought flitted into Dani's mind that she should quiz Ellie, and ask her why she came back to take her away after going to so much trouble to help her escape. Then she realised she didn't need to. She could tell the signs: the shivering, the hungry look. The woman in front of her *looked* like Ellie, but she was little more than a shell, a husk. Ellie had been an addict for far longer than Dani, and the pain of her withdrawal was accordingly more severe. Dani's head wanted to hate her for what she had done, but her heart couldn't.

How long they remained like that – Dani on the floor and Ellie pressed silently against the wall – she couldn't have said. But after a while she became vaguely aware of the sound of Baxter clattering around in the kitchen. It sounded for all the world as if he was preparing food and Dani's brow creased. Why would he be doing that? What was he up to? She glanced towards the kitchen door, and then back at Ellie. If she was aware of anything untoward, her face didn't reveal it. So Dani pushed herself to her feet and arched her head so that she could just see into the kitchen.

Baxter was standing at the worktop. He had opened a couple of drawers and not bothered to shut them again. Now he was rummaging in a third. As Dani watched, he soon found what he was looking for: a knife. Dani knew from having looked through those drawers herself that it was the largest one in the kitchen. As he pulled it out, Baxter seemed to examine the blade, his head fixed at a slight angle. He gave no indication that he realised Dani was watching him.

Once he had satisfied himself that this was the blade he wanted, Baxter moved to the old, greasy, stand-alone stove. He switched on one of the gas rings, and then tried to light it, using the orange button at the front. It clicked a few times, but the hob didn't ignite. Baxter swore before pulling a lighter from his pocket and sparking it in front of the gas ring. There was a brief whoosh of blue flame, and then the hob settled down. Baxter adjusted the control so that it was burning as fiercely as it was able, then he placed the knife directly over the flame.

He kept it there for some time, moving the blade up and down so that the heat covered all of the metal. It took a good two minutes, maybe three. Dani watched, wide-eyed, as he removed it and held it up again. She had half expected it to be red hot, but it wasn't. It looked completely normal, but she could tell from the way Baxter held it away from his face that it was very hot indeed.

He turned, and it was only then that he appeared to realise that Dani had been watching him. His lip curled and slowly he began to walk towards her, holding the knife up like a sword.

Dani stepped back, a sickening terror rising in her. Baxter didn't hurry. Far from it: he seemed to be taking his time. He didn't move his eyes off Dani, though. She continued edging backwards towards Ellie. Quite why, she didn't know. It wasn't as if Ellie was in much of a state to help her.

Dani was next to Ellie now and she felt the woman's trembling hand on her bony shoulder. Still Baxter walked towards them; still his pace remained slow, as if he was relishing what was about to happen. Dani found that she could not take her eyes off the knife. It was close now, and from this distance she could see that the blade was dull and had little nicks along its edge.

Baxter stopped. He was right in front of them.

'Leave it, Baxter,' she heard Ellie whisper in a rasping tone of voice. 'You got her back. Just leave it, eh?'

Baxter's eyes flickered towards her, and then back down at Dani. He lowered his knife arm fractionally and Dani couldn't help letting a whimper escape her throat. Ellie clutched her shoulder a little tighter, and Dani pressed harder against her body. She closed her eyes, waiting for it to happen, and then half opened them again, unable not to watch the knife approaching.

'What did you tell them?' he asked.

Dani shook her head. 'Nothing,' she whispered. 'Nothing. I promise.'

Baxter seemed to consider that. He examined her face, as though looking for the smallest sign that she was lying. The silence was stifling.

It happened with sudden, brutal swiftness. Baxter, who had bent down slightly to be more on Dani's level, straightened up. With his free hand he grabbed Ellie's hair and then, his face contorted with anger, he pressed the flat of the knife against the woman's cheek.

Ellie didn't scream immediately. It wasn't until Dani had scrambled away from between her and Baxter, and was looking back up at them both, that the sound escaped her throat. It was raw and bestial. Her whole body looked as if it was frozen in shock and pain; only the fact that Baxter's hands – both the one that was holding the knife and the one clutching Ellie's hair – were shaking told Dani that Ellie was struggling but was being overpowered by his superior strength.

The scream lasted for a long time – maybe ten seconds – before fading to nothingness as Ellie gasped for breath. The knife was still flattened against her skin and Baxter showed no sign that he was going to remove it. Ellie screwed her face up as if she was going to scream again and it was only then that Baxter gave her some relief. He pulled the blade away and then threw Ellie to the floor.

Dani backed up against the opposite wall. Her eyes kept flickering alternately between Baxter, who was surveying the scene with a look of calm approval, and Ellie, who was on her knees, her face buried in her hands, her whole body juddering and gasps of pain seeming to choke her. Dani wanted to do something, to comfort Ellie, to help her. But as she stepped towards her, she heard Baxter speak.

'If you ever,' he said in little more than a whisper, '*ever* try and run away again, you can expect the same treatment, lassie.'

She stared back at him. There was a glimmer of defiance in her and she struggled not to let it show in her face.

Baxter's eyes narrowed. He walked towards her, absently stepping round Ellie's shaking body, as though it was just a piece of litter in the street. The defiance that Dani had briefly felt melted away, to be replaced by the icy cold fear that had preceded it.

Before she knew what was happening, Baxter had *her* hair in his grip. She gasped as he squeezed it tightly and held the knife up to the side of her face. Faintly she shook her head, but she had lost all power of speech and was unable to beg him not to maim her as he had maimed Ellie.

The knife remained there, inches from her face. Baxter's hand was perfectly still.

Then he spoke again.

'I hope you don't think,' he breathed, 'that I wouldn't do it.'

Dani couldn't reply.

'What's the matter, lassie? Cat got your tongue?'

She shook her head. A brief flicker of a smile played across Baxter's face. A smile of satisfaction. He let go of her hair and then turned around to look back down at Ellie. She was still on the floor, her head still in her hands. Nonchalantly, Baxter reached into his coat pocket and pulled out a small wrap of heroin. He dropped it on the floor beside Ellie and then, briskly and without another word, he returned the knife to the kitchen and left the flat, locking the door behind him.

The sound of the key in the lock seemed to echo around the flat. Dani stared at the door. Everything seemed so unreal: that she should be back here, under Baxter's control again. It was like a waking nightmare.

Then she heard Ellie. The older woman had started to cry and slowly she straightened herself up and moved her hands away from her face.

It was all Dani could do to continue looking at her. Her cheek bore the brand of the knife just below where she had previously been cut, an exact replica of the blade's shape. The burn was puffy and red. In places it was bleeding and the blood had smeared somewhat over the rest of her cheek from where her hand had been pressed up against it. Her tears mingled with the blood. It looked as if she had been wearing gruesome make-up that had started to run in the rain.

It took a moment for Ellie to notice the wrap that Baxter had dropped on the floor next to her. When she did, she grabbed it hungrily. All of a sudden her tears stopped. She stood up and, almost as if Dani wasn't there, headed towards her room. Before she reached it, however, she paused and turned around. The two of them looked at each other. Ellie's face was more haunted than Dani had ever seen it.

'I'm sorry, titch,' she rasped weakly. 'I'm so, so sorry.'

And with that, she turned and disappeared into the sanctuary of her room.

Chapter Eighteen

Night fell.

Hayley was nervous: there was no doubt about that. Nervous to her very core. After leaving the hostel, she had returned straight home, where she had waited for the darkness to come. She did nothing while she was there, other than sit on the edge of her bed and look with a brow-furrowed intensity at the grainy CCTV picture in her hand.

Was it sensible, what she was about to do? Was it safe? Was it the right thing – for either of them? What if she found her? In her head, Hayley's reunion with her little girl was rose-tinted, a moment of unbridled joy for them both. But she was smart enough to know that it might not be like that at all. It was a million to one shot that she would find Dani anyway, but if she did there was a good chance that her daughter could be very far from being the sweet little kid she wanted to think she was. Hayley just had to look at the evidence: she had stolen money from the children's home; she'd been involved in prostitution; she had ended up in a hostel for recovering drug addicts; she had run away because she thought the police would come calling. And quite apart from that, Hayley had no idea if she would want to see her. Chances were that she'd take one look at her mother and walk away. The very thought made Hayley shudder.

Yet this was something she had to do. It would be easy now to walk away from the path she had embarked on. But whichever way she looked at it, Dani needed someone's help. Who would give it to her if Hayley didn't? She had, at the very least, to try to find her.

It was late when she left the house – gone ten o'clock. Hayley was going nowhere glamorous – far from it – but she had spent as much time deciding what to wear as if she was going to dine at the most exclusive restaurant in London. Rather than dressing up, however, she had dressed down. The people she was going to see would, she imagined, trust her more the less affluent she appeared. Hayley was hitting the streets and she had to look as if the street was where she was from. So it was that she caught a late-night bus wearing old jeans that were tight but frayed around the bottoms, and an old coat that had seen better days. As she sat at the back of the bus, ignoring a group of drunken kids just a few seats down, she stared impassively out of the window, still wondering if she was doing the right thing.

It took the best part of an hour to make it into the West End. Despite the fact that it was cold out, Trafalgar Square, where the bus stopped, was full of people, and the bustle only increased as she walked north up towards Leicester Square. Crowds were spilling out of the cinemas and there was a muffled thud from one or maybe more of the bars that surrounded the square. For a while, Hayley stood alone among the hurrying people, like a stone in a fast-flowing stream, at the bottom of Prince Charles Street. All she had to do was walk up here and she would be in the heart of Soho, in the red-light district – not as seedy now as once it was, but still the regular haunt of prostitutes and those who visited them.

Her nervousness increased. She could still turn back, and who would blame her if she did? Who would know? As that thought crossed her mind, she pulled the photograph out of her coat and looked at it. She shook her head. No. She wasn't going to give up now. Not when her daughter needed her. She stepped forward and headed up into Soho.

Hayley walked slowly, past the line of Chinese restaurants, which were full of customers. The air was heavy with the smell of the area – a mixture of food and dustbins – and Hayley kept her head down as she negotiated the network of streets. She knew what she was looking for, but it made her feel sick with anxiety to know that she would actually have to talk to one of those scary, abrasive-looking people.

She stopped outside an entrance to a building. It had been opened up to form a kind of alcove in the wall, in which there was a glass-fronted booth inhabited by a bored-looking woman with elaborate hair and a very low-cut top. Her face was heavily made up and she had a cigarette between her fingers. Above the booth a neon sign read 'Girls', and to the right of it, just by a black glass door that led into the building, there was another sign that read 'Show'. Hayley looked up at her from the pavement. The woman didn't seem to have noticed her and it took all Hayley's confidence not to walk away. She took a deep breath and stepped up to the booth.

The woman didn't notice her at first – close up it was clear that she was reading a magazine – so Hayley was forced to make her presence known. 'Excuse me,' she said.

The woman looked up slowly. She didn't appear surprised, exactly, to see another female approaching; but she looked unfriendly. Her gaze moved up and down, as though she was sizing Haley up, and rather than reply immediately she took another deep drag on her cigarette.

'Twenty,' she said at last.

Hayley was confused. 'What?'

'Twenty quid. To go in.'

She felt herself blushing. 'No,' she stuttered. 'No, I don't want to go in.'

The woman looked at her with a frown as, all fingers and thumbs, Hayley pressed the picture against the glass of the booth. 'I'm looking for someone,' she said. 'The woman in this picture. Do you know her, maybe?'

The woman barely glanced at it before looking back down at her magazine. 'It's not a bloody information booth, love,' she retorted.

Hayley blinked. 'No,' she said weakly. 'No, I know it isn't. I just wondered …' But the woman wasn't listening. Hayley bowed her head and turned away, her skin suddenly burning with embarrassment. As she walked away from the booth, a couple of lads across the road shouted something at her. Hayley couldn't hear what it was, but it was obviously lewd. She hurried down the road.

For about half an hour she just walked, feeling a bit stupid. In her mind, she had envisaged prostitutes on every street corner; but she'd been in this part of town enough times to know it really wasn't like that. And she'd typed up enough police reports about incidents in the area to realise that the people she wanted to find were more likely to be in places she didn't want to go. As she wandered past the dingy side streets where those places were, she plucked up her courage. From the corner of her eye she kept noticing the open doorways from which an orangey-red light glowed and finally, with a deep breath, she approached one of them.

There was nothing outside the door to suggest what went on up the steep flight of steps immediately beyond. Hayley was worldly enough, however, to know that the door was ajar for a reason. Timidly, her fingers tightly clutching the photograph, she stepped inside. The tiny hallway in which she found herself smelled of dirt and there was a thin, slightly sticky grey carpet beneath her feet. The red glow came from a solitary light bulb suspended from the ceiling halfway up the narrow flight of stairs; and at the top of the stairs was another door leading off to the left, also slightly open.

Hayley felt an overwhelming urge to turn and leave. This was a seedy place; a frightening place; a place not for her. It was not a place for her daughter either, and that thought spurred her on. She chewed absent-mindedly on her lower lip as she coyly walked up the stairs.

At the top, she knocked on the door and then felt faintly ridiculous for having done so. She pushed the door open a little further, and then peered into the room beyond. It wasn't big – maybe five metres by five metres – and it was almost empty. A couple of old armchairs, their cushions frayed and moth-eaten; there was wallpaper on the wall, peeling in places; and on the far side of the room was another door. As Hayley stood there, wondering what to do, the door opened and a man appeared. He had black skin and wore a tracksuit and baseball cap. When he saw Hayley he stopped.

Hayley immediately wished she could be anywhere else but there. When the man flashed her a lascivious smile, it didn't help matters.

'What can I do for you, darling?' he asked in a low voice. Something about him made Hayley's skin crawl.

'Nothing,' Hayley said quickly, glancing briefly back over her shoulder. 'I mean, I was just—' Her words tumbled out. She held out the photograph. 'I'm looking for someone,' she managed to say. 'The woman in the picture. I think she's a ...' Hayley looked around this seedy place. 'You know, I think she's ...'

The man's face had clouded over with suspicion. The unpleasant smile fell away and he jutted his chin towards the door. 'Fuck off,' he said shortly. His expression told Hayley that he meant it. She found herself nodding as she stepped backwards towards the door. Tripping slightly, she manoeuvred her way back onto the tiny landing; then she stumbled back down the stairs, her feet barely able to move as fast as she wanted them to. By the time she made it out on to the street, she was breathless. She was also tearful, scared and ashamed. Tears filled her eyes as she hurried back up the side street and half ran, half walked out of the heart of Soho.

What the hell had she been thinking of? She made her way to Trafalgar Square, where she waited for a night bus. It had been a fool's errand. The best thing she could do was go back home.

* * *

It was 1.00 a.m. Baxter had not returned since Dani had been stolen back, but she knew he would. This was just the quiet before the storm.

The silence and the waiting were so terrible. But not as terrible as the prospect of what she could expect when they ended. And so it was that, when Dani heard the sickening sound of a key in the lock of the front door, all feeling returned to her in the form of a wave of nauseating dread. Sitting in her lonely room, she closed her eyes, waiting for her own door to open, as she knew it most surely would.

It happened almost immediately. 'Couldn't stay away, eh?' a voice intoned. She knew the voice well, of course. It would be with her for as long as she lived, however long that might be. Slowly, heavily, she lifted her head and opened her eyes.

Mr Morgan's dead eyes were expressionless, his suit crumpled from the day's use and his tie slightly undone.

Dani felt a shudder of revulsion as he stepped inside and then, firmly, quietly and in a gesture full of horrible meaning, closed the door behind him. It was just him and her in the room, and she knew what was going to happen next.

Hayley couldn't sleep.

She felt disgusted. Disgusted by the places she'd seen that night and disgusted with herself. For being so hopeless: hopeless as a mother in the first place, and hopeless at what she'd just tried to do. In the warmth of her bed, though, her courage returned. She would try again tomorrow. She had to.

The next day passed quickly as she apprehensively waited for evening to come. When it did, she put on the same clothes as she had worn the previous night and took the same bus into town. As she tramped the same streets, she felt the same sense of embarrassment and shyness. She did her best to overcome it, though, and while she avoided the many dimly lit flights of stairs, she soon lost count of the number of women she had approached and shown the photograph. Their response was universally the same: an unfriendly look and a cold shoulder. Midnight came and went. One o'clock. Two o'clock. By the time Hayley was too cold and footsore to continue, she had tears in her eyes, just as she had the previous night.

On her third evening, some of the girls started to recognise her – Hayley was given aggressive, unfriendly glances even before she approached them. She had the feeling that word was spreading, that people knew about her and what she was asking. Gradually she started to become hardened to the constant rebukes; but it was not lost on her that the more people she asked and the more brick walls she came up against, the less chance of success she had. This crushed her resolve, and made the familiar sensation of despair flood over her yet again.

On the fourth night, she felt sick at the prospect of her evening's investigation before she even left home. By eleven o'clock she had shown the photograph to two people, both of whom had walked away from her without even a word. Now she was approaching a third. This woman was older than most; despite the cold weather she wore a low-cut top and tight trousers that did little to enhance her figure. She loitered outside what purported to be a 'bookshop', but one look at the frosted shop windows gave Hayley a clue as to what sort of 'books' it was likely to sell.

She held out the picture to the woman. 'Excuse me,' she said politely. 'I'm trying to find this person. Do you know who she is?'

The woman glanced without interest at the picture, and then at Hayley. It was only then that Hayley smelled the alcohol on her breath and saw the dangerous look in her eyes; and it was more by luck than judgement that she stepped back as the woman took a swing at her.

Hayley stumbled. 'I've fucking heard about you!' the woman shouted, her voice slurred. 'What are you? A fucking copper?' She hurled herself at Hayley, who turned and fled. She ran blindly, tears in her eyes; as she ran, she didn't look behind her, so when she ducked into a vaguely familiar side street, she had no way of knowing if she was being followed.

Stopping to catch her breath, Hayley rested her back against a brick wall. The encounter had shocked and scared her. There was no sign of the woman now, but as the sheer impossibility of what she was trying to do came crashing in on her, Hayley's back slid down the wall and she ended up in a heap on the ground, sobbing her eyes out. It was all so hopeless; so useless. She would never find her little girl. *Never*. And as that thought echoed round her head, her sobs became howls – howls of absolute hopelessness.

She didn't know how long she stayed like that, but gradually she became aware of a voice addressing her. It made her jump. Hayley looked up to see a woman standing in a doorway next to her, and with a start she realised it was the same doorway she had ventured into three nights previously.

Hayley couldn't tell if the woman was coming out or going in, but from the way she was dressed it was clear that she would be quite at home up those stairs.

'Shouldn't stay there,' the woman said in a tone of voice that made it clear she was repeating herself. She gave off a harsh, prickly aura.

Hayley quickly rubbed her hand across her eyes and pushed herself up to her feet. 'I'm going,' she muttered. Her voice was unsteady and wavering.

She turned to leave but then something – desperation probably – stopped her. She held out the photo. 'I'm looking for this person,' she said. 'Have you seen her?'

The woman looked at her curiously. 'You the one came up here the other night? He said someone came up, asking after a girl. Was it you?'

Hayley nodded her head.

'You stupid cow,' she said. Her words were harsh, but somehow she didn't sound entirely unkind. 'What you playing at, eh?'

'I'm just looking for someone.'

The woman's eyes narrowed. 'What are *you* doing, looking for someone round here?' She sounded genuinely amazed, but then she glanced with interest at the photo. After a moment she shook her head.

'Never seen them,' she stated. 'Neither of them.' She handed the picture back.

Hayley nodded once more, doing her best to avoid the woman's glance. 'Thanks,' she said briefly; then she made to leave.

'Hold up,' the woman called. Hayley turned again. 'Who is it, anyway?'

'Just … just someone I need to find.'

'She's a working girl?'

'I think so.'

The woman appeared to think about that.

'She in trouble?'

Hayley kept her lips tightly shut as she shook her head.

'You're not police, are you?'

'No.'

'You don't look like police,' the woman said thoughtfully. 'Give it here, then,' she added after a moment.

Hayley felt her brow furrow. She didn't want to hand the photo over again. The woman noticed her hesitation.

'Up to you,' she shrugged. 'I'll ask around, but no good without the photo. You can meet me back here at midnight tomorrow.'

'Midnight?' Hayley asked. 'Perhaps in the morning instead—'

The woman laughed briefly. 'Sorry, love,' she said. 'Don't do mornings. You going to give it to me or not?'

Hayley hesitated. She had no idea if she could trust this woman, and if she lost the picture it would be a disaster. Then she glanced briefly through the doorway and up the red-bathed stairs. The alternative was to keep hunting out those places, to keep climbing such stairs. She couldn't bear it.

'All right,' she replied. Before handing the picture over, however, she tore it, slowly and meticulously, dividing her daughter from the woman she was searching for. And with a profound sense of reluctance, she handed the fragment over to the prostitute in front of her. The woman nodded, and then disappeared back up the stairs.

Suddenly Hayley felt cold as she stood there, quite alone, holding the torn fragment of a photograph bearing the image of a pale and frightened little girl. She felt pale and frightened herself as she turned, walked out of the street and headed for home.

The following day passed intolerably slowly. Hayley paced the house in a frenzy of worry. The torn fragment of the picture lay on her table and she kept coming back to it, staring at it, wondering where the little girl was now.

She planned to leave the flat at ten thirty that night, but in the event she found she could not wait nearly that long, and it wasn't much past eight when she hopped on a bus to take her into the centre of town. Arriving at Trafalgar Square a good three hours early, she paced the pavements, occasionally passing the little side street that was her ultimate destination, but never walking up it. The chill got to her and she started to shiver. It crossed her mind to go and sit in a café and have a hot drink; but she didn't, because she knew she would never be able to stay still for long enough.

As midnight approached, time seemed to slow down and she found herself loitering at the end of the street. A quarter to. An age passed and then it was ten to. Five to. Hayley inhaled deeply and then walked to the doorway.

The woman wasn't there.

She looked at her watch. There were still a couple of minutes till midnight, so she stamped her feet against the cold and waited.

Midnight came and passed. A couple of men walked nearby, but Hayley sensed that they were avoiding the entrance because she was there. There was a bad vibe and she wanted to go.

Five past.

Ten past.

Hayley cursed herself. Cursed her stupidity at handing over the one link she had to her daughter. What would she do now? How would she ever find her? 'Damn it,' she muttered to herself as she prepared to walk away. '*Damn*—'

She stopped.

There was the sound of footsteps coming down the stairs. Timidly, Hayley peered in and saw her. The woman didn't seem to be hurrying and as she reached the foot of the stairs she did not seem in the slightest bit apologetic about her lateness. She simply raised her eyebrows in a curt greeting, handed over the fragment of the photograph that she was holding and then gave Hayley a small piece of paper.

Hayley opened it up. Written on it, in the spidery writing of someone unused to holding a pen, was an address, not far from where they were now.

'Her name's Ellie,' the woman brusquely. 'Least, that's what she calls herself.'

Ellie. A surge of hope rose in Hayley. Wasn't that the name Dani had given the hostel worker? Everything seemed to be fitting into place.

The woman sniffed. 'Word to the wise,' she mumbled. 'Don't go there by yourself, eh?'

Hayley looked at her quizzically.

'Her pimp,' the woman said briefly by way of explanation. 'Nasty fucker. Nasty piece of work.' She nodded and turned to walk back up the stairs. But before she disappeared, she spoke again.

'Don't do nothing stupid,' she said. 'Trust me, I've heard of the guy. Treats his girls like shit. He's not someone you want to get involved with. Her neither, from what I've heard.' She briefly mimed someone injecting themselves in the arm, and with that she was gone.

Hayley stared at the piece of paper as the woman's words echoed in her mind. *Not someone you want to get involved with.*

But it was too late. Hayley was already involved. More deeply than anyone could know.

She carefully folded the piece of paper in two and slipped it into her back pocket. The address that was written on it was only a few streets away and she walked there in a kind of daze, oblivious to the other pedestrians, oblivious to the cars on the road. Oblivious, really, to everything other than that her child could be so close. Within minutes she was there.

It was a quiet street, and narrow. The buildings were high. They seemed to close in on you. Hayley searched for the door number that had been scrawled on the scrap of paper. At first it didn't seem to exist, but she worked out from the surrounding numbers that it must be the door that was now in front of her. She stopped. It was a black door with no letterbox. There was a battered-looking intercom on one side, but other than that there was just a heavy stainless-steel handle and a lock. The paint was peeling a little and it looked somehow sinister.

For a long time Hayley stared at it. Occasionally her eyes would flicker up towards the top of the building, but they always came to rest once more on the door. It was like a barrier to so many things. She longed to knock it down, to break through it, but as she stood there, the warning she had just received seemed to reverberate in her mind.

She shook her head. She had taken it as far as she could by herself. Now she needed to go through the proper channels. She needed some help. And although she found the very idea hateful, there was only one person she could think of to go to.

It would have to wait till the morning. Regretfully she stepped away from the door and, feeling the separation from her daughter more keenly now than she ever had, she made her way home.

Hayley was in the office early the following morning. She sat at her desk and, though her in-tray was full, she made no pretence of doing any work. She just sat there, waiting.

DCI Barker arrived late, past ten o'clock. He looked tired, grumpy and dishevelled, and Hayley could instantly tell that he was in no mood to be helpful. But that didn't matter: she had to do what was necessary. She waited until he had settled down in his office with his suit jacket over the back of the chair; then she went and knocked on the door.

He looked up in annoyance. 'What is it?' he asked without ceremony as she walked inside.

She didn't tell him everything. Just that she had reason to believe that a crime had been committed and that she had the address of someone who knew about it. Barker listened with barely disguised contempt for her attempts to play detective, but she shut it out. Hayley wasn't going to be ignored. When she had finished speaking, she handed

Barker the piece of paper on which the address had been written, along with the fragment of the torn photograph that showed Dani outside the hostel.

A silence fell upon the room. As Hayley watched, she saw something change in DCI Barker. His lips thinned, and the colour seemed to drain from his face. She had seen her boss get angry before and she knew the signs. They were all there now. Everything she knew about him told her he was about to go off the scale.

He didn't shout. It would have been better if he had, Hayley thought. Instead, his voice dropped to a barely audible, sibilant hiss. 'You stupid girl,' he whispered. 'You stupid, *stupid* girl.'

Hayley blinked, but she jutted out her chin and stood firm.

'You're a secretary,' he said with burning contempt. 'What the hell do you think you're playing at? You think we're not busy as it is? You think we don't have enough on our plate?'

Hayley struggled to find her voice. 'But it's a little girl …'

'It's a junkie outside a hostel. You think I've got the time to start hunting down every fucked-up little …'

He didn't finish his sentence. He just grabbed the picture of Dani and crumpled it into a little ball in his big fist.

'No!' Hayley gasped. She stretched out to grab the picture back, but then she stopped. Barker had a dangerous look in his eyes. A mad look.

'Get out of here,' he spat. 'You're lucky I'm not firing you on the spot. Get back to doing the work you're supposed to be doing.'

There was something about the way he was staring at her that made Hayley take a step back. She found herself shaking with frustration and fury, but she did not dare do anything about it, so maniacal was the look in her boss's face. She didn't understand it. It didn't make sense. But she knew what she had to do. Trying her best to keep under control the tears that threatened to spring to her eyes, she stormed out of the room. And rather than go back to her desk, she simply left the office. She didn't bother to grab her coat from her desk; nor did she look back to see if Barker was watching her.

And so it was that she did not catch sight of the DCI pacing his room briefly, his knuckles white and his eyebrows crumpled in an expression of troubled concern, before pulling his mobile from his pocket, dialling a number and speaking briefly but urgently into the telephone.

Chapter Nineteen

Dani's eyes opened with a start.

Daylight had arrived. She had slept badly, of course. That went without saying. Towards morning, however, tiredness had overcome her discomfort and she had fallen asleep, covered with the brown blankets and with her head on the hard floor. When she awoke, there was a noise outside. The door had opened and there were footsteps.

She shook the sleep from her head and sat up. It could only be Baxter – no one ever visited, other than the clients, and even then they were always with him. But he never came in the mornings. *Never*. A sick feeling rose in her throat as she wondered what new terror he planned to inflict on her.

The door opened and he was there. His hair was wet – it must have been raining outside. Dani shrank back.

'You,' he pointed at her. 'Get up, we're leaving.'

Dani blinked. For the first time ever Baxter seemed agitated. She'd seen him angry, of course, but not nervous like this. He turned his back on her and she heard him move quickly into Ellie's room. 'Get the fuck up,' he instructed urgently. Then, when there was clearly no response from Ellie, he repeated, '*Get the fuck up!*'

There was a scuffling sound. Dani heard a whimper and she knew the woman had been hit. She made her way timidly to the door and saw Baxter in the hallway. Ellie staggered out. She was a terrible sight. Her hair was matted and tangled, her eyes panda-black. But it was the wound on her face that was the worst of all. It still bore the shape of Baxter's knife, but now it was weeping and bloody. There were flecks of white all across it where it had started to go septic. It turned Dani's stomach just to look at it. Her revulsion must have shown on her face, because when Ellie looked at her she immediately seemed embarrassed and turned her head away so that the wound was no longer in Dani's field of vision.

'What's the matter, Baxter?' she asked. Her voice sounded weak and unbelievably tired.

'We're going.'

'What do you mean, we're going?'

'Stop asking me fucking stupid questions,' Baxter barked. 'We're just going, all right?' He turned to Dani. 'You'd better listen to me, lassie,' he said, more quietly now, but no less threateningly. 'If you try anything – and I mean *anything* – then you know what'll happen, don't you?' He looked meaningfully over at Ellie. Dani nodded her head.

'Good. The car's outside. When we get down there, you get straight into the back. You don't talk to anyone, you don't even look—'

He stopped. A noise had filled the flat. The buzzer.

All three of them stared at the door. Baxter's silence made Dani feel on edge and she found herself holding her breath.

Finally Baxter spoke. 'You,' he said shortly to Dani. 'Get in there.' He pointed at the spare bedroom. 'Under the bed. If I hear a fucking peep out of you …'

Baxter didn't need to finish his threat. Dani scurried obediently into the room in which she had slept when she had hurt her hand as the buzzer sounded again. It was longer this time. Impatient. She was shaking as she crawled under the bed and pushed herself up against the corner of the room, her body curled up into a ball. She was cold with fear. She didn't know why Baxter was scared, but she knew that he was. Having seen what he was capable of when he was calm and in control, she could only guess what might happen to her now if she didn't do exactly as he said.

She felt tears coming, but she gulped them down. Because if anyone heard her now, Dani had no doubt that Baxter would kill her.

Hayley had run all the way to the black door. Just as she left the police station it had started to rain heavily. It almost blinded her as she negotiated the wet pavements with only one thought in her head. She had to find her daughter. No one else was going to do it for her. She *had* to find Dani.

Now she was there, pressing the buzzer. Her breath came in short, sharp gasps and she did what she could to regulate it. She needed to be in control. She closed her eyes momentarily, breathed deeply and then pressed the buzzer again.

She waited.

No one was answering, but she wasn't going away. She *couldn't* go away. This was all she had. Her only lead. There *had* to be someone here she could speak to. There *had* to be.

She pressed the buzzer again. And the moment she did so, the door opened.

It was a man.

He was well dressed, with a closely shaved head and a long nose that looked as if it had been broken at some point in the past. He wore blue jeans and a leather jacket. Hayley could smell his aftershave, strong and overpowering.

'Aye?' he asked. 'What do you want?' He spoke with a Scottish accent and he obviously wasn't pleased to have been disturbed.

Hayley took a deep breath and drew herself up to her full height. She could feel a strand of wet hair plastered across the side of her face, but she didn't move it. 'I'm looking for Ellie,' she said as confidently as she could.

Slowly the man nodded his head. 'Ellie, eh?' he said after a moment. 'Friend of hers, are you?'

'Not exactly,' Hayley said firmly in a tone of voice that she hoped suggested she didn't want to discuss it any further.

The man seemed to consider his options. Finally, he stepped back a couple of paces. 'You'd better go up, then,' he suggested quietly.

A chill shivered its way down Hayley's back. She peered inside. It was dark and unwelcoming. All she could see was a thin staircase leading upwards and every ounce of her being shrieked at her not to walk inside. She hesitated, aware that the man was looking at her through slightly narrowed eyes. Then, impulsively, she stepped over the threshold.

'All the way up,' the man said. Hayley walked towards the stairs. As she did so, she was aware of him shutting the door behind her. Locking it. She stopped and turned.

'Have to keep it locked,' the man said by way of explanation. He put the key into his pocket and then gestured with his head that she should carry on walking up the stairs.

Hayley grew colder and colder, but it was nothing to do with the temperature in the house. It was silent, tomb-like. The noise of London seemed to have been entirely eliminated by the closing of the door. On the first-floor landing there was another closed door and nothing else. Further up there was a toilet from which a foul smell emanated. All the while she could sense the man just a few steps behind her. She wanted to turn her head and look at him, but somehow she didn't dare. When she reached the top, she stopped. The man brushed past her and put another key in the lock of the door. He opened it and let her inside.

Hayley stepped into the dark, dingy top-floor flat. As she did so, she caught her breath.

There was a woman standing there. She looked like a ghost. Her hair was lank and dishevelled; her skin was ghostly pale. But what shocked Hayley more than anything was the mark on her face. It was sharp – pointed. The skin was raw. It seemed to weep. Her eyes, too, bore the signs of much weeping. They were red and bloodshot, with dark rings almost like bruises around them. She stood with her back against the wall and eyed Hayley with a look of the deepest suspicion.

It was only after a moment that Hayley realised who she was looking at.

'You're Ellie,' she whispered.

Behind her the door was being closed.

The woman didn't answer. She didn't even seem to register Hayley's comment.

Hayley stepped further into the flat, looking around her as she did so. It was a bleak, dark place. There were rooms leading off the main hallway, but they all had their doors shut, so she couldn't tell what was behind them.

'I'm looking for someone,' Hayley continued hesitantly. 'A little girl called Dani. I think you know her.'

At first Ellie didn't answer and Hayley saw that her gaze was concentrated on the man who had let her in. Hayley looked round to see him stare implacably at her. He looked severe. Dangerous.

'Don't know what you mean,' Ellie said in a thin, rasping voice.

Hayley looked from one to the other. 'Yes you do,' she breathed. 'I saw you together, in a picture.'

Again Ellie glanced nervously at the man; then she shook her head. Hayley noticed that her hands were trembling, and she could sense the fear coming from her. She could feel it. All of a sudden the room seemed to close in on her; the man stepped nearer. He had a flat, serious expression.

'So there you go,' he whispered. 'Time to leave, eh?'

It was not a question; it was an instruction. And it was one Hayley was pleased to obey. She wanted to be out of there. Away from the place. The man was scaring her, just as he was so obviously scaring Ellie. Doing her best not to let that fear show on her face, she made for the door. The man stepped aside and let her pass. She could feel the menace glowing from him and she had to force herself not to start running from that strange, terrifying place.

Then she stopped.

There was a sound. At first Hayley thought she might have been imagining it, but then she heard it again.

There was no doubting what it was. From one of the rooms at the far end of the hallway came the unmistakable noise of a child crying.

The others clearly heard it too, Ellie's face screwed up into a picture of torment, while the man grabbed Hayley by the arm and started to push her out of the flat.

'Time to leave,' he muttered.

But Hayley had found a sudden strength. She pulled her arm away and, ignoring a bark of warning from the man, ran towards the sound of the sobbing.

Bursting into the room from which it came, she looked around desperately. It was empty, and there was silence now. There was nothing in here except a table and a bed. Then, from under the bed, she heard not a sob but a panicked gasping. Hayley threw herself towards it and fell to her knees. From the hallway she heard Ellie's voice shouting out, 'Baxter!' But she paid no notice.

Her attention was grabbed by something else.

Hayley couldn't make out her daughter's face at first. She was curled up, facing the wall with her back towards her desperate mother, who saw with horror that her body was shaking with fear.

'Dani,' she said urgently. 'Dani, is that you?'

The sound of her name made the little girl turn immediately round. Her frightened eyes peered out. As they did so, an unnerving shock of recognition passed through Hayley's body. In that brief moment, she found herself back at the hospital, lying on the bed having given birth to that frail, premature little thing. She remembered watching helplessly as the child was taken away from her, how she wasn't even allowed to cuddle it. And she remembered going home that night and hiding under her bedclothes, wondering if she would ever see her baby again. Hayley was overwhelmed by a need to touch her child, to take her in her arms.

'I'm here,' she whispered. 'I'm here to take you away.'

She stretched out her hand underneath the bed. As she did so, Dani grabbed her. The little girl's tiny hand was cold and bony, but she held on to Hayley with a surprising vigour.

'Get up.'

The man's voice was behind her – the man Ellie had called Baxter – and it filled her with renewed dread. She looked over her shoulder to see that he was standing in the doorway. It took all her courage to ignore him and turn back to Dani. 'Come on, love,' she urged. 'Come on out. It's OK. Come on out.'

'I said, get up.'

She sensed him walking towards her and when she glanced over her shoulder again, she saw with a pang that he held a knife in his right hand.

It was not the weapon that made Hayley's blood run cold: it was the look in Baxter's eyes and the way she felt Dani's muscles tense even harder at the sight of him. His face was fixed in an expression of steely hate. 'Now you really shouldn't have done that,' he said, his voice little more than a whisper. 'You *really* shouldn't have done that.'

Hayley shrank back, but she didn't let go of her little girl's hand. 'Just let us leave,' she whispered. 'Let us leave and that's an end to it. We won't go to the police. We won't tell anyone.'

Baxter smiled. 'Of course you won't.' Then he opened his eyes wider, as though a sudden thought had struck him. 'But wait! Haven't you already done that? Haven't you already been to the police?' His smile turned into a dismissive sneer.

Hayley blinked. How could he tell? How did he know? The thought didn't have time to mature in her mind, however, because the man was approaching her, wielding his knife in such as way as to make it perfectly clear he was going to use it.

As he stepped forward, there was a screaming from beside her. '*No!*' yelled Dani, and the sound of her terrified voice was like an electric shock going through Hayley's bloodstream. '*Go away! Leave me alone! Don't do it!*'

The girl was hysterical. She was sobbing and screaming in equal measure, and now her body was shaking violently. Half of her was still under the bed, but she continued to cling tightly to Hayley's hand. Despite everything, the thought flashed through Hayley's mind that it was a good feeling. A feeling that made her whole. A feeling that gave her a bit of strength in the face of the monster who was bearing down on her with a knife.

He was barely a metre away now. And he was talking. 'I don't know who the fuck you are,' he growled. 'And I don't fucking care. You shouldn't have stepped into this room, lady, because we'll be taking you out in a bag.'

There was madness in his eyes. Absolute madness. It was only at that moment, as he raised his knife a little bit, and as Dani clutched on to her fractionally harder, that she realised he really was going to kill her.

Hayley's body went into a kind of spasm. Panic raced through her. But as she moved to ward off the sudden movement of the man's knife, it was not to protect herself. With a firm tug, she pulled Dani's body. The little girl slid with a whimper a little way from under the bed and Hayley found herself throwing her own body on to her daughter's. A human shield. She didn't know which one of them the man intended to attack, but there was no way Dani was going to come to harm while she could do a single thing to prevent it.

It didn't mean she wasn't scared, though. She was almost frozen with fear as she hid her face from the approaching blade, and now her screams were mingling with Dani's, in a horrid cacophony of dread.

Mother and daughter both knew what was coming.

Thinking it might be the last thing she did, Hayley turned her head to peek out at Baxter. Sure enough, he was almost upon them, bending down to their level. With his free hand, he grabbed Hayley's hair, a great clump of it in his fist. She gasped as he used it to tilt her head to one side, exposing the flesh of her neck; and her throat and stomach seemed to seize up as she watched the tip of the knife approach her skin.

She didn't see Ellie until the woman was right behind him.

If Baxter's eyes had been mad, Ellie's were psychotic. That, and the general disrepair of her face, made her look more like a ghoul than a human. Tears were streaming down her eyes, mixing with the weeping wound on her cheek to form a horrific, bloody mess; and her lip was curled into a snarl that displayed her teeth, which were yellowing. In her hand, which was raised just above her shoulder, she clutched a hypodermic syringe.

Hayley couldn't take her eyes off this apparition, and that fact was not lost on Baxter who, without letting go of her hair, momentarily turned to look over his shoulder.

Then Ellie struck him.

The needle slid into his neck with a silent ease. Baxter seemed to freeze. For a moment his grip remained firm on Hayley's hair, but as Ellie pulled the needle out again, his fist went limp and fell away. His knife hand dropped, and the blade thudded harmlessly to the floor. A sound escaped his throat – a strange, gurgling sound, like the dregs of a bath full of water swirling down the plughole. Baxter fell to his knees, and his hand covered the tiny puncture in his skin. As it did so, however, Ellie struck again, on the other side of the neck this time.

Holding her breath, Hayley watched in horror. Dani had fully pulled herself out from under the bed now, and Hayley instinctively pulled her arms around her, nestling her face against her body so that the little girl could not see the horrors that were unfolding in front of them.

Ellie had pulled the syringe out for a second time now and blood seemed to be flowing everywhere. All of a sudden she seemed to fly into a frenzy, stabbing the man repeatedly in the neck and screaming at the top of her voice, 'You bastard! You fucking, *fucking* bastard!'

Baxter weakly tried to ward off the blows, but without success. He fell completely to the floor, and within seconds he had stopped moving.

Ellie was on her knees, still stabbing the motionless body. But it was clear to Hayley that the woman in front of her was stabbing a corpse.

Hayley stayed completely still. Move now, she thought, and this woman might turn her violence on them.

It took perhaps thirty seconds for Ellie's frenzy of stabbing to subside, by which time Baxter's neck was a shredded mess. As she stabbed him for the last time, she left the needle in his body. Her hands were covered in his blood, but that did not stop her from using them to cover her face as she knelt before them, her body shaking with silent tears. Hayley gingerly stood up, pulling Dani to her feet as she did so and manoeuvring them both around the body.

Ellie appeared not to notice them, but as they edged towards the door of the room Hayley was aware that both she and Dani had their eyes fixed on her. Dani's breathing was heavy and frightened, and Hayley was overwhelmed by a need to get her out of that place. To get her out now.

They were just at the door when Ellie spoke. 'The key,' she said, her voice muffled because her hands were still over her mouth.

Hayley stopped and slowly Ellie turned around. Her face was now smeared in Baxter's blood as well as her own. She too looked like a corpse, but a waking one. 'You need the key,' she rasped. 'To get out of here.' She twisted uncomfortably back round and plunged her hand into Baxter's pocket, pulling out the keys he had used to let Hayley in. Then, pushing herself to her feet, she staggered towards them and dropped the keys into Hayley's waiting hand.

As Hayley curled her fingers around the keys, Ellie bent down so that her face was at Dani's level. Hayley's instinct was to pull her daughter away, but Dani did not seem as terrified of the gruesome figure as she thought she might be, so for a moment she hesitated.

Gingerly Ellie reached out the least bloodstained of her hands and touched Dani's cheek. Her hand left a little red smudge on the girl's skin, but Dani didn't seem to mind. 'I'm sorry, titch,' Ellie whispered.

Dani bit her lower lip.

'I'm so sorry,' Ellie continued. 'Sorry about all this. Shouldn't never have happened. You shouldn't never have been here. I could've—'

'Are you going to come with us?' Dani asked. For such a little girl, for someone who had been in such a state of terror only minutes ago, her voice was astonishingly calm. Grown-up, almost.

Ellie smiled, a rueful, painful smile. 'No, titch,' she replied. 'I can't come with you.'

'But we'll tell them,' Dani said, and now a little tremor had entered her voice. 'We'll tell them what he was going to do. It's all right, you won't be in trouble.'

The look Ellie gave her was sad, but somehow almost proud. 'You got to go, titch,' she whispered. 'Don't go worrying about me. I'll be fine. Always have been, haven't I?' As she spoke, she looked round at Baxter's dead form. 'He won't be coming after you no more. But you got to go quick.'

She took a step back, and then nodded curtly at Hayley. Hayley didn't know what to say. Something had passed between Dani and Ellie – that much was obvious. There was a bond between them, a bond she suspected she would never understand. For a moment she felt a pang of jealousy and almost involuntarily she pulled Dani a little closer to her.

'Go,' Ellie whispered. 'Now.'

Hayley nodded. She and Dani stepped out of the room and into the hallway. As they turned towards the main door, however, Hayley felt her daughter drag her heels slightly. They stopped, and Dani stared back into the bedroom. Ellie was standing there in front of Baxter's bleeding corpse, her arms limply by her side, watching them go. There was a look of such desolation in her face that it almost made Hayley want to grab the woman and drag her along with them. But she knew she couldn't.

'Come on, Dani,' she urged. 'We have to get out of here.'

Dani took a deep breath and nodded vaguely. A serious expression crossed her face; then she looked up at Hayley and nodded. Together they left the flat. Neither of them looked back, so they didn't know whether Ellie had stepped out into the hallway to see them leave.

Chapter Twenty

Hayley hurried through the streets of London, holding Dani's hand in hers and pulling her along. Both mother and daughter had tears in their eyes – tears of relief, tears of panic, tears of shock. They didn't talk, not for a good long while, and somewhere deep down Hayley was pleased about that. There was so much to explain to the little girl she had just rescued from God knows what. So much to explain. And when the child's questions started coming, Hayley wasn't sure how she'd find the words to answer them.

She didn't even know where she was leading her. In the back of her mind, she supposed, she wanted to get her back home; but it seemed impossible to sit quietly and patiently on a bus or a tube and make their slow way out of the centre of London. Instead, they wandered blindly and Hayley realised she was simply trying to leave that place of nightmares behind them. From Soho they hurried to Leicester Square and then down to Trafalgar Square. It started to rain heavily. Before long they were both soaked to the skin, but that didn't stop Hayley from hurrying. They negotiated the traffic and found themselves in the centre of the square, from which tourists were hurrying because of the rain, before Dani suddenly spoke.

'Wait!' she said. Her voice was hoarse and breathless.

Hayley turned round to look at her. The little girl's face was pale, her eyes frightened and confused. As the rain fell, it washed her hair down on to her face.

'Where are we going?' Dani demanded. 'Who are you?'

That simple question – who are you? – dug into Hayley like a knife. She bent down to Dani's level and gently stroked the hair off her face. Dani's head twitched in irritation – a peculiarly adult gesture.

'Dani,' whispered Hayley. They were practically alone now in the centre of the square, just them and the birds and a protective ring of traffic trundling its way through the rain. The thought flashed through Hayley's brain that this wasn't how she had imagined their reunion. This wasn't it at all.

'Who are you?' Dani demanded again, her voice more robust this time. More demanding. 'How do you know my name? How did you know where I was?'

'I've been looking for you,' Hayley whispered. 'I've been looking for you for such a long time.'

As she spoke, she felt Dani pulling herself away, as though trying to escape. Panicking at the thought of losing her again, Hayley gripped the girl's hand more tightly. She hoped it would make her feel safe, but it had the opposite effect. Dani started to struggle. She kicked Hayley in the shins and for a moment, in the rain and the noise, she looked like a wild child. Feral. Like someone unused to human company.

'Dani!' Hayley said sharply. 'Dani, stop it. I've got something to tell you.'

The words fell on deaf ears. Dani continued to struggle and it took all Hayley's strength to keep the little girl under control.

'Get off me!' Dani started to shriek. 'Get off me! *Leave me alone!*'

The more Dani struggled, the tighter Hayley's grip became. A desperate grip, as though she was holding on to the one thing that meant anything to her. Her ears were filled now with the sound of Dani's shouting. The noise made a flock of pigeons fly away from the area where they were standing. The little girl seemed completely out of control.

Hayley maintained her grip. 'Calm down, Dani,' she said, trying to keep her voice as level as possible. 'Calm down. I've got something to tell you.'

'Let me go! *Let me go!*'

'I can't let you go, Dani,' Hayley whispered. 'I can't ever let you go.'

The shrieking had stopped now, to be replaced with a shuddering whimper, a barely human sound. It was as though all the words had been sapped out of her, as if there was no way she could express her fear and her shock.

'Listen to me,' Hayley said. 'You've got to listen to me. I've been looking for you for such a long time. Ever since …'

She faltered.

Dani looked at her. Her ravaged eyes were wide, fearful. But they were gazing directly at Hayley. And in that instant, any doubt that she had that this was her daughter went out of the window. Call it what you like – a mother's instinct, or something even deeper – this little girl was hers, her flesh and blood. Her baby.

Something must have shown in her face, because Dani once more asked the question she had been repeating. This time, though, she sounded as if she was ready to hear the answer. 'Who *are* you?' she whispered.

Hayley closed her eyes for a moment, and then opened them again. Finally she said it: she spoke those words that she had rehearsed in her mind so many times. In her head, the situation had always been different. Happier. Rosier. But those had just been fantasies. This was real life.

'I'm your mum,' she breathed.

The words felt uncomfortable in her mouth, and her voice cracked slightly as she spoke.

So she tried again. *'I'm your mum.'*

At first she thought Dani hadn't heard her. The expression on the little girl's face didn't change; when it did, there was no clue to what she was thinking. No surprise. No joy. She just gazed out into the middle distance and didn't say a word.

Only then did her legs buckle. Dani fell slightly to the ground, but Hayley was there to hold her up. And as she did so, she smothered her daughter in a clumsy embrace.

It was awkward. Inappropriate, somehow. Dani's body felt bony and cold, stiff, as though she had found herself in a position she didn't want to maintain. But Hayley didn't let that stop her. She wrapped her arms tightly around her daughter and, as the rain fell and the traffic roared, hugged her for all she was worth.

Hugged her, with the boundless intensity of a woman making up for lost time.

* * *

The flat was silent. Like a tomb.

Ellie stood perfectly still.

How long she remained like that after Dani had walked out of the flat, she could never have said. A good few minutes anyway. She felt strangely calm, as though the madness that had overcome her when she was attacking Baxter had burned itself out, leaving nothing but a blank, emotionless husk. Although the burn wound on her face still hurt, it didn't seem to affect her. In fact she barely noticed it.

After a while, she turned round to look at him.

The bleeding had stopped, but there was still a meandering pool of blood on the floor around the corpse. Some of it had started to soak into the thin, unabsorbent carpet; much had been sponged up by Baxter's own clothes. He looked sinister in death – to Ellie's eyes even more sinister than he had looked in life. She gazed at him for a while, not quite able to believe that he was dead. That she had killed him. Half of her expected him suddenly to sit up, and then life would go on just as it always had. But that was never going to happen.

The past had been wiped out. The future, too. Ellie's future contained only one thing and without Baxter, that thing was gone forever. The dead man lying in front of her was loathsome to her. Poisonous. But it was a poison without which she could not live.

Almost in a daze she approached him, before bending down and, with an uncharacteristic thoroughness, searching his body. She started with the pockets of his trousers and then moved on to his jacket, where she wormed her fingers into all the little folds and cavities. It didn't take long for her to find what she was looking for. There were three of them, the little wraps of paper that he gave her on a daily basis. Ellie hungrily clutched them in her fist, and then stepped back and surveyed the body again.

The police would be here soon, she supposed. Dani and the woman – whoever she was – would be letting them know what had happened even as she stood there. When they arrived, there would be no doubt as to what had happened. She was covered in Baxter's blood. Oh, she could tell them it was provoked, but she knew the police well enough to realise that the word of a drug-addict hooker wasn't going to hold much weight. Even if they did believe her, there would be a spell in custody. And where would she get her junk from then?

'You bastard, Baxter,' she whispered as she looked down at him. 'Look what you did. Look what you did to both of us.' And with a look of contempt she spun round and left the room, slamming the door behind her.

For a couple of minutes she paced the flat. In the kitchen she remembered the first day little Dani had been here. She remembered how she had to tried to persuade herself that it was OK, that she would look after the girl, never mind what Baxter had in mind for her. They might even become friends, she had vaguely thought to herself. Her lip curled contritely at the thought.

Some friend she had turned out to be.

Ellie left the kitchen and wandered past Dani's room. For some reason she didn't feel comfortable going in there – she never really had – but she stood in the doorway and gazed at it for a moment. The mattress was there, where it always was, and the little pile of brown blankets was on the other side of the room. Ellie felt a surge of relief that the girl was finally out of here, finally out of the clutches of Baxter and the awful men who came to visit her. But in a stark moment of honesty, she realised she felt sad too. Sad that she would never see the child again.

Ellie had known she would never be a mother – that would be too much to inflict on any child – but it didn't stop her feeling the occasional pang of regret.

With a bowed head, she walked back to her own room and shut herself inside.

She was so calm. It amazed her how calm she was.

As she sat on the edge of her bed, her hand was still clutching the three little wraps that she had taken from Baxter's body. Now she opened up her palm and looked at them. Three wraps. Three days. And then what? She had no money, not without Baxter. Even if the police didn't take her away, even if she left here now and did not get picked up by them, her future without the pimp she loathed so much was unthinkable.

Ellie looked down at the wraps again. Three. It would be enough.

She went to the drawer of her dressing table and removed the equipment that was secreted inside. Almost on autopilot, like an assassin assembling his gun, she deposited the contents of the three wraps in her dish and started to prepare it. It didn't really take much longer to cook three doses of junk than it took to prepare one – Ellie was surprised by how quickly the syringe was ready.

Surprised by how quickly the time had come.

Ellie looked at herself in the mirror. It was a shock. Her fingers lightly touched the skin on her face and she remembered looking at herself in the mirror when she was a child.

It seemed like a lifetime away now, those days when she would steal her mum's make-up and try to make herself look prettier than she actually was. It often meant a beating when her mum found out what she was doing, but it was worth it – worth it to give herself the few minutes of fantasy of what it would like to be grown-up.

She shrugged her shoulders. Being grown-up wasn't all she had thought it would be. Not by a mile.

Her hands were trembling now. She almost dropped the syringe and her bootlace as she made her way back to the bed. She sat down on the mattress with her back straight against the wall, and then laid the syringe as gently as a baby on the bed, before tying the lace tightly around her upper arm, wincing slightly as she did so.

It took a while to get a vein. All her veins were collapsed and broken and she had to slap her skin a few times before one would show itself. It finally did, though.

Everything seemed to be happening in slow motion. She picked up the syringe and, with a deep sigh, laid the end of the needle against her vein.

A tear dripped down her cheek. It seemed to move infinitely slowly as she slid the needle into her skin.

Ellie closed her eyes, making more tears, tears that had been brimming, splash on to her face. She took a deep breath and then squeezed the syringe closed.

The relief was almost immediate. It washed over her, erasing everything. She even smiled faintly as she collapsed drowsily on to her bed. In just a few moments now, she knew, she would lose consciousness.

Oblivion. It was what she longed for. That was the last thought that crossed her mind as blackness engulfed it.

It took thirty seconds for Ellie's heart to stop, and another thirty seconds for her to die.

There were so many questions in Dani's head. A sea of questions, swirling around as though in the middle of a storm. She couldn't ask them, though. As she stood in the middle of Trafalgar Square, with this strange woman hugging her for all her life was worth, she seemed drained of energy. Unable to do anything. Unable even to run.

'*I'm your mum.*' When she lived at home – it seemed a lifetime away – she had sometimes fantasised about what it would be like to have a mother. A real mother. Someone who would hold her as she was being held at the moment. Now that it was happening, she didn't know what to think. Her veins were filled with a curious numbness. She wondered, vaguely, if she should be feeling something else. Something happier. But happiness seemed alien to her.

She thought of Baxter, lying dead on the floor. She was pleased he was gone, pleased he could never take her away again. Pleased he was no longer part of her life. Yet, when she thought of how he had died, she couldn't help shivering in revulsion. The image of Ellie standing behind him, syringe in hand, was one that she knew, even at that young age, would stay with her for the rest of her life.

Ellie.

With a pang she wondered what would happen to her. As she pictured the woman who had done her so much wrong but who had, nevertheless, been the closest thing she had to a friend, Dani felt a sudden need to see her. To help her. She would be in trouble for what she had done, and Dani wanted to be there for her. To help in whatever way she could.

But that would mean going back to the flat, and she knew in her heart that she could never, ever do that. Not willingly.

Her thoughts were interrupted by the woman's voice.

'This wasn't how I wanted it to be, Dani.' She pulled herself away.

'I don't know your name,' Dani said.

'Hayley,' she said weakly, before hesitating. 'We have to go, Dani. What happened back there, we have to tell the police about it.'

Instantly Dani felt herself freeze. She didn't want to talk to anyone about what had happened, least of all the police. She shook her head. 'I don't want to.'

'We have to, Dani.'

'*I don't want to, all right?*' Dani's temper flared up again. She couldn't help it. With a sudden tug she managed to free herself from Hayley's unsuspecting grasp. The woman gasped, as though she had just dropped an unspeakably precious vase; but though Dani's intention was to run, something stopped her. She looked up at Hayley. She didn't know if it was true, what the woman had said to her about being her mum. But in that instant Dani realised one thing: this woman was not going to do her any harm.

'What about Ellie?' she asked. 'What's going to happen to her?'

The woman blinked. 'I don't know, Dani,' she said. 'But if we go to the police, maybe we can help her. Maybe we can tell them what happened.'

'I don't want her to be in trouble,' Dani said in a small voice. 'I—' She faltered. 'I just don't want her to be in trouble, that's all.'

Hayley approached her and put one hand on Dani's shoulder. This time her touch didn't feel so uncomfortable. 'I can't promise you that, Dani,' she said. 'I can't promise you anything, except that I'm going to look after you. I don't know what you've been through, and you don't have to tell me if you don't feel ready. But listen. I work at a police station. There's a guy there, his name's Ryan and he's …' She struggled to find the word. 'He's nice,' she concluded a bit weakly. 'He'll help you. He'll help *us*. I promise.'

The rain continued to fall and Dani realised that she was shivering with the cold.

'Do we have to go now?'

'I think we should.'

Dani bowed her head. 'How far is it?'

'It's very close.' The woman squeezed Dani's shoulder gently. 'Just come with me, Dani, and it'll all be over.'

Dani looked up at her. 'Do you promise?'

Hayley paused. 'I'm not going to lie to you, Dani,' she said finally. 'I'm never going to lie to you.' She took a deep breath. 'And yes,' she said. 'I promise. I absolutely promise.'

Sergeant Ryan Heller had a mound of paperwork and not much time to do it in. Barker was on the warpath, biting the head of anybody who dared so much as look at him, so the young sergeant just kept his head down and ploughed through the work. He'd been at it an hour already and his hand hurt from writing. He allowed himself a moment to sit back and stretch the muscles in his hand, and it was at that precise moment that he saw them.

Hayley was a nice-looking girl. Ryan had come to terms with the fact that there was nothing doing romantically, but he still liked her. As she walked into the office, however, he was startled by the way she looked. Her clothes were drenched and so was her hair. Her face was pale and there were dark rings around her eyes. And by her side there was a child, a little girl who was also soaked to the skin but whose gaunt features and haunted look made Hayley look like a supermodel. The kid – Ryan couldn't tell how old she was – seemed to shrink behind Hayley, fearfully clutching her hand.

Their eyes met and Hayley threw him a serious kind of look. A look that gave him an uneasy feeling in the pit of his stomach. He remembered the conversation they'd had in the pub, the information he'd found out for her. His eyes flickered down to the girl by her side, and then back to Hayley.

She nodded.

Ryan took a heavy breath. Something told him that she was in trouble. A lot of trouble. He scraped his chair out from under the desk and quickly approached her.

'We need to talk,' she hissed as soon as he was in earshot.

'Damn right we do,' Ryan murmured. 'Where've you been? Who's this?'

Both adults looked down at the little girl. 'I'll tell you everything,' she said. 'But not here. We need somewhere private.'

Ryan nodded curtly. 'All right,' he said. 'We'll—'

As he spoke he was interrupted, not by a voice but by the fact that Hayley was looking past him, over his shoulder, with an alarmed expression. Ryan sighed deeply. He knew what it meant and he heard Barker's voice even before he turned to see him.

'Where the hell have you been?' the DCI barked. 'What are you doing?'

'It's all right, boss,' Ryan said wearily as he tried to think of something to say that would get Hayley out of the hole she was so obviously in. Slowly he turned to face Barker, fully prepared for the force of the man's peeved fury.

What he wasn't expecting, however, was the look on his boss's face.

Barker had stopped, statue-still. To look at him, you wouldn't think that either Ryan or Hayley were even there. Because Detective Chief Inspector Barker's attention was focused on only one person.

That person was the little girl who even now was cowering behind Hayley.

Barker's face had gone white. Ryan could sense him holding his breath. His eyes twitched, but apart from that he made no other movement.

Ryan hadn't been a police officer for long. A few years, that was all. He was at the bottom of the slippery pole and there was a great deal about police work that he had yet to learn. He knew that.

But he also knew that you didn't have to be Sherlock Holmes to realise one stunningly obvious fact. He didn't know who this bedraggled little girl was, but it was abundantly clear that this was not the first time DCI Barker had set eyes on her.

* * *

Dani had walked into the station suffused with nervousness. All eyes seemed to be on her. They seemed to accuse her, to know what she had done. It made her want to hide, to curl up in a little ball and conceal her face from the world. It made her want to disappear.

She couldn't, however. Hayley had her hand firmly in hers and was pulling her further into the building. And besides, she had promised, hadn't she? She had promised everything would be all right.

They entered a big, open-plan office and for a moment Hayley stood in the doorway, scanning the room. There were even more people here, more people to hide from, and Dani felt increasingly nervous. She edged behind Hayley, trying to hide herself from the accusing glares that were no doubt being cast in her direction. As she did so, a man approached. He had a nice face, but he looked worried. He talked to Hayley in hushed, urgent whispers. Dani couldn't really tell what they were saying, but it sounded important.

Then there was the voice.

That voice.

The one she knew so well. The one that would haunt her dreams for the rest of her life.

'Where the hell have you been?' it demanded. 'What are you doing?'

It took every ounce of bravery that Dani Sinclair possessed to peep out from behind the protection of Hayley's body. She had to, though. She had to be sure it was him.

Mr Morgan looked out of place here. She had only ever seen him in the flat, in her room, when he was doing those horrible things. Dani froze with fear and as she did so Mr

Morgan stopped too. Stopped in his tracks, looking at her with an unknowable expression in his face.

How could this be happening? How could he be here? The man with the nice face was calling him boss. It was all a trick. Dani pulled her hand from Hayley's grasp and stepped backwards. She wanted to run, but as if in a dream she found there was no speed in her legs. No strength.

'Dani!' Hayley's voice entered her swarming consciousness. 'Dani, what is it? What's the matter?'

Dani couldn't pull her terrified gaze away from Mr Morgan. Her abuser just stood there, staring at her now with disbelief in his face.

She had never known he was a policeman, but suddenly so many things made sense. The way he talked to Baxter; the way Baxter treated him differently to the others. She had to run away. She *had* to. How would anyone believe her? How would anyone not believe *him*?

'Get me out of here,' Dani said. Her breath was coming in short, panicked gasps. 'It's him. Get me out of here.'

Hayley had her arm around her now. 'What do you mean, it's him?'

But Dani shook her head. She couldn't say it. She was too embarrassed, too scared. She couldn't speak about the horrors in front of everyone. And he would stop her, anyway. Hit her. They would never believe her. They would only believe him, whoever he was.

Dani felt her knees buckle underneath her as she stepped back. She was aware of Hayley looking up at Mr Morgan; and she could feel the fury of the stare that he returned. She could feel the danger.

Everything happened so quickly. She was being whisked away, almost carried, to a room. The door was slammed shut. Then there was just the two of them, her and Hayley, her and the woman who claimed to be her mother.

Only now that they were alone could she speak. But still the words were difficult to find. Her skin burned with shame. 'It's him,' she wailed. 'The man who … who used to come. One of them, anyway. He was always there. He knew Baxter. He …' Her words tumbled out incoherently, finally collapsing into nothingness, into weeping.

'Dani …' Hayley tried to say.

'Get me out of here!' Dani whispered, quietly because she was so scared, because she didn't want anyone to hear. 'I don't want to be here! *Get me out of here!*'

As she spoke, there was a clattering. The door burst open and he was there. His tie was slightly undone, just as it always was, and a thin trickle of sweat dripped down the side of his face. His eyes were wild.

Dani shrank back and so, she noticed, did Hayley.

'It's a lie,' Morgan hissed, his voice full of violence. 'Whatever she's saying, it's a lie.'

He took a step into the room. His face was steely and set.

'What's she been saying?' he demanded.

No one spoke. Dani found herself clinging on to Hayley, but they both took a fearful step back.

'Look at her,' he spat. 'She's a fucking urchin. She's never seen me before in her life. She's a liar.'

As he spoke, Dani felt Hayley's muscles clench.

'Get her out of my police station,' Mr Morgan continued. 'Get her out of here, or you're out of a job, you stupid bitch.'

Another silence. Dani heard Hayley taking deep breaths, as though trying to be calm.

Suddenly Mr Morgan approached them quickly. He was only a metre away from them now and Dani could smell him. Smell the scent she recognised too well.

He raised his hand and then pointed a finger accusingly at Hayley. When he spoke, he accentuated each word with a sharp poke on Hayley's chest. 'She's a *dirty … little … liar!*'

'*No!*'

Hayley's outburst was sudden and terrible. With a force that belied her slight frame she raised her arm with astonishing sharpness and thumped it down on the side of Mr Morgan's head. It knocked him sideways and when he looked back there was a thin stream of blood seeping from his nose.

'Listen to me, *Barker*,' she hissed, pronouncing his name with heavy contempt. 'This little girl has been through hell and it's going to carry on over my dead body.'

Morgan – or whatever his name was – looked amazed at her sudden confidence. He stepped back and for the first time since he had entered the room, he looked less sure of himself. He looked scared.

'Seems to me,' Hayley continued, 'that it's about time someone started believing what Dani is saying to them. It starts now.' She stepped forward, past Mr Morgan, firmly pulling Dani along with her. In the doorway was the policeman with the nice face. He too looked shocked at what was going on.

When Hayley spoke again, it was in little more than a whisper.

'You're going to pay for this, *sir*,' she said. 'If I've got anything to do with it – and believe me, I will do – you're going to pay for what you've done.'

Mr Morgan's eyes narrowed. His lips curled up into an expression of utter loathing. But he didn't say anything. There was, after all, very little to say.

Hayley looked down at Dani. 'We're going home now,' she said. Her voice was still trembling slightly, but it was softer now that she was speaking to her. 'Your real home, I mean. With me. Would you like that?'

For a moment Dani didn't reply. She looked over at the form of Mr Morgan. He was in the corner now and for the first time ever he seemed smaller. Less of a threat. Less terrifying. In an instant Dani seemed to relive all the times he had visited her. All the things he had done. She tried to block those awful memories out, but as she did so others came flooding in. She remembered her foster mother and the things that had happened. She remembered the children's home, and the street. She remembered Baxter, lying dead on the floor of the flat. And of course she remembered Ellie. Poor Ellie, who had done so much for her, and so much to hurt her. She hoped she was all right, but some sinister intuition told Dani that she wasn't. How could she be, after everything that had happened?

Then she looked up at Hayley. At her mother. Her real mother.

'Yes,' she said quietly, her voice unusually calm despite everything. 'Yes. I'd like that.'

Hayley nodded and, without even looking back at Mr Morgan, she led Dani from the room.

They walked together out of the police station, and into whatever the future held.

Epilogue

Three months later

The room in which they sat was rather bland, not unlike the many doctors' waiting rooms Dani had seemed to spend half her time in over the past few weeks. Hayley – Dani couldn't yet quite bring herself to call her Mum – sat by her. They both wore new clothes. Not expensive, but new. Hayley had a smile fixed on her face, but Dani could tell that her mother was at least as nervous as she was.

'You all right, love?' she asked.

Dani nodded.

'You sure you want to go through with this? It's not too late to change your mind, you know. They can set up a video link – you don't have to see him.' She sounded almost as if she hoped Dani *would* change her mind. But Dani knew there was no going back now.

She looked up. On the other side of the room was Ryan. As their eyes met, he gave Dani an encouraging look. *You're going to do just fine*, he seemed to say. It made her feel a bit better. She smiled at him. Dani was glad when Ryan was around, and she could tell that Hayley was too.

It had been a big decision, saying she would go up in front of the court. Lots of people didn't want her to do it – the social workers, the child psychiatrists, the endless stream of people who seemed to be around her. And at first she had agreed with them. The idea of standing up in a crowded courtroom, having to answer questions about what that man had done to her – the very idea terrified her. Made her want to shrink away. And when they had said that the chances of him being convicted on Dani's say-so were small, it had only added to the feeling that she wanted nothing to do with it. Nothing at all.

But then they had told her about Ellie. About how they had found her. Nobody really wanted to talk to Dani about her at first – everyone spoke in hushed voices, as though she would be somehow damaged by hearing the words they were saying. It made her cross, so in the end Hayley had sat her down and told her everything.

She cried, of course, when she first heard. She cried inconsolably. The memory of Baxter's corpse was distressing enough, but to think of Ellie, alone and dead in that flat – it was almost too much to bear. And at night, when she slept in the comfortable single bed Hayley had provided for her, Dani would hear her voice. 'Don't worry about me, titch,' Ellie would say to her, her voice as clear as if she was whispering in her ear. 'Don't you go worrying about me.'

But Dani did worry. She knew Ellie was dead, but that didn't stop her worrying. And it didn't stop her from starting to hear Ellie's voice at the strangest times of both the day and night. From nowhere she would remember words that she had spoken when they first met.

It's what we're here for. It's what we do. It's what we are.

Best not to fight them, titch. Best just to let it happen.

Those words haunted her. In her own troubled way, Ellie *had* done her best to fight them. Prison or no prison, Dani would be repaying her poorly if she didn't do the same thing.

A court official stepped into the room. She nodded at Hayley and then looked down at Dani with that expression of sympathy that the girl was so used to now. 'They've called you, dear,' she said. 'You need to go through now.'

Dani bit her lower lip, and then looked up at her mother.

'He won't ever do it again, will he?' she asked in a small voice. 'He won't ever be able to come near me again?'

Hayley looked at her daughter with a serious expression.

'He won't be able to come near you,' she said quietly. 'Or anybody. I promise.'

Dani nodded. 'Good.'

She took a deep breath, stood up from her chair and followed the court official into the court room.

As she walked, she heard Ellie's voice once more. *Best not to fight them, titch. Best to let it happen.*

But Dani Sinclair wasn't going to let it happen.

Not again.